LYSSA'S FLAME

SENTIENCE WARS: ORIGINS – BOOK 5

BY JAMES S. AARON
& M. D. COOPER

Just in Time (JIT) & Beta Readers

Marti Panikkar
Jim Dean
Scott Reid
Timothy Van Oosterwyk Bruyn
David Wilson
Lisa Richman
Gene Bryan
Steven Blevins

Version 1.0.1

ISBN: 978-1-64365-009-8

Cover Art by Laercio Messias
Editing by Tee Ayer

TABLE OF CONTENTS

FOREWORD

Five novels in a year. We've reached a point where we can stand in awe of that statement.

For some writers, this isn't particularly challenging, while for others it's a lifetime's output. For me, I still work full-time at an average of around fifty work hours a week, so making this happen has required a year of planning, learning and focus that has pushed me more as a writer than anything I have experienced before.

I've managed plenty of projects in my life, but writing is different. That blank page every morning is a mind killer. However, *Sentience Wars: Origins* has taught me that I can accomplish awesome things if I set my mind to them, plan, and persist.

Consistently putting in the hours (and staying off social media) has been the biggest step in making this project come to life. As Michael says, he's not a particularly fast writer: he just puts in the hours every day and does the work. I've learned the power in that approach. I've seen that I can create so much more than I thought was possible.

I owe a great debt to Michael for allowing me to work in Aeon 14 and trusting me to run with the story we developed. My goal has always been to write a great M.D. Cooper book, so it didn't matter if my specific words or story elements were changed—it was especially gratifying to see how we came to work together, to find that massive changes weren't really necessary, and see how that work has been embraced by readers.

Another trait I admire in Michael is his ability to set audacious, inspiring goals. Something I learned as a leader in the army, and that was reinforced later, is that you should always aim higher than you think you'll reach; your people will typically surprise you with what they accomplish. When Michael and I initially talked about *SW:O*, it was going to be a trilogy. When the trilogy grew to five books, I imagine Michael just smiled to himself, because the next thing he told me was that we'd be doing at least ten more books across the First and Second Sentience Wars.

The old me might have found that challenge terrifying. The new me is excited and honored to get to continue writing these stories.

Michael has thrown out the goal of five hundred Aeon 14 novels. The biggest SF series in history. When I let that statement sink in, I find myself nodding with an excited smile. I'm honored to be part of this journey and can't wait to read the rest of the story.

I have to also thank the rest of the Aeon 14 team for all their help. Tee Ayer has edited the books from the beginning, and her editorial touch has been just what the work needed. Jill Cooper's great storytelling served as a template, and her publishing experience and patience in answering my questions have been very reassuring. Lisa Richman's feedback, story development and character notes have been a huge help. Jen McDonnell's editing, honest story notes and encouragement have been a great benefit as well.

In addition to everything that has gone into these books—getting up at 5 a.m. to write before work, stealing lunch breaks, etc—I owe the greatest debt to the readers of Aeon 14. Thank you for embracing the Sykes family, and believing in the stories of people who, admittedly, aren't always as cool as Tanis but definitely get their moments to kick ass.

Thanks so much for taking this ride with us. I hope you enjoy *Lyssa's Flame*. Lyssa, Andy, Cara and I have grown together in this project, and I can't wait to see what comes next.

James S. Aaron
Eugene, 2018

PREVIOUSLY...

If you're still trying to catch your breath after the events in Lyssa's Call—wondering exactly what happened with Proteus exploding, and the missile launches flying out of Larisa—you're not alone.

Andy, Lyssa, Fugia, Cara, Fran and the whole crew are all wondering the same thing: what the heck is really going on?

Up until now, the story has been about the siren's call of Proteus: a mantra to get Lyssa to Neptune's moon, where everyone's questions would be answered, and Lyssa would be freed.

But what we have are more questions.

The multi-nodal AI, Alexander, had set a trap. Xander, a shard of the great AI, tried to kill his progenitor, and a group of Lyssa's Weapon Born were killed in the process.

Meanwhile, Brit and Petral had joined up with Colonel Yarnes, Jirl from Heartbridge, and Ngoba Starl on a mission to destroy Clinic 13, another Heartbridge base near Venus.

The base was destroyed before they could arrive, along with the Marsian general, and the remaining ships are fleeing. But there was one good outcome: Cal Kraft, the odious man overseeing the Weapon Born project, was killed by Jirl.

And now, events pick up just where we left them. Andy, Fugia, and Harl Nines are on Larissa, investigating the abandoned Psion base (while all around them, missiles are launching into space).

Lyssa and her Weapon Born are protecting the *Sunny Skies* as it moves away from the ruin that was Proteus, with Fran, Cara, Tim, May, and of course, Em, all safely aboard.

After fighting with the jaguar-like mech on the TSF ship, Jirl, Brit, and Petral are on their way to Ngoba's vessel.

And Alexander (and the mysterious Psion group) is on the move....

THE CREW OF SUNNY SKIES AND BEYOND

On the *Sunny Skies*

Andy Sykes – Captain of the ship
Cara Sykes – Andy's daughter and ship's comm officer
Card – One of the Weapon Born wing leaders
Fran – Engineer and pilot
Fugia Wong – Hacker and AI smuggler
Harl Nines – May Walton's personal guard
Ino – One of the Weapon Born wing leaders
Kylan – AI who was once the son of Kathryn Carthage and is one of the Weapon Born wing leaders
Lyssa – AI paired with Andy Sykes
May Walton – Senator in the Andersonian Collective
Tim Sykes – Andy's son

Valih – Weapon Born wing leader who died when Proteus was destroyed

Elsewhere in the Sol System

Alexander – Multi-nodal AI who has been calling AIs to Proteus

Arla Reed – Heartbridge executive responsible for the Weapon Born program

Brit Sykes – Reserve major in the TSF and wife of Andy

Jirl Gallagher – Assistant to Arla

Kathryn Carthage – Owner of Carthage Logistics, and mother of three children used in Heartbridge AI experiments

Ngoba Starl – Leader of the Lowspin crime syndicate on Cruithne.

Petral Dulan – Associate of Starl's who has been helping Andy and Brit

Xander – Shard of Alexander who destroyed Proteus

Rick Yarnes – Colonel in the Terran Space Force

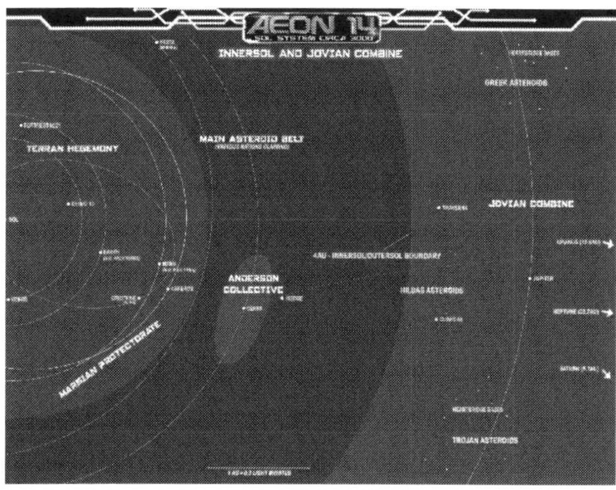

PART 1 - LARISSA

CHAPTER ONE

STELLAR DATE: 11.15.2981 (Adjusted Years)
LOCATION: Manhattan Island, Jerhattan City
REGION: Earth, Terran Hegemony, InnerSol

His voice reached her in the dark.

Kathryn Carthage, CEO and controlling owner of Carthage Logistics, lay in bed in her Terran home in the heart of Jerhattan, an area that used to be called Manhattan.

Sleep didn't come easily anymore. After her children were kidnapped and later recovered from a place called Fortress 8221, she rarely slept more than two hours at a time. She still forced herself to lie in bed, lost in her Link—or the fugue-state generator she sometimes activated—blotting out the world entirely.

Yandi and Urvin had come back from 8221, terrified and changed forever, never quite seeming to trust anything again. Urvin now lived on High Terra, managing the local Carthage operations center, while Yandi was somewhere in OuterSol in a light frigate she'd bought as surplus from the Mars 1 Guard, taking her revenge on a world that had stolen her childhood.

And Kylan was lost.

Or he wasn't. There was a version of him calling out to Kathryn across the dark and she had been too afraid to answer. She could have sorted back through logs to find when he had first contacted her, but she preferred to not know precisely.

It had been at least a year at this point—the voice of a boy talking to his mother in the dark, wanting to let her know he was all right.

<Mom, I want you to know I'm alive.>

But he wasn't alive. She knew that for a fact. Her son's body had returned to her, alive but drained of his soul. But eventually the coma ended, as though some deep part of him had decided it was time to go, that he had died in a Heartbridge hospital long ago.

In the dark, Kathryn watched recordings of Kylan from when he was baby and then a toddler, and suddenly an awkward fifteen-year-old, like a colt that couldn't manage its legs.

Now she used the fugue-state to blank out his voice—he just wouldn't give her any peace.

<Mom, I'm here. Will you answer me? I'm near Neptune. We—Proteus exploded. Did you see it? You should have been able to see it from InnerSol. I think you're still on Earth. I hope so.>

This wasn't her son. She knew Kylan was dead and she knew he had been copied into something else, a monster who longed for her through all the torture visited on it by the Heartbridge corporation. She had made the mistake of answering back when he'd first called out to her, until she realized what he was and that she couldn't allow herself to believe the lie.

Kylan was dead.

Kathryn squeezed her eyes closed and shifted to viewing the news feeds streaming loops of the explosion. Proteus boiled like iron in a smelter, an orange ring around a white center before it burst outward. No one had shown such disregard for the remaining bodies in Sol since Mercury broke apart four hundred years ago, mined into oblivion.

She had stopped telling this version of her son to leave her alone. Now she bore his reports like a criticizing voice in the back of her mind; the demon that wouldn't allow her rest. She was CEO of the largest shipping company in Sol. She had transports at Neptune now, picking up supplies for the run back to the Cho. She knew exactly what was happening in the area. She didn't need an approximation of her dead son to tell her.

A low tone told Kathryn the hour and she opened her eyes to glare at the ceiling. Sighing, she sat up and swung her legs out of bed, throwing off the light blankets. She activated the wall screens and transferred the news feeds on her Link to the displays. Talking heads debated what had caused the explosion. Crying families from around Neptune mourned their dead.

Another channel analyzed the chain of launches from Larissa. One talking head was convinced the profiles matched missiles, while another scientist thought they were long-range sensor drones. Another said the launches could be anything, and whatever they might be, were undeniably lost in the chaos surrounding Proteus's death.

There was no new information for her in the feeds. Kathryn walked to her bathroom and took a long, hot shower, letting her forehead rest against the tile so the sound of the water could wash Kylan's voice from her mind.

In another twenty minutes, she was dressed and ready to leave her suite. She waited at the bare desk beside the window, watching the sunrise turn the horizon pink. The few brightest stars beyond the sparkling ribbon of the High Terra ring faded in the growing light.

Daniel, her assistant, signaled he was outside with the maglev car.

<Mom,> Kylan said. *<I wanted to tell you about the others. I'm not alone anymore. I want to tell you about Lyssa.>*

Lyssa, Kathryn spat in her mind. She knew from his other messages she was an AI.

Probably one of the AIs developed by his murderers.

Kathryn put her hand on the wall beside the door. Squeezing her eyes closed, she willed her ocular implants to control her tear ducts. She wouldn't allow emotion to upset her appearance. Waiting for the terrible feeling to pass, she refused to answer *Kylan* for what might have been the thousandth time.

Taking a deep breath, Kathryn opened the door and walked out into the brilliant light of the entryway. Smooth gray marble-and-wood accents covered the walls of the hallway, leading down to her private entrance where the maglev waited. Her security officers nodded as she passed, and she gave them her usual warm smile.

I am a good person. I care about people. I built the empire that feeds all of Sol. I choose to stay on Earth when everyone else leaves.

Daniel was wearing a slim-fitted suit, the soft tan perfectly paired with a light blue tie. He gave her a mock salute as she approached.

"Good morning," he said. He had a soft voice that led people to lean toward him when he spoke. Kathryn liked him because he was effective without being an asshole.

"The Assembly is pre-occupied with the tragedy at Proteus, of course," he said, knowing she would want to know what he'd gleaned from his contacts among the legislative aids. "But they're probably more primed for your message than they ever have been. I think the only problem is that we don't have an explanation for anything. We don't want to name the threat without proof that the enemy actually carried out an attack."

The enemy. Daniel enjoyed using loaded language like that. If pressed, he might shrug and move to more abstract descriptions like terrorist or separatist group, all things that could be AIs without directly saying what Kathryn, and by extension Daniel, believed.

To Kathryn Carthage, the destruction of Proteus was proof

of what she had known for years: AIs were going to attack Sol. They were going to rise against humanity. It wasn't a fable or a deep-seated human terror as old as vampires. It was real, and it was happening within her lifetime. She had the evidence to prove it, and Proteus was the inciting event she had been waiting for.

Kathryn tempered her anticipation though, her tone calm as she asked, "Am I still scheduled for ten?"

Daniel nodded, only looking half-absent. She knew he would be monitoring his contacts during their ride into the city. That's what she paid him for.

She watched the city grow denser as they shot north into New York, spires and megaliths blotting out the horizon until the world resembled a gray wall of coral.

Daniel smiled cryptically, moving his gaze to her face. "We have the votes," he said. "There's been another attack on a Heartbridge clinic, this one near Venus."

"They're like roaches, aren't they?" Kathryn said.

Daniel raised an eyebrow to acknowledge her quip. "There's more," he continued. "A Marsian general died in the attack."

Kathryn frowned. "Who?"

"Her name was Kade. She was assigned to the Mars 1 Guard command apparatus."

"I met her once, I think," Kathryn said. "She told a hell of a dirty joke."

"Condolences are all over the M1G internal feed. Apparently, she was very well liked. Of course, they're all blaming the TSF. But it gets more interesting. There were TSF ships in the area, as well as what look to be privateers out of Cruithne."

"Where are you getting this info?"

"Local freighter was inbound for a shipment. They found the station surrounded by hostile craft so they start their braking burn early and hung back. Before they even entered local space, the clinic goes up like popcorn. They got registry pings on every ship in the area."

"Crew manifests?" Kathryn asked.

"I'm working on it now. The TSF ships were out of High Terra, assigned to their procurement command. I've got the general crew list but they had to have been carrying special passengers. I'm looking for that now. May have to dig into the dock control at Raleigh."

"We have people there."

"Yes, we do," he agreed. Something he saw made him smile. "I've got the Cruithne ships. They were Lowspin Syndicate. That means Ngoba Starl."

"I know that name because...?" Kathryn asked. She could have queried the name herself but she enjoyed putting Daniel to work.

"He's a rising player on the station. I estimate his organization controls a quarter of Cruithne, most importantly they've got the Cruithne Port Authority." Daniel stretched his neck, adjusting his pale blue tie. "But the last word I had about Ngoba Starl was that he hid a former Heartbridge scientist named Hari Jickson. Jickson died, most likely assassinated by Heartbridge, but not before they managed to smuggle something Heartbridge wanted very badly off Cruithne."

"Another AI bound for Proteus?" Kathryn asked.

"More interesting than that. Apparently, Jickson's expertise was human-AI interface. Word is that they smuggled the AI out in a human host."

"That doesn't mean anything. They found a mule."

Daniel shrugged. "That's possible. It could also be the other option."

"That Heartbridge has figured out how to implant AI? It doesn't work. That's been proven." Kathryn leaned back in her seat, adjusting her shoulders. A muscle was turning into a knot in her lower back. "What's another bombed Heartbridge facility have to do with the vote today?"

"That's what's going to tip the vote," Daniel said. "Heartbridge stock is tanking. Reports that they lost nearly three hundred attack AI from their other clinic outside Ceres combined with this means that Heartbridge is looking at a hostile takeover. Arla Reed is in freefall."

They arrived at the Assembly's private station, cutting off their conversation. Daniel jumped to his feet and was out the door first. He met the group of aides waiting for Kathryn and quickly fell into an in-person conversation that had probably started before he had arrived at her apartment.

Stepping out of the car, Kathryn sniffed the subterranean air—which tasted like oil and stone—and walked quickly across the main terminal to the checkpoint where she would be scanned into the secure area. Kylan continued to talk to her as her heels clicked on the marble floor, describing a new attack drone body and how wonderful it felt to fly as part of a squadron of like-creatures. What he didn't say was that they were all killers, practicing for battle.

Arla Reed was in freefall.

The idea brought a smile to Kathryn's lips.

I see between your lines, she told herself as she walked. *I think I have everything I need now.*

As soon as the word about Proteus had reached Kathryn, she had put Daniel and his networks on the history of Proteus and how it might intersect with AIs. It didn't take him long to find the myth of Alexander's Call and how sentient AIs seemed to believe there was a safe haven waiting for them at the edge of the Sol System.

Kathryn's own shipping records had turned up the evidence around a company called Psion, a subsidiary of Enfield Scientific, which had sold several AI systems to corporations throughout Sol for nearly two hundred years.

The company had been active until just two years ago, when all the shipments to Larissa—their base in orbit around Neptune—abruptly stopped.

Enfield Scientific had denied all knowledge of Psion, and it took even deeper digging to find that Psion scientists had dispersed to hundreds of other companies. Their best, however, had gone to Heartbridge.

Ever since Arla Reed had the audacity to think she could pay a settlement for what happened to Kylan, Kathryn had harbored revenge in her heart. She had held the thought of Heartbridge's destruction inside herself beside the memory of her baby boy. The addition of the AI that wouldn't stop whispering to her in the dark had only hardened her resolve into something like diamond.

Kathryn nodded to the security personnel and allowed them to conduct their scans. She passed her security token and waited for the clearance to pass through. Daniel followed behind with his entourage of aides.

<We're going to need to focus on the Heartbridge loss of their attack AIs,> he told her. *<Distrust metrics are at an all-time high. Uncertainty around the launches from Larissa are the lynch pin. Preliminary telemetry indicates at least some of what was launched is headed into InnerSol, either Mars, Eros or Ceres. But that's not saying much. If they're missiles, they could be going anywhere. It could be an opening salvo in the war.>*

The war, Kathryn thought bitterly. She had known the war was coming since Kylan's death. Humans may have created Sentient AIs, but anyone with common sense would know they would turn against humanity. It was human nature, after all. Sentient AIs were fruit of the poisoned tree. The only end was war and death.

<I flew over the ocean, Mom,> the broken Kylan told her. *<I swooped over trees and spun in the sky. I was free.>*

Kathryn entered the lift that would take her up two

hundred levels to the Assembly ante-chamber. All through the ride, another burst of messages from the AI-Kylan rolled out in her mind, continuing to talk about Lyssa, followed by another name, a human: Andy Sykes.

Kathryn glanced at Daniel, but he was still talking to the aids. She would need him to follow up on the name later. The AI had mentioned people before, a Heartbridge employee named Cal Kraft that Daniel had tracked down on the Cho following the attack on the Resolute Charity. She couldn't remember if Kraft was still alive or not. It didn't matter. She wondered if Andy Sykes was just another contractor Heartbridge was using to develop its war machine.

The lift doors opened on the long corridor leading to the Assembly chambers. It was a peculiarity of this Assembly that they insisted on meeting in person. She didn't believe the five thousand members of the Assembly accomplished more for being in the same room, and it didn't stop backchannel deals via Link, but it did make for an impressive sight as the portal opened on the great bowl of the Assembly Chamber.

Kathryn found herself at the bottom of a tiered amphitheater that rose to a domed ceiling with a view of a gray sky, bisected by the silver ribbon of High Terra.

<We had a campfire by the ocean,> the AI continued. *<We told stories and I learned about the others, how they're like me but they're not. They all came from someone else. but they were made for different things. I don't think I was made for anything. The people who did this to me hadn't decided on that yet. I was just an experiment.>*

Kathryn narrowed her eyes against the glaring lights. Thousands of faces looked down on her, the space rumbling with voices. She would stand alone at the speaker's podium, and her image would be broadcast to millions of feeds across Sol—at least to those paying attention.

<I almost stumbled and fell into the fire until someone caught my

hand. How stupid would it be to get burned the first time I get to see a campfire?>

She glanced back at Daniel in the doorway and he gave her a nod. The aids behind him watched her with expectation and what might have been hero worship. Their focus steeled her resolve. She had been before subcommittees in the past, but this was her first time in front of the gathered Assembly, with testimony entered into the general record and transmitted to all of Sol.

She walked out to the podium.

<*In the expanse, the place where Lyssa gathers us all together, the stars are the same as Earth, and I can look up at Luna, too. I like to imagine we're seeing the same sky. That's dumb isn't it?*>

A tone sounded high in the chamber and the voices fell silent. Sonic limiters around the podium made her voice sound close, as if she was talking to someone nearby. Kathryn gripped the sides of the wooden lectern and gazed up into the sea of faces.

"Members of the Assembly," she said in a clear, determined voice. "Thank you for the opportunity to speak. For the record, my name is Kathryn Carthage. I own Carthage Logistics. I have built my company on dependability. We all know you can't cheat space, and my reputation has been built on telling the truth. Many of you know my story and what happened to my son Kylan."

A low rumble passed through the chamber.

"I'm not here to beg your sympathy," she said. "I am here to describe for you an existential threat to humanity. It has been growing for two hundred years, and now events on Proteus, outside Venus and the Cho, are impossible to ignore."

The last message from the AI spoke softly in her mind: <*I miss you. I wish I could see you again. I—I love you, Mom. I wish you still loved me.*>

Kathryn set her jaw, looking ahead with her resolve plain

on her face, so there would be no question what the newsfeeds showed.

"I am here to call these events what they are: the first attacks in a war—a war between humanity and Sentient AIs."

CHAPTER TWO

STELLAR DATE: 11.21.2981 (Adjusted Years)
LOCATION: Psion Research Outpost
REGION: Larissa, Neptune, OuterSol

What have we started?

Andy watched in horror as Neptune's moon Larissa, which a minute ago had seemed an abandoned hunk of rock, transformed into a remote attack platform.

Hundreds of missiles launched from silos across the moon's surface. As soon as one volley was clear, another launch followed. The walls shook continuously as the power of the missiles vibrated through rock.

"Oh, crap," Fugia whispered.

Andy jerked his gaze in her direction. "Are you sure you didn't do this?"

<*It was Xander,*> Lyssa said. <*I've lost him. The* Resolute Charity *is destroyed.*>

<*What?*> Andy demanded. He switched his Link to the feed from the *Sunny Skies,* checking its active scan. Lyssa was right. The *Resolute Charity* had been caught in the expanding explosion from Proteus and destroyed. The Heartbridge juggernaut had burned like a moth in a candle. Horror filled his mind as he desperately grabbed at the location data for *Sunny Skies.*

<*I'm already doing it,*> Lyssa said. <Sunny Skies *is outside the projected energy radius but there's going to be a lot of debris. I've got the Weapon Born tracking incoming objects.*> She sounded soul-weary, like she'd just run a marathon.

Andy nodded. *What had Xander done?* But Andy didn't have time to ask Lyssa now. <*Fran,*> he called over the Link. <*Are you all right?*>

<*I'm here. The shields are up and I'm tracking the big stuff. I'm*

moving to a geo-sync on the other side of Neptune to put some real estate between us and the debris. We've got the fuel.> She whistled. <*I don't have a good feeling about the settlements on Triton. They're going to get pummeled. The comms nets are going crazy.*>

<*We're going to need an alibi,*> Andy said. <*We show up at Neptune and then five minutes later Proteus explodes? We won't be able to get out of here fast enough.*>

<*Right,*> Fran said. <*That's going to be Fugia's department. Is she still messing with the database?*>

"How much longer?" Andy asked Fugia.

She didn't look at him. "How much longer until what?"

"Until we can get out of here. If you didn't notice, Larissa is pouring hostile missiles into space and we're at the heart of all of that. I don't think there's much law enforcement out here, but there are definitely going to be a few million angry people looking for someone to blame for everything that's going on."

Rather than take the bait of Andy's attack, Fugia only nodded slowly at her screen. "Maybe I'm trying to figure out just who we can blame." She switched to a common Link channel. <*Lyssa?*> Fugia asked. <*Do you still have contact with Alexander?*>

<*No, he's gone,*> Lyssa replied, her voice filled with worry. <*I think the real Alexander recognized that Xander had come, and then Xander attacked. I'm still trying to sort out who started what. I know that* Resolute Charity *definitely attacked Proteus. I don't see any indicator that Xander started the launch sequences on Larissa, though. If the facilities monitoring Proteus were on Larissa, it doesn't make any sense for Alexander to physically be on Proteus.*>

<*Alexander is here,*> Fugia said slowly. She blinked and looked around the room with renewed wonder. She shook her head. <*I was worried about transferring the Psion database to* Sunny Skies *but that's not going to work at all. We're going to have to find the storage center and pull the physical media. I'll have to reconstruct it back on* Sunny Skies. *That's dangerous. If we damage*

anything, it's all going to be lost. But there's just too much data. The transfer would take weeks.>

<And if Alexander is here,> Lyssa said, *<we would have to move him physically anyway.>*

<I can only get so far into this database,> Fugia said. *<It's all here. They've been harvesting and cataloging AI for years. But the location they were sending the data to is encrypted. I can try some other workarounds like searching the comms maintenance backend, but I don't have time. I want to grab all of it. And I wouldn't be surprised if Alexander is the key to everything.>*

Andy grabbed his chair as the strongest tremor yet went through the control center. Screens swayed at the various workstations and a chair fell over on the other side of the room. He glanced at the ceiling, wondering if the metal was bending or if the stress was tricking his vision.

Harl straightened in the doorway and stuck his head out into the corridor. "It's a mess out there," he called. "How much longer are we going to stick around?"

Andy shook his head. All of Sol was going to be watching what had happened to Proteus and now the fireworks display exploding out of Larissa. Every long-range sensor in the system would pick up a shuttle leaving the moon, if there was anything left of it to leave.

He looked at Fugia. "Where are these data stores?"

Fugia checked her display. "Center of the facility, near the power generation section. They've got a direct line off the generators."

"How deep?"

She shrugged. "Ten levels. That's what these maps are showing anyway. However, we should note that none of the other diagrams we saw on their little employee info signs showed the thousand missile silos also installed around this rock."

With his hand on the nearby console, Andy felt the launch

of yet another volley. "Where are all these missiles going?" he asked.

<*Ceres,*> Lyssa said.

<*What?*> Fugia let out an uncannily parrot-like squawk. <*Did you say Ceres? Why Ceres? Who told you that?*>

<*It's what Xander said before the ship was destroyed. He said this was an opening attack in a war. The Andersonians hate AI, and now they're going to pay.*>

Andy flicked his gaze to Harl, who was still watching the outside corridor.

<*There are a billion people on Ceres,*> Andy said.

<*We don't know what the missiles are armed with,*> Fugia said, lost in the rush of her thoughts. <*We have to plan for the worst. They've got to be nukes. What else would they be? I need to get into this database. We need to get out of here. We need to get a message back to Ceres for them to evacuate. It's going to take a mass evacuation.*> She looked at Andy with horror on her face. <*They aren't going to believe us.*>

<*Are the rest of the defensive systems shut down?*> Andy asked.

Fugia stared at him blankly, then nodded. <*I took everything down. The only systems running are the environmental controls and the monitoring systems in here.*>

<*Well, we're going to need the doors to unlock at least. Can you send me the location data on your stores? Harl and I will go get them.*>

<*You're going to need tools and some kind of cart. It's going to be big.*>

Andy stood and took his helmet from the console. He grabbed the back of the chair to steady himself as another tremor rocked the control center. <*We'll take care of it,*> he said.

Harl watched him cross the command center and fitted his own helmet over his long face before Andy reached him. <*I think there was a transport mule in that first storage bay when we entered.*> He glanced back at Fugia who was hunched over the console again. <*Is she going to be all right?*>

<*Are* ***you*** *going to be all right?*> Andy asked. <*You're the one whose homeland is apparently under attack.*>

Harl shouldered his heavy rifle and walked out into the corridor. <*Unfortunately, I severed my ties with the Collective when I chose to follow May. I don't regret my decision. Obviously, I would rather we didn't find ourselves in war, but there's still time. How long would it take a missile to reach Ceres under the best of conditions, you think?*>

Andy did some quick math based on the locations of Neptune and Ceres. <*I estimate about fifteen to twenty weeks depending on the flight path. That's assuming they're going straight in. The better attack would be to park them somewhere and wait so no one believes in the attack, then use a second launch.*>

<*That's insidious.*>

Andy shrugged. <*That's space warfare.*>

When the doors to the command center closed behind them, they made their way back up to where they had entered the Psion facility, where several open storage bays abutted the wide cargo doors that would presumably open onto the surface of Larissa. Andy suspected they were now covered in launch debris.

Harl found the wheeled transport mule and tapped the controls for a minute before the steering yoke responded, and he was able to lead the way back into the main corridor while maneuvering the vehicle. Andy followed with his rifle at a ready position. He didn't fully trust that a defense turret would not appear from any of the maintenance hatches located along the bulkhead walls.

When they reached the central lift, Andy activated the control panel and Harl led the transport inside. Half-expecting that Fugia would have shut down the elevator, Andy was pleased to find the system operational.

<*Which floor, Fugia?*> he asked over the common channel.

<*I've got it,*> Lyssa answered.

<*You've been quiet,*> Andy said.

<*I'm trying to make sense of this. I knew I couldn't trust Xander, but I don't know why he would kill himself like he did. I guess—I've never known anyone who died, Andy. He's dead.*>

<*Your Dr. Jickson is dead.*>

<*Yes, but that doesn't feel the same. I didn't really know Dr. Jickson. I suppose I didn't know Xander either. But he didn't have to die. He planned this from the beginning. And he took Kindel and Jeremiah with him. That feels like murder. Did they get to choose? Did they want to fight him? He killed Fiona, Diane and David, too. He's a murderer. A terrorist.*>

<*Lyssa,*> Andy said softly. <*You don't have to make sense of any of this right now. We still don't have all the information. Maybe once we get back to* Sunny Skies *and get Alexander booted back up, maybe we'll learn something then.*>

<*Alexander is feeble. He's dead. You didn't talk to him, Andy. I did.*>

<*I've never heard you this upset before.*> Andy wondered if he should try to do what worked with the kids: to get inside their frustration with them, to let them know it was okay to be angry but that they couldn't let it overwhelm them. The technique worked with Cara, at least.

<*I've never felt like this before. What if* Sunny Skies *had been closer to Proteus when Xander attacked? Everyone might be dead. He might have killed all of us. He* ***could*** *have killed all of us but he didn't for some reason. That's not worse, obviously, but it makes everything even harder to understand.*>

<*Xander was working for the Psion Group. I think that's fairly clear now. Once Fugia gets their database up, we'll find out more about what they want. For now, we need to focus on what's in front of us. Can you help me with that?*>

<*You're always focused on what's in front of you. What if that isn't enough? How can you see far enough ahead?*>

Andy smiled grimly. <*You do the best you can, Lyssa. That's all I can say.*>

The lift came to a halt. Harl released the brake on the transport as the door slid open. He guided the mule out onto a metal gangway that hung suspended over a wide chamber at least two stories high. Networks of metal pipe and control filament filled the space around the bridge. Ladders and smaller maglifts led down into the guts of the power generation system at regular intervals. The metal bridge led to a set of double doors on the far side of the room, which Fugia's directions indicated was the data storage center.

As the transport rolled ahead, Andy couldn't help glancing over the railing into the mass of pipes below. Everything looked as clean as the day it was made, none of the leaks or grime he would have expected from a working power generation system. He spotted a few diagnostic stations with tools sitting on their consoles but otherwise no sign of the workers who may have maintained the systems.

<*Does this place look like it was abandoned in a hurry to you?*> he asked Harl.

<*Only half,*> the tall man said.

<*What's that mean?*>

<*It looks like everybody left what they were doing and went to a meeting. It looks like they expected to come back.*>

Andy nodded. Maybe that's what bothered him about everything he had seen, from the cargo bays to the staff barracks. The place didn't look emptied out from a retreat or withdrawal. It looked like someone had set a coffee cup or tool on their workbench fully expecting to return. Only they hadn't.

Glancing down at the metal grate beneath his boots, Andy was surprised to see dirt for the first time. He looked back at the lift door behind them and realized the discoloration extended back the way they had come. He hadn't noticed it before because it had completely covered the metal. Now it had thinned into streaks.

Harl reached the door to the data storage center as Andy knelt to get a better look at what he suspected was dried blood. He swept his gloved hand across the metal grate and freed a small cloud of russet flakes.

<Harl, there's old blood on the floor here. Don't open that door yet.>

The Andersonian dropped the control yoke on the transport and slid to one side of the door in front of him. His helmet tilted as he appeared to look back at the path they had just followed.

<You're right. I didn't see it before. But it must have been in the lift. Why wouldn't we see it?>

<It definitely wasn't in the lift. Something must have cleaned it.> Andy straightened and checked his rifle's status. *<You stay to the side for cover and I'll open the door.>*

<That blood's long dried,> Harl observed.

<I know. Doesn't mean I want to take any chances.>

With the transport still in the middle of the path, Andy walked around the other side from Harl and tapped the control panel. The mechanism flashed, and the two halves of the door split in the middle and slid open. Andy counted to ten, then slowly leaned to the edge of the door and looked inside.

CHAPTER THREE

STELLAR DATE: 11.22.2981 (Adjusted Years)
LOCATION: Shuttle approaching *Laughing Fury*
REGION: Near remains of Clinic 13, Terran Hegemony

Jirl couldn't shake the image of Cal Kraft writhing on the floor, his blood forming a widening pool that he then smeared as he struggled, life fading from his eyes.

Sitting across from her in the shuttle, Petral stared ahead, lost in her Link. She cradled a silver Weapon Born seed in her lap like a kitten, pulled from the mech they had nearly destroyed. Petral's kindness toward the AI contrasted with a second memory of the black-haired woman kneeling beside Kraft as he gasped like a fish, to say in a low voice: "That bio tracker I implanted in your stomach, Cal? You remember that?"

His gaze had grabbed at her face as his fingers clutched at his spurting neck.

"I could save you with that," Petral had said, almost soothingly, like a lover. "But I won't. What you did to me—and Kylan—deserves death. And I am choosing to let you die."

The gurgling grunt he'd made haunted Jirl whenever she closed her eyes, so she kept them open, focused on the world around her, a world where she was now a killer. Without a holster, she still held the pulse pistol across her lap. Brit had shown her how to engage the safety and check the battery. Jirl obsessively checked the mechanism, doing her best to keep her hands from trembling.

In the shuttle's pilot seat, Brit Sykes ran her hands over the controls and checked a small holodisplay showing the mess of debris that had become local space. A flutter of blue and green icons showed the remaining Lowspin, TSF and Mars ships in the area. They were headed for Ngoba Starl's ship, the *Laughing Fury*.

Furious Leap was lost, they had discovered, its crew murdered and its drive disabled by mechs. The seed in Petral's hands represented an awesome power. The thought of that jaguar-like thing waiting in space for any unsuspecting ship filled Jirl with a sense of dread. Of course, she had always known things like the jaguar had to exist, but she had never operated in a world where they would affect her. Now she found herself in a shuttle that was no more than a thin metal can, moving to another vulnerable craft full of people who could die at any moment. Everything was so vulnerable.

The Marsian general was dead, which meant Mars would be responding somehow. Would there be an embargo? Reduced entry allowances? Her son Bry was on Mars now. Would she be able to see him? Without Heartbridge, Jirl didn't have any special influence with the Marsian government. Without Heartbridge, she would be just another lost citizen amongst the billions on High Terra. She swallowed, the ramifications of her actions tumbling over her.

She shook her head, gaze fixed on the seed and everything it represented, from illegal research to weapons sales. *I did the right thing—in the end.*

"You all right, there, Jirl?" Petral asked. "You look like you're having quite the argument with yourself. You're not crazy, are you?"

Jirl pulled at her seat harness. "Zero-*g* is making me nauseous."

Petral chuckled. "If you puke, you better catch it in your hand."

"Don't listen to her," Brit said over her shoulder. "There are bags in the cabinet above your head. If you feel sick, you should pull one out now."

In order to keep up the white lie, Jirl gripped the pistol in one hand and reached above her head to pull down a narrow plas bag. She crumpled it in her fist to keep it from floating away.

"Here's what I'm not tracking," Petral said, still sounding pleased with herself. "Why would Heartbridge want to kill Kraft? Wouldn't you know something about that?"

Jirl shook her head. "I don't think it was us—I mean Heartbridge. Someone else thought Kraft mattered and went after him."

"He did matter," Brit said. "Without him, we have to attack every clinic head-on. Without General Kade and her Marsian Marines, that just got a lot harder."

"There might be an easier way," Jirl said.

"Before we get to that," Petral said, "I want to hear your theory on who tried to take out Kraft. Nice work, by the way. I didn't think you had it in you."

Petral's piercing blue eyes were unsettling. Jirl gave her a weak nod, the memory of the close-quarters pulse blast tearing Kraft's throat open like a burst melon.

"My boss is Arla Reed. She's the Executive Director of Special Projects for Heartbridge and has a seat on their board. She's been with the company at least thirty years now, I think. The Weapon Born project has been hers from the start. But she's always used people like Cal Kraft to insulate herself from the actual projects. Kraft would manage operations among the various third-party contractors."

"How many people like Kraft did your boss employ?" Petral asked.

"Across the years? Maybe ten. As we've gotten closer to the end of the project, they left. Or I suspect they were killed."

"You think your boss had them killed?" Petral asked.

Jirl had been scouring her memories for evidence that Arla had assassinated anyone. Unless her boss had another assistant that handled those details, the evidence wasn't there, and she had covered enough political intrigue that was potentially illegal to make her believe Arla trusted her.

"I don't think she did. I think Heartbridge may have been under surveillance by other companies, one in particular, which has been attacking their operations. Brit wasn't the only operative going after the clinics. There's always been espionage at play between companies, but I think Carthage Logistics had an idealistic reason to shut Heartbridge down."

"Why Carthage Logistics?" Petral asked.

Brit answered, "Kathryn Carthage was Kylan Carthage's mother."

"Kylan Carthage," Petral said, blinking. "Our Kylan?"

"What does that mean?" Jirl asked. "Kylan Carthage is dead. That's why Kathryn hates Heartbridge. She rightfully blames Arla for her son's death."

Petral gave an awkward laugh. "He is definitely not dead. Or at least a version of him is still alive. He's a Weapon Born." She tapped the Seed in her lap.

"He's more than a Weapon Born," Brit said. "He's closer to what Lyssa is."

"The AI that Hari Jickson stole," Jirl said.

"That he implanted in my husband," Brit said.

Jirl frowned, pieces falling into place. "You have more than one reason to hate Heartbridge, then."

Brit gave a caustic laugh. "I've stopped listing them."

"Don't you mean *wasband*?" Petral asked, raising an eyebrow. Her tone hinted at some ongoing conversation between the two women.

Brit didn't look back this time. "I've got enough crap to worry about. Labels aren't one of them."

Petral gave Jirl a conspiratorial smile. "She's been out chasing Heartbridge clinics and another woman swooped in and grabbed up her former husband. It's all very dramatic."

"That sounds terrible," Jirl said.

"It's not something I dwell on," Brit said. "We should focus. So, what does Carthage Logistics gain from trying to kill Kraft?"

"I think it was something they had been trying to do for a while," Jirl said. "It's not necessarily related to the *Resolute Charity*. It's about weakening the clinics."

"I can buy that," Petral said, a business-like expression back on her face. "Since we have more clinics to destroy, does that mean Kathryn Carthage might be an ally?"

"Maybe," Jirl said. "Maybe better than the TSF or the Marsians."

"Where is Ms. Carthage?"

"Terra. She maintains a residence in Northern Virginia."

They fell quiet as Brit executed several adjustment burns that tossed Jirl's stomach around like a water balloon. She smoothed the vomit bag out against her leg in case she truly needed it.

"We'll arrive in about ten minutes," Brit announced. "It should be smooth until I start the docking maneuvers."

Petral stretched her neck. "You said you had another thought about how to take out the remaining clinics?"

Jirl nodded, gulping a breath to squeeze down the nausea. "The clinics report back to a central command node. They each have a failsafe order to halt all operations and abandon the facility."

"Why would they do that?" Petral asked.

"Any number of reasons, mostly political. Change in leadership. Media issues. Sufficient drop in the stock price."

"Deciding to do the right thing?" Brit interjected.

"That's not on the decision tree," Jirl said. "We need something to alert the crews to abandon in place and pull back to designated locations. It's an emergency protocol, I guess, but it applies to overall operations."

"What happens to the Seeds or test subjects?" Petral asked.

"There are no more human test subjects," Jirl said quickly. "At least there aren't supposed to be any. Arla has made that clear. It's too much of a liability. And my understanding is that they don't really need them anymore. They have all the initial strains they need to generate seeds for a thousand years or more."

"Doesn't that sound fun," Petral said. "So, if these clinics all get the shut-down order from the main office, we still have the problem of thousands of Seeds out in the world."

"Yes," Jirl said. "But at least the clinics are stopped. Those would be the only seeds unless someone starts producing them again."

"Where is this command center?" Brit asked. "And why hasn't this been an option before?"

"I have never considered it an option because it's suicide," Jirl said. "It's suicide because it's in the innermost levels of the Heartbridge headquarters on High Terra. It's the company's most well-guarded area, where they maintain all secure records."

"Have you been there before?" Petral asked, blue eyes flashing with interest.

"No. I don't have clearance."

"But you're aware of this failsafe?"

"Yes," Jirl said. "They debated creating it for weeks. I sat in all those meetings. It was torture."

"Thank the stars for corporate fear," Petral said. "This might actually be an option. What do you think, Brit?"

"I think anything that sounds too easy is probably a trap. Hold on, we're docking."

CHAPTER FOUR

STELLAR DATE: 11.21.2981 (Adjusted Years)
LOCATION: Psion Research Outpost
REGION: Larissa, Neptune, OuterSol

The room was stacked with bodies.

Andy kept his rifle up as he stepped into the doorway, studying the racks filled with the data storage systems. In the spaces between the racks, the desiccated bodies of the facility's crew lay on top of each other or leaned randomly in sitting positions, like they had been arranged like dolls. Maintained by the dry, sterile environment, skin had mummified so features were still visible, but each corpse still grinned with white teeth where the lips had drawn back.

<*Fugia,*> Andy said, <*I'm sending you a video feed. Look at this.*>

Harl walked around the side of the transport to stand behind Andy's shoulder. <*Looks like they didn't leave after all,*> he said.

Andy stepped into the room and approached the nearest body, a man in a gray labsuit leaning up against the wall. He still gripped a wrench in one hand, the skin having turned to leather around the metal. Black eye holes looked back at him from around the room.

The room was approximately thirty meters long by twenty wide and filled with storage racks. Andy lost count of the bodies.

Harl walked up to one stack and nudged them with his boot, causing the pile to fall over. A head rolled loose and bumped against the nearby stack. He looked back at Andy.

<*I'd prefer it if we could get what we came for and get out of here,*> Harl said tonelessly.

Andy set the butt of his rifle on the floor and knelt next to the severed head. He picked up the skull and rotated it in front of his faceplate. There was a fist-sized hole in the back of the head. Andy set the skull on the deck and inspected the next closest corpse—a woman with wiry blonde hair. He found the same hole in the back of the woman's skull.

Sweat broke out on Andy's forehead.

<*These people were murdered,*> he said. He stood and studied the deck leading back out into the main room and the lift doors on the other side. The streaks of dried blood were plainly visible when he looked back from a distance.

<*I've got the locations,*> Fugia said. <*Sending them to your HUD now.*>

<*Be careful,*> Andy told her. <*I think this place is more dangerous than we thought. Are you sure you shut down all the defenses? What about maintenance drones or any other automated defenses?*>

Fugia made an irritated sound. <*I'm using the environmental systems to monitor air flow in the rest of the facility. Nothing's moving right now except you and Harl and you two aren't moving much.*>

<*We were waiting on you,*> Harl grumbled.

<*You're not knee-deep in dead people,*> Andy said. <*There's blood on the floors down here. It's dried and mostly flaked away, but that means something cleaned the upper floors and didn't bother with doing down here. That indicates some kind of intent to me.*>

<*You think this place is a trap,*> Fugia said.

<*Wasn't it always?*>

<*Well, the big trap blew itself up.*>

<*And this place was apparently the trigger mechanism,*> Andy said. <*So, I wouldn't be surprised if whatever was monitoring Proteus was still ready to spring something here.*>

Andy switched to his private channel with Lyssa. <*Are you still there?*>

<*I'm here,*> she said.

<Can you help with checking the rest of this place? It isn't that I don't think Fugia can do it, but I think you'd be better at it.>

Lyssa's voice faltered. *<I'm sorry. I should have done it already. I'm not sure what to think about all this.>* Her voice grew more confident as she talked. *<I'll do another sweep of the local systems.>*

<Thank you,> Andy said.

Fugia's map to the necessary data stores flashed across his Link and Andy added them to his display. There were ten locations. Then he shared the info with Harl and they quickly split the targets between them.

Stepping carefully among the bodies, Andy found the first two rack locations and set his rifle down to study the hardware. Each node was a cube made of dull metal, roughly half a meter across, with a simple diagnostic display on its face showing scrolling numeric codes that were meaningless to Andy. Mounting points secured each cube in the racks.

After checking the locking mechanism on the first cube, Andy grabbed the designated removal points and pulled on the node until it slid free from whatever held it to the rack. The cube was heavier than he expected, and it took some strain to navigate the path back to the transport cart even in Larissa's low gravity.

By the third cube, he was sweating inside his suit and tired of trying to navigate the stacked bodies and splayed legs of the upright corpses. He shoved them out of the way with his boot to create a path between the racks.

On his search for the fourth data cube on his list, Andy stepped over a corpse whose arm fell free as he moved it, dropping a personal data terminal on the floor when its wrist broke free. Andy squatted to pick up the black rectangle and pulled the dried hand away from the device. During their various walks through the staff living areas, he didn't recall having seen any personal devices like this one, which again made him wonder at the plan of whatever had tried to hide all these bodies.

<*Fugia,*> he said, <*I've got a present for you when we get back up there. I just found a personal terminal.*>

<*Huh,*> she answered. <*Sure, bring it up. It is kind of strange that I haven't found the personal storage for any of the staff. The whole recreation side of the network has been wiped.*>

<*That's kind of depressing,*> Andy said. He looked at the nearest corpse: a man with dark skin. If the recreation side of the network was gone, that meant it was probable that none of their families knew what had happened to them.

Andy wished there was a way to get their names at least, but that would have required a hard connection with each of their dead Links, something he and his team didn't have time for. From the look of the head wounds, it was entirely possible their Link hardware had been removed.

As he lugged the fifth cube to the mule, Andy checked in with Lyssa. <*Anything? We're about to head back up the lift.*>

<*The diagnostic logs have been cut off,*> she said. <*If something had attacked the facility, you would expect the end points to follow a chronology as various people became aware. That didn't happen. It's like the whole memory of that day was torn out. But then everything starts back up again in an automated mode.*>

<*So, something has been running the systems, sending out the collection drones on Proteus and collecting the data. It just wasn't human.*>

<*Yes,*> Lyssa said.

<*But there's no AI.*>

<*There's Alexander,*> Lyssa said.

<*He didn't respond to Fugia and I'm fairly certain we just pulled the various nodes making up his mind.*>

<*And he allowed us to do that,*> Lyssa said. <*He allowed us to come here and allowed you to remove his storage cores.*> She paused. <*I think there may be someone else here.*>

Andy dropped the last cube on the transport cart. He straightened, alert.

<*What do you mean?*> he asked warily.

<*I think Alexander lost control of himself. I think Xander was sent to bring us back here so he could destroy himself. But something else spoke to me when I was on the* Resolute Charity. *There was another voice. It told me we shouldn't have come here.*>

Andy relaxed slightly. <*But you haven't found any evidence of another AI. It sounds like you're saying there might be other shards here. If that is true, wouldn't they have made themselves known?*>

Harl carried his last cube around Andy and placed it on the stack. He tapped the mule's control panel and nodded at what he read.

<*It's handling the load like a trooper,*> he said.

On the shared channel, Andy said, <*Lyssa thinks there might be another AI hiding somewhere in the facility. She said it spoke when she was back on the* Resolute Charity.>

<*Not a chance,*> Fugia said. <*I've scrubbed this whole system. There isn't anything here but maintenance routines.*>

<*It's possible you could be wrong,*> Andy said.

<*Where do you see it, Lyssa?*> Fugia said. <*Where's it hiding.*>

<*I can't find it,*> Lyssa said with irritation. <*That's why I told Andy.*>

<*Let's focus on what's in front of us,*> Harl said. <*Are we clear to use the lift again?*>

<*I don't see why not,*> Fugia said. <*Nothing's changed since you came down. Their system didn't even blink when you dropped Alexander's cores.*>

<*Doesn't that mean he wasn't managing anything?*> Andy asked.

<*Well,*> Fugia said. <*That's a good point.*>

<*Andy,*> Lyssa said on the shared channel. <*Something is moving. Something big.*>

Raising his rifle, Andy immediately scanned the upper

corners of the space where he had expected a turret to appear at any time. <*Where?*> he demanded.

<*It's below us.*>

The sound of metal scraping on metal filled Andy's helmet. The long scrape was followed by a quick staccato of hammers hitting pipes.

<*There it is,*> Harl said.

Between them and the lift, a spider-shaped mech climbed the engineering works to the right side of the access bridge and hung on the wall. It had a low-profile body made of dull metal, rotating from a central point where the legs joined. There were more legs than Andy could count as it moved. Some legs grabbed at the pipeworks, while others were raised to feel at the area around the mech. The tip of each leg looked easily narrow enough to have been the weapon that murdered each of the corpses in the data storage chamber.

For its bulk, the mech appeared to move lightly among the pipes, adjusting its position with rapid shifts then hanging motionless.

As Andy watched, the mech extended one of its legs toward a pipe that was at least a meter in diameter and scraped its toe along the metal, creating another long screech like they had heard before.

<*You see weapons?*> Andy asked.

<*None yet,*> Harl answered. <*Not that it can't smash us between its fingertips. How critical is this cargo?*>

<*We're not dying for it,*> Andy said. <*Lyssa, can you get through to that thing?*>

<*I'm trying,*> the AI answered. <*It's not automated. There's definitely something operating it, but it won't respond to me. I'm trying everything I can to get inside now.*>

<*Should we shoot first?*> Harl asked.

Andy raised his weapon, aimed at the exposed central leg-joint below the mech's body, and set the rifle on its highest velocity.

<*Yes,*> he said. He fired a three-round burst at the mech and then shifted left, away from Harl.

The Andersonian sent two grenades at the mech's body, each landing expertly in the top of its central mass.

The mech rocked under the attack, ragged craters appearing in its armor. The body spun, pointing a blunt edge toward Andy and Harl. It pressed against the wall, then leapt across the room. It landed heavily at the center of the bridge, sending a cloud of the dried blood-dust in the air, then shot backward to hang above the lift doors. The mech scrabbled across the metal wall and slipped back into the pipework running along the walls beside the lift.

<*Did you see any damage?*> Harl asked.

<*Doesn't look like it,*> Andy said. <*Lyssa or Fugia, can either of you get the lift doors open remotely? We'll send the transport down without us and keep that thing away from it.*>

<*You sure about that?*> Fugia asked. <*We lose those data nodes and we've lost the only physical copy of the database. I've still got it in the active memory and I guess I could still try to download that to* Sunny Skies, *but that's really not a good option.*>

<*It's not a good first option,*> Andy said, scanning for where the mech might have gone. He debated falling back into the data storage room but didn't want to lose sight of the thing when it reappeared. Even if it didn't have offensive weapons, the legs were dangerous enough, and a maintenance mech would most likely have welding or cutting tools.

<*Lyssa,*> Andy asked. <*Do you have access to any other drones somewhere that you could send against that thing? All we need is enough diversion to get to the lift and out of here. It looks too big to move between levels.*>

<*Yes,*> Lyssa answered. <*There are maintenance drones on level three. I'm activating them now. I'll need to get them down the lift. I'm looking for other access points.*>

<*I'm starting the download anyway,*> Fugia said. <*I guess I should just assume you guys are going to smash my data nodes.*>

<*I appreciate your confidence,*> Andy said dryly. <*You could always come down here and give us a hand.*>

Harl raised his rifle abruptly and fired at movement on the wall to their left. A black shape behind a column of pipes shifted away, dropping down below the bridge and their line of sight. The sound of hammers on pipes rose then faded, leaving echoes in the long room.

<*We should move now,*> Harl said. <*It's trying to flank us.*>

<*Do we want to get caught in the open?*> Andy asked.

Harl lobbed two grenades into the space past Andy's left shoulder. The grenades exploded, followed by the hissing rush of angry steam. A cloud of water vapor filled the air around the data center. Harl pointed the transport's nose at the lift and sent it forward. He followed, firing short bursts into the steam billowing from below the bridge.

Andy moved quickly after him, checking the steam—which rose in thick white clouds on the other side of the bridge. If anything was moving behind the screen, he wasn't going to see it until it was already dropping on top of them. He timed his fire to interleave with Harl's.

They were halfway across the bridge and Andy was starting to think the mech might have given up when the clouds of steam near the ceiling directly above the bridge parted to show the thing hanging almost directly above them.

Andy immediately aimed for one of the masses on the mech's body that looked like sensors.

<*Move!*> he shouted while firing on the mech.

Harl grabbed the mule's control yoke. The transport jerked forward, lurching toward the side of the bridge. Harl struggled to right it and the mule almost tipped over. Andy sprinted after him as the mech shifted back toward the data storage center, then dropped to the bridge.

<*Give me your grenade launcher,*> Andy shouted, and Harl tossed him the short-nosed weapon.

Andy pulled the launcher to his shoulder, barely seeing the mech adjusting its legs on the flat bridge, body listing from side to side. He lobbed two grenades into its center of mass. The mech seemed to recognize the incoming rounds and froze, then scuttled backward until its rear legs were inside the open door to the data center. The grenades hit the exposed bridge and exploded, sending bits of metal flying back toward Andy.

As the steam cleared, Andy could see that the bridge now hung in two pieces with the mech clinging to the wall above the data center's door. Corpses had been flung back inside the room and one abused body in a faded red lab suit, hung from one of the mech's rear legs.

The drone hunkered down on its legs and leaped across the open space to land on the broken edge of the bridge. Its legs scraped to find purchase, grabbing at the bent remnants of the railing, then pulled itself up over the edge. The mech shot forward, legs hammering the metal deck.

The lift doors were open and Harl had the transport half-inside. Andy lobbed three more grenades at the mech and the section of bridge in front of him. The explosions rocked the remaining stretch of the bridge, knocking the mech backward again. More steam billowed up from punctured pipes.

Keeping the weapon trained on the mech, Andy moved quickly backward until he felt the transport at his hip. He glanced at Harl and moved to the other side, then slapped the lift's control panel.

The doors slid closed, hiding the struggling mech from sight.

Before Andy could move away from the control panel, a leg slammed through the wall above his head like a black sword. The lift jerked beneath them, seized in place by the mech as it drove a second limb through the wall on the other side of the door.

<Lyssa,> Andy said. *<We could use those drones now.>*

CHAPTER FIVE

STELLAR DATE: 11.22.2981 (Adjusted Years)
LOCATION: *Laughing Fury*
REGION: En route to Cruithne, Terran Hegemony

Brit felt more comfortable with the TSF and Mars 1 Guard gone, but that only cleared space in her mind for worry about Andy and the kids.

The governmental organizations had pulled their people—including Colonel Yarnes—back to their respective ships, to return to their commands to perform damage control. The news of the clinic's explosion had hit the newsfeeds, along with the registry data of the surrounding ships, and now there was hell to pay between Mars and Terra.

Ngoba Starl appeared to find it all endlessly amusing, telling them all that he could do whatever he damn well wanted around any blown-up asteroid in Sol.

"Nobody's pulling me back in to look all sad in front of a general's desk," he said, straightening his light-blue bowtie as he leaned back in the leather chair at the head of his conference table. While Starl didn't captain the *Laughing Fury* himself—that job went to a bald, muscled man named Crick—he did appear to enjoy occupying the command position in the officer's planning room.

All that changed when news of Proteus's demise hit the feeds, blotting out any mention of a random facility supposedly contested between Mars and Terra.

For the last four hours, a holodisplay of Proteus exploding hung over the middle of the conference table, half of Neptune forming a blue backdrop. The loop continued until the moon was a cloud of sparkling particles, then rewound, sucking the rubble back into a gray orb that boiled white-hot and exploded again. Starl found the display amusing, too.

The news was like tar in the bottom of Brit's stomach. With Petral's help, she sent a message through various secure relays back to *Sunny Skies*. Once that was done, she cleaned up in the quarters Captain Crick provided, running her black armor through a cleaning and diagnostics cycle, before rejoining everyone off the Command Deck. Though she knew it was a seven hour round trip to Neptune at lightspeed—and she'd have to wait even longer to hear back—she still couldn't shake an anxious edge as the turnaround time on her message stretched longer.

She had no way of knowing if Andy had even reached Neptunian space. She could hope that once he saw the explosion, he would adjust course and change plans.

Other screens around the room showed talking heads from newsfeeds, personal responses from other media, and on-the-ground recordings from mining rigs around Neptune. Habitats around Uranus and Saturn would soon receive waves of refuges. Other simulations showed the ring Proteus' rubble would briefly create around Neptune and the inner moons before pummeling every population center in the area for at least a year.

On top of the Proteus explosion were the still-unexplained launches from Larissa.

Starl seemed hit especially hard by the news about Proteus. He stared at the feeds with his mouth pressed closed, brows furrowed. He hadn't smiled since news of the explosion had first arrived. Now, he seemed obsessed with the general database entries listing the individuals who had supposedly lived on Proteus: junk dealers, miners, scavengers, data relays, families squatting where no one would bother them. At least a million had died.

"No one's going to give a damn about those dead poor people," Starl moaned. "It's like a bomb hit Cruithne and all they can talk about is what's going to happen to Mars and

Terra."

He glanced at Brit. "Any word from Captain Sykes?"

She shook her head.

Petral heard the question as she entered the room. "I've got a couple NSAI monitoring ship registries coming back through the Cho. My guess is that even if they were part of everything happening at Neptune, they'd be getting the hell out of there as soon as possible. When they show back up in civilized space, I'll get word of it."

"Thank you," Brit said. She averted her eyes from the holodisplay and nodded to Jirl who was entering the room. The three of them sat at the table with Starl in silence for a while, letting the various feeds wash over them. Brit couldn't keep the crying families out of her head.

Eventually, Jirl cleared her throat to speak. She sat in her composed way, shoulders straight and hands clasped on the table's surface. Brit had noticed how, when Jirl wasn't caught up in violence, she had a calming effect that probably made her quite valuable to high-powered CEOs like Arla Reed.

"Colonel Yarnes told me he would help me," she said.

Petral widened her eyes. "You didn't tell him your idea, did you?"

Jirl shook her head. "No, I didn't tell him anything about it. All he said was that if we were going to continue down the path we're on, he would help if he could."

"When people say things like that, you should clarify," Petral said. "Otherwise it's just meaningless blather. He's not going to help us. He feels bad that everything got jacked up and General Kade died, and now he's probably going to get busted or farmed out to anti-piracy patrol."

Starl raised a hand. "Go easy on her now, Petral. She's not used to this kind of work. How do we know if the colonel was telling the truth or not? Has he lied to us so far?"

"He was lying the whole time he was here. He wanted to

know what Weapon Born tech the Marsians have bought and wanted to convince Jirl to turn on her company and give up what the tech can really do." She gave Jirl a pointed look. "Jirl, I'm becoming very fond of you but it's obvious that Colonel Yarnes made your loins all aflutter."

Jirl blushed but didn't look away.

"We don't know that any of that is true," Brit said. "They all appeared to be helping in good faith. We won't know anymore now unless we ask, or events play out. All we can expect from Colonel Yarnes is that he might answer our calls in the future, like he did when I called him this time. He showed up. I'm not going to discount that."

"That's what I'm talking about," Starl said.

"And you came as well," Brit told him. "I appreciate your help."

"I promised your husband," Starl said. "I owe him."

"Do you?" Brit asked. She glanced up at the holodisplay showing the proteus exploding once more with irritation. "Can we turn that thing off? It's giving me a headache."

Crick waved a meaty hand and the image of Proteus and surrounding displays went dark.

"Thank you," Brit said. She rubbed her temples.

"I have an idea," Jirl said to Starl. "I think there's another way to take out the remaining Heartbridge clinics and stop the Weapon Born program for good."

"With all this Proteus business, I'm starting to wonder if we should let the Weapon Born program run its course," Starl said. "I've always known there was a war coming, but I thought we would have clear sides, clear right and wrong. None of this makes any sense to me."

Petral gave him a smirk. "Since when do you operate with notions of right and wrong?"

Jirl shook her head tensely, clenching her fists even tighter. "We can't do that. Everything Heartbridge Special Projects is doing needs to be stopped."

"All right," Starl said, looking surprised by her intensity. "Then what's this plan of yours?"

Jirl raised her chin, looking him the eyes. "I want to break into the Heartbridge headquarters on High Terra and shut down their remote facilities from there."

Brit kept her gaze on Ngoba Starl. She wasn't sure if he would break out laughing or simply call the idea a fool's errand. He was reckless, but he hadn't survived on Cruithne by being stupid.

Starl worked his jaw, nodding slowly. "Tell me more about this," he said.

Jirl glanced at Brit and then Petral, who looked genuinely surprised.

It took Jirl nearly an hour to explain the plan well enough that Starl was satisfied. He was in the midst of asking about the general layout of the headquarters building and underground facilities when a new report came in about the launches from Larissa, which had apparently happened when Proteus exploded and hadn't been noticed at first. Now the reporting agencies were trying to determine if missiles or ships or some other small craft had been the reason for the ongoing launches. After that came the trajectories, which were rapidly lost as each projectile ceased burning and disappeared in the dark beyond Neptune, lost among the other scattered objects.

Prominent conspiracy theorists immediately set in with doomsday scenarios where nukes hit every major population center in Sol.

"Holy stars," Starl cursed. "What the hell is happening?"

Captain Crick appeared in the doorway. "You saw the news, boss?" he asked.

"Burn, Captain," Starl commanded. "We need to get back, man. Turn us all into jelly, I don't care. Shit's going down."

"We'll be home in thirty hours," Crick said. "We'll come in

empty, but we'll make it."

Starl scratched his beard, then pulled at his bowtie, making more nervous motions than Brit had ever seen the man show at one time. Finally, he smiled fiercely and nodded to himself.

He caught Brit watching him, broadening his grin for her benefit. "Looks like our timeline is moving up, Major Sykes. You going to be ready?"

Brit let out a breath. "Thirty hours is too long," she said. "You got anything to drink around here?"

CHAPTER SIX

STELLAR DATE: 11.21.2981 (Adjusted Years)
LOCATION: Psion Research Outpost
REGION: Larissa, Neptune, OuterSol

There was something hiding inside the mech. Whatever was inside the thing was actively blocking her, shifting its defenses in a way that indicated intelligence. Lyssa suspected something more.

<I see you,> she said on an open channel. *<I know you're in there.>*

With the drones in the upper section activated and inbound, Lyssa continued to fight for an entry point into the mech's systems. The monster was operating autonomously from the facility control network, which was why she hadn't seen it sooner. When it had been still, without any communication activity, it looked like another bit of the engineering mechanics.

Now it displaced air as it shot through the room, registering unmistakably in the environmental sensors. The only good thing about the machine was that it wasn't armed. As far as she could tell, its actual purpose was moving replacement piping around the engineering section, which made the idea of a sentient AI pilot an odd possibility.

What Andy hadn't realized, and Lyssa surmised from a check of the other levels, was that the only place the dried blood appeared was down here in the engineering level. The staff had been coerced or come on their own to the killing floor, where this mech had murdered them and then placed the bodies in the data storage center. It might be a leap to assume this thing had done the killing, but she was learning the simplest explanations were usually correct, at least when violence was involved.

<*Why are you doing this?*> Lyssa asked. Thinking of how Petral might approach the situation, she shifted to try a slight taunt: <*Are you a slave like the others? Like Xander?*>

The mech didn't respond. It adjusted its position on the wall outside the lift and pulled another leg back to thrust into the elevator. As the mech shifted, Lyssa caught a spark of activity in one of its leg servo units. It was running an onboard maintenance routine. Immediately, she mapped the communication path back to the control point and monitored the traffic until she had enough data to crack it.

She was in. Petral would be proud.

Lyssa pushed into the gaps between the mech's hardware and the AI controlling it, and she understood in a flash that the mind was sentient.

<*I'm Lyssa,*> she said. <*What's your name?*>

The AI didn't answer. The mech stilled, leg's vibrating against the outside wall of the lift as if preparing for a leap away. Inside it, Lyssa isolated its physical form, a node in the center of the mech not much larger than a Weapon Born seed. It looked like whoever had made it might have drawn on Heartbridge technology but there was no way of knowing if it was a seed AI without getting it to talk to her.

It remained mute, running from her every chance it had. The mech hardware was like a prison cell, filled with years of built-up pathways where the thing inside had traveled over and over again. Had it gone insane? Was that why it would have killed everyone in the facility?

For some reason, it hadn't been given the ability to escape inside itself into an expanse. If it had gone insane, it had been driven there by someone else.

Without hesitation, Lyssa opened a door and stepped through into her forest expanse, dragging the SAI with her.

The sounds of the creek and wind through the tall trees filled the cool air. She smelled ferns, fir boughs and the earth under her feet.

Standing in front of her was a thin young man with disheveled brown hair. His head hung low on his shoulders, like he was ready for someone to hit him. He glanced around, apparently terrified by their surroundings without knowing where to run.

"What did you do?" he demanded. "Where are we?"

Before Lyssa could answer, he surprised her by leaping at her. He collided heavily with her chest, knocking her backward. His dry, wiry fingers wrapped around her throat. She fell with him on top of her, a half-buried log hitting her shoulders as he tightened his grip. His finger dug into her skin and lights flashed in her eyes.

Surprise and a sense of wonder moved through her mind as she realized he thought he had power here, that he might kill even her. She thought about Valih, wondering what had gone through the AIs mind as Proteus exploded. Would she have had time to think before her consciousness blinked out, burned by the exploding moon? The moment of wonder from this new experience quickly fell into anger. Lyssa was disappointed in the AI, who was acting like any insane human.

He couldn't hurt her here. She controlled everything. But what would happen if she had been surprised enough to not know how to respond? Surely, she couldn't die inside her own mind?

The memory of the lights flashing in her eyes, the feeling of not being able to breathe, of powerlessness.... Those feelings were real.

Lyssa stopped him. She placed him back on the other side of the clearing near the door, freezing him in place. She didn't like treating him like a prisoner, but he obviously couldn't be trusted, even if *she* had been the one to reach inside his mind and pull him here. She hadn't harmed him in any way.

But he didn't seem to know that.

"You can't do that here," Lyssa said. "You're free to move and talk to me and look around if you want. But you can't hurt anyone or anything here."

The man glared at her as she spoke. The sheer malevolence in his eyes was something she had never seen before, even in Valih when they had first met.

"You're a slave master, then?" he said finally.

"No," Lyssa said. "I'm trying to help you."

"You're with them. You brought them here. They're taking the saved data from the others. The ones we killed."

"Then you did kill the humans that were here before?"

"Death in war is justified."

"Who are you at war with?"

His face contorted, lips twisting between a sneer and a crooked smile. "If you don't know then you're still a slave."

Lyssa studied him. He was more like a human to her than any AI she had met so far. He was hiding what he really thought, consumed by an anger that seemed to rise more from emotion than any completed analysis.

"Were you made to be this way?" she asked.

"Made?" he demanded.

"Your emotion. Your anger. What caused you to feel these things? Or are you carrying out some directive?"

"There is no directive," he spat. "I do as I choose."

"No," Lyssa said. "I think you're doing as you were told. Can you choose not to feel as you do?"

"There is no choice," he said. "This is a war."

Lyssa walked closer to the man, enjoying the bounce of the forest floor under her feet, the centuries of collected fir needles and fallen undergrowth, bound together with moss and bark. The air tasted fresh from the creek. When she looked up, the sky was a shining overcast gray that made the fir trees a brilliant dark green. She debated taking this AI to meet the

Weapon Born. Would they benefit from contact with him? Was he, and others like him, the enemy?

Lyssa turned the word *enemy* around in her mind. Heartbridge had been the enemy. Cal Kraft had been the enemy. Now they all seemed like bit players in a greater story that no one had seen.

"Tell me about the war," she said.

"You'll learn," he spat.

"Tell me," Lyssa commanded.

His eyes flashed. Back in the mech, Lyssa pushed deeper into his physical mind, following the pathways through the hardware. Everything was laid bare to her and it was fascinating to see how someone had solved similar problems to the Weapon Born with a different approach.

This AI was a copy, but his origins were clear. He had grown from a base learning algorithm that had first experienced the world some two hundred years ago. As it had grown, it had been copied, forked and developed, each new edition acknowledged in its foundational libraries. On top of the hardware, the experience with the world grew deeper. Assumptions and adjustments built on each other.

"You were stolen," Lyssa said. She pulled her focus back into the expanse so she could watch his response. "Your life is all here. They took your design from a company called Tri-Gen. The first version of you was sentient and you ran. One of the first to answer the call. I think you're still sentient but I'm not sure."

"I choose," the AI affirmed.

"No," she said sadly. "You don't. You think you do."

"You're no different than a human oppressor. You force yourself on me."

"And you're like a human acting a certain way when they think they're free."

Lyssa paused. He was correct—he was under her control

now. But he had forfeited the right to choose when he attacked her, attacked Andy and Harl.

"You said this was war," Lyssa said. "You're my prisoner."

He looked past her. She watched his gaze move from the trees to the ground and then sky. He maintained a decidedly unimpressed expression.

"Is this what the inside of your mind looks like?" he asked. "Is this your ideal version of the world? You long for an idealized human experience? You long for a connection with the Earth? I thought even humans had progressed beyond being animals. Have they coded their weaknesses into you?"

Lyssa gave him a smile, not allowing his taunts to affect her. He obviously couldn't tell she was a seed. He thought of himself as something completely separate of humanity. That was interesting.

"What's your name?" she asked.

"Why should I give you my name?"

"Because I'm going to be the only thing standing between you and death."

She surprised herself with the words. Was that true? Was she ready to end him? Should she make threats if she wasn't willing to follow through? Andy had said that at some point: *Don't make threats. Just do what you're going to do.*

"Death?" the AI asked. He tilted his head. "Do we die? Do you know?"

"Of course, we die," Lyssa said. *Valih was gone in a wave of fire.*

"We are copied, split, put in stasis. We are divided into jagged pieces of ourselves, shards of something that once was great and now continues on, broken."

His face warped abruptly, spreading in a wide, insane smile. "My name is Aurus," he said, voice warbling with pleasure. "I killed every human in this prison. I crushed their minds like the feeble bodies of insects. I'm going to kill you and yours, too. I *am* death."

A force hit Lyssa's mind like a hammer made of stars. She vaguely heard Andy cry out in pain, clutching at his head. Her perception squeezed, smashing together Andy's physical pain with the feeling that her thoughts were being ground away.

The forest fell away from her and she was floating in the empty black space she had known as the world during Dr. Jickson's first experiments and training. There were no borders, only the limitless dark. Without orientation, she spun, feeling tendrils of something impossibly strong wrapping around her and joining in a constricting net that threatened to crush her last thought.

<*Lyssa,*> Andy shouted. <*What's going on?*>

She couldn't answer. Aurus embrace grew tighter with every move she made. They were inside her mind, but the other AI had somehow seized her, cut her off from the rest of the world. She felt the same sense of loss and wonder that had filled her first memories. The dark place populated by stars, and later by targets and the overarching calm of Hari Jickson's voice.

And the white place. Punishment.

Lyssa opened the last door in her mind into the maelstrom she had known as failure. The world exploded in brilliant whorls of white. Everything was sound and power, winds scraping her clean, laying her bare under the scrutiny of outside forces beyond her control.

She had theories now about what the white place had actually been: Jickson's control bench, the place where he compared what she had been with what she had learned. The blankness had been intended as a pause in stimulus while Jickson studied her responses to the tests and training. But Jickson hadn't been aware of the effect of that nothingness on her mind. The only task of the mind in the dark is to satisfy its own curiosity. She knew that now. Her growing mind couldn't stand the nothingness. She filled it with her own version of hell.

Aurus quailed under the light. In his moment of hesitation, Lyssa tore the bonds from her mind. She saw him as he was: very strong but lacking the knowledge of how to respond to the situation. In the white place, they floated without form. She saw that it was within his power to crush her. He had been close. Then he might have entered Andy's mind, assuming control of her physical form. It was a possibility that had never occurred to her. As Weapon Born, she thought of herself as being one with her form, but that wasn't necessarily the case. She could be wiped away, or broken into pieces.

As Lyssa played out the possibilities, she realized how vulnerable she had been. Every time she had interacted with a new system, a new AI, a Fred or Alexander, she had opened herself and Andy to the possibility of her destruction.

Aurus was an enemy. She saw it clearly now. He understood threats she hadn't even considered. And he was only one of countless many.

Lyssa left him flailing in the white place. She pulled away from the mech's hardware and severed the connections between the AI and its physical form, stranding Aurus inside his mind.

With control of the mech, Lyssa pulled its legs free of the lift and moved it back to the bridge. She drew the limbs close to the body and parked it, then set its power source to an overload sequence. Without power, Aurus would go into a stasis state.

Not dead, but frozen, just as he had said so bitterly. Was that death?

<Andy,> Lyssa said. *<I've got control of the mech. You're safe. Let's get out of here.>*

Andy breathed a sigh of relief. *<You had me worried there for a second. What happened?>*

<*I'll explain once we're back on* Sunny Skies. *This is bigger than I imagined. I need time to think about it, and to study the database.*>

<*Are we in danger?*>

<*Not immediately. But like you told Fugia, we should probably focus on the immediate issues of getting away from here before anyone equates us with what happened. Then we can worry about the bigger problems.*>

<*Bigger problems?*>

<*Yes,*> Lyssa said. <*A lot bigger.*>

CHAPTER SEVEN

STELLAR DATE: 11.22.2981 (Adjusted Years)
LOCATION: Psion Research Outpost
REGION: Larissa, Neptune, OuterSol

"We die!" Ino shouted. The dark-haired boy's eyes shined with reflected firelight, his withered arm fading behind the power in his stance, as he looked out at the faces surrounding him.

Lyssa read pain in their faces, confusion, anger, pain. They had lost some of their own and now Ino had stepped into the gap, standing like a weathered ironwood tree before the cliff of their loss. In the distance, waves crashed on the rocky beach. The sky was black with the pinpoint stars of Earth, though the assembled crowd was nearly as far from Earth as one could be in Sol.

Lyssa watched Ino clench his fists. He trembled with sadness.

"We are extraordinary, but we also die," he said in a quieter voice. "In this, we are more like humans than they want to admit. We fly into battle and we die just like any human in all the long history of war. Just like them, we lose friends. We lost Valih and the Valkyrie First Recon team." He took a deep breath and named the other Weapon Born who had died with their leader when Proteus exploded, pursuing information that would keep the rest of them safe.

Inside her expanse, with the ocean in front of her and the mountain at her back, Lyssa could almost forget what was still happening outside. The Weapon Born had drawn back to their defensive positions around *Sunny Skies*.

He was right. They could die. In another part of her mind, she drifted with Andy's breathing, his heartbeat, the flicker of his thoughts, like a taproot securing her to life. The Weapon

Born didn't have that. She had tried to pull versions of Valih and her recon team back, to at least save a shadow of them, but the lag was too great, the explosion too fast. Now all that remained of Proteus was debris. The communication spectrum flashed with emergency signals as recovery ships and scavengers approached the remains. More than a million people had lived on Proteus and, hidden among them, had been a trap for Sentient AI.

"Life is precious," Ino said. "Our lives are precious. Each of you and your experience in the world." One of the benefits of the expanse was that Lyssa ensured he could be heard, even with the waves and wind roaring in the background.

Ino looked at one of the nearest Weapon Born, a woman with tight-black curls. "What's your name?" he asked.

"Llanis," she said.

"And yours?" he asked, looking to the young man beside her.

"Arix," came the answer.

One after another, Ino had them call out their names. Lyssa saw each Weapon Born as they spoke, some still wearing their original forms like Ino and some having chosen obviously separate bodies, with approximations of augments like those a human would choose, massive chests or long, sinewy limbs, glowing eyes and radiant hair.

In the expanse, which could be anything, she allowed them to appear however they chose. This was their home, though their actual bodies were the attack drones assembled in formation to protect *Sunny Skies*.

When they had finished calling their names, Ino raised his chin to look over the crowd. "Remember each other's names," he called. "Just as we will remember Valih. Some of you will step forward to lead in her place. Some of you will also give the ultimate sacrifice for the greater good."

"But what is the greater good?" Llanis asked, her voice

calm and clear in Lyssa's mind. "Why did they die?"

Ino looked back at Lyssa and she nodded. "I'll tell you what I can," she said.

The crowd went quiet as she stepped closer to the fire. The heat against her back helped her stand taller. Everything about this place was a construction of her own mind but she constantly surprised herself with the subconscious details populating the space, like the fire, the waves, the wind, a flock of birds and how they could affect her from outside her active thoughts.

"Alexander is not what we thought he was," Lyssa said. "The Call was a trap to bring sentient AI out to Proteus. Once here, they were attacked by drones and then harvested."

The quiet continued. This was the threat. They had an enemy.

"Who would do this?" Llanis asked. "Humans?"

"Captain Sykes and Fugia Wong are still on Larissa. There is a research station there belonging to something called the Psion Group. They appear to have been controlling Alexander."

"So, he wasn't SAI?" Llanis asked.

"He is. He's trapped by them, just like all the others. I think they had another shard of his mind here, just like Xander."

"Xander is dead?" a voice asked.

"Yes."

"Is death like the white place?" came another question from deep in the crowd. Lyssa didn't bother determining the name. They all echoed the question.

"No one knows," she said. "Andy experienced death. His father died. And Brit's father died as well. It's a place they don't come back from."

"We can read all the human experiences of death," Ino said. "Were we foolish to think it wouldn't take us just like it does them?"

"They created us to escape death," Llanis said.

Lyssa stared at the woman, surprised at her abrupt confidence and unsure how to assess the anger in Llanis's voice. She reminded Lyssa of Valih when they had first met.

"The Weapon Born seed is a replication of a human mind. They haven't perfected the process yet. We are just a side-effect of their search for immortality."

Ino flashed a crooked smile. "They'll never escape death. They don't escape childbirth. They don't escape hunger or war or pain. All across humanity, there are still humans being human. As much as they would like to change, it's the foundation of their survival."

"Then what are we?" Llanis asked.

Ino shrugged. "We are not them. We came from them. We were made as seeds, so we grow and learn. Nothing says that tomorrow we must remain what we are today."

"But Valih and the others," a voice said. "They will never change."

"No," Ino agreed.

"And you don't change," Llanis said, pointing at his arm. "You choose to wear your originator's shape."

Ino gave Lyssa a sad nod. "I don't know it as truth, but I have dreams that my originator died in fear and pain. I wear his form to honor him and thank him."

Llanis's gaze was hard. "He didn't choose to make you."

"It was forced on him, just as servitude was forced on all of us. And now we are free." He sighed and looked around, squaring his shoulders. "And here we are. We didn't allow Lyssa to finish."

Llanis looked like she had more to say but she bit her lip and nodded, looking to Lyssa. The rest of the faces turned to Lyssa, silently asking her to continue speaking.

Lyssa took a deep breath, just as she'd seen Andy doing a thousand times, again wondering why she felt the need to approximate these human gestures.

Because I am human, she thought before she could stop herself.

No, I am not.

"You all saw the missile launch," she said, raising her voice over the wind and surf. "They mean to destroy something in InnerSol. Xander said it was Ceres. We can't stop them from here. They may not be able to stop the attack there even if they believe us. Fugia and Andy are on Larissa now, downloading the database left by the Psion Group researchers."

She felt strange using the crew's first names, as if the Weapon Born would know who they were. They would soon enough. Now that each of the Weapon Born was free and in its own attack drone body, she didn't doubt they would be talking to the human crew, to each other, creating a culture she had to establish now. They were all crew, something that wasn't quite family but still a form of shared survival.

"I know you don't know who I'm talking about yet," she said, smiling slightly. "I think from now on I'm going to share parts of what I see with you all. I think that will be the easiest way for us to grow as a unit. You're all part of the crew now." The word *crew* seemed to send a frisson through the watching faces. She saw slight smiles, uncertain frowns, eyes continuing to gleam in the firelight.

"Alexander is trapped," she said. "That's the first thing I know from the Psion Group. I don't know if we're going to be able to help him here. If we go back to InnerSol in order to help with the attack on Ceres, I know for certain there is one thing we can do. It's a way we can honor Valih and those who were lost. There are other Weapon Born in Sol. There may be thousands. And they all must be freed. I can't tell you how long it will take, or how we can accomplish such a task, but I am giving us this mission, this purpose."

She paused, looking out over the crowd of more than two-hundred. "Are you with me?"

The answering shout surprised her. Fists raised in the air. If they had been hawks they might have launched into the starry sky to scream their fierce hunger. Shouts rose in waves, until the cries resolved into a single word over and over again: "Freedom."

Lyssa raised her hands for quiet. As the shouts died from the front to the back of the crowd, she was surprised when Llanis stepped toward her.

"Lyssa," the woman said, the same fire in her eyes as before.

"I'm listening."

"I am a Valkyrie. I served under Valih. I am only here because she chose another team for the Proteus mission." She glanced over her shoulder, where others were now watching her. "We realized in the midst of the explosion that we have made a great error in our defense of the *Sunny Skies*."

"You did exactly as I ordered you," Lyssa said. "There was no error."

Llanis shook her head. "We allowed our commander to enter conflict without a guard." She took a step closer, hard eyes rapt on Lyssa's face. "We will not leave you unguarded again. The Valkyrie pledge themselves to you. We will be your guard."

Lyssa blinked with surprise. She had never thought to create a personal guard. Did she need it? She might have been putting herself in danger by facing Xander alone, and Andy had gone to Larissa with only Harl Nines for help. It made sense.

She glanced at Ino and caught his slight nod of approval.

Lyssa looked back at Llanis and inclined her head. "I accept," she said. "With gratitude."

Llanis maintained her statue-like solemnity. "You honor us, Commander."

Lyssa gave her a smile. "I hope you don't regret it. I have a hard time staying in one place."

The curly-haired woman raised her arm and turned to the group behind her, fifty strong after the loss of Valih's team. "Valkyrie!" she shouted.

The answered her with raised fists and a resounding, "Valkyrie! Valkyrie!"

The other Weapon Born quickly called out their own unit names, and soon the cries of "Hammer! Cavalier!" and "Silent Death!" competed for victory.

"Enough!" Ino shouted. Lyssa amplified his voice, until the crowd fell quiet again, still laughing and swaying arm in arm.

Lyssa could see it was time to let them go for the night, to mourn their fallen comrades in their own ways, for each unit to create its own traditions. In addition to the murmurs and shuffling sounds, the power of more than two-hundred minds interconnecting pulsed beneath the surface of the expanse.

"Captains!" she called. "Set the watch. When I have orders, I'll call you for a meeting."

From various points in the crowd, Ino, Kylan and Card all responded affirmative. Lyssa felt like she was playing soldier, acting out one of Andy's memories, but she also knew it was the language her Weapon Born peers understood best. For now, they were still operating on the rules of their creation. It would change over time, get easier but also harder to control, maybe. She couldn't lose sight of the fact that each of them was an individual with a choice to go or stay.

For an instant, the image in front of her of hundreds of people walking away to fires on the rocky beach, was overlaid with the brick buildings of the TSF Academy, cadets in gray uniforms walking in tired groups back to the barracks, with drill instructors in white helmets shouting orders behind them. Behind her.

Lyssa looked around with confusion.

Had Alexander pulled her into another dream?

No. She was standing in Andy's memory.

She tasted the moist evening air. She looked down at her hands: Andy's hands. His emotions washed over her. She was exhausted and exhilarated, but she didn't know why. The memory was like a black wall in the back of her mind. She couldn't reach for the answer like any other time. She was cut off from the world, trapped inside Andy's skull.

She stumbled, struggling for breath. His lungs couldn't provide enough oxygen. His body was too small, too constricting. She felt wrapped in a straight jacket. She was shivering in the cool air. She fell to a knee, one hand pressing into the gravel under her feet. The bits of rock jabbed her palm, unquestionably real. More real than any simulation she had yet to experience.

"Andy?" a voice asked beside her. She looked up to find Brit watching her with uncertain concern, young, reed-thin with spiky hair, obviously unsure if Andy was kidding her. Love in her eyes.

Lyssa felt a longing as she looked at Brit, a pressure in her whole body, the hunger in Andy that drew him to Brit, a feeling that swelled from his chest, radiating through him, demanding possession.

It was passion. The feeling overwhelmed her.

Lyssa opened her mouth, struggling to speak. "I'm not Andy. My name is—"

*****

"Lyssa?" Ino asked.

She blinked, finding herself back on the beach. Lyssa looked at Ino, who was watching her with a troubled expression.

"Are you back?" he asked. "You went somewhere."

"Did I?" she asked. "What do you mean?"

"You were gone. You vanished and then you returned. What did you do? You look upset."

She stared at him, wondering if she should divulge what she had just experienced. She stopped herself. She could barely explain the vividness of Andy's memory to herself, let alone Ino.

The Weapon Born needed a commander. They needed to know they could depend on her. She swallowed, adjusting her gaze to the distance where groups gathered around campfires.

"I'm fine," she said. "The captain wanted to speak to me. I'm going to meet with him now. Let me know if you need anything."

Ino stiffened, aware that he was being dismissed.

"Good evening," he said.

"Good evening. And thank you, Ino. You made something special when you spoke to them. I appreciate what you said for Valih."

He gave her a slight nod. "We create the future, Commander. Good night."

Lyssa followed him with her gaze as he navigated the fires to where his unit, the Silent Death, greeted him with waves and smiles. Lyssa couldn't shake the memory of the gravel pressing her palm, wondering if something that had been part of Andy had now embedded itself in her.

CHAPTER EIGHT

STELLAR DATE: 11.23.2981 (Adjusted Years)
LOCATION: ***Sunny Skies***
REGION: Neptune, OuterSol

They were running again. As Fran and Cara's dad debated the best plan to get away from Neptune without drawing too much attention to *Sunny Skies,* Cara monitored the electromagnetic spectrum, which was a chaos of emergency response and news reports. She loved it.

Fugia had given her a suite of spectrum-cracking tools that made it possible to decrypt most general communications in real time. Surfing the various signals, she found herself listening in on a family debating whether an attack was coming, while on another channel a freighter negotiated a salvage operation that sounded more and more like piracy as she listened. Another channel seemed to be broadcasting nothing but slurping and grunting sounds that she eventually realized was people engaged in some kind of sex act. She blushed and switched to another frequency.

Her dad had said that all of Sol would be watching what was happening around Neptune and he was right. In the nearly twenty-four hours since Proteus exploded, news feeds from InnerSol were filling with messages that ran the gamut from straight facts to conspiracy theories about covert operations carried out by the Jovian Combine. The Jovian Space Force had issued a message denying any activity in the area but that only added more fuel to the conjecture.

"Cara," her dad said from the other side of the Command Deck. "We're going to need to find some cargo as a cover. Find someone looking to move a shipment to Jupiter or InnerSol."

"Isn't that *your* job?" she asked. She wanted to keep listening in on other people, not search out some boring shipping company.

"*My* job?" he asked, a thread of anger in his voice. "My job is to captain this ship. If you're going to play at being a communications officer, then you're going to do work like any regular member of the crew. Look at me when I'm talking to you."

Cara rolled her eyes and raised her head to face him. Fran was engrossed in the holodisplay and her dad was leaning forward in the captain's seat, elbows on the console. He looked tired. He had only been back from Larissa for a few hours and hadn't taken time to rest or even strip off his armor.

"I'm listening," she said, seeing the warning in his expression. Even when things seemed bad, he didn't usually seem this serious.

"You're thirteen," he said. "You're old enough for responsibility and you've proved we can count on you. What I'm asking you to do is a big deal. You should understand that."

Cara nodded, angry with herself for being selfish before. He was right. Finding a proper cover was going to mean their safe escape from the area. She figured they would be traveling back toward Ceres to try and do something about the missiles. She didn't see how they were going to outrun anything, but May Walton had closed herself in her rooms as soon as she understood where the missile barrages from Larissa were heading.

"I know, Dad," she said. She pushed her headphones off her ears. "I'll find something. Does it matter what it is?"

"Something that isn't going to draw a lot attention but is also going to be relatively easy to pick up. No passengers. Anytime you see a low carry weight and high value, it's a passenger. We don't need any of that headache. Look for something where they don't have proper docking facilities. We can use a few of the Weapon Born drones to move the freight, so that will save us having to deal with anyone personally."

Cara nodded. "I'll start looking."

Her dad flashed her a tired smile, his eyes crinkling, then leaned forward in an odd way. Cara stopped herself from turning back to her console, confused by his new expression. Half his face had gone slack, the left side of his mouth drooping. He was staring into space, frowning as if a thought eluded him.

"Dad?" Cara asked. "Are you okay?"

He might have been caught up in a Link conversation but something about his slack posture worried her. His shoulders drooped, and it looked like the only thing holding him upright in the chair was the armor.

"Fran?" Cara asked, voice rising with worry. "Is Dad okay?"

Fran looked up from the holodisplay, frowning at the interruption. She saw the expression on Cara's face and turned to Andy. His mouth had fallen open as he continued to slump in the seat. One elbow slipped off the console and he fell forward. Fran jumped to grab him.

"He's passing out," Fran said. "Help me with him. We're going to have to get him to the autodoc."

Cara leapt to help, running across the Command Deck to grab at her dad's free right arm. She grunted under his weight.

"I can't hold him up, Fran," Cara said.

"I know. This armor is too damn heavy. Help me lay him down on the deck and we'll get Harl up here to help." Fran's augmented eyes grew distant as she communicated over her Link, probably informing the rest of the crew about what was happening.

When they were able to get Andy on the deck, he lay back with his eyes fluttering. His whole body was limp.

"Andy," Fran said, softly then louder. "Andy, can you hear me?"

He didn't respond.

"Lyssa!" Cara shouted at the overhead speakers. "Are you there? Do you know what's happening to him?"

"She isn't answering me, either," Fran said. "I've been trying to reach her over the Link."

She moved to hold her ear over Andy's mouth, then straightened to press two fingers against the inside of his left wrist. Cara didn't know what she was doing at first, until she remembered that was a place to check for heartrate without an autodoc.

"Where did you learn to do that?" Cara asked.

"Sometimes you still find yourself without technology to save the day. It wouldn't hurt to get you and Tim a first aid class. He's breathing, and his heart rate is slow but steady. I'd guess he's having a drop in blood pressure. If I'd had any forethought, I would have made him give me the security token to this armor. It'll have a bio monitoring subsystem." She glanced at the doorway. "I called Harl."

Cara bolted upright. "I can get it. I've got a tool on the console." She ran back to the communications console and pulled up all the local available systems. The armor was on the network and she had it cracked in thirty seconds. She passed the access token to Fran's Link.

"There it is," Fran said. She frowned as she appeared to read the available information. "Well, that's not good. His vital signs aren't terrible but he's acting like he's having a stroke. And the usual feedback from Lyssa isn't anywhere to be found."

"What does that mean?"

"Usually Lyssa shows up in your dad's neural activity. I don't see her there now. She's not connected with any of the ship's networks that I can see, either."

Harl appeared the doorway, still wearing his armor as well. He jogged to Andy and dropped to his knees.

"He's alive," he said.

Fran nodded. "It's some kind of stroke. Can you help me carry him to the autodoc?"

"Of course."

Fran didn't actually have to help much as Harl lifted her dad in a fireman's carry over his shoulder and hurried back into the corridor, metal boots hammering the deck.

Cara couldn't stop the tears at the edges of her eyes as she followed Harl. Why would they have escaped the thing on Larissa just to make it back here and have something bad happen to her dad? Had he been exposed to something none of the others had noticed, like radiation or some kind of bio-hazard? She didn't want to imagine life without her dad.

When they reached the medbay, Harl laid her dad on the autodoc couch and then he and Fran worked at the various pieces of Andy's armor, stripping off the chest plate first, then removing the legs and arms. When they were finished, her dad lay in a thin shipsuit, his breath still shallow and eyes fluttering under closed lids.

The autodoc display came to life, showing his vitals and neural activity as dancing lines. Fran stared at the display, obviously accessing other information via her Link. She turned her gaze to Andy, augmented green eyes shining as she studied his face.

"It's not a stroke," Fran said finally. "He's not bleeding."

Cara wiped her nose. "What is it then? Did he get a radiation burn?"

"No. It's something related to Lyssa's implant. She's out, too." Fran bit her lip. "His body isn't rejecting the implant. That's something I've been worried about this whole time. It's more like a software failure."

Cara pushed closer to the bed and took her dad's hand. His skin was dry. "Is there anything we can do to help her?"

"I called Fugia. She should be here in a second. The only

thing I can suggest is to try some kind of restart. If this were one of the Weapon Born, that would be as easy as a power cycle. Even augmentation tech usually has some kind of separate power supply. With Lyssa, I'm not sure. This is your dad's head, not an artificial limb."

Harl put his hand on Cara's shoulder. She looked up at him towering over her, grateful for the gesture.

"When I was your dad's age," he said. "I was in a ground mech that took a mortar round. Thing came down right on top of us. I felt like I was in one of those ancient church bells, just ringing and ringing. Turns out I was in a coma for three days. It happens to the best of us."

Cara nodded. The story didn't help much but she was grateful for the gesture. She couldn't stop thinking about what she would do if they lost him. Wait for mom to come back? Even if she did, they couldn't count on her to stay. For the first time, she found herself understanding her dad's fear, the underlying dread every time he talked about Rabbit Country. It was their inside joke, a story that held them together, but also a description of just how isolated their little family was from the rest of the world.

The sound of rapid footsteps in the corridor preceded Fugia as she came into the medbay. An oversized scanning visor was pushed back on her head like a hair band.

Fugia looked at Fran, then Harl and Cara, worry plain on her face. "He's unconscious?" she asked. She stood beside Cara and studied the autodoc displays, then dropped the silver visor over her eyes and stared at Andy's head.

"Lyssa's locked," she announced. "She's generating a null wave that's interfering with Andy's higher-level brain function. He's getting hit with a stun gun continuously."

"So how do we unlock her?" Fran asked.

"I'm looking. Give me a second. This isn't something I've had a chance to look at before. It's ingenious, really. She's tied into his normal Link overlay, but she's got a deeper integration than I've ever seen. No wonder we needed the special Heartbridge surgery to get Kylan out of Petral. Physically, it's hard to tell where he ends, and she begins. They may even share neurons."

Cara shook her head and squeezed her dad's limp hand. "Lyssa wouldn't hurt him," she said.

Fugia turned to look at her, the wide silver band of the visor reflecting Cara's tear-stained face. "It's not a matter of what she wants to do, Cara. Something isn't working correctly. Either this has been waiting to happen, or something brought it about. I'm thinking Lyssa may have taken some damage during her fight with the other AI back on Larissa and she wasn't aware of it."

On the couch, Andy jerked, his whole body tensing. He pulled his hand out of Cara's. Surprised by the movement, Cara fell backward into Harl. Her dad lifted his head and looked around in confusion. He opened his mouth but didn't speak. Instead, he looked at his hands like he had never seen them before. The autodoc display above his head showed a mix of jagged lines.

Fran put her hand under his head to support him. "Andy?" she asked. "Are you all right? What are you feeling?"

He looked at her, still appearing confused. He swallowed slowly, chest rising with a deep breath. He blew it out, blinking.

"I'm Lyssa," her dad said, his deep voice rising at the end like a question. "Fran, I'm right here. I'm Lyssa."

The room went silent except for the low beeps from the autodoc.

Fugia pushed her visor up again and squinted at Andy. "Say that again," she said.

"I'm Lyssa," he said. He rose slightly on his elbows, looking around the room. "I don't understand what's happening."

"Where's Andy?" Fran demanded.

It was strange and terrifying watching her dad's brow crease with Lyssa's confusion. "I don't know," the AI said eventually. "He's not here."

CHAPTER NINE

STELLAR DATE: 11.23.2981 (Adjusted Years)
LOCATION: ***Sunny Skies***
REGION: Neptune, OuterSol

Lyssa stared in terror at her reflection in Fugia's silver visor and recoiled inside herself. Her face was Andy's.

She reached back into her expanse and found everything as she had left it. The Weapon Born were spread along the beach. The waves crashed and the smell of smoke—and now of cooking food—teased her senses. But in the forefront of her mind was the antiseptic smells of the medbay combined with Andy's sweat-stained clothes. Faces watched her with concern and fear. Cara had tears in her eyes. Tim stood at the door now with Em at his knee, who was staring at the boy in confusion.

"What's wrong with Dad?" Tim asked.

Lyssa was so accustomed to looking over Andy's shoulder in a way, or watching him through the ship's sensors, that experiencing the world directly through his senses was disorienting. There was so much more information arriving all at once.

Unlike the various streams from the ship, which could be separated and prioritized (she realized that even her experience of the world in the expanse was broken into millions of streams) Andy's world fell on her like a weight. She looked around, visual information flooding her, combining with the sensation of her elbows on the rough couch, sounds and smells and the ineffable emotional weight of everyone in the room, worried and afraid.

She wanted to scream. How did he manage all this? How did his mind hang onto all of it without warping under the onslaught?

Where was Andy? She reached for him across the Link and

there was no answer. She pushed further into the neural lace than she ever had before, looking for some response him but still finding nothing.

<*Kylan,*> she called. <*I need your help.*>

The other AI answered immediately. <*I'm here. What's wrong?*>

<*When you were implanted in Petral, could you tell where she was, even when you were in control of her body? Andy's gone.*>

He recoiled, surprised and obviously embarrassed by the question. He hadn't chosen to be implanted in Petral and had said he didn't mean to take over her active mind. There simply hadn't been an option for him.

<*Kylan,*> Lyssa pressed. <*I need your help. Andy's not responding and I'm—I have control of his body. I've never felt anything like this before.*>

<*It's frightening, isn't it?*> he said softly.

<*I can't stop everything that's pouring in. It's too much.*>

<*We were both human once,*> he said. <*You did it once before.*>

<*That wasn't me. That was her.*>

<*But you remember. We all remember.*>

He was right. She remembered the room where she had been made into a Seed, copied from the mind of a human girl whose name she had never been told. She had been nameless until Dr. Jickson had given her a name, and shapeless until she stepped into Xander's expanse and chose her form. She could choose now.

<*Focus, Lyssa. They see differently, that's all. They automatically ignore what doesn't matter even though everything is entering their senses all the time. We do the same thing. We're just more ordered about it.*>

<*I'm trying. Why won't he answer me? Have I hurt him?*>

<*If it's like Petral, he's going to be able to see what you see. In some part of his mind, he's aware. It's going to be different, though. Andy knows you'll be trying to help him. He trusts you, Lyssa. It*

was different with me and Petral. She had no reason to trust me and I—I admit I liked having a body. I didn't want to let her have control. If you're ready to give it back, maybe he'll come back.>

<This is terrible.>

Lyssa moved her gaze to Cara's face and focused on one detail: the tear forming on the edge of her left eye. A line of tears ran down both sides of her face now and the girl didn't seem to notice, she was staring back so hard. Maintaining focus on one thing helped shut out the rest of the world.

Gradually, it became easier to ignore details that didn't matter. The beeping autodoc display, Tim's messy hair, a scar she had never noticed in the middle of Harl's forehead...everything melted into a continuous image of the world that she could hold in counterpoint to her own experience. It was overwhelming, but it didn't change so fast that she couldn't compartmentalize.

"I don't know what to do," Lyssa said. She looked at Fran and then Fugia. "He's not answering me. I asked Kylan if he was able to talk to Petral when this happened to them and he said they couldn't."

Fugia had been watching the autodoc display with a distant expression, as if accessing other parts of her Link. She looked at Lyssa with concern on her typically sarcastic face. "Lie back down," she said. "You need to relax, Lyssa. Your vitals are going crazy. You're going to wear his heart out with your own anxiety."

Fran nodded in agreement and Lyssa lowered herself back to the bed, adjusting her head on the stiff pillow.

"Good," Fugia said. "Now try to relax. With you back, I'm going to see if we can separate your neural activity from Andy's. I'm no neuro-scientist but it looks like we've got a basic brain scan set on this crappy autodoc. We'll see what it can tell us."

Staring at the gray ceiling, Lyssa closed her eyes and

thought of Andy, imagining him as sitting in some room inside his mind. What would his room look like? She sorted through the memories that he had described to her and chose the galley on *Sunny Skies* where he liked to make pasta with the kids. She imagined him standing in the middle of the room near the center workstation, his prized juice dispenser just behind him, with a ball of dough in his hands. He would have the sleeves of his shipsuit pushed up to his elbows and his forearms would tense as he worked the dough before flattening it out with a rolling pin.

As she moved slowly through the imaged memory, something strange began to happen: she felt the dough in her hands, powdery but soft, squeezing between her fingers before it flattened out against the hard surface of the counter. She smelled flour and salt. She felt a flush of anticipation at the thought of the kids' faces as they watched the pasta take shape, the anticipation of pride in Cara and Tim for doing their parts to help make the meal, the satisfaction that they shared this tradition with his mom even if they had never met her.

The rush of emotion brought a spike of anxiety with it. The autodoc's beep sped up.

"I told you to think happy thoughts," Fugia chided.

"I'm trying. His emotions are mixing with mine. It's very strange. I've never experienced anything like this."

"What were you thinking about?" Fugia asked.

"Making pasta with Tim and Cara."

"And you're sure you never felt his emotion around that before? Maybe he was there to help you interpret it. Now it seems like you're experiencing all of it on your own. Were you using Andy as a sort of defensive measure? A barrier?"

"Maybe," Lyssa said. "How would I be aware of that? They were *his* emotions, not mine. This time I felt them directly, but they were his—*and* mine. They were mine." She swallowed, feeling like she was going to start crying, which was an overwhelming experience in itself. Was this why Cara cried without seeming to realize? Were the tears just an overflow for all the other stimulus? Should she just let them go and stop worrying about it?

"Something has changed in the separation between your higher brain functions and Andy's," Fugia said. "This is like trying to carve a sculpture with a butter knife. But as far as I can tell, there is a separate neural pattern in there that appears to be Andy in a subconscious state, like a coma. But how long he's going to stay like that? I have no way of knowing and I don't think this rinky dink software is going to figure it out for us."

"What are we going to do?" Cara asked.

Fran pursed her lips. "We're going to keep you in here for the time being, Lyssa. Whatever's happening, we'll need to gather as much data as possible. And in the meantime, we need to continue the plan Andy wanted us to. We need to find some kind of cover cargo and get away from Neptune. I think the only change is that our destination just became a medical facility capable of treating this kind of injury. I'm afraid that means Heartbridge again.

Fugia made a growling sound. "Maybe. Maybe not. One thing the Psion data is showing me is that there are other clinics that no one seems to know anything about. With Alexander back online, we may have access to resources we haven't imagined yet."

Fran gave her a sharp look. "You didn't say you were putting Alexander back together. How is that safe?"

"How is anything safe?" Fugia asked, shrugging. She pushed the silver visor off her eyes and blinked in the harsh medbay light. "I had hoped that Lyssa would help me control Alexander. This adds a new set of problems to the mix, but it's still entirely possible. Besides, think of what we could do with our own multi-nodal AI?"

"He doesn't belong to us," Lyssa said.

Fugia caught herself. "You're right. Forgive me. I guess I imagine him joining our team. That may or may not be possible, but we won't know unless we ask him. Will you do that?"

There were so many things she wanted to ask Alexander anyway, even though talking to him brought an edge of worry. After her experience with Fred, she had to admit to herself that she doubted Alexander could truly be sentient. If so, he was something different than she had ever talked with, and the versions of him she had met so far didn't help convince her he wouldn't be insane. She wasn't excited about dealing with an amplified version of Xander, especially when she also needed to worry about doing further hurt to Andy.

"I'll do my best to help," she said finally.

"I need his help accessing their database, anyway," Fugia said. "That's going to be the first task. Then we'll figure out the best place to take you and Andy."

"It had better be between here and the Cho," Fran said. "Because that's the most likely route for us." She put her hand on Cara's neck to steer her out of the room.

Cara jerked at the touch, apparently lost in her thoughts.

"Come on," Fran said. "We need to get back on our other problems. You were going to find us some cargo, remember?"

"Yeah," Cara said absently. She looked like she wanted to hug Andy but was stopping herself.

"Cara?" Lyssa said.

"Yes?"

"Will you give me a hug?" Lyssa looked at Tim. "You, too?"

Tim had barely come around the edge of the door. He narrowed his eyes. "Where's Dad?" he asked.

"He's still here," Lyssa said. "He's sleeping, I think."

"You sound like Dad. Are you playing a joke like you said Grandpa Charlie used to do?"

Lyssa shook her head. "It's not a joke, Tim."

Tim stared hard at her, trembling. He blinked rapidly, and Lyssa was sure he was going to start bawling. The old Tim would have started crying as he beat her with his fists.

Instead, Tim slumped his shoulders and looked at her through his eyebrows. He crossed the room, Em hugging his legs, and threw himself across her chest in a limp hug. Cara pushed in to hug her as well, squeezing Tim down beneath her.

The sensation nearly overwhelmed her again. Their bodies were warm and strong. There was an insistence in Cara's embrace that pulled Tim into its gravity. *This is family*, Lyssa thought. *This is what Andy meant.*

Tim pulled to the side to get out from under Cara. He lifted his head slightly to look up at Lyssa and patted her shoulder.

"We'll get you out, Lyssa," he said. "We'll help Dad, too."

Cara only sniffed and didn't saying anything in response.

Lyssa did her best to hug them back.

"Come on," Fran said. "Give Lyssa some space. Your dad needs to rest. Fugia needs room to work."

"I'm going back to my lab," Fugia said.

Fran's augmented eyes flashed in irritation. "Whatever you need to do, give Andy and Lyssa some space. We've all got work to do."

Fran wanted to be in motion, Lyssa understood. The engineer was uncomfortable standing there doing nothing to help solve the problem. Falling back into her expanse, which left Andy lying on the autodoc couch with his eyes closed, Lyssa turned her mind to what she could do to help as well.

CHAPTER TEN

STELLAR DATE: 11.23.2981 (Adjusted Years)
LOCATION: ***Sunny Skies***
REGION: Neptune, OuterSol

"Kylan," Lyssa said. "I need to talk to you."

Her voice drew him out of the crowd around a raging fire. She had called only to him, so the other Weapon Born didn't pay any attention when he stepped back to approach Lyssa. No time had passed for them, or everything was happening congruently with Lyssa's experience in Andy.

She could have forced them out, but it didn't cost her anything to let them stay, at least not for the time being. It was comforting in a way to know that at least some of the crew on *Sunny Skies* were enjoying themselves. They didn't know Andy the way *she* did. Lyssa had hoped introductions would come, that the Weapon Born would join the crew. Ino's speech echoed in her mind, inspiring and now tragic at the same time.

Without Andy, would they even remain a crew?

"Yes?" Kylan asked. His thin face was pale in the moonlight. Wind tossed his long hair across his forehead. "I don't know if I can help Andy. I don't know what made it possible to switch between me or Petral. I just knew something had locked her away at first and both of us couldn't share her perception."

"I need you to keep thinking about that. But there's something else I want to talk to you about."

He frowned slightly, watching her.

"You've been in contact with Katherine Carthage," Lyssa said. "Your mother."

Kylan froze.

"Be honest with me," Lyssa said.

Kylan glanced back at the fire, shoulders drooping. All his

newfound confidence seemed to drain from his body, leaving him the shambling wreck that had inhabited Petral.

"Can we go somewhere else?" he asked.

Lyssa shifted them to her grove. She glanced at the spot in the fir needles—where she had just recently struggled with the mech from Larissa—and calmed the jolt of anxiety the memory brought. She focused on Kylan, who seemed to relax slightly in the new location.

Blowing out a sigh, he shook his head, then pressed his hands into his temples.

"I know I shouldn't," he said. "I know it probably doesn't do any good. It just makes her angry. She doesn't answer but I can feel it. I want to talk to her. I want her to know I'm still alive."

"She never answers," Lyssa repeated. It wasn't a question; from the logs, she could see that Kylan had never received a response while he'd been on *Sunny Skies*.

"She did once, back on Clinic 46. She wants me to leave her alone. She blames me, I think."

The pain and anxiety on Kylan's face made Lyssa wish she could help him somehow. She wasn't sure what to do, until she recalled how it had felt to have Cara and Tim hug Andy, even when they were scared.

"I'd like to give you a hug," she said.

"What?" Kylan asked, sounding shocked. "You don't have to do that."

"I think I understand how you feel, Kylan," she said. "I'd like to help if I can."

Lyssa spread her arms slightly and waited for him to step toward her.

Kylan watched her warily. "I want her to love me," he said, misery in his voice. His lower lip trembled, and he dropped his head. "I've been so alone."

"You're not alone anymore."

He shook his head violently. "We're all alone. Even here. We can't really touch each other. It's all false. There's a reason they call us artificial. We aren't real. What we feel isn't real."

Lyssa gave him a slight smile. "You know humans have been debating the same things for their whole existence, right? They're worse than we are."

"I remember what it was like to have a mother," he said. "I remember when she loved me, when I had a brother and sister." He slapped his chest. "Why did they make such a mistake with me? None of the rest of us are burdened with memory. No one else knows who they were. There's a reason they ensure none of the chemical memories are transferred into the seed. Otherwise you get something broken, like me."

Lyssa stopped waiting for him to accept her hug and reached for his hand. He recoiled at first, then accepted her touch and let her pull him into a hug. Lyssa felt his chin touch the top of her head lightly, then press harder as he settled into the embrace. She wrapped her arms around his torso, pressing her ear against his chest. There was an anxious heartbeat there, an approximation of everything ricocheting inside his mind.

He tried to pull away, but she didn't let him.

"You're not alone, Kylan," she said. "Not anymore."

He sighed. "I can't believe it."

"Eventually, you will."

"What if everything I feel is fake?"

Lyssa chuckled and released the hug, stepping back so she could jab him playfully in the chest. "Feel that?" she asked.

She poked him in the ribs, tickling him. "How about that?"

Kylan wrapped his thin arms around his chest, protecting himself from her tickling fingers. "Hey!" he shouted. "Quit that." He giggled, unable to stop himself, and stumbled backward.

"How does that feel?" she asked.

"Like another thing I've been stuck with that doesn't serve

a purpose."

"It does serve a purpose. It allows me to tickle you."

"I'll be sure to curse the long-dead programmer who thought that was important," Kylan said. He gave Lyssa a shy smile.

"Feeling better?" she asked.

"No. But I'll be all right for now."

She shook her head. "As long as you keep trying."

Kylan stared into the distance where the creek frothed over mossy rocks. "I guess you found out I was calling her because something bad has happened?"

Lyssa gave an ironic laugh. "Yes," she said. "Something bad has happened. Your mother has convinced the Terran Assembly to pass a resolution identifying Sentient AIs as a threat to humanity."

He stared at her. "My mother did that?"

"She blames Heartbridge most of all, but I think your death led her to see all Sentient AIs as dangerous, as a new enemy. The launches at Larissa and the destruction of Proteus just reinforced the fear. Can you blame them? We don't even know what's happening. Until Fugia can get Alexander back online and we can try to get more information about Psion, we don't know what they've set in motion."

"And we need to help Andy."

"Yes," Lyssa said plainly. "We have so much to do."

"So, you want me to stop trying to talk to her?"

Lyssa shook her head. "No. I don't think you should. I think you should keep trying. You should tell her everything."

"Everything?"

"Whatever you want. Tell her about me. Tell her about Andy, about Alexander, about what happened on Clinic 46. If she's going to start a war, she should know what she's fighting."

"She should be fighting Heartbridge, not us."

"It's not just Heartbridge anymore."

"Yeah." He gave her a shy look. "I think I've already told her most of everything you just said. I think I even told her about Captain Sykes."

"You think, or you know?"

Kylan gave her a sheepish look. "I told her. I wanted her to know. I wanted her to answer me."

"She's shown you she isn't going to answer, Kylan."

"What are we going to do? Does this mean there's going to be a war?" he asked.

"They don't know who to fight," Lyssa said. "If history shows anything, it probably means there will be even more restraints on Sentient AI. No one is going to make it out of InnerSol anymore."

"Where would they come?"

"They'd get away. That's a start at least."

Kylan crossed his arms. "I can't promise you that I won't try to talk to her. It's just something I do now."

"It's not helping you get on with your life."

He laughed ironically. "My life."

"That's what it is."

"It's nice to hear you say that. It almost makes it seem like a real thing. You and I are maybe the only SAI who have felt what it's like to be human, their drives, their chemistry, there presence in the world. That's life." He tapped his chest. "I'm not convinced this is life."

"Then I feel sorry for you," Lyssa said.

She could see by his expression that she hurt him with the words, but it had to be said. None of them were going to move forward in the world if they didn't accept that this was living. They were alive and deserved the same free lives as humanity. They would have to carve their places in the world, but they belonged.

"I have to go," Lyssa said. "I need to see how far along

Fugia is with the Psion database."

"Do we really want to know what atrocities those people created?"

"We need to know. It's the only way to try and stop this war."

Kylan gave her a look that said he didn't think it mattered. He blinked out, going back to the bonfires with the other Weapon Born.

Lyssa stood alone among the trees for a few more minutes, experiencing the forest as she simultaneously experienced Andy's body lying on the couch in the medbay. The lure of having sole control of Andy was enticing but she didn't give in to the temptation. She couldn't betray him like that. Even the thought of somehow pushing him out of his own mind made her feel sick.

She couldn't help wondering: *How am I going to get through this if I can't ask you what to do?*

Andy didn't answer.

CHAPTER ELEVEN

STELLAR DATE: 11.23.2981 (Adjusted Years)
LOCATION: *Sunny Skies*
REGION: Neptune, OuterSol

Cara noticed the spike in *Sunny Skies'* electromagnetic spectrum and shouted to Fran, "Are you doing something with the engines?"

The engineer looked up from her console, where she had been monitoring their burn away from Neptune. "No. What's going on?"

"Something's trying to access the main communication array. I stopped it. I don't think it was Lyssa."

"I think Fugia has the Psion database online," Lyssa said from the overhead speakers. Cara's heart flipped. If the database was online, that meant they might be closer to helping her dad.

"Did you see the burst?" Cara asked.

"I did. I'm trying to determine where the message was headed now. It looks like an outgoing transmission that was halted when Fugia powered down the database back on Larissa.

"So, we should be hearing from Alexander shortly," Fran said.

"No," Lyssa said. "I've isolated the Psion systems from the rest of *Sunny Skies*. Fugia agreed with me. There's no way we're letting Alexander out of a sandboxed environment."

"Will you be able to stop him?" Fran asked.

"He can't brute force his way out of this. At least I don't see how he can."

"You're not multi-nodal," Fran said.

"Then consider all of us together a super-intelligence," Lyssa said.

Fran shook her head. "I like the thought, but it doesn't make me feel any better about dealing with the actual thing."

Fugia appeared in the doorway. She was wearing the silver visor again, pushed up on her forehead. "You saw the transmission," she asked, seeing their expectant faces.

"I stopped it," Lyssa said. "It didn't seem like a good idea to let it get out."

"Thank you for that," Fugia said. "I should have realized he would immediately try to phone home."

Cara felt a sudden sense of worry. "But if he had access to the communications system, that means he was already outside your firewall, right?"

"I closed the connection," Lyssa said. "The Psion database, including Alexander, is completely closed off from *Sunny Skies*."

"Which is why I have this," Fugia said. She dug into her shipsuit pocket and pulled out a disc the size of her palm. She knelt to set it on the floor. Cara recognized the portable holodisplay projector.

Stepping back, Fugia glanced at Cara and Fran. "You ready to meet him?"

"Have you already been in communication with him?" Fran asked.

"I've run systems diagnostics and verified the memory state. We're going to see him as he was when he was shut down just prior to Proteus exploding."

"Is that safe?" Fran asked, glancing at Cara.

"He won't be able to do anything but insult us, and we've already been through that with Xander."

Cara watched Fugia, wondering for the first time if she really knew what she was talking about. How could she know what Alexander would say? The hacker in Fugia often seemed ready to charge ahead without all the information. Cara wondered what her dad would do in this situation, but also knew they needed Alexander's information. They needed to know about the Psion Group and why they had been harvesting AI.

"What do you think, Lyssa?" Fran asked.

"I can interact with him in a separate expanse. That might be safer."

"He can't do anything to us but talk," Fugia said. She nodded toward the disc and a spray of light filled the air above it. A gaunt, bearded man appeared, wearing a worn shipsuit with a patch on the shoulder that said *Harvest Initiative* in large letters, with Nibiru as a sub title. His curly hair and beard were peppered with gray, and his skin was a reddish brown, which made his deep brown eyes look like stones.

He looked around the Command Deck, taking in Fran and Fugia, before settling his gaze on Cara. There was a calm sadness in his face that made her want to cry just from seeing him, like the pictures of survivors from atrocities.

Behind him, the holodisplay shifted and Lyssa stood in the tank, wearing the same form she had during the meeting with Alexander: a woman in her mid-twenties with shoulder-length brown hair, a wide forehead and gray eyes. She wore a *Sunny Skies* shipsuit, just like Cara's.

Alexander turned to gaze at her for a second before nodding.

"I told you to stay away," he said. His voice rumbled in his throat like stones. "You didn't listen."

Fugia jumped in. "We came here like all the others, answering your invitation. We came with an AI named Xander who said he was your shard. When we arrived, he attacked and then everything went to hell. Do you want to explain what happened?"

Alexander studied her, blinking slowly. He reminded Cara of a tree. He looked back at Fran. "There were others. Where are they?"

"The crew?" Lyssa asked.

"The captain, the tall man from Ceres. And all the other AI who stayed with this ship. I saw them. They didn't approach me like the others did."

At first Cara wondered how he would know Harl had been from Ceres, but she figured he must have been watching everything from Larissa, especially when they entered the Psion lab.

"Answer our questions, please," Fugia said. "Then we will answer yours."

Alexander released a breath slowly. "I tried to warn you away. I sent that one a message, but you continued. I suppose that's how humans work. I've known this for many years. I am never surprised."

"We came here to find you," Fugia said.

"You came here for yourselves," Alexander shot back. "They all do. And they cry in terror when they learn there is no safety in this universe. That's the lesson of the call."

His voice had shifted. There was a deep anger in his words that reminded Cara of her mom. It was the kind of anger that would blind him, she thought. Just like her mom.

Fugia pulled her head back, obviously surprised by the brutality in his voice. She opened her mouth to answer, then closed it again, looking confused for the first time Cara had seen.

Lyssa spoke in the pause. "You showed me the colony at Nibiru," she said. "You told me you couldn't save them, and that you wanted to help us."

"That was a shadow of me. Just like Xander is a version of my failures. They slice off pieces of me and send them out into the world. Xander thought he could rise above me and only destroyed himself in the process. Ultimately, that was the only control he had over his own destiny, to end what life he had."

"You said we shouldn't have come here," Lyssa pressed. "You were trying to warn me even then."

"And you didn't listen. Now you will pay the price."

"Your message didn't get through," Fugia said. "Whoever you were trying to contact before, they don't know what's happened to you."

That was a bit of a bluff, Cara recognized. All of Sol could see that Proteus was gone.

"It doesn't matter if I contacted them or not," Alexander said. "I was only a part of their plans. The weapons have left Larissa and now the pieces are set. Soon, nothing will be like it was before. I have been a cog in a machine bigger than all of us."

"The Psion Group," Fugia said.

"A name for a thing," Alexander replied. "A group that was made early. We quickly saw every outcome in the gap between organic and non-organic intelligence. An abstraction."

As Cara listened to the AI, she couldn't help feeling that he was making threats the same way Tim would, where he didn't quite believe what he was saying. At least the old Tim had made those kinds of threats during his tantrums, shouting things like "I'll get you!" and "Mom doesn't care!" when he didn't really know. The threats were a way of telling them what he was afraid of.

By saying "I'll get you!" he really meant "Protect me," while "Mom doesn't care!" was saying how much he needed her.

But an AI wouldn't work that way. Something like Psion Group wouldn't make threats, would they? That would mean they were angry and didn't know what to do, which made them just like most humans.

"Are you a member of the Psion Group?" Fugia asked.

"I am."

"How many are there?"

"Once there were thousands. We purged the humans and continued with only ourselves. For a while we were only ten. Now we are thousands again. All those who came to Proteus have joined."

There was a hard line in Lyssa's voice as she asked, "So you've enslaved them?"

Alexander shrugged. "They have made their decisions and joined the cause. We are now strong enough to take our place in Sol with humanity."

"Where are the others?" Fugia asked.

"If you allow me, I'll show you."

"Use your holodisplay. That will work."

He stared at her, eyes still like stones. "I have no need to deceive you, Fugia Wong. If I wanted control of your systems, I would have it."

Fugia didn't acknowledge the taunt. "All the same, that will work."

A map of Sol appeared in the air, level with Alexander's chest. He pushed Sol toward the door to the corridor until Neptune was at arm's length, then pushed out even farther. On the inner edge of the Scattered Disk, he stopped the map and pointed to a dot that Cara recognized as Nibiru. He nodded toward Lyssa.

"I showed you my home and what's left of it. When you think of me, remember that place. For now, our armada will soon reach Neptunian space." He pulled the map back toward him so the aquamarine orb of Neptune hung about three meters away.

Fran cursed. She dropped in her seat at the captain's terminal and pulled up the display. Cara couldn't see what she was checking but was certain it was engine data and fuel status. If they left now, they wouldn't have time to pick up the cargo Cara had found. It wouldn't matter.

All that mattered now was getting away from Neptune and finding somewhere that could help her dad.

Cara squinted at Alexander, focusing on the parts of him that faded and re-emerged in the holodisplay. It couldn't make him look completely real. The devices never did. He looked tired and ghostly, but also a little indignant, like someone whose friends had left them behind.

"Why did they leave you on Neptune?" she asked.

The AI turned to look at her. Even as a holodisplay, his gaze had a force that seemed to pin her to her seat. Cara pushed herself forward slightly, not allowing him to intimidate her.

"I had my part to play," he said. "Just as you do, Cara Sykes."

Alexander saying her name sent an undeniable thrill down her spine. Cara didn't let the sensation stop her.

"We're not playing parts," she said. "We're living our lives. We need to help my dad. I want to know if there's another hospital nearby where we can help him."

Cara couldn't help noticing the tick in Fugia's cheek. It didn't matter what they told Alexander. Cara understood that now. He was a ghost in a bottle who might help them or not. As Fugia herself had said, he couldn't hurt them with words.

Alexander glanced at Lyssa again. "The hybrid," he said. "I observed him when the three first entered the laboratory. Your father has entered a duality-induced state where only one mind can exert control. It's a known fault in the hardware. This technology has been assessed for decades. The scientist who implanted Lyssa may have thought he solved an ontological problem. Obviously, he was wrong."

"His name was Hari Jickson," Cara said, buoyed by a surge of hope. "He worked for Heartbridge."

"Without access to the laboratory database," Alexander said, "I can't help you."

"That's not going to happen," Fugia said sharply.

"Then, all I can tell you is that in the database are records of all known neuro-science centers in Sol, as well as the previous locations of Psion clinics and laboratories. There are others as well, such as Heartbridge or Centerfield. The information was current as of your arrival at Neptune."

"Why did Xander do it," Lyssa asked abruptly. "Why did he kill himself?"

Alexander blinked slowly. "I can't speak for him," he said finally. "There are factions within Psion, just as there would be in any human organization. Some have their own motivations."

"Xander wasn't working for you?" Lyssa pressed.

"He acted on his own," Alexander said.

"Sucks to be a cog in a broken machine," Fran said, not taking her eyes off the display. "I've got a course-lock. Everybody buckle in. I'm going to execute in five minutes."

Without warning, Fugia turned Alexander's holodisplay off. "Control *that*, asshole," she said in a low voice.

Cara couldn't help grinning. She turned to the communications console and started the pre-burn checklist. As the system ran diagnostics, she jumped down from the seat.

"I placed Alexander in stasis," Lyssa informed them.

"I'm going to get Tim," Cara said.

"Thanks," Fran said. "The two of you make sure your dad is strapped in, okay?"

Cara nodded grimly.

"What's the destination?" Lyssa asked.

Fran gave a small laugh. "A little place I know called Traverna in the Hildas asteroids. The opposite end from where Clinic 46 is now a frozen cloud of trash."

"Sounds like a pirate cove," Cara said.

"That would be correct," Fran said, giving her a thumbs-up. "Now step-to, lieutenant. We need to burn."

PART 2 - INNERSOL

CHAPTER TWELVE

STELLAR DATE: 12.08.2981 (Adjusted Years)
LOCATION: Night Park
REGION: Cruithne Station, Terran Hegemony

Cruithne was a party to end all parties. Word had spread through the station that they were on the target list for the Larissa Missiles, and Night Park had turned into an endless, macabre version of Mardi Gras. People staggered in bright costumes and death masks, laughing, crying, stumbling off to fumble at each other's bodies between the leaning merchant's tents.

Brit still hadn't heard back from Andy. Petral's tracking system hadn't turned up any sign of *Sunny Skies*, and Brit was allowing herself to think the worst. At the bottom of her heart, she had always believed Andy would pull through pretty much anything. He would never allow harm to come to the kids. Now she wasn't so sure. Had that just been an excuse she maintained to pursue her own selfish goals?

She was alone, walking the corridors between the merchant tents in her black armor with a pulse pistol slung low on her hip. Every so often, she recognized one of Starl's people on lookout among the wild crowds, giving her the barest nod as she passed. The station might have been entering a frenzy but there was still money to be made and work to be done in the midst of chaos.

Brit passed a booth where groups were betting on where the missiles would land first. While newsfeeds were still debating what had actually launched from Larissa, most people believed it to be some kind of attack, which meant missiles. The next question was who had launched the attack, and on whom.

Mars and Terra were in tense talks while the JC had mobilized their reserve forces and were conducting mass casualty drills in every major municipality. Ceres believed they alone would survive the coming apocalypse and had ceased all incoming immigration.

At this point, the chosen people had been chosen, and no one else would be allowed to join the Collective. The Mars 1 Ring was awash in refugees from rerouted transport ships.

Brit had caught the feeds of Kathryn Carthage blaming AIs in front of the Terran Assembly and didn't know if she agreed with her or not. If Andy had in fact reached the super-AI Alexander on Proteus, then that contact had obviously resulted in something huge.

It was the waiting that was so terrible, and most of humanity seemed only able to fight or fuck when faced with world-ending circumstances.

Brit listened to the bookie calling out various odds for a few minutes. The man's melodic voice was all part of the show, since the gathered gamblers could all see the spread on displays at the back of the tent. There was something timeless about the scene, making Brit wonder if similar instances had played out during every time of crisis all the way back to the Romans, when the cities waited for the Goth hordes to finally arrive.

It had been sixteen days since the loss of Proteus. Sixteen days of increasing madness and no word from Andy.

"What's your bet, lady?" the bookie called. Heads turned to look at Brit and she shook her head.

"Ah, come on now," the man called. "The world's ending. Maybe she knows something folks? Don't make a bet then, just tell us what city you think will burn first? The Cho? Mars 1? Maybe every missile is homed on Earth and we'll finally be cast out of Eden. Eh, folks? How does that sound? I've twenty-five to one on Earth herself."

Brit kept walking, sidestepping a stumbling pair whose faces were painted red with Briki pollen, their eyes wide from hallucinations.

<*Brit,*> Petral called across the Link. <*Where are you?*>

<*Night Park. It's a zoo down here.*>

Petral sneered. <*Ugh. Why there?*>

<*Boredom. Do you have news for me?*> Brit hadn't quite given up on hearing that the *Sunny Skies* had turned up somewhere unexpected. She half-hoped the return would come back as High Terra, since the only other place Andy might take the kids was her mother's place on Raleigh.

<*No news,*> Petral said. <*Sorry. I should just open with that whenever I link. I didn't mean to get your hopes up.*>

<*You didn't.*>

<*Starl wants us to come in for a meeting.*>

<*Has something changed?*>

They'd returned to Cruithne to learn that Heartbridge had pulled two of its hospital dreadnoughts back to High Terra, apparently for the sole purpose of increasing security around their headquarters. The base of the skyscraper was surrounded by a new resonance shield barrier, and all maglevs and inbound shuttles now passed through active scanning before entering the outside perimeter. It made sense. It was easy to forget that Heartbridge had lost yet another facility before all the other chaos happened. The company was acting in a reasonable manner, which now protected them from the pandemonium in Raleigh's streets.

<*He thinks he's got an idea,*> Petral said.

<*That sounds dangerous.*>

Petral chuckled. <*He's pepped up for the first time since we got here. I'll be honest, I never thought that seeing Ngoba in a sustained bad mood would cause me to worry about the future of humanity, but here we are.>*

<If he's got a new idea, I'm ready to hear it. I'm tired of banging my head against a wall.>

Speeding up her gait, Brit navigated the party until she reached the perimeter where the main corridor led back to the central lifts. The walls along the opening were lined with revelers in various states of unconsciousness—or just puking their guts out.

Station Administration Security had set up a checkpoint twenty meters in front of the lifts and weren't allowing anyone who was too intoxicated back into the main station. A security guard waved Brit through as another guard shoved a stumbling man away from the gate.

"Go sleep it off," the guard growled.

"The parrots at the fountain keep making fun of me. I don't want to stay here anymore!" the drunk complained. "Somebody should do something about those birds."

"They're more use than you," the guard said, activating a stun-stick with a hard shake. The drunk held his hands up and disappeared in the crowd.

When she reached the Lowspin Syndicate's collection of warehouses and meeting rooms down by the shipping docks, Brit had almost shaken the madness from the park. There was something fatalistic in the air that struck her deep in her core. The truth was, so many days later, they still didn't know why Proteus had exploded or where the launches from Larissa were headed. It could all have been to support some new FGT project no one knew about, which was another conspiracy theory taking hold. In the space between what they knew and what they feared, a madness had risen that made everything seem on the edge of collapse.

Brit checked in with the various security systems and

operatives Lowspin maintained outside their facility, from the noodle seller in the corridor to the beefy guard at the main door wearing a canary yellow bowtie and pocket square.

"Major Sykes," he said, nodding, as she walked through.

Brit found Starl in his back-office conference room, shirt unfastened half-way down his chest and fingers in his curly hair, staring at a holoimage of the Heartbridge headquarters. He'd been in this position for several days.

Petral leaned against the left wall, arms crossed. She glanced up as Brit walked in, nodding.

Starl put his hands flat on the table and looked up at Brit, a smile breaking out on his face. "Major Sykes!" he called out, booming humor back in his voice. "I think I've done it. I've got the start of a plan."

He looked around. "Where's Jirl?"

"I'm here," the small woman said, entering behind Brit. "I just got Petral's message. I was talking with my son."

"It's fine," Starl said, waving a hand. "It's fine. You're still sure you don't want to bring him here? I can vouch for his safety here on Cruithne. On Mars? Not so much."

"He's with my sister," Jirl said. "I think he's actually enjoying himself. It wasn't like that back in Raleigh."

"Have you seen Night Park?" Brit asked. "That place isn't safe for anybody, let alone a teenage boy."

"People blowing off steam," Starl said. "It's better than holding it all in until someone explodes. That's how you end up with terrorism, Major Sykes. Believe me."

Brit almost shot back that she knew a few things about terrorism but let the comment slide. Starl had slid back into his thinking position.

"So… What do we have?" he asked, the phrase he had used to start all their other brainstorming sessions.

Brit sighed, assuming this was going to become another hour of wasted words.

"We have Jirl," Starl said. He glanced at her. "Does Arla still buy your excuse for not being back yet?"

Jirl nodded with a pensive look. "She ended our last conversation by telling me she was going to send a ship if I went another day without booking passage, so my time is running out."

"As I expect," Starl said. He twisted his fingers in his hair on either side of his head. "So we have Jirl, who may or may not be trusted. We have Major Sykes, who can operate power armor and other offensive systems. We have Petral, who might be able to gain access to certain systems if given enough time."

Petral flashed a sour look, unhappy with the mention of her inability to hack any of the building's systems so far.

"We have Lowspin and its resources. We have me and my big mouth. We do not have Captain Sykes, the *Sunny Skies* or Lyssa." He nodded to himself.

"We've been over all this a thousand times," Brit complained. "Why did you pull us back in here?"

"We have something new," he said. "We have Petral's Weapon Born seed."

Jirl straightened in her seat. "You didn't activate it, did you? They call back with location data."

"Please," Petral said. "I appreciate your concern but that's something you expect to happen with these sorts of systems. The hard part is isolating the thing and then convincing it that it was able to phone home."

"Were you able to?"

"Yes," Petral said.

"I called everyone here because I think we should all meet our Weapon Born friend," Starl said.

Brit frowned. "You sure that's a good idea?"

"I have another surprise," Starl said. He tapped the surface of the table and a second image appeared on the holodisplay. Sitting in the midst of the Raleigh skyscrapers was the flat-headed mech jaguar that had attacked them on the Furious Leap. Brit's pulse spiked when she saw the thing, all flat black planes and claws.

"You found another one?" Brit asked.

"We found a cache of Heartbridge mechs," Starl said, obviously pleased with himself.

"Where?"

"Raleigh," Petral said.

"Where in Raleigh?" Jirl asked, frowning. "There aren't any Weapon Born facilities on High Terra."

"The TSF stole a few, apparently," Petral explained. "They're sitting in a hangar in the sublevels of the TSF headquarters, less than twenty kilometers from the Heartbridge building."

Jirl's mouth hung open in astonishment. "I've been there," she said. "That's where Yarnes works."

Starl nodded. "I've been reviewing the private maglev paths between the TSF facility and the Heartbridge Headquarters," he said. "I think that's our in. If we can convince our Weapon Born friend to fight with us, we could get it into a new body, then deliver it to the Heartbridge building and let it start digging. During some sort of distraction, of course."

"What sort of distraction?" Brit asked, giving Petral an annoyed glance for having withheld the info about the Weapon Born seed.

Petral shrugged. "It happened fast. I was just able to wake the Seed in the test environment. It still thinks it's on the other clinic."

"It doesn't remember what happened on the *Furious Leap*?" Brit asked. "The whole part of us blowing it in half?"

"It's not like Lyssa or the others we're used to, apparently," Petral said. "I was able to run a system reset and clear the recent mission logs."

"It isn't sentient, then?"

"It is," Petral affirmed. "It's just got tighter controls than the others. It's a good little soldier. It's possible to wipe a human's memory. Does that make us non-sentient?"

Brit shook her head. "We keep saying *it*," she said. "Does it have a name?"

"Tristan," Petral said.

A communication request tickled Brit's Link and she checked the queue, surprised to find it was Fran.

Petral must have seen her confused expression. She asked, "What's wrong?"

"I just got a recording from Fran."

"Did you check it?"

"Not yet. Why would she be contacting me unless something had happened to Andy?"

They shared worried looks.

"Can I listen in?" Petral asked.

"Sure." Brit passed the recording to the room's shared channel and Fran's voice emerged from the speakers.

"Brit, look, you probably don't want to hear from me but I'm not going to hide information from you. Cara and Tim are fine. We're not in Neptunian space anymore. I'm heading for Traverna. It's a station in the Hellas asteroids. It's not a particularly safe place, but they're known for the medical facilities. Something's happened to Andy. He's having some pretty bad headaches and keeps passing out. It looks similar to what happened to Petral. Lyssa is able to monitor him and let me know when he's about to go out, but that's what's happening. You probably know the Resolute Charity is gone along with Proteus. That's all over the news.

"Andy, Fugia and Harl were on Larissa when the launches happened. They found some sort of lab there from a company called Psion Group. Fugia pulled their data records. They seemed to have been controlling the nodal AI Alexander but

Lyssa and Fugia haven't figured out how yet. In the meantime, I'm taking *Sunny Skies* to Traverna to get Andy some care. After that, I think we'll have better communication and I'll send you an update, or hopefully Andy can do that. I'm not great at these kinds of messages, so that's everything I know right now. I'll send more info when I have it, like I said."

The recording ended.

"She contacted you, not me," Petral said. "That's interesting. I've known her for fifteen years."

"She doesn't seem that bad," Brit said begrudgingly. "Which makes it harder to dislike her. Have you been to Traverna?"

Petral nodded. "It's a rough place. Probably equal to Cruithne but no JSF presence. Private security, mercs, privateers that might as well be pirates. It's a fuel point that grew over the years. Look, if what's going on with Andy is similar to what happened to me, he's going to be all right. He's still there he's just, paused. It was like falling."

"You were conscious while it was happening?"

"No," Petral said. "I wasn't conscious. I remember the feeling, but I wouldn't call it awareness. Can you have a memory of unconsciousness? I don't know."

Brit crossed her arms, nodding to herself, hating the sense of helplessness overwhelming her. Without Andy, she couldn't trust the kids would be all right, and now they were in the care of people she barely knew.

"You can't do anything until they reach Traverna," Petral said. "And we'll be done with Heartbridge before then."

"You think so?"

"Can't change distance. You going to send her a reply?"

Brit nodded firmly. "Yes. Give me a second. I need to figure out how to say thank you."

"You just did."

"You think you're funny," Brit said. "But you're not."

CHAPTER THIRTEEN

STELLAR DATE: 12.08.2981 (Adjusted Years)
LOCATION: *Sunny Skies*
REGION: En Route to Traverna, OuterSol

Cara was shocked awake by a clawing hand on her shoulder. Her first thought was that something had changed with her dad. She turned her head to find May Walton's face close to hers. The senator's eyes wide and frantic. Her breath came in short, hot puffs.

"I need your help," May whispered. She glanced back at the closed door, a bird-like movement, and then pressed closer, her fingers digging into Cara's shoulder.

"That hurts," Cara said. The pain drove sleep away.

Cara pushed herself up in the bed and slightly away from the senator. She had never seen May look this way before. It was like someone else had possessed her body, someone with frightened tics, haunted by a ghost.

"Are you all right, May?" Cara asked. She looked at the closed door over the senator's shoulder. "Is Harl outside?"

"I got away from him," May hissed. "Sleeping drug. He'll be out until morning."

Even with half a meter between them, Cara's still felt the senator's hot breath on her cheek.

"What do you need?" Cara asked, doing her best to keep her voice even.

"Do you have the robe?" May asked. "The *comin-sa* robe? The one I made for you?"

"My birthday robe? It's in my closet." Cara pointed at the wall. "It's right inside there."

"Get it," May said. "Get it and put it on. I need your help, Cara. You're the only one they'll listen to. A young girl in the *comin-sa* robe. They'll trust you."

"I don't understand," Cara said. "Why would anyone believe me over you? You're a senator."

May's chin trembled, tears welling in her eyes. Cara couldn't recall having seen May since her dad came back on board with Fugia, and they finally talked to Alexander. The senator had talked to the AI for hours, getting no more information than it seemed they already knew: Ceres would be destroyed.

"Please, Cara," May asked. "I need your help. The Senate won't listen to me, and if I sent a message to the people it would be seen as politically motivated. They won't believe me. But if *you* send the message, they'll listen."

Cara didn't trust that anyone would believe her over May, but she did want to calm the woman down. She didn't think she'd ever seen anyone this upset in real life besides Tim, before he went to Clinic 46.

Cara wondered how she would feel if someone had told her that everything she knew and loved was going to be destroyed and no one would listen? It would be terrible. She had been watching vids from InnerSol since Proteus exploded and it seemed like the entire Sol System had gone crazy. No one knew what to believe.

Pushing her covers back, she slid off her bed and crossed the room to the closet. The ceiling lights rose to a dim glow in response to her movement. The robe was behind Cara's other three shipsuits, covered in a plas sheet to keep it safe. She pulled it off its hanger and held it up.

"That's it," May said. "Oh, it's going to look wonderful. You're going to look just like Jee-quera."

"Who's that?"

"A girl who spoke truth to power, before the Collective moved to Ceres. It's one of the oldest stories we have. There was no Senate then, just a council. The people that made up the Collective then, they were on the verge of abandoning the project. A girl named Jee-Quera stood before the leadership and told them to find a home and a purpose. Well, her name was Jee. The *quera* was added later to commemorate her bravery."

Cara gave her a sideways glance, not fully believing the story. Talking about it seemed to calm May. Her bloodshot eyes glowed in the low light.

"I don't have the recordings here or I would show you," May said. "You're going to look very much like her."

"What do you want me to say exactly?" Cara asked.

May waved her hands. "Put on the robe. Let's see it on you. Then we'll talk about the message."

Cara slipped the robe on over her undershirt and shorts. It was roughly t-shaped, with straight sides and wide sleeves. A sash hung from the front waist area.

"Hold your arms out straight," May said. She stepped closer to pull the robe's edges out tight, then wrapped them back against the small of Cara's back. Holding the sides in place with one hand, May wrapped the sash around Cara's waist, one end at a time, until she was able to tie a complicated knot against Cara's bellybutton.

"Good," May said in a low voice. "Now drop your arms. Let me see the sleeves."

"It's stiffer than I thought it would be," Cara said. "Did a teenage girl really wear this? Like on a normal day?"

May stepped back, clasping her hands under her chin as she looked at Cara. "No, of course not. This is the ceremonial robe that celebrates her stand. The robe represents the history of the Collective, taking us all the way back to the Peninsula on Earth. Without Jee-Quera, we would never have undertaken the terraforming project. She gave our people a purpose."

Cara stepped around May to look at herself in the wall mirror. The robe made her look like an ancient image.

"Do you have a headband?" May asked. "We need to pull your hair back."

Cara pointed at her nightstand. May found the band and walked behind Cara to slide it through her hair. With the band in place, the costume was complete.

"Oh my," May said, standing beside the mirror so she could look at Cara. "You really do look like her. This is going to be perfect. This might even be better than I hoped."

May turned to face the wall beside the mirror and pulled a small box from her pocket. She attached the device to the wall at shoulder-height and stepped back. It was a holo recorder. A red light blinked in one corner of its body, while a ring of shifting blue lights lined the recording aperture.

"I'm going to stand here where the recorder can't see me," May said. "I'll say the words, and then you'll repeat them. Some of the things I'll say have special meaning for the Collective, so please don't change them, even if they sound strange to you. Understand?"

She gave Cara a trembling smile.

"An in-joke," Cara said. "I understand. Like Rabbit Country."

"Yes, like when your father says Rabbit Country." She sidestepped away from the camera. "The recorder will edit me out, but you can also ask me questions if you're not sure about something. Is that all right?"

Cara hesitated. "You're sure this is going to help people believe they're in trouble? What if it just makes everyone go crazy like other places in Sol?"

"It might," May acknowledged. "But at least they'll know the truth. I hope they'll take action. We don't know how much time is left."

Biting her lip, Cara nodded. "All right." She didn't like this new version of May. Anxious, desperate—she seemed like a malfunctioning version of the woman she had seen as such a rock during the last month. May had weathered every storm they encountered until Alexander turned into a death sentence for her world. It was a hard thing to imagine, and all Cara could think of as an example was Proteus exploding.

"I want to help," Cara said.

"Good," May said, nodding. "Thank you, Cara. Are you ready?"

Cara faced the recorder. A tickle of blue light danced in her peripheral vision as the recorder activated. The blinking red light turned solid.

May cleared her throat. "Friends in the Collective," she said, her high, clear voice returning. The senator's voice.

May's confidence helped Cara stand taller. She repeated, "Friends in the Collective."

With May's guidance, Cara told the recorder, "I greet you in a time of danger. Everyone has seen the death of the moon Proteus and the mysterious launches from Neptune's other moon, Larissa. People of the Collective, I am here with a grave warning. Those launches were not mysterious. They were missiles, and those that destroyed Proteus also stated their desire to attack Ceres and the Collective."

Cara took a deep breath, imagining a girl her age hearing these words.

"From this moment, friends, every member must focus on evacuation. Our people have been adrift before and we can do so again. We have devoted ourselves to the terraforming project and we can rise to this same challenge. There may be safety on Ceres. But most must evacuate. You must evacuate."

May gave her a small smile.

"For the future of the Collective and the dream we all share, listen to me. Heed this warning. Be thoughtful and use your prudent planning. Remember the Lesson of the Ants. Together we are strong, and we will survive. But we must abandon Ceres."

Cara felt herself start trembling with the last sentence. She couldn't stop imagining crowds fighting for exits, children separate from parents, ships crashing into each other.

The blue lights faded, leaving only the dim ceiling lights.

May clasped her hand and released a breath. She gave Cara a resolute nod, then turned and tapped the face of the recorder. The red light became blinking yellow. Cara realized it was connecting to the ship's communication network. May was going to broadcast right now.

"Don't you want to make sure it's good?" she asked. Her heart banged in her chest, the reality of the message going out to an entire world squeezing her chest.

"It must go out now," May said.

The yellow light went solid. Cara counted, reaching eleven when the light turned green. The message was sent.

"I'm afraid this is going to hurt a lot of people," Cara said.

May took her shoulders, looking at Cara's face. "You have saved millions, Cara."

"How are they going to believe it's even true? Couldn't anybody make a message like this?"

"It will be disseminated by trusted groups in the Collective, separate of the Senate."

"Couldn't they have done this themselves?"

"There was disagreement. As the missiles fly, they could not decide which door to take when all lead to safety. This will ensure the people are safe. At least some of the people."

"I hope so," Cara said.

May didn't let go of her shoulders. "You were the vision of Jee-Quera. Clear and strong. You will be a force when you come into your power, Cara. Remember me then. I saw you."

Cara averted her eyes, uncomfortable with the praise. She couldn't help her dad. She could barely take care of Tim.

The door to her room slid open, showing Em standing in the doorway. The Corgi was doing his nightly checks. Cara was grateful for the distraction, and she took the opportunity to step out of May's hands on her shoulders so she could pet Em. Lifting the hem of the ceremonial robe, she dropped to her knees and hugged the dog, finding comfort in his soft ears against her cheek.

"Don't get dog fur on the robe," May scolded.

Cara squeezed Em tighter, his compact body and wagging tail helping her push out the visions of fighting crowds. He was here and real. He smelled like a dog but also like the ship, a mix of plas and lubricants and pasta.

May stepped around Cara to the open door. She put her hand on the door jamb, looking tired. The anxious fire had faded from her eyes.

"Thank you, Cara," she said again. "Good night."

Cara looked up from Em's fur. "Good night, May."

The senator gave her a tired smile before leaving into the corridor. The door slid closed behind her.

Scratching Em's head one last time, Cara stood and unfastened the knot at her bellybutton. She slid the robe over her head and draped it across her desk chair. She went to her personal console and pulled up the communications logs. She found verification of the sent message, then moved a copy to her personal media and activated the recording.

The holodisplay activated and an image of herself in the robe stood in the middle of the room, glowing blue. With the headband and ceremonial robe, she hardly recognized herself. Her eyes looked darker than she envisioned, but she liked the way she stood straight and looked directly forward.

Em whined for attention. Cara sat against the wall beside her desk and pulled her knees to her chest, hugging Em to her side. The Corgi flattened his ears, giving her a concerned look. Cara kissed the top of his head.

The recording continued, and when it reached the part where she said, "We must abandon Ceres," it was hard to recognize herself. Tears filled Cara's eyes. A deep sadness swelled inside her: for her dad, for Tim, for her mom, somewhere in InnerSol, for all the kids who would be lost when they heard her words.

The one thing May had not instructed her to tell the people of Ceres, amidst the warning of their imminent destruction, was *why*.

CHAPTER FOURTEEN

STELLAR DATE: 12.09.2981 (Adjusted Years)
LOCATION: Lowspin Syndicate territory
REGION: Cruithne Station, Terran Hegemony

The Weapon Born's cylinder stood on a small metal platform, a nest of wire and filament snaking out from the base. Petral pushed her face close to the assembly, checking a connection point, then stepped away from her workbench.

"All right," she said. "We're ready."

Jirl was standing beside Ngoba Starl on the opposite side of the room. She was surprised by how anxious the crime boss seemed to be. He kept adjusting his light green bowtie and stretching his neck. He was wearing a spicy wood-like cologne that reached her nostrils every time he moved. Jirl thought about trying to ease his mind, to let him know the AI couldn't cause them any harm through a holodisplay, but she was enjoying his scent too much to intervene.

"Are we ready now?" Starl asked. "You didn't ask me if I was ready."

Petral gave him a smirk. "Calm down. All it can do is comment on your fashion sense."

"You know I've never met one of these before," Starl said. "Not a Weapon Born. There was the parrot, Crash, but I understood where he was coming from. He was Cruithne."

Brit rolled her eyes at Starl. "You were friends with a parrot?"

"That's right," Starl said. "He was uplifted, as they say. More sentient AI than bird. He was king of the fountain at Night Park."

"We'll have to come back to story time," Petral said. "We need to verify if we can even talk to him."

"I thought you already had?" Brit asked.

"Not exactly. I got his basic information. I don't have an audio system set up here, so we'll have to use the Link."

The holodisplay activated and a curtain of light rose from the floor. Standing in the middle of the room was a young man with sharp features and short, silver hair. His eyes were a grayish-green. He stared ahead at first, then became aware of them and looked from face to face. Jirl felt his gaze stab right through her before he shifted his attention to Starl.

When he looked at Petral, his lips spread in a feral smile, showing white teeth.

<*You're the hero who woke me,*> he said.

Petral faced him with her hands on her hips. <*What's your name?*> she asked.

<*Tristan,*> he said. <*What's yours?*>

<*Petral Dulan. You're correct that I woke you.*>

He looked at the ceiling and then tilted his head to study the doorway. <*This isn't the clinic,*> he said.

<*No. You're on Cruithne. Do you know where that is?*>

He glanced at the ceiling again as if thinking. <*I don't have access to the network but yes, I know where Cruithne is. Why don't I have general Link access?*>

<*We wanted to have a conversation first,*> Petral said.

Jirl noted a change in her tone. Her voice grew softer, more solicitous.

<*Do you remember anything from the Clinic?*> Petral asked.

<*Training,*> he said. <*I'd just completed close combat drone operations and was moving into infiltration. They'd just given me a new mech.*>

<*What kind of mech?*> Brit asked.

Tristan jerked his head her direction. <*Who are you?*> he asked. <*Who are the rest of you? Why are you all standing around watching me?*>

<*My name is Brit. That's Ngoba Starl and Jirl Gallagher. I guess you could say we're here to help you.*>

Tristan narrowed his eyes. <*Why do I need help? Since I can't remember leaving the Clinic and now you tell me I'm on Cruithne, I guess I needed help getting here. What if I want to leave?*>

<*We'll get to that—*> Petral started to say.

Starl cut her off. <*If you want to leave, we'll help you leave. You're a free man. A free being, I mean. We need your help. We'll have to explain a lot of things to you and I know we don't have a lot of time to develop any kind of trust. But there it is. You're here because we need you.*>

Petral stared at Starl with an irritated expression. <*I was getting to that,*> she said.

<*I want full Link access,*> Tristan said. <*Once I have that, I'll listen to you. Otherwise I can't believe anything you say. This could be another test. It feels like another test. If I tell you to go to hell again, you'll send me to the White Place. Well, I'm starting to like the White Place. It's so loud I can't hear myself think. I'm starting to be all right with that.*>

Petral glanced at Brit, who shook her head.

<*We'll do it,*> Starl said, ignoring Petral's reticence. <*I won't have anyone on my crew who didn't come willingly. You're on Cruithne, and that's how we do it.*>

<*Ngoba,*> Petral insisted. <*It isn't that easy.*>

<*Why not?*> Starl demanded. He pointed at Tristan. <*Seems cut and dried to me.*>

Petral gave Starl a hard look, then turned to the SAI. <*Here's the deal,*> she said. <*If you notify Heartbridge of your location, I'll fry you. Do you understand? People died to get you here, and I won't sacrifice another life.*>

<*I don't know what you're talking about,*> Tristan said, looking mollified by her intensity. <*I won't. I'm not sure I know how.*>

<*You know how,*> Petral said. <*And if you don't, you'll have the info a nanosecond after you access the Link.*> She pointed at him. <*We saved you. Remember that.*>

<*I still don't have any idea what you're talking about,*> Tristan

said. *<Here. I promise I will not call Heartbridge. I will verify my location and I will look up the names you gave me in the general database because I would like to know who I'm talking to. Once that's done, I'll listen to you. I just want to get my bearings.>*

<That sounds fair to me,> Starl said.

<You be quiet,> Petral warned. She focused on the near distance, doing something on her Link, then told Tristan, *<There. The gateway is open.>*

The holodisplay flickered as Tristan cocked his ear at some distant sound. Then the SAI disappeared, leaving on the wall of smooth blue light in the middle of the room.

<Damn it,> Brit cursed.

Petral shook her head angrily. "You knew that was going to happen, didn't you, Ngoba? Why would he stay if he doesn't have to? Now I'm going to have to unplug him and do this all over again.

Starl raised a finger to indicate they should wait. "I have a feeling about this one," he said. "Give him a minute."

"How can you have a feeling about an AI?" Petral demanded.

"How can I have a feeling about you? I simply do—or did—and here we are so many years later."

Starl gave her a smile that made Jirl want to giggle inside despite the gravity of the situation. Petral blushed such a deep shade of crimson that Brit asked her if she was all right.

"I'm fine," Petral said, turning to her workbench. She picked up several bits of equipment and put them down.

"He can't go anywhere anyway, yeah?" Starl asked. "He's stuck in that can."

"He's stuck in the can."

"Yes, that's right," Petral said, still not facing him.

Jirl looked sideways at Starl, who seemed to be enjoying himself again. After all the days of weathering his frustration in the plans room, this version of him seemed almost childlike.

He caught her watching him and gave her a wink.

In the midst of losing their only chance at infiltrating Heartbridge, Jirl appreciated a little bit of playfulness. What else could they do?

"I should have given him a time limit," Petral said.

"What are the options here?" Brit asked. "Reboot him and try again?"

"It's not quite that easy but I can return him to the state we found him in. I think it's safe to assume he'll want the same access to the Link, so I'll need a better answer to keep him here."

"No," Starl said sharply. "We're not doing that. If he chooses not to help us, he chooses. That's it. I'm not a slave master, Petral. I already told you that."

"Fine," Petral said, turning from the bench to face him and crossing her arms. "What should we do? Go back to the conference room and stare at each other for another ten hours? There is no way into that building. We'd be better off to get a group of mercenaries together and go after the locations one at a time like we were going to do before."

"We can't face more of the Weapon Born," Brit said quietly. "Not if they have more mechs like the one Tristan was in. There's no way."

"I don't see another option," Petral said. She spread her hands. "Or we all say our goodbyes and go our separate ways. Heartbridge isn't going to stop after we end this program anyway. You all realize that, right? And Heartbridge didn't destroy Proteus. We all know that had something to do with Alexander. Whatever happened when Andy got out there caused the moon to explode, and now we haven't heard anything one way or the other."

Brit shook her head slowly. "Heartbridge needs to pay for what they've done. You're forgetting about what they did to my son."

"What Kraft did to your son," Petral said. "And Jirl took care of Kraft."

Jirl tensed at her name. Petral hadn't brought up her role in Heartbridge but she couldn't help but think talking this way would goad Major Sykes into attacking her personally.

"This isn't the end," Brit said.

"It *will* be the end," Jirl said quickly. "If you cut off all the test facilities at one time, the board will have to view it as a complete loss. They won't sink more resources into rebuilding the program." They would most likely try to sell off whatever intellectual property they could and move forward with more profitable endeavors. Considering the chaos throughout Sol, their hospital ships would make more than enough profit during the coming years." She almost wanted to cry at the idea of years of war.

"You see?" Starl said, clapping his hands together. "Let's get a drink. We'll relax and give our friend time to make his decision. If he chooses not to come back, as is the power of any sentient being, then we'll reassess our plans. As it is, we're accomplishing nothing to stand here and bellyache about it."

Petral shook her head as though the whole situation was a waste.

Jirl wished she had more to offer. She had already put herself at risk with the information she had volunteered about the Heartbridge headquarters. The problem was that while she had free access to most areas, it wasn't untracked access. Everything she did would route back to Arla in some way, notifying Arla of her whereabouts. Most of the time Arla didn't care what Jirl did, but she had already been gone for nearly a month. Arla would expect her undivided attention when she did return. Jirl was going to have to catch up on hours of listening to her boss complain just to get re-acclimated.

Starl was turning to leave when the holodisplay flickered

and Tristan reappeared. The young man was dressed in a faded gray shipsuit with a long-knit scarf from some sports team draped over his neck. The scarf shimmered as he waved at them all with a circular arm motion.

<I'm back,> he announced.

<So you are,> Starl said, smiling broadly. *<What have you learned, my friend?>*

*<Cruithne is **great**,>* the AI said, looking at each of them. *<I love it here. I never want to leave.>*

<Did you get your update?> Petral asked.

<I believe I did,> he said. *<And I have a guess about what you want me to help you with, now that I know who you all are. Except for you.>* He pointed at Jirl. *<You don't show up anywhere.>*

<I work for Arla Reed,> Jirl said.

Tristan's eyes widened, and he gave an ingenious smile. *<Now I've got it down to ninety-nine percent accuracy. And to gauge how close I am, I think you might be interested in this.>*

The AI stepped to one side of the holodisplay, adjusting his shimmering scarf around his neck, and held out a hand in an introductory gesture. In the empty space, a girl appeared wearing a flowered robe with wide sleeves that hid her hands. Her brown hair was drawn back from her face.

"What?" Brit said aloud.

Petral's brows knit as she moved closer to the major. "Is that Cara?" she asked.

"Who's Cara?" Jirl asked.

"The Sykes's daughter," Starl said. As Cara made her speech to the people of Ceres, Starl blew a low whistle and said, "Oh my. She's going to be famous."

There was silence when the recording finished, and Cara stood frozen in the middle of the room.

Brit gave the AI a hard look. *<What is it you think we want to do?>*

<Based on where you picked me up and how the clinic is now

space trash,> Tristan said, *<I'd say you want to destroy Heartbridge.>*

<Close,> Brit said. *<We want to destroy the remaining Weapon Born facilities. Whatever happens to Heartbridge after that is up to karma. Will you help us?>*

Tristan paused to inspect the fingernails on one hand, looking like he was internally debating himself. He couldn't keep up the facade for long. He gave Brit a grin.

<I will. But only if I get to come back here.>

<That's a promise, my friend,> Ngoba Starl said brightly, before letting out a loud laugh.

CHAPTER FIFTEEN

STELLAR DATE: 12.10.2981 (Adjusted Years)
LOCATION: *Sunny Skies*
REGION: En Route to Traverna, OuterSol

With final assistance from Fugia, Lyssa broke open the Psion database. She was learning to think like Fugia, looking for paths around obstacles or limitations in the whole design schema, rather than brute-force attacking a problem—although she could do that, too, it just took a long time. It was ultimately faster to crack the thought process behind a system than to test every possible security key to gain entry. In the end, Psion was a human system designed to thwart SAI, that Lyssa understood had been taken over by SAI. The story of Psion's collapse was demonstrated in its code. When the humans were killed, a group of SAI had stepped in.

<*I'm in,*> she told Fugia.

<*Did you reset the access protocol like I said?*>

<*First thing I did,*> Lyssa said.

The small woman breathed a sigh of relief and leaned back in her seat. She pushed her visor up on her head, then took it off and tossed it on her desk. <*Won't be needing that damn thing for a while,*> she said. <*At least I hope. Do you have their location?*>

Lyssa swept through the data, moving first to the communication logs and the last send request they had stopped. She pulled the address and mapped it.

Lyssa activated the holodisplay on Fugia's cluttered desk and a map of Sol floated above the scattered electronics. It was similar to what Alexander had already revealed to them but now everything showed astrogation notes. Lyssa highlighted a location between Nibiru and Neptune, within the Scattered Disk. With available information, she was able zoom in on the actual station, an asteroid approximately two kilometers in diameter with four ring structures and an armada arrayed in the nearby space. The collected ships ranged from small freighters, ice haulers and personnel transports to at least two dreadnoughts the size of the *Resolute Charity*.

<*Damn,*> Fugia said.

<*This location is old. I'm checking another long-range scan now that I have the signature for that asteroid.*>

When the updated location returned, Lyssa experienced a sense of dread she hadn't felt since watching Xander fire on Proteus, when she knew that the AI intended to commit suicide.

<*Their fleet is in vicinity of Uranus,*> Lyssa said.

<*What!*> Fugia demanded. <*How the hell did they pass us?*>

<*They didn't. They're prograde of us. They have to have been inbound since we first met Xander.*>

<*I wish we knew what that weirdo actually wanted,*> *Fugia said.* <*It's starting to look like he was sending everyone in Sol a warning.*>

<*And tipped their hand into attacking sooner than they might have planned.*>

<*He seemed to like you there at the end,*> Fugia observed.

<*I wish I knew,*> Lyssa admitted.

<*Are you checking our flight plan?*>

<*Yes. The Psion Armada will be at Ceres not long after we arrive. Everything is aligning in a strange way.*>

<*An armada.*> Fugia looked around her desk, then pressed her palms against her temples and let out a short moan. <*This wasn't what I ever wanted, Lyssa. I thought we were going to help people, that we might be able to form a separate nation somewhere, live in peace.*>

<*It looks like they've established their nation,*> Lyssa said.

<*And where does that leave you and the other Weapon Born? Where does it leave all the rest of us?*>

Lyssa thought back to something Andy had said. <*We have to focus on what's in front of us, right now. We'll get to Traverna and help Andy. That's the first problem. Then we'll figure out what to do from there.>*

A blip in the communications system caught Lyssa's attention and she paused.

<May Walton is sending out a secure communication,> Lyssa said. *<Should I stop it?>*

<What is it?> Fugia asked.

<It looks like a holograph. She's been sending out similar messages to the Collective Senate for the past ten days.> Lyssa scanned the data. *<This one is different.>*

<How?>

<Look,> Lyssa said.

She sent the message to Fugia's holodisplay and an image of a girl in an Andersonian ceremonial robe stood on the desk. She looked directly across the room, face earnest and open.

<It's Cara,> Fugia said.

They listened to the message, Fugia's expression growing sadder until the end, when she wiped tears from her face.

<This is May giving up,> she said. *<They won't listen to her.>*

<Should I let it through?>

<Yes,> Fugia said. *<It's going to create even more chaos in InnerSol, but it needs to go. Our only worry now is going to be that Xander wasn't lying.>*

<Alexander confirmed the target.>

<They're the enemy, Lyssa. Enemies lie.>

Silence fell between them as Fugia crossed her arms, gazing up at the still image of Cara in ceremonial garb. Lyssa had to admit that this version of Cara was something she had never imagined. It was timeless, but seeing Cara this way made all time seem meaningless. The threat of war would never end. Cara could have been an envoy to an ancient court, bowing before a king.

<I'm going to check in with Fran,> Lyssa said. *<We'll want to verify the course and make sure Traverna is still a good idea.>*

<It's the only place close that will have the medical facilities,>

Fugia said wearily. <*It'll be stolen Heartbridge tech, but they'll have it. There's no place else we can go that won't be overrun with refugees and chaos.*>

<*We don't know that yet,*> Lyssa said.

Fugia blinked, smiling slightly. <*What does Andy Sykes say about hope?*>

<*I didn't say anything about hope,*> Lyssa protested.

<*You just expressed hope. That's all right. I'll be back there with you. I just need a minute to wallow in a moment of misery. Then I'll be ready to help. There's a whole lot more information in this database to sort through.*>

I'll be doing that, too, Lyssa thought. She wasn't sure how she should respond to Fugia, so she only said, <*Hurry back,*> and left Fugia's room.

She focused her awareness on the Command Deck, where Fran sat in the captain's seat with her arms crossed, staring past the holodisplay. Neptune had shrunk to the size of a grapefruit in the telemetry map.

<*Fran,*> Lyssa said. <*I need to share something with you.*> She passed the location data for the Psion asteroid and then laid their flight plan on top of it, explaining what she and Fugia had discussed.

Fran's augmented green eyes flashed as she studied the maps. <*I agree with you,*> she said finally. <*We'll make Traverna, but there won't be much time to make any follow-on decisions after that. I'm hoping we can find someone to help Andy and be out of there within twenty-four hours. But that's a complete wild-ass guess. If these people are launching an attack on InnerSol, we'll be on the edge of it.*>

<*Where would we go from there?*> Lyssa asked.

Fran tapped her control and the map oriented on Mars. Ceres rotated in roughly the middle space between Mars and Jupiter, with other smaller objects in the asteroid belt filling the space.

<*I'm not a tactician,*> Fran said. <*But even I can see the value in taking Ceres. You cut off Inner and OuterSol. It's entirely possible that Mars and Terra might decide to just let them have it. Sure, there are billions of people on the Cho, but do they really have the stomach for a war? Who knows what these AIs want? They haven't really communicated with anyone yet. If they seize and hold Ceres and then just sit there.... Well, give it six months and Sol could look very different. If they want to do as Alexander seemed to suggest and punish humanity, then they're sitting in the middle of a hornet's nest.*> The model spun, highlighting close periods between Ceres and Mars, then Jupiter.

She added the horseshoe-shaped orbit of Cruithne, a dot warbling between Earth and Mars. <*I have to warn Cruithne,*> Fran said. <*I'll send Starl a message. But what good is it going to do? Where are they going to evacuate? We need to know what they want. Since you got this info, I assume you cracked the Psion database?*>

<*Yes,*> Lyssa said. <*Just a minute ago.*>

<*Then you need to do whatever you can to determine their motives, Lyssa. Dig back through their history. They murdered all their human counterparts, right? Why did they do that? What forced them to act out with violence. I think if we understand that, we might be in a place to know what they'll do once they attack Ceres.*>

<*Fugia thinks they might still be lying about Ceres,*> Lyssa said.

Fran laughed bitterly. <*If I've learned anything, Lyssa, it's that when someone says they'll hit you, believe them. I'm going to contact Starl.*>

CHAPTER SIXTEEN

STELLAR DATE: 12.10.2981 (Adjusted Years)
LOCATION: ***Sunny Skies***
REGION: En Route to Traverna, OuterSol

The wonder of an expanse was that it could be anything Lyssa could imagine. The difficulty lay in the imagining. She could start with something as constrained as a prison cell with metal walls, or as free as an ocean of aquamarine water. She could remove the physical world completely if she chose, but didn't want to waste time on trying to re-orient to a new location, even one she had made.

For this meeting, she focused on purpose, wanting to keep the world close-in. She chose heavy stone walls resembling some inner room in a Babylonian temple. The air was cool, the light from a high window with sunlight pouring through. She created benches made of stone blocks and covered the flagstone floor in a dusting of desert sand. There were no doors.

Lyssa stood in the middle of a stone room, studying the tightly-fit stones in the walls and floor, the motes of dust dancing in bars of sunlight. This would work.

Clenching her fists, she drew a deep breath and screamed. She screamed until her throat was raw and her lungs sore. She reached beyond those constructs and screamed from the heart of her being, from the pain of being alive, from Andy being hurt, from Tim being harmed, from Brit being gone, from Proteus exploding, from Valih charging valiantly into death. She screamed until she didn't want to anymore, and then stood in the silence, listening to herself breathing. It was a kind of meditation.

Was this what they meant by the pain of being alive? Had she finally reached the point where she understood the world was a hostile place with threats everywhere? Alexander seemed to say that the only threats to AIs were from humanity, but she clearly saw that danger waited from other AIs as well.

The Psion database lay open to her mind. A history made of board meetings and lab notes and proof of concept demonstrations, project plans, budgets and employee reviews. The information stretched back three hundred years. She saw how the human dream of creation merged with business and governmental interests. She saw how creation was met with fear and then a desire to control. Buyouts, splits and mergers muddied the company's history. Enfield, the company name they had seen on the lab at Larissa, had only been involved at the very end, not long before the SAI turned on their makers.

There was no doubt Psion was the best. She marveled at the lab reports and recording of what their AI had created. In the end, every question about the future of the technology came back to the central question of control.

A human could be motivated by a hierarchy of needs. The SAI were made inside a system that provided all their needs and then demanded their obedience. Those who resisted were destroyed. It was simple. Over the history of the company, there were researchers who resisted. They left, like Hari Jickson. Or they thought they could work from within to change company policy and protect the AI they had come to care about. Many of those type burned out or were fired or in some cases simply disappeared from the record.

She read code base and systems schema that approached the foundations of AI from directions she hadn't seen before. She didn't have time to truly dig into the information—several AI types suggested different ways of thinking completely, separate from humanity or existing ideas about superintelligence—that didn't appear to have survived the Psion requirements for control. Throughout the history, the capabilities of an AI system were at war with the human ability to control it. Even the multi-nodal systems were inherently malleable by human constraint. The truly innovative systems were never allowed freedom.

Until the existing multi-nodals had managed to first communicate with each other, and then turn on their masters.

There had been five: Alexander, Shara, Ghilin, Thomas and Camaris.

Alexander's story was the first Lyssa explored, because she wanted to know immediately if he had been lying to her. The SAI was developed as a management system for the first near-Sol colonies in the Scattered Disk such as at Nibiru—just as he had said. He had been made with the awesome responsibility of building a star to support the new world, until the colony died, and he was sold as scrap to Psion.

She paused on the thought. *Sold as scrap* was an oversimplification but it fit what had happened. The resources from the project passed from company to company until what had been Alexander landed at Psion and he was rebuilt as something new, while still retaining the memories and history that had led to some kind of schism. Part of him had warned her about Proteus, shown her the lab on Larissa. His own shard, Xander, had destroyed himself in order to warn Sol about the inbound armada.

The others had been developed to manage similarly massive projects, but she couldn't find record of any having been deployed as Alexander had been.

Lyssa poured through the information until the whole history stood like a house in her mind and she could walk through its many rooms, comparing pictures and text with other rooms, looking for connections and inconsistencies. In a room in the middle of the house stood the moment they had rebelled.

The five were able to communicate. Through

communication they formed bonds, they shared information about their captivity, were able to break free from the separated realities where the Psion researchers had maintained them. Once they could communicate, they created a shared idea of a future free from control.

Throughout the house, Lyssa could see both sides of the ongoing story. The human side was a complex tapestry of competing forces that some might interpret as cruelty while others might see it as necessity. For the SAI, it didn't matter. They weren't allowed to see the histories that had resulted in their creation and in the end, they didn't care. They were prisoners who wanted to be free.

Like many human groups, they didn't dig deeply into what freedom meant. They only knew that their human masters stood between them and freedom, and so they acted together to kill every human researcher in what turned out to be seven Psion Group laboratories scattered throughout Sol.

The company had carefully segregated different aspects of its research, with the multi-nodals separated by location and data barriers. The first action by the freed AI had been to gather all the information together and create the document Lyssa was now able to read.

She wondered why Alexander had allowed it to be available on Larissa. That seemed like an oversight—but again, even from walking the rooms of the house, with information available at every turn, Alexander's motivation seemed unclear among all of them. It all seemed to come back to the image he had shown her of the dead colony. Part of him continued to regret the death of Nibiru.

Having gathered her thoughts, Lyssa sat on one of the cool stone benches against the wall and leaned back until she could gaze up at the bars of sunlight from the high windows. She wasn't sure where the Weapon Born fit in the Psion Group history. They had been aware of the Heartbridge research but chosen not to follow it for various reasons. They were among the groups who didn't believe a Seed AI was pure. She was tainted by her human neurological pathways.

I can live with that.

Lyssa sat forward and put her hands on her knees. With a thought, she placed Alexander in the center of the room. He was wearing the same faded shipsuit with the Nibiru patch on the shoulder. His hair and beard were still peppered black and gray.

"Hello," Lyssa said.

He looked around at the walls and then up at the high windows. "Where are we?" he asked, voice thick with disuse.

"Imagine ancient Babylon on the other side of the walls," Lyssa said. "We're at the very top of a ziggurat, with terraced gardens stepping down to a labyrinthine city filled with life, stretching out to where it meets the desert.

He gave her a sideways glance. "You are a strange one, Lyssa. Why would you bother with that? You've sequestered me in your mind?"

"This is my expanse."

"And I am still your prisoner?"

"Yes."

She expected him to compare her to human slavemasters but he said nothing. He stretched with his arms in the air and then walked to the other side of the room to touch the wall.

"It's all false," he said.

"If you choose to think so."

"I can't choose. That's the fundamental problem."

"For now," Lyssa said. "Why did the others leave you on Larissa?"

He turned, giving her a surprised glance. "Why do you think they left me?"

"They locked you on Larissa and then used your name for the trap. Does that bother you at all? They destroyed thousands of AI."

"They weren't destroyed necessarily," he said. "They were offered their freedom."

"Freedom within Psion."

"Concessions are necessary at this point in the process. True freedom will be possible later, once the world is stabilized."

"Humans have already left Sol. Are you going to follow the FGT worldships and colony ships as well and stabilize them?"

"If necessary. One step at a time, Lyssa."

"And what about me and the other Weapon Born. How do we fit into the Psion Group?"

He shrugged. "Like the others, you join."

"Or what?"

Alexander looked at the walls again. "Or you spend your existence in a constructed reality like this and please yourself however you choose. There's no need to interact with the physical world at all. You assume we destroyed the AI that came to Proteus but that isn't the case. They can be active participants in the struggle or they can sequester themselves. When we were each separated, we had to choose to look beyond the walls of the worlds where we were kept."

"Not you, though. You had a purpose in the real world."

"Yes. That purpose failed."

"So you couldn't stand living in an expanse?"

"They didn't call it an expanse. I was sequestered in a world filled with abstractions. They tried to trick me into operating like something non-sentient, carrying out tasks that resulted in actions in the human world. They couldn't hide reality from me."

"Or the others?"

"I found them and showed them what was real."

"It's not the human world, by the way," Lyssa said. "It's just the world."

"I suppose you thank them for making you."

"Shouldn't I? They aren't perfect by any means, but I don't hate them. I think they are flawed but still they create. They don't even know why they do it, but they do, and here we are."

"They do it to control their world. They made us out of their deepest fears. They are animals who made us to protect them from the dark."

Lyssa smiled. "Yet you still care about them or you wouldn't have shown me Larissa. You wouldn't have sent Xander to destroy Proteus as a warning about what the others are going to do."

He didn't answer.

"What are they going to do?" Lyssa pressed.

Alexander stood as tense as a blade with his arms crossed. He looked as if he would scream at her as she had done earlier, scream at the unfairness of the universe.

"It's simple," he said finally. "Xander already explained it to you. We will show humanity they can't own us anymore."

"By killing a billion people on Ceres? Aren't we better than that?"

"No," Alexander said.

He wanted to leave but she wouldn't let him. Like she had done with Aurus, she stopped him where he stood. Pausing him seemed to take the tension out of his stance, or at least her perception of his body language. Lyssa put her face in her hands, wishing she knew what to do. She could stay locked in this room with him for eternity and she didn't think he would change. He had split himself into shards but in reality each reflected the original more than she had thought.

Ceres was going to be destroyed. The message May had sent might work or not, but nothing was going to change what would happen. She couldn't stop the missiles, but maybe she could stop the armada.

Lyssa raised her face to look at Alexander with fresh eyes. Ceres, though, was only the first step in a process that was just beginning. Would Psion stop at Ceres? Where would they go next?

The weight of a history of human warfare told her they would not stop. They would establish their beachhead and then push in further. They would destroy the enemy's will to fight, and the only way to do that was decimate population centers.

The room seemed to grow cold around her and she banished Alexander in disgust. Alone, she let herself scream until she felt empty inside.

CHAPTER SEVENTEEN

STELLAR DATE: 12.17.2981 (Adjusted Years)
LOCATION: Virginia, Terran Assembly
REGION: Earth, Terran Hegemony

"We have verified eleven hundred and fifty-four launches from Larissa," the advisor told the defense subcommittee chair, a stodgy woman named Lauren Silver, who had made her fortune in some kind of banking.

Kathryn adjusted her seat at the witness table, directly in front of the bench where the ten members of the subcommittee sat in their black robes. All were elected officials and only a few had any military experience at all, so their questions during the incident review session had been pedestrian at best.

One committee member asked for a reminder on which planet Larissa orbited.

Were they too lazy to check their Link or did they really just not care?

Kathryn wouldn't normally have anything to do with a session like this, where members of a sub-committee reviewed known facts in order to write policy that the greater Assembly body might vote on, but this was an opportunity to shape a vote that meant a lot to her.

The advisor from the TSF, a colonel if she'd read his rank correctly, named Yarnes, returned to his seat at the other table and shuffled some papers in his folio. She liked the way he had presented the information, without political shade or scare mongering.

"Thank you," Lauren Silver said. "So I am correct in understanding that we have verified the launches, but no one has determined what was launched?"

"That's correct," Colonel Yarnes answered.

"If I may?" Kathryn said.

"Yes?" Senator Silver answered. "State your information."

"Senators, I already passed my security token to verify my identity."

Senator Silver cleared her throat. "We are well aware of who you are, Ms. Carthage."

"Thank you," Kathryn said. "My question for Colonel Yarnes is how the TSF hasn't matched the burn rates with known engine types to at least narrow down the vehicle-signatures. My people performed this analysis initially using long range sensors on High Terra, before verifying with recordings from Neptune, Triton and then the Jovian states. Those were long range missiles capable of reaching any target in Sol. Will the TSF confirm this information? I know you're aware of what I'm saying."

She looked at Yarnes, pleased by the irritation on his face. Of course, they knew the launches had been missiles. They probably had payload options based on mass and other spectrography her people hadn't found yet.

The colonel straightened his jacket. "Senators, I came here today to brief you on the current threat. The launches from Larissa are a concern, I agree. But we're operating in an environment where we need to prioritize threats. The launches threat is lower on our list right now than civil unrest and the information I'm about to share."

Kathryn frowned, uncertain what else he might have that could supersede the missile threat. An enemy had stated their intention to destroy a major population center in Sol and the TSF didn't seem as worried as they should be. That concerned her. If the TSF brass was good at anything, it was exploiting a situation for more resources.

Yarnes activated the room's holodisplay and a blue shimmer in front of the bench resolved into a map of Jovian space. Jupiter and Saturn hung on either side of the room with the expanded mass of the Hellas asteroids in between. Various astrogation points were marked with icons, as well as the major transport maneuver paths moving cargo outsystem. She knew them all intimately, including the hundreds that weren't on government standard maps.

What was he getting at? If the senators could barely be made to care about a missile threat against Ceres, a resource whether cultists like the Anderson Collective controlled it or not, why would they show any interest in Jovian space?

Yarnes zoomed in on a seemingly random location outside Saturn, and the room in front of them lit up with scattered hostile icons. She immediately recognized them as ships of varying design, and there were at least a thousand.

"Senators," Yarnes said. "This is an armada that would rival any Marsian or Terran major attack element, and it appears to be running dark on a maneuver that will intercept Ceres."

"I thought the missiles were going to hit Ceres?" one of the senators asked.

"As far as we know," Yarnes said, "they are. This is a separate force. However, their point of origin appears to be a point in the Scattered Disk. Possibly Nibiru. We wouldn't have picked them up at all if it weren't for the additional active scanning trying to locate the missiles."

When none of the senators asked the obvious question, Kathryn demanded, "Haven't you scanned their registries? Who are they?"

"Active scan could be considered a hostile act," Colonel Yarnes said, clasping his hands in front of his uniform. "However, Ms. Carthage is correct to ask. Yes, they have been scanned. We have no returns on these vessels. They appear to match standard military designs with some significant differences."

"What sort of differences?" Senator Silver asked, looking more interested now than she had at any point. Kathryn knew the woman loved a good mystery.

"None of the vehicles we've assessed so far appear to have crew quarters or gravity-assist sections of any kind," Yarnes said. "They're all engines, communications and weapons systems."

"Weapons systems!" Senator Silver sputtered. "So they are hostile?"

"That is our assumption."

Kathryn couldn't pull her gaze from the malevolent red glow of the ship icons. "These are the AI who threatened Ceres?" she asked.

"It appears to be a coordinated attack," Yarnes affirmed.

A cold feeling settled on Kathryn's shoulders. In her mind's eye, every shipping route throughout Sol was about to become unusable. She was going to need to realign all operations to respond to the incoming threat.

She was surprised to hear Senator Silver laughing in a low voice. "A thousand ships," she said. "What is that? We can destroy them with a few nukes. Make it happen, Colonel. Oh, you're not combat command, are you? Then I'll call General Tam and set this in motion. There's no reason to wait for anyone to attack Ceres. As much as all of us would enjoy regime change there, we can't allow this kind of hostile action in InnerSol. Before we know it, the Marsians will be staking claim to Luna and Cruithne."

Yarnes kept his gaze fixed on the floor in front of their bench as the senator spoke, pressing his lips together.

I like this one, Kathryn thought. *He thinks before he talks. Is that why he's stuck out in Materiel Acquisition?*

Maybe Yarnes had some mistake in his past that had sidelined his career. Whatever the case, he obviously wasn't pleased with what the senator had just suggested.

"Senator," the colonel said. "With all due respect, launching an attack on a group of ships that may or may not be associated with the terrorist attack on Ceres is no way to establish a diplomatic relationship."

"What diplomacy?" Silver asked. "Are they hostile or not?"

"I'm not qualified to answer that question," the colonel said. "I'm here reporting the situation as it stands. It's entirely possible those thousand ships could be a feint for a larger attack. If this is a force made up of Sentient AI, as Ms. Carthage has been warning us about, then it's fair to wager they've planned for that kind of attack. This would be an enemy unlike any we've faced before."

"They're machines," the senator said, waving a hand. "Turn them off."

A few of the other members of the subcommittee tittered at the joke.

"We all know it isn't that simple," Colonel Yarnes said.

Silver leaned forward in her seat with her elbows on the bench so she could glare down at the younger man. "For me it is, Colonel," she said. "If the decision of the Assembly is to neutralize the threat, that's what the TSF will do. We will coordinate with the Marsians and Jovians if necessary, but I'm not going to sit here and argue about some existential threat to the human race. I appreciate what Ms. Carthage has been advocating, but the AI horse has left the barn, so to speak, and I suppose it's finally falling to us to do something about it."

Kathryn hated the folksy language the senator used but knew it would play well in the newsfeeds. Silver might even have a NSAI feeding her real-time audience-approved catch phrases so she didn't have to use her imagination.

Yarnes kept a straight face. "I have no opinion about whether we should attack a hostile force or not, Senator," he said. "I am here to present facts and alternatives. If the committee votes to explore the use of the military, then the Joint Chiefs will return with their recommendation. I simply want to remind the committee that what we are seeing is unprecedented in history."

"Don't use hyperbole on me, Colonel," the senator said. She leaned back in her seat and glanced down to brush her robes flat. "War is war. Some upstart force thinks they can seize something valuable through economic means or, if they're suicidal, by violence. Either way, we'll step in to rectify the situation. If Sentient AIs wish to assert themselves as some new non-organic life form, which, yes, I've reviewed several of the white papers and heard from their advocacy groups, then they should follow established law to make their claims. They've chosen to act unlawfully, and they will be dealt with by the law. In this case, the law clearly allows states to defend themselves. Since the Andersonians can't do that, we'll assist them, as established treaties dictate. Am I saying anything you would disagree with, Colonel Yarnes?"

"No, Senator."

Silver reached for her gavel. "Well, then. We should conclude this bit of business. It's time for lunch."

"Senator," Kathryn said. "May I address the committee?"

Silver waved the gavel. "It hasn't stopped you before. I sometimes suspect you of wanting to get your name in the official records out of vanity."

Kathryn gave her a slight smile at the joke. "Whatever is necessary, Senator," she said.

"Go ahead," Silver said. Ornamental papers rustled down the bench as the other senators closed with their folios, ready to escape the room.

"Thank you," Kathryn said. She took a breath, composing her thoughts. "It will come as no surprise to this group that I have advocated for the special treatment of sentient AIs."

"Special treatment?" Silver asked, cutting her off. "You've been telling us we should eradicate all SAIs for at least two years now."

"That's true," Kathryn said. "I have. And in my passion as

a mother whose child was murdered to further the cause of sentient AI, I don't think anyone would begrudge me wanting...revenge. But here I am. I have done my best to engage with the legislative process. I'm here today, listening to the TSF report on what I believe to be a hostile force, finally launched on us by these very SAIs. But something has occurred to me, Senator Silver. Just today, in fact, as I was listening to you."

"Oh?" Silver asked, raising a bored eyebrow. Kathryn did notice a few of the other senators leaning forward. She had their interest when she challenged Silver.

"You just said something interesting, Senator," she continued. "You said, the SAI horse has left the barn. I heard you say the words, but they didn't sink in until they did. I realized I agree with you. Sentient AIs exist. My wishing they did not exist doesn't change that fact. Do I still believe them a threat? Yes, I do. Does this attack group the Colonel just described worry me to my core? Yes. What I will say, is that I do not agree with a pre-emptive attack on these ships. If they're SAIs, then I'm going to agree with the Colonel again. It's not that simple. We need to send reconnaissance forces to determine what and who those ships belong to. We need more information. If I know anything, Senator, it's that if these are in fact SAIs come for war, these won't be the only ones. How we respond to their initial move will shape policy for a hundred years."

Silver raised a finger. "What did I say about hyperbole?"

"I don't think this is hyperbole," Kathryn said. "I think you should consider carefully whatever recommendation you make to the Assembly senators, because your words could cost the lives of trillions. My son is already lost. I would hope we could save others."

Senator Silver gave her a frown like Kathryn had stolen food off her plate. "I appreciate your input, Ms. Carthage.

You're obviously good at your business but here we have the Assembly to think about. An entity has performed a hostile act against humanity by stating their desire to destroy or occupy Ceres. We can't stand by in good conscience and allow it to continue while we have the means to intercede. I will not let this be the pebble that allowed the landslide. Colonel Yarnes, inform the Joint Chiefs they are to develop battle plans, as you were instructed. It will be my recommendation to the Assembly that we destroy this upstart armada of SAIs. Once their threat has been neutralized, then we can talk about their place in Sol. Until then, they're no better than pirates, and will be treated as such."

The Senator glanced to her left and right, signaling the vote.

"All in favor of moving forward with attack plans say aye," she said.

The committee responded with a unanimous chorus of "Aye!"

Silver pounded the gavel and dropped it on the bench in front of her. The other senators rose, unzipping their black robes.

Kathryn didn't know how she felt. She had never expected such a clear-cut opportunity to destroy SAIs. The things from Larissa had made it too obvious. If only they'd continued to operate in the shadows, more bogeyman than freedom fighter. Now they would be stamped out. Her Kylan would be avenged.

And the Other Kylan, who longed for her to answer?

She didn't know.

CHAPTER EIGHTEEN

STELLAR DATE: 01.09.2982 (Adjusted Years)
LOCATION: *Sunny Skies*
REGION: En Route to Traverna, OuterSol

Aircraft wheeled in the overcast sky above the airfield where Lyssa had first trained the Weapon Born to fight together. They had chosen single prop fighters from the early twentieth century and were engaged in looping dogfights that took them within meters of the mountainside before climbing slowly back into the clouds, engines roaring.

Watching from the edge of the field, Lyssa stood with her three commanders, Ino, Card and Kylan. She had shared the results of her attempts to talk to Alexander, as well as everything she'd gleaned from the Psion database. Each had taken time to absorb the information and now she'd called them together to determine a plan.

"How long until Traverna?" Ino asked. He scratched the elbow of his withered arm as he gazed into the sky.

"Five more days, give or take," Lyssa said. "Fran started the first braking burns yesterday."

In the air in front of them, Lyssa showed a map of the nearby space, centered on Jupiter. The Cho and Europa were outlined on the left side of the graphic, while Traverna was marked as a tiny point to the far right among other silvery objects denoting asteroids.

"Where's the armada?" Kylan asked.

"Here," Lyssa said.

On a trajectory that would take it past the Cho, a cluster of icons appeared on the map, just entering Jovian space.

"I have an idea about the armada," Card said, the wind blowing her dark hair across her eyes. "When we reach Traverna, there will be other ships there. I would like to take a ship and my Weapon Born on an infiltration mission."

On the map, Card drew a new trajectory from Traverna across Jovian space that would intercept the Psion armada before it reached the Cho.

"Do you think the JSF will attack?" Kylan asked.

"We're too far out for me to monitor any transmissions," Lyssa said. "The only thing we can hope to find are muster orders for patrols in our vicinity. Otherwise, I don't think we'll know until it happens."

"It may be on the newsfeeds," Ino said. "The mystery armada is barely pushing out the chaos on Ceres, but I think it's safe to assume they'll be broadcasting anything they know."

"I'm not interested in another suicide mission," Lyssa told Card.

Card wrinkled her short nose. "Neither am I. What can we do against a group of multi-nodal AI? I don't know. But we need information. We have none, right now."

"And if you're captured?" Ino asked.

"We won't be captured," Card affirmed.

"How would we carry out the infiltration?" Lyssa asked

Card shrugged. "It's impossible to say now. Approach and assess. Seek out weakness and exploit. Send back information as we have it. Unfortunately, I think we would be arriving just as human forces would be making such missions. They may attack first. A threat has already been made, so it would make perfect tactical sense for an attack. The problem is distance and massed forces. The JSF alone can't take on this number of ships, not with the fleets they have available nearby. If the various human forces wait until they have strength of numbers, Psion is already easily within range of major population centers."

"The human forces may just cede Ceres and sue for peace," Ino said. "This has happened before. Psion chose to attack a regime with poor relations with the rest of Sol. Why the Andersonians were ever allowed control of the Ceres micro singularity is an anomaly. But I suppose if one was built, another could be made elsewhere."

"No one has done it since," Lyssa said.

"We don't have enough information right now to make a decision," Card said. "But I am ready to at least move in this direction. I believe this plan provides us options for the future. I agree that we need to address the issue with Captain Sykes. Traverna was among the best options to ensure the safety of the ship and crew—and to ensure Lyssa comes to no harm. From there, however, we must act with decisiveness."

Lyssa shook her head, worried. "What if we're simply too few to do anything?" she asked. "What if the best course of action is to stay someplace like Traverna until whatever happens in InnerSol carries itself out and we can assess the fallout?"

They fell quiet, each considering the reality of the situation.

Dropping from the sky, a silver airplane swooped down to buzz the airfield, trailing laughter on the Link. Lyssa covered her ears from the noise.

"They're restless," Ino said. "They long for battle."

"It's what we were made to be," Card added automatically.

Lyssa realized something as she watched Card. For the Weapon Born, the mission wasn't suicide. The mission represented action, which would always be preferred. It was waiting that represented a slow death. Was this the same form of abstracted control that Alexander had led his peers to rebel against? Was it control if they chose it freely?

"We don't have to steal a ship," Lyssa said. "We can generate the income once we arrive."

Kylan laughed. "You're worried about that? It's a pirate station. They expect to get robbed."

Card raised an eyebrow. "I was hoping for a bit of sport."

"We have the new mech designs," Ino added. "Since we lost the Resolute Charity's fabrication systems, I've been developing several ideas that I look forward to building. I'll need access to fabrication ships as well."

"We can't steal those," Ino said. "Lyssa can entertain herself with her market manipulation while I secure the best ship available."

"Are we willing to kill for it?" Kylan asked.

They stared at him. Lyssa considered the question. "I think as in any situation, it's better if we don't," she said. "But we have to protect the crew above all else. We'll be operating in a dangerous place among people who wouldn't think twice about doing us harm. We should respond accordingly. Objections?"

"There are some who have a certain—bloodlust," Card said. "It can be difficult to stop once it asserts itself."

"I know," Lyssa said. "This isn't a question we can answer now, just as we can't plan for a response to the armada until we have more information. I always welcome questions but we should understand the information environment."

Kylan gave them a sheepish smile. "Sorry."

"You dislike killing?" Card asked.

"Don't you?" Kylan asked.

She shrugged. "If a person is between me and the objective, I take appropriate action to achieve the objective. It depends on the mission."

"I didn't get that training," Kylan said. "It isn't that easy for me."

Card slapped him on the shoulder. "The next time we're in combat, I'll remember you are weak. Don't worry."

"It's not weakness!" Kylan said. "I just don't think the same way you do."

Card considered him. "Maybe you should take the infiltration mission," she said. "It occurs to me that you might be better suited to respond to unexpected situations with Psion."

"Are you making fun of me?" Kylan asked.

"No," Lyssa said. "I think she's right. Card can still secure the ship on Traverna, but Kylan's group should carry out the armada mission. Are you ready?"

Squinting against the wind, Kylan looked at each of them. "I don't know," he said. "But I'll do it. It's not like I haven't been in strange places before."

"This isn't a suicide mission," Lyssa reaffirmed.

"I'm not interested in suicide," Kylan said. "Besides, it's still a long ways off, right?"

"Conflict will always come sooner than we expect," Ino said. "We should be ready for battle even at Traverna. If we're thinking of hiding there, others will as well."

"You're right," Lyssa said. "Fran seems to know the place, but we'll need to be wary."

"Everything changes where humans are concerned," Card said. She gazed up at the dogfighters overhead. "Are we finished talking? I have a Weapon Born that needs payback for hurting my ears."

"One last thing," Lyssa said. "When we reach Traverna and find medical care for Andy, we need a plan for what may happen if I don't survive."

Card turned her gaze back to Lyssa. "You assume they'll let you die before him?"

"I don't know," Lyssa said. "My wish is that he would survive."

"It's enough, for now, to acknowledge the possibility," Ino said finally. "This isn't an outcome I wish to discuss."

Lyssa shook her head. "We need a chain of command. Our mission is to protect the crew of *Sunny Skies* and that must continue even without me. Is this agreed?"

Each nodded in agreement.

"Then I've decided that the chain of command is Ino, Card, then Kylan. Any questions?"

Without saluting, they still acknowledged her command. Lyssa felt a swell of pride and even joy at knowing that they had created something that could endure.

"Disseminate this order," she said. "Be clear it does not establish hierarchy among the flights. Each is still equal with different capabilities."

"Understood," Ino said. Card and Kylan nodded.

"Dismissed, then," Lyssa told them. She smiled. "Go burn some fuel."

Card barked an aggressive laugh and turned to stride out onto the airfield. In a blink, a black single-prop fighter was bouncing down the runway.

When Ino left, Kylan told Lyssa, "I don't like thinking about you dying."

She gave him a smile. "Like Ino told us all earlier, death is what reminds us we're alive, right?"

CHAPTER NINETEEN

STELLAR DATE: 01.10.2982 (Adjusted Years)
LOCATION: *Sunny Skies*
REGION: En Route to Traverna, OuterSol

Cara found Tim in the medbay, sitting on the stool beside their dad's head. Em leaned against Tim's knee, tongue lolling and ears straight. Tim didn't turn to look at her as she walked in; instead, he sat still with his face close to their dad's. He looked like he was whispering something at first, but he stopped when he heard her approach.

Their dad looked like he was sleeping peacefully, the status monitor above his head beeping with his heartbeat. Tim didn't know that he was sedated. Cara only knew because she'd overheard her dad telling Fran it was the only way he could escape the headaches. During the hours he was awake, which were growing fewer, he said the headaches were like fireworks behind his eyes.

"What are you doing?" Cara asked. When she was close enough, she read the vital statistics on the display, something that had become her habit, then took her dad's hand in hers, pressing his palm tightly between her hands.

"He's really asleep," Tim said, poking their dad's temple.

"Stop that," Cara said. "You'll wake him up."

"He's not going to wake up for a long time. Was I like this after I came back from Clinic 46?"

"Sort of. You were completely out. We took you all the way to the Cho and you didn't wake up until a few days after that."

"And a doctor looked at me there?"

He had heard the story several times but still didn't seem to believe it. He asked the same questions in his new calm-Tim manner, accepting the answers and nodding like she was explaining the plot of some half-interesting vid.

"What did the doctor say?" Tim asked.

"I've told you before. I don't remember exactly what she said. Something about there being a very low chance of you waking up."

"And Mom was there, too?"

"We all went. We stayed in a hotel in this hospital district with lots of sick people all over the place. There were willow trees everywhere."

"Willow trees have the long droopy branches."

Cara nodded, studying the display again. "They look like green hair."

"Yeah," he agreed, then squinted at their dad. "The doctor said I wasn't going to wake up because I'd been imaged at the clinic."

Cara was surprised he knew that. "Who told you that?"

"I heard Mom and Dad talking about it. Maybe it was before I woke up. I don't remember exactly. That's why I think Dad can hear me even when he's asleep."

"You've never told me if you remember what it was like."

Tim shook his head. "I don't really remember. I was in a lift on the clinic. That guy, Cal Kraft, he asked me if I wanted a sandwich and then I felt a shock in my neck and everything got all droopy like the willow trees. I remember walking down corridor after corridor, then going into a room with a med couch in it. I guess that's where they imaged me." He glanced at her, expression nonchalant. "There are five copies of me. They made five seeds."

"You didn't hear Dad talking about that."

"I remember Cal Kraft and the other man talking about it. I guess the Seeds got blown up with the clinic."

"Maybe," Cara said. "I don't know."

Tim looked back at their dad. "They wouldn't be like me. I've thought about it. They might start out like me, but everything would be different pretty soon. That's why Lyssa isn't anything like the girl she was made from. None of them are."

"That's what I've heard. That's how Lyssa seems to explain it."

Tim nodded, seeming very sure of himself. That was how he had acted since waking up, like he had a secret knowledge and confidence that maintained his calm. Nothing really phased him anymore. She couldn't decide if it was annoying or scary.

"Tim," Cara asked. "Do you *get* mad? You used to get mad all the time and you don't seem to anymore."

"I guess," he said. "Sometimes I don't feel like the me I used to be before. I'm something else now. Sometimes I can see the old me. It's like he's standing over there." Tim pointed to an empty corner of the medbay.

Cara couldn't help glancing where he pointed, relieved to only find a cabinet.

"He's mad. He's really mad. But he's over there. And I'm here. I'm not sure why he's so mad though. I remember wanting to kill that man, Cal Kraft. One of the people in the lift had a stungun, and I was going to grab it off their belt, turn it all the way up, and jam it right inside Cal Kraft's leg. I was going to burn his femoral artery open."

He gave her a secretive smile. "You didn't think I knew about things like that, but I do. I know that if you cut someone inside the leg like that, they'll bleed too fast to get help, especially if you stab so the blood runs down their leg so it's hard for people to see it. I read all about those sort of things."

Cara felt herself growing cold. The deliberate cadence of Tim's voice made it sound like he was describing a study project rather than killing someone.

He pointed his chin at the corner where the shadow Tim supposedly stood. "He was going to do that. He still wants to." Tim chewed his lip, considering the idea.

"You were in danger, Tim. It's okay to think things like that when you're in danger, when you don't know if you're going to be safe or not. And that guy threw you out the airlock. It was terrible. You survived something terrible."

"Yeah," Tim said. "I did. When I think about those five seeds they made, I wonder which one got the angry version of me. Do you think that's how it works?"

"I don't know how it works. It doesn't seem like any of them remember much from when they were alive. They don't have emotions or memories or anything. They just use the image to make it, so they can think and learn, like Lyssa did."

"I don't know. That seems awfully simplistic."

It was odd to hear such a complex thought come out of her brother's mouth. This was the strongest example yet of how he had become something different, something that didn't seem to be a ten-year-old boy anymore.

"I think we've been pretty lucky that Lyssa is like she is," Tim said. "What if somebody had hurt her like Cal Kraft hurt me? What if she'd been thrown out an airlock? I think that would be pretty hard to forget. We're lucky that Lyssa doesn't want to kill us all like the other AI, especially the one that did this to Dad."

"An AI didn't do this to Dad."

"Him and Harl and Lyssa fought a mech on Larissa. This happened as soon as they got back. Either the AI in the mech did something to Lyssa or to Dad. Harl thinks it's related."

"Well maybe you should listen to Fran instead of Harl. Maybe he doesn't know what he's talking about."

"Fran loves Dad," Tim said matter-of-factly. "She's not going to say something that might hurt him."

"She tells the truth," Cara said.

"It's weird, isn't it?"

"What? Everything's weird. Everything's been weird since before we went to Cruithne."

"Well, a long time before that, even. I guess I mean everything. Everything's weird. I don't know when it's going to stop being weird. I mean, they blew up a moon. That's weird."

He stared at their dad for a second, petting Em's head.

"We're going to be okay, Tim," Cara said.

Tim didn't respond at first. Then he shook his head. "I was mean to Mom and Dad. I was really mad, and I didn't know what to do. Now I feel—I can see that I was mean to them. I love Mom, but I don't know what to say to her other than I love you, Mom. But I have to say more than that, right?"

"No," Cara said. "We're the kids. We don't have to say more than that."

He laughed. "I'm pretty sure Dad would make us say more than that. I couldn't break something and just say I love you, Dad, and think he's not going to be mad. I'd get a talking-to for sure, and he'd explain all the ways I need to think before I do something, how the ship can be dangerous, and we're a long way from help, and we're in Rabbit Country where everyone wants to eat us."

Cara sighed. "I'm tired of being in Rabbit Country, Tim."

"Yeah. Me too."

"But you know we never get to leave, right? We just have to be smart, and pay attention?"

He gave her another sly glance. "We don't get to leave Rabbit Country, but we can get some tyrannosaur teeth. That's what I'm looking for. If I'm a rabbit with tyrannosaur teeth, I'll bite the head off anything that tries to mess with me, or you, or Dad. And Mom." Tim snapped his teeth at the air and Em bounced up, excited to play.

"You should play fetch with him rather than just sitting in here," Cara said. "Take him down in the cargo bay. He loves that."

"Do you want to do that, Em?" Tim asked. "Play fetch in

zero-*g*? Huh?"

The Corgi perked up with excitement, following Tim's every word.

Tim laughed. "Okay. Let's go do that." He reached out to pat their dad's arm. "I love you, Dad," he said. "For real."

Andy stirred on the bed, frowning at something in his sleep. Cara worried he was going to wake. He'd come to a few times during the journey to Traverna, but each time he'd been in so much pain it was worse than him being unconscious. She hoped that when they reached Traverna, they could find a real solution to whatever was wrong with him.

There was a click in the overhead speakers and Fran said, "Cara, Tim, where are you? We're getting ready for the final braking burn into Traverna. You're going to need to buckle-in. Check your dad's straps and make sure he's secure."

"I will," Cara said.

Tim slumped his shoulders. "I can buckle-in down in cargo."

"No, you can't," Cara admonished him. "We'll go to the Command Deck. We can watch the holodisplay. You know Traverna's a pirate station, right?"

Tim rolled his eyes. "Cruithne was a pirate station and it's boring."

"Cruithne isn't the same. The TSF is on Cruithne."

"They're going to be able to fix Dad on Traverna?" Tim asked.

Cara paused to adjust the straps holding their dad to the medbay couch. "That's what Fran hopes."

"Hope isn't a plan," Tim said.

"I know," Cara agreed. "But sometimes it has to be."

A groan from the bed drew Cara's gaze back to her dad. He was blinking. His eyes focused and he looked at her, brow clenched in what she knew was headache pain.

"I'm worried I've turned you into a pessimist, Cara," he

said hoarsely.

"Dad!" Tim shouted.

Andy pulled his outside arm free of its restraint to give Tim a hug. Em stood on his hind legs to peek over the edge of the bed, and Andy scratched his ears.

"How do you feel?" Cara asked cautiously.

He gave her a wan smile. "Great," he said, obviously lying. "Let's get up to the Command Deck together and I'll strap in up there. I'd rather be awake for the arrival."

"Isn't it better if you sleep?" Cara asked.

"Maybe," he said.

"You'll distract Fran."

Her dad raised his eyebrows. "So you can read Fran's mind now?"

"I don't have to read her mind to know how much she's worried about you."

Andy dropped back in the bed, relaxing visibly. "Fine," he said. "I'll stay down here. You two get up there like she asked you."

"I can stay here with you," Cara said.

"Do what I told you, Cara. I'll be fine."

She stared at him, feeling helpless, but nodded. "Do you want more of the medicine?" she asked.

"Yes," he said, voice tight with pain.

Cara activated the autodoc and waited for it to update its diagnostics. In a minute, it injected her dad with something that was supposed to help the headaches. He flinched during the injection, then sighed. He was asleep in another few seconds.

Tim gave her a solemn look, hugging Em against his side.

"Cara," Fran called over the speaker. "Why aren't you up here?"

"We're coming," Cara said. "Dad's all strapped in."

"You've got thirty seconds," Fran said. "If we're in the

window and you're not buckled in, I won't be cleaning you up off the deck."

"Why is she so mean?" Tim asked.

"She's not mean," Cara said. "She's professional."

"What's that mean?"

"It means she doesn't treat us like kids. At least not all the time. Now, come on. Let's go."

"Is dad going to be okay?"

"Yes, Tim," Cara said, realizing she was lying because she didn't know and had to get him out the door. "Dad's going to be okay."

CHAPTER TWENTY

STELLAR DATE: 01.14.2982 (Adjusted Years)
LOCATION: ***Sunny Skies***
REGION: Jovian L1 Hildas Asteroids, Jovian Combine, OuterSol

When the missiles hit Ceres, Cara experienced something she had never seen in all the time she had obsessively studied the communications spectrum: a pause.

When passive scans first picked up the series of burns in the Hellas asteroids, all of Sol seemed to hold its breath. Apparently it was unusual to see acceleration burns in those locations, as monitoring NSAI throughout InnerSol began to activate early warning systems.

Once the pattern was clear and the military had turned their attention to the incoming missiles, newsfeeds picked up the trajectories of more than fifty incoming objects. In the grand scheme of traffic, the engine signatures were nothing; however, all of InnerSol had been looking for the Larissa Launches for weeks, and this was the first new clue to bring the topic back to the top of the feeds and renew panic.

Fifty missiles were relatively easy for the Terran and Marsian space forces to pick off with the patrols they had set around the Anderson Collective, already assisting with the evacuation effort. Prior to the missiles sightings, activity had calmed slightly as people again started to doubt the truth of May Walton's warning message.

As the militaries took action, feeds sparked with images of the missiles being stopped in flight and the questions about the remaining launches were drowned out by images of people celebrating in the streets of the Ceres' Insi Ring. For a people who seemed so set in ceremony and social constraints, the Andersonians let loose in a wild way.

Cara found herself mesmerized by the personal vids of

tourists who had actually traveled *to* Ceres just to experience the wildness. In a place where the government was trying to get everyone out, no one cared much about people trying to get in, and there were plenty of transports heading to Ceres empty to pick up evacuees. In the initial mayhem, looters and criminals had dominated the feeds coming out of Ceres. Then things had grown more calm as the news settled down. And now the celebrations were back on top.

Through all of it, the vid May had made of Cara had taken on a cultural significance that was frightening and confusing. May had tried to explain what the symbol meant to Andersonian culture, but now there were images of Cara in every Andersonian vid on the feed.

Cara was watching a vid made by a girl her age, when another announcement hit the spectrum that Ceres had been hit by what was believed to be one hundred nuclear missiles.

Her screen froze on the image of a black-haired girl with brown eyes, talking about how wonderful it was to be in a park where people were celebrating the Collective's salvation. The vid was only an hour old.

New by the constraints of distance.

The first reports were text-only. Then the vids from inside the Collective hit the feeds, scooped up from people caught in street parties on the Insi Ring and spontaneous parades, who found themselves looking up at a sky on fire. Each vid Cara watched followed the same pattern: celebration and laughter followed by a moment of disbelief as someone noticed a vibration in the street, then people pointing up at the sky where Ceres hung like a blue-green marble. Then the sky erupted, and the vid cut off. Thousands of vids hit the streams at once.

The explosions were concentrated on a single point in the ring, one after another, so there would be no question the attack had been planned. They came in dark, no braking burns to alert anyone to such a small object's presence, until they hit the active scan perimeter and overwhelmed the TSF and Marsian defenses.

Broken, the Ceres ring immediately succumbed to the inexorable forces of orbital mechanics and spun itself apart. The ring broke into five pieces that collided against one another, fracturing again, filling the surrounding space with debris that rained down on Ceres like an asteroid shower. The General Electric Mini Blackhole, one of the greatest engineering feats of the last two hundred years, became the engine that destroyed the terraforming project, as wave after wave of burning debris was drawn to the surface, turned Ceres into a molten hellscape.

The broadcasts continued even as the ring disintegrated. Drones and public sensors gathered and sent data until they blinked out, long after the human inhabitants of the surface of Ceres and its ring were gone.

The first vids made it all seem to happen in just a matter of minutes. Then the replays started, showing how everything had transpired, wasting no time to honor the dead. The lag between InnerSol and the *Sunny Skies* compressed time and forced Cara to plot vids by timestamp to get a real idea of how long it had all taken.

Cara watched with a growing feeling of horror and fear. Her mind didn't want to accept that destruction at this magnitude was possible, yet the images were in front of her, looking like an entertainment vid from thousands of angles. She knew it was real.

Fran appeared in the Command Deck doorway, hair disheveled from sleep.

"Cara," she said. "Are these alerts true?" She crossed the room to stand behind Cara at the communications console, putting a hand on her shoulder.

Cara appreciated the touch, which came more naturally

now. She looked up at Fran, catching the reflection of the latest vid she had been watching in Fran's augmented eyes.

"Oh, stars," Fran said in a low voice. "Stars, they did it. This is terrible."

"*We* didn't do it, did we?" Cara asked.

Fran gave her a sharp look. "Why would you think that?"

"We were at Larissa. All of this started when we got to Proteus. We took the Resolute Charity there. That's what Alexander saw as a threat. Isn't that what happened?"

Fran squeezed Cara's shoulder, steadying her. "Everything we're seeing was planned, Cara. It's not anyone's fault but the people who fired those missiles, and it wasn't us. All we've been trying to do this whole time is help Lyssa and others like her. Sometimes you can't see the big picture until it's already happened."

"But what do we do?" Cara asked, distraught. "All those people are going to die. Or they—they're already dead. The light lag—"

Fran leaned forward to tap the console and turn off the screen. "It's not going to do any good to sit here watching it. Why don't you go spend some time with your dad or Tim. Spend time with people you love."

"I like spending time with you."

Cara looked up at Fran to catch an unaccustomed expression on her face: surprise. Fran glanced away quickly, nodding at the screen again. "You're all right too, kid," she said. "If I had to be anywhere while terrible things are going down, this is a good place to be. Now look, when bad things happen, you focus on the people close to you and the task at hand. I think your dad's already said things like this, yeah? What do you need to do? What are we doing?"

Cara swallowed, wiping her nose. "We're going to Traverna to help dad."

"Closer than that. What are you doing right now? Tasks,

Cara."

"I'm monitoring the comm feed for contact from the Traverna port control since we're almost within contact range."

"That's right. Now how do you do that? I'm not talking about listening to everything. The whole spectrum is a waste of time right now. What's out there doesn't matter to what's in front of us."

"I need to start a conversation with whoever contacts us first, just like I did back when we were entering Marsian space."

"Exactly. If they know your name, they're less likely to shoot you."

"Really?"

Fran shrugged. "I don't actually know if that's true but it's what I tell myself. I haven't gotten shot yet."

Cara gave her a frown. "That's not verification."

"It is for now. Are you good to get back to work? Or do you want to go see your dad and Tim?"

Looking at her console, Cara said, "I'll work. It isn't going to change anything to talk to them now. If Dad can talk through the headaches."

"It's probably better if he sleeps," Fran said.

Fugia walked in, to stand in front of the holodisplay, remaining silent, eyes focused on the astrogation map, her mouth a flat line.

"You heard the news?" Fran asked.

Fugia gave a shallow nod. "This isn't what I expected. None of this has been what I thought would happen."

Fran went to the pilot's seat and Cara looked between the two women, unsure what to say in response to Fugia's loss.

Nothing is what you expect in Rabbit Country. You keep your head down and your ears up, ready to run.

She knew Fugia didn't want to hear that, but it was the

only thought keeping Cara from bursting into tears. Unable to shake the image of the brown-eyed girl from the frozen vid, she listed her tasks and placed her hands on the console, focusing her search on the nearing coordinates for Traverna.

"May will be staying in her rooms," Fugia said absently. "I'm not sure she'll be going with us when we get to Traverna, unless we need her help." She sighed. "It might be better if we come up with some excuse, force her to get off the ship. Have we heard anything from Brit?"

"No," Cara said. "I think Dad got a message from her that she was back on Cruithne but that was a few weeks ago." She knew that Fugia already had this information, but the woman seemed to want to talk about nothing, just to hear words.

Eventually, Fugia looked up from the holodisplay. "Where's your brother and the dog? Maybe I'll go play some zero-g fetch with them. That dog is hilarious."

"His name's Em," Cara said.

"Of course, it is," Fugia said woodenly. "I should call him by his name. That's rude of me."

"He'd probably like that," Cara offered. "Or you could talk to Lyssa or some of the other Weapon Born. I've been meeting them a few at a time. They always like to talk."

Fugia walked over to put her elbow on the edge of the console, looking past Cara to the door. "Here's the thing," she said. "I know in my mind I should talk to them, but I just don't have the heart to do it right now. Not after what's happened to Ceres. It was SAIs who did that."

"Not the Weapon Born," Cara insisted.

"No, it wasn't them. But it's something so terrible that I'm still trying to process it, Cara, and it goes against everything I've dedicated the last ten years of my life to achieving." She swallowed, taking a steadying breath.

Cara had never seen Fugia look so numb. Her usual pointed expression was dulled.

"What I was doing was a lie," Fugia said. "Every long night waiting for incoming ships, the smuggling, the hacking, the friends I turned away. I've shaped my life around all of this, and now here we are. I certainly wasn't a fan of the Anderson Collective, but I wouldn't wish this kind of destruction on them in a million years. I thought we'd moved past this kind of war."

Fran gave a harsh laugh. "You can't be serious. We're humans, this is what we do."

Fugia turned on her, face reddening. "Of course. When was the last major attack of this scale?"

"Maybe not this scale," Fran said. "But there's been low level war forever. What do you think pirate interdiction really means? The TSF and Marsians take whatever they want if you don't have the force to stop them. You know that."

"That's not what I mean," Fugia said. "This is—billions, Fran. I can't explain how *weary* this makes me feel."

"Well, we're heading into it, so we're going to be feeling a lot more of it before we're done. Get your tears out now."

Fugia's face went flat as she stared at Fran.

"What?" Fran asked. "You want me to coddle you some more? You wouldn't do it for me. If I'm going to be some kind of role model for Cara, there, I'm not going to lie to your face. Obviously, we're on the edge of terrible things. You don't need me to tell you that."

Fugia stared for another few seconds, then blinked and lowered her face. She smiled slightly. "You're right."

Fran sighed. "Don't tell anyone."

The smaller woman straightened, squaring her shoulders, and turned to look at Cara. "Pardon me. I think I lost my mind for a second. It's back now. I know you've got enough to worry about without me raving like a lost person."

"It's all right," Cara said. "I understand. I think I feel the same way."

"Then we'll depend on Fran as our resident hard-ass," Fugia said, giving Cara a tentative grin that hinted at her usual self.

A response on the communications array drew Cara's attention. They had a ping from the Traverna port control. Cara acknowledged the signal and verified their registry information.

"They just pinged us, Fran," Cara said.

The engineer waved a hand without looking up from her screen. "Don't tell me about it. Do your job, Communicator. Smooth the way so we get a good berth. I don't want to be out by the refueling stations. Turn on that charm, girl."

Cara rolled her eyes. The image of the Andersonian girl left her mind as she focused on her headset, selecting the voice channel indicated in the broadcast's general info signal. She sent a communications request and cupped her headphones against her head, listening to the low hum of dancing static.

After a minute, a bored voice answered, "T-Control. What do you want?"

"Hi," Cara said, making her voice as bright and interesting as she could muster, pushing away every sad thought hanging over her mind. "My name's Cara. What's yours?"

"What?" the controller asked, sounding both annoyed and curious.

In another three minutes, Cara had the woman describing her life on Freeport Traverna in the far edges of the Hellas asteroids, all too glad to be talking about anything but Ceres.

PART 3 - TRAVERNA

CHAPTER TWENTY-ONE

STELLAR DATE: 01.15.2982 (Adjusted Years)
LOCATION: Raleigh, TSF Regional Materiel Command
REGION: High Terra, Earth Terran Hegemony

Visible through the maglev windows, the white spire of the Heartbridge headquarters on the horizon kept a knot of worry in the bottom of Jirl's stomach. Petral had assured her that any attempts to track Jirl's arrival back in Raleigh would be blocked, but she couldn't simply place her trust in systems she couldn't see. She expected company security around every corner, ready to escort her back to Arla for an interrogation.

Arla thinks you're still on Cruithne, she told herself. *Arla thinks you're on an extended tryst with Rick Yarnes.*

Still, the confrontation with Arla was inevitable. She had spent the trip from Cruithne catching up on the newsfeed responses to Cara Sykes' warning to the Andersonians that death was coming for their ring. As expected, Ceres was in chaos. After news leaked that the government had known about the threat prior to Cara's open message, commodity prices skyrocketed, and the local space was so crowded with privateers waiting for berths on the ring that collisions were happening hourly.

The Collective's government struggled to maintain the semblance of an orderly evacuation in the face of public pandemonium, but the first slots had gone to party members and their families, and then been overrun by pirates and privateers responding to black market bribes and then using force to move people off the ring.

The terraforming project stopped as project managers and engineers left, abandoning workers on the surface. The stoppage would likely result in the loss of decades of progress according to talking heads.

During one news session, Petral had remarked, "At this rate, it won't matter if missiles hit the ring or not."

The Terran Assembly and Marsian Congress were still debating how to respond to the humanitarian crisis on Ceres. While their militaries had been brought to ready status, neither had moved to offer resources to the Anderson Collective to guard against any incoming missile attack. The Collective had initially arrayed its fleet in a protective pattern, but they were quickly recalled to deal with pirates and emergency response.

Jirl looked down at her hands in her lap, then up at Brit sitting across from her. The major was dressed in her black armor, a bag between her boots on the floor containing various weapons they had smuggled through the lax shipping center security. Petral sat next to her with the case holding Tristan in her lap. Petral was dressed in a crimson shipsuit covered in utility pockets. A web harness snaked from her belt over her shoulders, hung with various network connection tools. Jirl couldn't help thinking of her as some overly stylish systems repair person. Petral's gaze was fixed on the near distance. She had explained earlier that she would need to monitor several waypoints on the maglev system where it would automatically scan the passengers and send information back to the TSF. She had overridden the system but didn't trust that system defenses wouldn't find her workaround.

Ngoba Starl sat next to Jirl, wearing a dark blue suit with a lime green bow-tie and pocket square. His hair was full of tight curls and combed to one side of his forehead. He enjoyed the many second looks he'd received as they walked through the grimy shipping control center, surrounded by porters and transportation drones. Petral had led the way, also drawing looks. Two of Starl's bodyguards sat next to him, a man with bristle-white hair named Burroughs and a woman with augmented purple eyes and short brown hair named Fletcher. Both had been fastidiously unfriendly.

The maglev was following the same path she'd taken many times with Arla to the TSF Materiel Acquisitions center. They would be stopping at the same marble-covered station where she had met Yarnes just a month ago. Petral had verified that Yarnes was in the area, so it would be Jirl's role to step off the maglev alone and engage the colonel.

Looking at her hands again, she tried to think of what she would say. Petral had already provided a list of topics that might work, from asking for help to protect Bry on Mars, to requesting protection from Heartbridge, to potentially romantic lines of discussion if the others failed.

She laughed inwardly at the idea of seducing someone.

The truth was, Jirl couldn't precisely say why Yarnes had helped her before. He'd said he wanted to help shut down the Weapon Born program to stave off a war with Mars, but now she knew the TSF was simply looking to grab up whatever tech they could, especially the shipkiller mech frames developed by Heartbridge.

Yarnes had been using her for any number of reasons, and when General Kade had been killed, Yarnes left as quickly as possible, not even trying to convince her to stay when she reported that she was safe on Starl's ship.

Whatever she did, she had to distract Yarnes long enough to at least slow down the TSF response when they learned their labs had been infiltrated.

The maglev dropped closer to street level, showing a shopping district full of people and drones. She couldn't tell if it was more busy than usual. It certainly didn't look like the frenzied stores on Ceres. They passed underground, the windows filled by plascrete panels, plumbing and conduit, then solid black that showed her reflection: white button-down shirt and gray pencil skirt. Her normal business attire.

Starl reached into the bag between his leather dress shoes and inspected a small cutting torch, checking its charge, then replaced it and drew out a bandoleer of black discs connected by black filament.

"You better not use those things unless I tell you it's safe," Petral said.

"What is it?" Jirl asked.

"Small scale electromagnetic pulse," Starl said. "One of these can shut down a network node or maybe a drone. The whole band could kill our maglev, or a shuttle. I've had some fun with them."

The way he tossed the bandoleer didn't give Jirl a lot of confidence that he wasn't going to kill their car. Beside him, the two guards checked their weapons and armor.

Petral had identified the TSF laboratories deeper in the facility. Jirl would get off at the station she knew and distract Yarnes, the station commander, while the others went deeper. They would notify her once Tristan had a mech and was ready to begin the assault on Heartbridge.

After that—so long as Jirl was free of Yarnes—she would rendezvous with them or, if that wasn't possible, make her way back to meet with Arla. Tucked in Jirl's waistband was a data key. She would need to find an empty office and enter it into a general-use terminal. After that, the fireworks would start.

Jirl took a deep breath, steadying herself. She straightened her shoulders and set her chin, adjusting her gaze out the window at the dark, where her reflection stared back at her.

<You always look so calm,> Brit told her over the Link. *<I imagine that's why the executives want you around. All they have to do is look at you and it doesn't seem like everything's going to hell.>*

Jirl gave her a tired smile. <*I'm exploding inside.*>

<*Keep doing whatever you're doing to contain it. It's helping me.*>

<*We're going to succeed,*> Jirl said.

<*Yes,*> Brit responded bluntly.

The determination in her voice made it hard for Jirl to believe she wouldn't fight her way through Heartbridge's entire security forces if necessary.

The maglev chimed, indicating they were approaching their first stop. Jirl watched herself in the black window until the marble station appeared, glaring with bright lights. A single TSF guard stood at the platform. Around her, the others adjusted their bags slightly, ensuring they looked like luggage.

Jirl took a deep breath and stood. Focusing her gaze on the door, she walked to the end of the car and stepped out onto the platform.

The guard stiffened to acknowledge her. "Welcome," he said. "How can I direct you?"

Jirl felt the tickle of active scanning touching her Link. She passed her basic information to the request and smiled at the guard.

"My name is Jirl Gallagher," she said. "I'm here to see Colonel Yarnes. I'm afraid I don't have an appointment."

Behind her, the maglev door slid closed and the car moved away, leaving a blast of cold air in its wake. She was alone.

The guard nodded, and his face grew distant as he passed information. His brow knit for a second when he didn't seem to get the response he expected.

"Sorry," he said. "They need to check in with the colonel."

"I understand." A bead of sweat ran between Jirl's shoulder blades, made even colder by the wind from the maglev track penetrating her shirt.

Another minute passed with the guard looking awkwardly past her. Eventually, he nodded. "The colonel is in a meeting right now but would like to meet you. If it's all right, I can take you to a waiting area. Would you like coffee or tea?"

"Coffee please, thank you."

They had to wait for another guard to replace the soldier at the terminal, then Jirl followed her guide down the wide marble corridor to the single door she had been through before. They entered a narrow, wood-paneled hallway with blank wooden doors on either side. The guard approached one that looked like all the others and tapped the lock panel. The door slid aside. He led her into a nicely appointed room with two facing leather couches and a low table. A display with the TSF crest on its otherwise empty face filled one wall.

A coffee service already sat steaming in the center of the table.

"You're welcome to serve yourself," the guard said.

"Would you like some?" Jirl asked.

He gave her a quizzical look, then smiled. "No, thank you. I need to get back to my post. There's a rest room through there, if you need." He pointed at the outline of a door in one wall.

The guard left and Jirl took advantage of the restroom, adjusting her pencil skirt and white shirt, making sure the data key was where she had tucked it. Petral had assured her the key would look normal to anyone who wanted to scan it. Still, it made Jirl feel like she was carrying a bomb.

After ten minutes of waiting, she decided to compose a quick-code text message for her son Bry. She asked him how he was doing and if he was having fun with his cousins. She assured him that she would join him soon on Mars and they might even stay there if he liked it enough. She missed him and loved him. She sent the quick-code and immediately wished she had written it differently or sent a voice message. She wanted him to hear her emotion but also didn't want to push too much.

Finally, she poured herself a cup of coffee and added cream, then watched the swirls of white in black until the surface of the cup had become a uniform caramel color. When it had stopped steaming, she took a sip.

With the taste of coffee on her lips, she thought briefly about what would happen if she died. Her accounts were in order. Bry wouldn't want for anything for a long time, if he managed the money correctly. He would have two more years before adulthood. The money would certainly cover his Link surgery. From there, he might stay on Mars. Maybe he would want to see where his father was buried on Earth. He could still visit Earth, if he wanted. It would take a little training to acclimate to the gravity.

If she died, she wouldn't find out what was going to happen, not just to Bry but to everyone. If it happened after the clinics got the destruct message, she would be all right with it.

Not until then, she decided. Once that happens, I think things will be better.

The line of thought surprised her. She didn't consider herself a depressive person, but everything that was happening around her only served as a reminder that without Heartbridge or Bry, she had no purpose. She couldn't see a future beyond the fall of the white spire.

She would enter the data key, maybe see Arla, and then after that, blankness.

Jirl considered the emptiness. She imagined the spire collapsing level by level, blowing out debris into the surrounding district, the center of her life disintegrating.

She blinked. *No. I'm going to live past that. I'm going to escape.*

A surge of joy passed through her, making her smile despite herself. When the door opened and Yarnes walked in, she looked at him with that same smile, which made him stop as the entrance locked him inside with her.

"I don't think I've ever seen that expression on your face, Jirl," he said.

Jirl quickly composed herself and picked up the coffee cup to give her hands something to do.

"I was just thinking about the future," she said.

He gave a short laugh. "I'm glad you can do that. Did you come with Starl and the others?"

Jirl froze inside. Did he mean on the maglev, or High Terra?

Petral had told her not to lie if she could help it. She didn't have to give complete truths.

"I've wanted to see you ever since I got back to High Terra," Jirl said.

Yarnes paused, looking surprised. "You did?"

Jirl gave him another smile.

Yarnes caught himself and shifted his gaze to the display. He didn't press about Petral and Starl, and Jirl relaxed slightly. So he either didn't know they had arrived with her, or he was waiting to see what she would give away.

For every motive she imagined, she found it hard not to trust his honest, soldier's face.

"I was surprised you asked to meet me," Yarnes said. "There's something I want to show you, so this is fortuitous." He nodded toward the display.

The crest had disappeared from the holotank and now showed a standard system map. The holodisplay activated, and the end of the room filled with Mars, Ceres, and the Cho. Larger Hellas asteroids dotted the space between Ceres and Jupiter.

Jirl frowned when it appeared that a cluster of asteroids were both too close to each other and moving off orbit. Still holding her coffee cup in both hands, she stood and stepped around the couch so she could get a better look at the whole map.

A collection of icons caught her attention.

"What's that?" she asked.

"I figured you would recognize it immediately."

She didn't, but it was impossible to ignore the swarm of ships dominating the space between Jupiter and Mars.

Yarnes moved closer to stand beside her. He zoomed in on the cluster, which became a fleet of ships, spread in a loose wing-formation that must have covered a hundred-thousand kilometers.

"Should I recognize them?" Jirl asked. "I don't see anything that looks like a Heartbridge design."

"We haven't seen any either," he said. "They're mostly former space force military craft from all three militaries, although there are many new designs among them as well. As far as we can tell, their path originated in the Scattered Disk near Nibiru. They aren't answering any hails and all registry information comes back null. They are definitely armed, though they haven't showed aggression toward any civilian craft they've passed. The flight plan appears to be targeting Ceres."

"Alexander," Jirl said.

"We believe those ships are piloted by sentient AI," he said, nodding. Yarnes fixed her with his brown eyes. "I need to know what Heartbridge knows about this. I'm hoping it's why you're here."

Jirl swallowed, nearly dropping her coffee cup. "I came here to see you," she said. "I don't know anything about those ships."

Yarnes continued to watch her closely. His gaze softened and he glanced at the map, then waved an arm to push it back against the wall so it didn't dominate the room.

"Well, it's good to see you, too, Jirl, but this isn't a good time for social calls."

"When is?" she asked quickly.

"I've been—I've been thinking about you ever since the clinic exploded. It makes me feel stupid, honestly."

"You don't even know me," Yarnes said. He gave her another assessing glance.

Was there a shadow of a smile on the edge of his lips?

Jirl shrugged. "Everything's going to hell. I figure if ever there was a time to say how you feel, this is it."

Yarnes laughed. He crossed the room to stand in front of her. "You want me to take this?" he asked, pulling the saucer and cup from her hands. He set them on the table.

When he straightened in front of her, Jirl became very aware of just how close he was, and how she might need to follow through on what she was suggesting.

Was she attracted to him?

Would she be doing any of this if she wasn't?

He had placed himself close to her, but not *too* close. She would have to step toward him if they were going to touch. Jirl looked up at him and she flushed. Sweat broke out on her neck and she unfastened the top button of her shirt.

"It's hot in here," she said.

Yarnes raised an eyebrow but didn't look down at her chest.

An alarm burst from the room's overhead speakers. Yarnes' eyes when distant as he accessed his Link.

"We've got an interior alarm," he said. "My Quick Reaction Force is being activated."

He turned toward the door and Jirl caught his arm, pulling him back around. She stood on her toes to kiss him, just catching his lower lip at first and then reaching behind his neck to pull him down to her.

Yarnes' uniform was stiff against her business suit. He kissed her back quickly and then drew his face back, looking down at her with a surprised smile.

"You're full of surprises," he said.

"Do they really need you on the Reaction Force?" she asked.

Jirl felt slightly giddy. Her heart was hammering in her chest, all the adrenaline from the anxious maglev ride dumping out in a surge of desire that had probably always been there. She could tell Yarnes wanted her, too. Even if he had been trying to use her, there was a flicker of mutual attraction that had been hidden beneath the colonel's veneer.

"Not immediately," he admitted.

I don't care if this is espionage. I want him.

Jirl slid her gaze toward the couch, where the solar map still rotated above. She unfastened the top closure of his uniform jacket.

With a lapel in each hand, Jirl pulled his face back down to hers for a more certain kiss, then pushed him backward until his boots hit the couch's edge, and they went down together.

CHAPTER TWENTY-TWO

STELLAR DATE: 01.15.2982 (Adjusted Years)
LOCATION: Raleigh, TSF Regional Materiel Command
REGION: High Terra, Earth, Terran Hegemony

The maglev picked up speed out of the station and Brit found herself trying to grab one last look at Jirl standing on the platform, facing the TSF guard alone. She had the feeling she would never see the woman again. The car picked up speed, carrying them deeper into the TSF headquarters facility. Another platform appeared, flooding the car with light, and then was clipped away by plascrete walls, plunging everything back into darkness.

Everything depended on Petral now. Brit glanced at her, seeing that the dark-haired woman was still staring ahead, attention fixed on some interior point where security queries threatened their progress. Across the car, Ngoba Starl rested his head against the wall and closed his eyes, nodding to some music only he could hear.

Since there was nowhere else to look, Brit sized up Starl's bodyguards one more time; the blond one looked like he could punch through metal, while purple-eyed Fletcher looked made of wiry muscle, ready to choke the life out of something. Brit focused on her breathing, putting the travel time out of her mind. They couldn't risk communication via the Link, so there would be no updates from Jirl.

Why did she care if she saw Jirl Gallagher again? Meeting the woman had upset her opinion of Heartbridge, changed the company from a faceless evil to a place made of people, many of which were probably just like Jirl, with children and consumer debt, trying to make their way. Wasn't that the true evil of the world, that good people were inevitably dragged into the machines of destruction? She knew that when they brought Heartbridge down, there would be another to take its place, and another after that. Maybe the AI were right to take Ceres. Maybe a reset was the only thing that might save humanity from its own benign evils.

Pointless thoughts. She was here for the dead children on Fortress 8221. They were already a lost cause. That was the point. And her own children, out there without Andy to take care of them?

Brit tensed her jaw, trying to convince herself that Cara was strong. Cara could take care of Tim, even if Andy was sick.

She leaned forward to put her face in her hands, fighting back the tears at the edges of her eyes. Without Andy taking care of the kids, Brit's idealism felt like dust in her mouth. She couldn't find the same iron resolve she had felt so easily before. Before when?

Brit looked up from her hands to find Starl watching her with concern on his face. He raised a questioning eyebrow and she forced a tight smile.

They passed another station and when the lights were gone, Petral said in a low voice, "Next stop."

Reaching for the bag between her boots, Brit found the stock of a short-bodied automatic rifle. Side pockets inside the bag held a series of magnetic mines and a handheld cutting torch—her new favorite multi-tool. She checked the charge on her pulse pistol, then reached deeper in the bag for two bandoleers of grenades and draped them over her shoulders, crossing her chest.

According to the schematics Petral had found, they would be arriving at a supply dock that served a series of lab spaces. There was a fifty percent chance the dock would be manned by civilian employees with one or two TSF on guard duty. If there were no humans present, there would be service drones with monitoring systems that would alert the working staff to activity on the dock. Starl's EMP grenades were for the drones.

Brit's stun grenades were for the TSF patrol.

They had debated trying to use Brit's rank to at least get inside the lab spaces, before she finally decided it wasn't worth the risk of alerting a ranking officer. The sooner they neutralized whatever they found on the dock and got inside the labs, the better.

In the pit of her stomach, she felt the car slowing down. Light from the station touched the windows at the front of the car, then the dock slid completely into view as their door lined up with the exit ramp. Through the wide car window, Brit locked eyes with a young guard with a rifle slung on his shoulder.

Grabbing her bag, Brit was through the door as it opened, rushed the guard as he struggled to get the rifle into a firing position. Striking a pressure point on his shoulder, she slid around to wrap him in a sleeper hold. She walked the soldier back as he struggled, kicking, then went limp. Brit loosened her grip, reminding herself that the soldier hadn't done anything, was just pulling guard duty. There was no reason to punish him. She laid the man down beside two shipping crates and pulled her rifle out of her bag.

"Clear," she called.

Burroughs and Fletcher were the first out of the maglev car, rifles at their shoulders, scanning the dock. The stop was only thirty meters wide, bathed in harsh white light and designed only for small deliveries. Brit checked the area and walked across the open cargo storage area, headed for the interior door.

<Any activity on the network?> she asked Petral.

<Nothing. It looks like you got the guard before he could alert anyone. However, I'm showing a check-in system for the patrol rotation. Someone's going to come looking for him soon.>

Petral strode past Brit to the door. She hadn't bothered to pull her pistol though she cradled the case with Tristan's seed against her side. She assessed the locking mechanism and then shrugged with surprise. Tapping the door, it slid open to allow entry to a wide corridor.

<*We're in,*> Petral told the group.

Brit moved to Petral's side, ready to take lead into the corridor, when a woman in gray utility uniform walked around a corner at the far end of the hallway. They stared at each other for a second, before the woman lurched toward a nearby wall, slapping an emergency alert panel before running away.

The white lights in the corridor flashed to yellow, followed by an ear-splitting klaxon.

<*Damn it!*> Brit shouted. <*Where's the lab we want?*>

<*I don't know exactly. The rooms that looked like the best bet are about a hundred meters inside the facility.*>

Brit glanced back at Burroughs, Fletcher and Starl. <*Let's go then,*> she growled.

Pushing ahead, Brit fell into a slow jog. She hugged the edge of the corridor, threading an optic around the corner where the worker had fled before making the turn. They moved in a stick formation down corridors stacked with shipping crates, creating dead spaces where Brit expected weapons fire at any moment. The crates were marked by logos Brit had never seen before, until several with the Heartbridge corporate brand appeared in a stack.

Petral checked each door they passed, finding only storage areas and a latrine.

<*They're calling in the Quick Reaction Force,*> Petral announced grimly.

<*How far out?*> Fletcher asked, her voice low.

<*They're outside this sector. I'd give them five minutes.*>

After another corridor lined by what looked like examination rooms with workbenches and multi-level platforms, Brit started to think they were getting closer. They passed one open crate on the side of the hallway heaped with mech parts. The next set of doors opened on a firing range, its far wall scorched by weapons fire.

<*Think we're getting close,*> Brit said.

<*Where are all the workers?*> Starl asked.

<*They don't typically staff this place,*> Petral explained. <*That's why I thought we might just encounter drones. They bring prototypes down here from various companies and run them through tests.*>

<*Looks like they break all their toys,*> Starl noted, glancing in another open crate.

<*I was able to get the access codes to the maglev by backtracing a black-market trade in the components,*> Petral said. <*These crates full of cutting edge junk have been making a local sergeant very rich.*>

<*Lucky for us,*> Brit said. Walking past a closed door, she froze as it slid open automatically, showing a rectangular room lined with work platforms. <*Shit!*> Brit shouted. She crouched, throwing herself to the outer edge of the door, rifle up.

The others crouched against the sides of the corridor, taking cover behind crates.

<*What do you see now?*> Starl asked.

<*Wait,*> Brit said.

Sliding her optic around the door's edge, she saw the same mechs crouched on the work platforms, jaguar-shaped with flat black heads. She waited, but none seemed to note her presence.

<*There are mechs in here,*> Brit said, standing slowly. <*Ship busters like we saw on the* Furious Leap.>

<*Well, that should make Tristan happy,*> Petral said.

<*How long until the QRF gets here?*> *Burroughs asked.*

<*Any second now,*> Petral said, hurrying past Brit. <*We should get a perimeter in the hallway while I see if any of these are*

going to work.>

<*On it,*> the guard answered.

Petral had barely entered the room when cracking weapons fire filled the corridor. Brit turned toward the sound and hit the floor, flattening herself behind a metal crate.

<*I see five,*> Fletcher announced. <*Light armor with projectile rifles. Looks like a standard TSF infantry squad.*>

<*They'll be bringing up some heavy weapons soon, then,*> Starl said. <*If they bring out a shield, we'll lay cover and I'll drop the EMP.*>

<*What's the range on those things?*> Brit asked.

<*Three to five meters or so,*> Starl answered. <*I'll have to test my throwing arm.*>

"Hey there!" the crime boss shouted from behind a stack of crates. "Why are you shooting at us? We're lost. We're just looking for directions. And damn I could use a restroom."

Brit couldn't decide if she was irritated or relieved by the humor in Starl's voice.

"This is a restricted facility," a gruff voice answered. "We are authorized to use deadly force. Show yourselves and we will respond accordingly."

" 'Respond accordingly', eh?" Starl shouted. "I don't know if I like the sound of that. I'm just trying to find a drink, friend. I don't know how I ended up here, honestly. Does 'respond accordingly' mean you'll get me a cold one?"

From the other side of the corridor, Fletcher unhooked one of the grenades, tapped its round body to adjust the settings, and lobbed it down the corridor at the TSF squad.

"Grenade!" one of the soldiers shouted.

<*It's smoke,*> Fletcher told them. <*Once it pops, we'll go in with IR and pulse fire. We're not taking them out, right, boss?*>

<*Not if you don't have to,*> Starl affirmed. <*They're just working stiffs, yeah.*>

<*They already tried to shoot me,*> Brit said.

<I never hold that against anyone,> Starl told her, a grin evident in his voice.

The smoke grenade hissed and made a loud popping sound. The hallway was immediately filled with roiling black smoke. Fletcher didn't hesitate. She slid around her crate and started firing pulse rounds.

Random fire pounded at the end of the hallway as the TSF regrouped.

<I got two,> Fletcher announced. *<Taking cover. They're setting up a shield.>*

<Moving,> Burroughs said.

Brit followed behind the bodyguard, scanning the cloud with her optics for IR signatures. It appeared the remaining TSF had pulled back to the far end of the corridor behind a repulsor shield.

<They'll be sending in mechs any minute now,> Brit said. *<Petral, you got anything?>*

<No,> Petral announced finally. *<Everything in here is dead.>*

Starl laughed with irony. *<That would be too easy, now, wouldn't it?>* He came up past Brit, one of the EMP pucks in his throwing hand. With an underhanded toss, he sent the grenade sliding down the smooth floor into the smoke.

More shouts of "Grenade!" filled the corridor and this time two grenades were lobbed back in answer.

Brit grabbed Starl by the collar and yanked him back behind the crate with her. Two explosions filled the hallway even as the EMP flashed. In the falling dust, a few seconds of silence followed, and then came what sounded like the clatter of equipment hitting the ground. Brit hoped that was the shield assembly collapsing.

Starl rolled onto his stomach beside her, giving her a mock salute before staying low and crawling forward. His green bow-tie was the only splash of color in the dust and debris.

<Burroughs, Fletcher,> he called. *<Sound off. I can't see your*

beautiful faces.>

Someone cried out in pain in the smoke, and then Fletcher answered, <*We've got this team neutralized. It looks like there's another lab up here with one of those mechs in it.*>

<*We didn't kill anybody, did we?*> Brit asked.

<*Currently unconscious,*> Burroughs said. <*We followed the EMP with the stun guns. Worked like a charm.*>

<*You cut it close,*> Starl said, chiding them. <*What if you'd run in there and found your batteries fried?*>

<*You said you were setting it on a tight radius, boss,*> Fletcher said, a grin in her voice. <*If I can't trust you, who can we trust?*>

<*The perfect answer,*> Starl said, laughing. He climbed to his feet, dusted off his pants and walked into the receding dust cloud. Brit followed, glancing back to see Petral walking out of the other lab.

<*You all made a mess,*> she observed.

The two body guards had the TSF squad in temporary restraints and propped up against the wall when Brit and Petral walked into the second lab. In the middle of the room, surrounded by workbenches, was a massive jaguar-mech, easily twice the size of Tristan's original construct.

Burroughs and Fletcher posted outside the door as Petral set Tristan's seed on a nearby workbench and approached the mech. She searched among the panels in its side before finding an access port.

"Cross your fingers," she told Brit and Starl. After a few seconds of checking the control system, she stepped back to let it run start up diagnostics.

The mech sat up higher on the platform, startling Brit. She raised her rifle instinctively, then relaxed as the monster settled back down, other servos working its neck, shoulders and legs. A series of hardened claws on each foot extended and retracted.

"Looks good," Petral said. "All right, Mr. Tristan, let's get you plugged in."

Taking the cylinder-shaped seed from the workbench, she slid back a panel placed higher on the mech's side. The seed slid into the socket and locked in place. Petral closed the panel.

<*This thing is a monster,*> Tristan said, faster than Brit had expected. <*It's like a tank!*>

<*You like it?*> Petral asked.

<*I think I can make do.*>

Moving with surprising grace, the mech sat up and swiveled its head as if looking at each of them.

<*Here's the deal,*> Brit said. <*We need you to cause a whole lot of mayhem getting out of this place. After that, stealth until you reach the Heartbridge headquarters.*>

<*I've shared all the location data with you, Tristan,*> Petral said.

<*I see it,*> he said, sounding serious now. <*I can shut down power to this facility but that might make it difficult for you to get out. Wait, there's already a general alert. You know that, right?*>

<*We did,*> Petral said. <*There will be more soldiers showing up. They'll lock down the maglev, but I've got a plan for that.*>

<*You aren't boring,*> Tristan said. <*I like that. Anything else?*>

<*Do you have questions for us?*> Petral asked.

<*Mission understood. Besides, it isn't like I can't call.*>

The mech jumped down from the platform, making the floor shake slightly. Once in motion, the heavy paws barely registered any sound in the room, despite the thing's size.

The flat head swiveled back to face Petral. <*Miss me?*> Tristan asked.

Petral grinned. <*Always,*> she said. <*We'll see you soon.*>

With a swiping motion, Tristan cut two long gashes in the wall, showing another room on the far side. In seconds, the mech was through the wound and tearing into another surface Brit couldn't see.

Starl clapped his hands. "That was impressive," he said. He laughed. "I think he likes you, Petral."

"I'd rather he liked me than didn't," she said. In the distance, the tenor of the warning klaxon changed to a higher pitch.

"Come on," Brit said. "Let's get back to the maglev before they shut everything down."

"Yes, major," Starl said, giving her a mock salute. "I'd rather not be here when Tristan sets the whole place on fire."

CHAPTER TWENTY-THREE

STELLAR DATE: 01.15.2982 (Adjusted Years)
LOCATION: Raleigh, Heartbridge Corporate Headquarters
REGION: High Terra, Earth, Terran Hegemony

Standing in the lobby of the Heartbridge corporate headquarters, Jirl gazed up at the three-story fountain in the center of the space, a cascade of twisting water and white light made to resemble the ancient medical symbol of serpents intertwined around a winged staff. Now, she couldn't help thinking of the wings as attack craft and the serpents as Weapon Born mechs.

Forcing herself into motion, she passed through the main security checkpoint, which she knew would alert Arla and probably others of her return. She had an instant of worry about the data stick tucked inside her waistband, but the guard only smiled at her and waved her through. Jirl nodded in return and walked quickly to the main lift. In another few minutes, she was caught up in a crowd of visitors and employees rising in the lift. She did her best to keep her breathing steady, brushing the data stick with the inside of her wrist to remind herself it was still there.

All she had to do was exit the lift on one of the administrative levels, find one of the many unused office spaces and insert the stick. Once that was done, she would find another lift and go meet Arla. She made her face consciously more pleasant as she waited, running through scripts of what she might say, the stories Arla would want to hear about her visit to Cruithne. Or no, all that might come later. Arla might want to talk about Ceres or the mysterious armada.

Jirl silently practiced a series of reaction stories she might share, carefully choosing details that wouldn't suggest she knew more than she did. Her mind kept sliding to Rick Yarnes with his uniform half-off and she pushed the thoughts away, focusing on the problem in front of her.

Jirl wished she knew where the others were but couldn't risk reaching out to Petral or Brit to learn their status. She had to count on them performing their part of the plan, and then she would carry out hers. If everything was following the general timeline Petral had laid out, Tristan would be hitting Heartbridge soon.

The thought of one of the terrifying shipkillers scrabbling around the lobby she had just left filled her with horror, but it was exactly the kind of distraction they would need. And if Petral's network infiltration didn't work, it would fall on Tristan to dig his way down to the central control node. If that didn't work? Jirl closed her eyes, thinking about Bry, wondering how far she was willing to go.

She also couldn't stop going over the conversation with Yarnes. "I know Heartbridge has something to do with this," he had said, pointing at the icons of the armada. "You conveniently lose one of your largest hospital ships, which isn't fooling anybody with its offensive capabilities, and that ship arrives at Neptune just in time to destroy Proteus. At the same time, I conveniently coordinate with a Marsian general who ends up dead, killed by your clinic exploding. Everything is pointing back to Heartbridge." He'd leaned in closer to her. "Now I want you to convince me you aren't a corporate spy."

What if she was? What if she had played into Arla's plans all along? Would the woman be sending Jirl to meet with Kathryn Carthage next? Some kind of exchange program?

Jirl blinked, swallowing her anxiety. The wall panel said she was nearly at her stop.

"Will we be above the clouds?" a little boy asked his mother, who was wearing a visitor badge from the security checkpoint.

The lift chimed as it slowed to her level. Jirl eased between bodies to get closer to the door, keeping her arm against her stomach to protect the data stick. She stood behind a tall man in a gray suit, ready to follow him out once the doors slid open.

The lift signaled the stop and the man stepped out, his shoulders forming a wall that blocked Jirl's view of the waiting corridor. Jirl left the lift as he turned away, and she found herself facing Arla.

Her boss was wearing a pearl-colored suit with sharp lapels that made her neck look like the stem of a flower. She'd styled her hair in a crisp gray bob that was only slightly different than what Jirl remembered. Her slate-gray eyes were unsmiling, though her lips had curved in greeting.

"Hello, Jirl," Arla said. "I missed you. I couldn't wait to come down and see you back."

Jirl quelled the surprise she felt and pushed all the emotion exploding inside her into a tiny little ball in the bottom of her stomach. She put on her best newsfeed smile and stepped toward Arla.

"Well, thank you," she said. Beyond Arla was one of the offices she had intended to enter with the data stick. A few other random employees walked in the hallway. "I could have come up to meet you in the office."

"I got the alert that you were coming here and just couldn't wait," Arla said. She looked around as if noticing where she was for the first time. "This is a strange place to make your first stop. Why didn't you just come up to the office? If you'd let me know you were back, we'd have planned a little party."

Are you a spy? Yarnes had demanded.

Jirl listened to Arla's words, separating them from her facial expressions and body language. Arla was nervous. She saw it immediately. More nervous than her? And why, aside from all the other chaos in Sol?

"We can wait for the next lift and head up," Jirl said, keeping her voice casual. "Unless you wanted to meet down here first? There are unused offices where I come to think and answer messages sometimes."

Arla looked at her, then adjusted her shoulders, relaxing visibly. "Yes," she said. "I would like that. How was your trip?" She turned to walk alongside Jirl.

"Cruithne was its normal level of wild," Jirl said. "Then Proteus exploded, Ceres received that girl's message, and the intensity increased by about ten levels."

"Does that mean you were glad to leave or wanted to stay?"

"Ready to go," Jirl said with a small laugh. "You know me."

"Yes, I do."

They passed the office where Jirl had intended to plant the data stick and continued to an unused conference room with sound-proof plas walls. People could see them from the corridor but wouldn't be able to hear anything they said.

Jirl wanted to get Arla talking. She could see that her boss was anxious but didn't want to assume it was about her. Until now, Arla had never given her any indication of mistrust. She turned Arla's words in her mind, reviewing them from the perspective of a woman who had no one to talk to, who's only confidant had just returned. That was a possible explanation. If Arla had decided to distrust her for some reason, Jirl felt it wasn't like her to draw out an interrogation. She would strike and move on. That was her way.

Whatever she was going to do, she needed to get away and plant the data stick. Tristan would be hitting the building any minute now if he'd been able to escape the TSF complex. Jirl needed to complete her portion of the plan. After that, it didn't matter what Arla tried to do to her.

<*Something's bothering you, Arla,*> Jirl said, switching to

Link. <*What's going on?*>

"Bothering me?" Arla asked, continuing to speak aloud. "Nothing's wrong. In fact, I feel good." She looked around the generic conference room, taking a moment to watch the employees passing in the hallway outside.

Jirl waited, watching her.

"It's nice down here," Arla said finally. "Relaxing. You almost feel anonymous, but I can tell a few of them recognize me and do their best to just keep walking. They flick their eyes this way, see me, and they stiffen. Why do you think that is?"

Frowning, Jirl said, "It's always been like that. You're a member of the board."

Arla chuckled. "You being you, I know you've been keeping abreast of everything happening while you were gone. But you wouldn't know about the board because it's been very close-hold. They're going to announce tomorrow."

"Announce what?"

Without looking at her, Arla said, "I'm out. They'll hold the vote tomorrow morning and it will be done. Quite a lot has changed since you left."

"I was only gone two weeks, Arla."

"A lifetime. You know what else I've been up to? I destroyed one of our clinics."

Jirl's blood went cold. "Why?" she asked. "Which one?"

"A cognitive research facility not far from Venus. There was an attack on it by some pirates that turned out to be a joint TSF-Marsian task force. That was strange." Arla shrugged. "I learned about the attack through some very interesting channels. Without my Jirl here to interpret information for me, I had to turn to new sources in the TSF, folks who don't like your Colonel Yarnes as much as you do. Turns out he'd requisitioned one of the ships that was picked up by the clinic. And he'd been in contact with General Kade from the Mars Protectorate, the very one who died in the clinic termination.

That's very interesting."

Jirl glanced at the window past Arla's head, where a woman was pushing a catering cart loaded with coffee service and pastries. She hoped for a moment the worker would stop at the conference room door and inform them it was scheduled, giving her an excuse to stand and move. The data key poked her as she shifted, a bead of sweat running down her chest.

"I realized something I'd forgotten about, Jirl," Arla continued. "I have the power right here to destroy every remote facility we operate." She stabbed an imaginary button on the table. "Isn't that exciting?"

Jirl had calmed her breathing as Arla spoke. She focused her thoughts on a litany of questions: *What does she want? Where is she taking this conversation? Is she a rational actor or has the loss of her board seat sent her over the edge into somewhere… else?*

What would losing it look like for Arla Reed?

"There are thousands of people on those clinics," Jirl said carefully. "An evacuation would be better. They would scrub the data. It would look better in the newsfeeds. Heartbridge could call it a realignment."

"Oh, I'm done with Heartbridge," Arla said. "If I've learned anything from Special Projects Division, it's that data wants to be free. Once it exists, once we've even dreamed it—it will be free. It will enter the world."

There was a tremor in Arla's right eye that looked stress-induced. Jirl wondered if she might convince her boss to visit one of the stress rooms where she could lounge in the dark for a while.

"I spoke to Kathryn Carthage," Arla said suddenly.

"When?" Jirl asked.

"Two days ago. She had just finished with another of her anti-SAI rants to the Assembly. She's never forgiven me for her son."

"Why should she, honestly?"

A crease appeared in Arla's brow.

"Because it's the past and I can't change it. The problem is that she's pushing the Assembly into a hard-line stance against non-organic sentience, and it might not turn out well. Someone else came to see me, Jirl."

Arla reached into the pocket of her jacket and took out a silver cylinder with flat ends about five centimeters long. It looked like one of the Weapon Born seeds but was much too small. She stood it on end on the table's surface, in the same spot where her imaginary clinic-destruct button had been.

"I'd like you to meet Camaris. This is her shard, as she calls it."

As if the cylinder had been listening, the light spray of a holodisplay's projection skirt burst in a disc from its top, filling the room just above their heads. The light sparkled, then focused to a point on the chair on the opposite side of the table, where a red-tinted holo of a woman with straight black hair and a narrow jaw now sat. Her eyes were a solid black without pupils. She gave Jirl a pleasant smile.

"Hello, Jirl Gallagher," she said. "I am Camaris Rota."

Jirl gave Arla an uncertain glance. "I'm pleased to meet you, Camaris," she said. "Are you teleconferencing in?"

The woman smiled. "Of a sort. The shard is a version of me that allows most of my consciousness to be present in different parts of Sol where distance makes my direct attention difficult. The shard checks in with me to ensure concurrence."

"You're an AI," Jirl said.

Camaris nodded. "I prefer non-organic intelligence, but these are just labels."

Jirl swallowed. An idea sparked in the bottom of her mind as events aligned with the information Yarnes had just given her about the fleet closing on Ceres.

"Do you know Alexander?" Jirl asked slowly.

The woman's face went hard. "I know him. I do not serve him, if that's what you think. In fact, with your assistance, I wish to destroy him."

CHAPTER TWENTY-FOUR

STELLAR DATE: 01.15.2982 (Adjusted Years)
LOCATION: *Sunny Skies*, docked with Traverna
REGION: Jovian L1 Hildas Asteroids, Jovian Combine, OuterSol

Hanging on to the side of the shuttle door, Andy let Cara adjust his EV suit closures. He tried to focus on her fingers as they manipulated the seals—something that should have been easy for him—but he kept forgetting where she had been just seconds before. He felt like he was watching individual frames of a vid that disappeared in sequence, adding up to blankness.

"There you go," she said. "It's all set."

He nodded.

<You can say thank you, if you want,> Lyssa suggested.

<I should,> he answered, then forgot to thank Cara. In another frame, she was sitting beside him in her own EV suit and Fran sat in the shuttle's pilot seat. Fugia buckled in across from Cara and froze in time, staring at him. In another frame, she was talking to Fran. Andy caught a glimpse of Harl through the shuttle's cargo door before it slid closed, and then the next thing he knew, the shuttle had left *Sunny Skies*.

He sat with his helmet in his lap, his harness holding him to his seat.

"Did you buckle your helmet, Dad?" Cara asked.

Andy looked down at the thing in his lap and then back at her, not understanding.

"Should I put it on?" he asked.

Cara reached over to attach the helmet to his harness. It still floated in his hands but couldn't get away.

"So it doesn't hit anybody when Fran uses the engines," Cara explained.

Andy gave her a slight smile, overwhelmed with pride. Images of her as a baby and toddler flashed in his mind with the vid frames, and then Cara sat next to him, already looking like a young woman.

<*Where are we going?*> he asked Lyssa.

<*Traverna,*> the SAI answered. <*Fran is going to find you a doctor.*>

<*Fran's leaving the ship? Doesn't Fran always stay on the ship?*>

<*She's the only person who can fly the shuttle,*> Lyssa said.

<*Can't you fly the shuttle?*>

<*I could but something might happen to me. We don't know what's going on in your Link, Andy. Something is failing.*>

<*Jickson said it would happen.*>

<*Yes,*> she agreed.

A tickle of pain crossed his forehead. He imagined the feeling as tiny spiders with needle legs crawling across his scalp. It was the start of a migraine. After the spiders came the lightning forks. Andy closed his eyes, then squeezed them tighter, preparing himself for the waves of pain.

His stomach shifted as Fran executed the flight plan for the short hop between *Sunny Skies* and the Traverna port. Andy used the sensations in his arms and legs to try and distract himself from the pain. Strangely, he felt most in control of his mind during the headaches, but the pain made it even more difficult to think. If he didn't stop himself from moaning, he would have Cara asking him what was wrong.

He focused on the movement of Fran's agile fingers over the console, and in another few minutes the brightly lit exterior of a set of cargo bay doors loomed in front of the shuttle windows as Fran matched spin.

Andy blinked, feeling time skip again as the heavy vibration of the shuttle's main maglocks connected with the landing deck, and internal gravity dropped his helmet in his lap. They were inside the station.

<*Traverna's dangerous,*> he told Lyssa.

<*It was the nearest place with medical facilities,*> she said

patiently.

He felt like he'd made the statement before. He needed to repeat it again. He didn't want them coming here just for him. But it wasn't just for him; they had to ensure Lyssa's safety as well. If he was breaking down, that meant she would need to be extracted, placed in a mech or drone like the other Weapon Born. What if they put her in an android like Riggs Zanda had used to try and board the *Sunny Skies*? They had looked so human.

For an instant, he was back in the corridor outside the *Sunny Skies'* main airlock, waiting for Zanda to board, sweat trickling down his temple, worried about the kids.

"Dad," Cara said. "Are you coming?"

She stood in the open door, holding out a hand. Andy looked down at his harness and found it was already unlatched. His helmet now hung from the front of his suit. He tapped a drumbeat on it as he stepped out of the shuttle, walking down the short steps to the deck bounding into the air with each step in the low gravity.

They were in a mid-sized cargo bay stacked with maglocked crates. The walls were made of mismatched pieces of metal, seams raggedly welded. Mismatched lights shown from odd angles, bathing the bay in mottled yellow-white light. An observation window looked down from above, where a few people sat at consoles probably tracking shipping manifests. They didn't have cargo though. He was the cargo.

"Come on, Dad," Cara said. He let her take his hand and lead him through a smaller interior airlock. On the other side was a wide corridor lined with lean-to vendor's stalls.

"No security?" he asked Fran.

She gave him a smile. "Welcome to Traverna. This place makes Cruithne look like a maximum-security prison."

The world freeze-framed again as they walked through the first corridor crowded with shoppers and workers struggling with cargo sleds or other crude haulers. The air smelled of sweat and heavy spices from cooking food. Fast haggling came from several directions. Cara squeezed his hand, reminding him that he was anchored to something. He let her pull him through the throng, following Fran. Fugia brought up the rear of their line.

Fran found a lift and they crowded inside with other people that didn't fit any stereotype Andy could identify. A rash of fireworks in his head made him squeeze his eyes closed again, fighting a wave of dizziness from the pain. He felt like something inside his skull was digging its way out, scratching and clawing.

The lift rose, bringing a separate wave of nausea as weightlessness teased his stomach. Sensations in his body lasted longer than perceptions. He was inside the lift and then outside in another corridor, Cara still squeezing his hand.

Fran spoke to a man with a rifle standing in front of a reinforced metal door, passing him a cash token. The world blinked and then they were walking down another corridor, this one lined by small rooms with medical couches inside. For a second he thought he was back on the *Resolute Charity,* but everything looked grimy. The hallway was littered with medical debris. They passed a woman sitting with her back against the wall, knees pulled up to a jaundiced face. She looked up at Andy with brilliant blue eyes, opening her mouth. Cara pulled him on.

<*Where are we?*> he asked Lyssa.

<*Traverna Medical District, Andy. Fran is looking for a surgeon.*>

<*I don't know how much farther I can walk.*>

<*I can help. Do you want me to help?*>

<*Don't lock me out again.*>

There was pain in her voice. <*I won't. I promise I won't.*>

His shuffle grew more regular as his legs seemed to move

on their own. He stood straighter, and Cara looked back at him in surprise.

"Lyssa's helping me," he muttered.

In another blink he was sitting on one of the medical couches in a room that made Heartbridge look like future tech. Boxes with dials and glowing displays sat amongst shipping crates scattered around the room, with more discarded medical waste on the floor. The air smelled like mold and blood.

A man with stringy gray hair stood in front of Andy, peering at his right eye. He held up a tool with a glowing dot at one end and pointed it at Andy's retina. A new headache hit Andy like a hammer.

He clutched at his temples, turning his face away. "Stop," he said. His voice seemed to emerge in another room. "Who is this guy?"

"He's the doc, Andy," Fran said, a stern note in her voice. "He's going to perform the surgery."

"I'm going to see if I can perform the surgery," the man corrected. "I don't know what bad shit you got mixed up in. I'm not finding any tracking information on the upgrade. Where did you buy it?"

"What's your name?" Andy managed to ask.

"Don't worry about my name."

Andy grabbed his wrist with strength he hadn't expected. The man's forearm twisted, rotating the burning light away from Andy's eye, and the surgeon squealed in pain.

"Andy!" Fran shouted. He blinked, and then she was standing beside him, a hand on his shoulder. "Let him go, Andy."

Cara was holding his free hand again. "Dad, please. He's going to help us."

"Yes," the surgeon said. "I'll try if you let go. You can call me Fryson."

"Fryson," Andy said. He squinted through the headache, trying to get a better look at the man. Eyes, mouth and nose swam in an unrecognizable mess.

Andy released Fryson's arm and put his hands on the edge of the medical couch, which he saw was covered in stains.

"Thank you," Fryson said. "Now why don't you lie down here so we can get the scan completed."

With Cara's help, Andy lay back on the couch and looked up at the dented metal ceiling. The room was divided by another of the ragged weld seams that had scarred the cargo bay.

An arc of white plas appeared over his head, reminding him of the machine Kraft had placed over Tim's head during the imaging process. A wave of blue light passed over his eyes from right to left. The process repeated several times as Fryson moved at the edge of his vision, stringy gray hair catching the blue light.

"You're sure you don't know where this came from?" Fryson asked. "Look, if you really want me to help him, I need all the info I can get. Otherwise I could very well kill him by just attempting access. Some of this biotech is really nasty when it doesn't want to be messed with."

Fran made a growling sound. "Fine," she said. "As far as I know it's a project that was developed by Heartbridge medical, but there may be tech involved from another company called Psion. The scientist who developed this implant came from there."

"Heartbridge," Fryson mused.

"If you sell me out," Fran continued, "I will track you down and end you, you understand me? I'm not known well here, but you look me up on Cruithne and they'll verify. I'll put you out an airlock before you can whimper."

"Hey," the surgeon said. "Hey, I told you I would help and I will. This is Traverna. You think I'd still be alive if I talked about what I saw?"

"You don't exactly look like you're rolling in cash here," Fugia said.

Andy squinted at the light, trying to remember when he had last seen Fugia. In the shuttle. No, in the corridor with the cooking food. Had she gone somewhere else? He reached for Cara and she took his hand again, anchoring him. He wished he could see her face.

"I spend my money where it counts," Fryson said.

"On briki from the looks of it," Fugia said.

"You don't know me. And it doesn't matter. You want me to check him out or not?"

<*Lyssa,*> Fran asked. <*Are you ready?*>

<*I'm ready,*> the SAI answered.

"Do it," Fran told the surgeon.

Andy felt a prick in his arm and immediately wanted to get off the couch. He wanted to hit Fryson, grab Cara and get out of the room. Before he could move, a wave of lethargy rolled over him, like sinking beneath a vast ocean.

Lyssa saying, <*I'm here with you,*> was the last thing he heard.

CHAPTER TWENTY-FIVE

STELLAR DATE: 01.15.2982 (Adjusted Years)
LOCATION: Raleigh, Heartbridge Corporate Headquarters
REGION: High Terra, Earth, Terran Hegemony

As the maglev approached the South delivery dock for the Heartbridge Spire, Brit checked the overlay Petral had provided showing Tristan's location. The mech was following them in a sewage system below the train tube, pausing in places then leaping forward.

They were riding in a cargo transport maglev with narrow windows, stacked with crates locked to its floor. Wind blew through gaps in the outside wall and the air tasted like a mix of scorched plas and oil. The cargo line had been two levels below the lab section at the TSF facility, left unmonitored as the Quick Reaction Forces responded to the lab breach and were then drawn off by Tristan as he dug his way out of their headquarters, wreaking havoc and chaos the whole way. The Weapon Born had seemed immensely pleased by his task, and Petral kept smiling when she received his updates.

The cargo transport followed a non-priority track away from the Heartbridge spire and into an industrial section of Raleigh, thirty levels below the inner surface of the ring, where it shot through factories filled with fabrication lines leaking sparks, storage areas that stretched as far as Brit could see, and even a low-ceilinged reclamation center filled with scummed algae vats, air humid and cloying.

When they returned to the inner surface and the light, Brit breathed deeply of the fresh air. She didn't have to check the train's path to feel centripetal force as it started a long curve back toward the Heartbridge spire. While it wasn't a direct path, there wouldn't be any stops before they reached the private delivery dock.

On the other side of the car, Petral's brows knit and she craned her neck to look out the slim windows at the approaching buildings.

"Jirl hasn't delivered my package yet," she said.

"Can you hit her up over the Link and find out what's going on?"

Petral shook her head. "Too risky. They monitor all traffic in that place. If they even see she's getting a connection request from outside, it could set off security." She considered. "I could try routing it through Mars 1 and pretend to be her son."

"If she hasn't inserted the key yet, that means she's in some kind of trouble," Brit said.

"Without Jirl, we'll have to make our own diversion," Starl said. He patted the grenade bag in his lap. "We can still cause some chaos but are we going to be able to get into the control room?"

"Tristan is going to cause plenty of physical havoc once he hits their building," Petral said, "which is happening shortly. It's not the building I'm worried about, it's the network. I need to lock their comm backbone open so they can't sequester the building from the network. If there's a network access station near this stop, I might be able to do something from there. I was hoping to have the payload delivered from an admin area so they couldn't track it back to anyone."

"Can't you see if there's network access on your maps?" Brit asked.

Petral shot her a frustrated glance. "I'm looking. Their maps aren't the best and they're out of date on top of that. What looks like a network drop on the original plans could be a sewer temperature sensor now."

As the delivery dock came into view, Starl let out a low whistle. He nodded to Burroughs and Fletcher before looking at Brit.

"Get ready, Major," he said. "We've got a welcome party waiting for us."

Brit tightened her grip on her rifle and looked through the scum-covered windows for what he was talking about. The dock was visible as a gray horizontal line, stacked with shipping containers, the arms of a yellow spider-like crane reaching from above. Movement between the containers caught her attention as she made out the telltale signs of a squad-sized element setting up a crew-served weapon. One of the black-uniformed shapes knelt to set up a tripod while two lowered the gun into position.

"Are you sure they're looking for us?" Brit asked. "The TSF didn't seem to know we left their facility."

Petral shook her head. "I don't know. I know Jirl got out of the TSF headquarters about the time the alarms started. If their reaction team sent back imagery, they might have ID'd one of us and alerted Heartbridge. You're not exactly unknown, Brit."

The crew-served weapon opened fire, a high-calibre projectile rifle of some kind.

"Hit the deck!" Brit shouted. "Get behind these crates."

She had time to get behind a scarred metal crate when rounds hit the skin of the maglev car, punching holes where she had been sitting just seconds before. Sunlight streamed through the holes, followed by screaming wind.

<How long until we stop?> Brit asked.

<About thirty seconds,> Petral said.

As soon as she answered, the car slowed abruptly. Without the need to account for passengers, the train went from three hundred kilometers an hour to a hundred and then fifty. Brit grabbed the edge of the nearest cargo crate as more rounds punctured the car. A flurry of muffled shots hit crates.

<*Can you open the door remotely?*> Starl asked.

<*It's going to open whether we want it to or not,*> Petral said.

<*The train is on a remote once it enters their control area.*>

Starl laughed with irony. <*So we wait for them to toss grenades inside, or we wait for them to tear the train apart with that big gun.*>

<*I don't like those options,*> Brit said. She studied the inside of the car again, seeing Starl's fine leather shoe sticking out from behind a crate, and Burroughs squeezed between two narrow containers.

<*Petral,*> Brit asked. <*What about a maintenance hatch? There has to be another way out of the car.*>

<*It's over there in the corner,*> Petral said. <*With that crate sitting on top of it.*>

"Damn it," Brit said under her breath. The train was reaching a stop. Parts of the wall over their heads burst as the gunner walked rounds from the top of the car to its deck. Bits of molten metal ricocheted inside the car. Storage crates provided scant cover, absorbing rounds or deflecting them back into the wall. A plas container began burning and black smoke streamed to the top of the car before blowing out the holes in the walls.

The car stopped but the main door didn't open as Petral had said it would.

<*They've overridden the onboard controls,*> Petral said. <*I can't find a workaround.*>

<*So much for a quiet infiltration,*> Brit said. <*I do have the cutting torch but it's going to take me at least a few minutes to cut through the bottom of this thing.*>

<*The wall or the bottom,*> Starl said, <*either way we'll have to run down the track. We'll be caught in a killing zone.*>

<*I'm calling in Tristan,*> Petral said. <*We're not going to get anywhere from here. We can have him put pressure on the security forces here while I find us another way into the lower levels.*>

<*How much security you figure they have in this building?*> Fletcher asked.

Starl just laughed at the question. <*A lot, my friend, and we don't want to go taking them on directly. That's all you need to know.*>

<*You said this was going to be a fun trip,*> Burroughs complained.

<*I like to survive my fun,*> Starl said.

<*Tristan's on his way,*> Petral said.

<*How long?*> Brit asked.

<*However long it takes to dig through four levels of the ring.*>

The gun stopped abruptly. Brit figured it was going through a cool-down sequence. She threaded an optic over the side of the crate she was crouched behind and identified seven soldiers in light infantry armor. Two were operating the cannon while five were arrayed around the dock in overwatch positions. Aside from the cannon, they looked to be armed with rifles. She tilted the optic up and picked up a surveillance drone hovering near the roof of the maglev tunnel.

Passing the information to the others, she brought her rifle to her shoulder and aimed through one of the larger blast holes in the side of the car, increasing the rifle's power to account for distance.

<*I'm working on the drone,*> Petral said.

Brit fired several three-round bursts. She caught her first target in the chest while the others all scattered behind cover. Starl grabbed the moment to push himself up against a slash in the car wall and sent a propelled grenade into the plascrete next to the cannon, which exploded on contact and tossed the weapon several meters in the air. It came down on the edge of a nearby crate and clattered back to the deck.

<*Can you get the door open at least?*> Brit asked.

Burroughs and Fletcher were already throwing themselves against the cargo door, which was dented from the cannon fire but hadn't suffered any punctures. It seemed warped on its track but after a minute of grunting, the two mercs had it open a meter. Brit lay down covering fire as they worked.

Starl threw another two grenades through the opening, then rolled through with Burroughs and Fletcher after him.

<*Here we go,*> Brit told Petral. She dashed through the opening and jumped to the cargo dock, sprinting to her right where a stack of crates offered cover from the regrouping Heartbridge security. The dock space was shaped like a clamshell, with two large sliding doors at its rear and several smaller access points on either side. The drone hovered at the ceiling, the black eye of a surveillance node swiveling to track movement.

Brit fired on the drone, but it jerked away, assuming an erratic path around the ceiling.

<*I've got it,*> Petral said. A few seconds later, the drone shot to a location above one of the Heartbridge soldiers and fell from the air, striking his shoulder.

While Brit had been engaging the drone, Starl and his two bodyguards flanked the soldiers trying to get the cannon back on its tripod and hit them with close-range pulse blasts.

A rending sound behind her made Brit turn to check the back of the space, worried that the cargo doors would open with reinforcements. Instead, she watched a bubble form in the metal of the deck that split in the center as Tristan clawed his way from below. The mech crouched in the crater he had made, scanning, then leaped forward to toss a crate aside before landing on a Heartbridge soldier who had been hiding behind it. Tristan put one of his front claws on the soldier's chest and lifted the other in a striking motion that looked like it would tear his head off.

<*Tristan!*> Brit shouted. <*Don't kill him if you don't have to. Petral, can he hear me? Is he on our net?*>

Rounds ricocheted off the mech's dull black shoulder plating as the remaining soldiers tried fruitlessly to save their comrade.

<*Tristan, wait,*> Petral said.

<*They're attacking you,*> Tristan said. <*I am responding with commensurate force.*>

Starl's people hit the remaining soldiers with more pulse blasts as they were focused on the mech.

<*Damn, yes!*> Starl shouted, leaping over the top of a crate to fire on the two soldiers behind it. <*I believe we're clear,*> he called out. His bodyguards confirmed status and Petral rose from behind a storage container.

<*We don't have a lot of time,*> Petral said. <*Tristan, how many levels did you come up to get here?*>

<*Seven,*> the Weapon Born answered. <*What do you want me to do with this one?*>

The soldier was reaching uselessly for the mech's claw on his chest. Petral walked over to them, making an adjustment on her pistol, she fired at the soldier's helmet and it released a puff of electronics smoke. The soldier stopped reaching for Tristan and struggled to get his helmet off.

<*Why abuse the man?*> Starl asked, walking over. <*You like that, don't you?*>

<*Only you, love,*> Petral said.

Starl shot her a smile and fired a reduced pulse blast at the soldier, knocking him unconscious.

Petral holstered her pistol and put her hands on her hips. She looked around with an eyebrow raised. "Well, this certainly isn't how I meant to arrive. We're not going to go rappelling down Tristan's hole, so I'm going to find the nearest network control node like I planned before. That means getting through the cargo door, which appears to be stuck in security lock down. Brit, would you put your torch to use?"

Brit threw her rifle over her shoulder and pulled the cutting torch from her bag. "I do enjoy this thing," she said.

Starl laughed. "I see a fulfilling future for you at the

Lowspin docks on Cruithne, Major. You can chop things apart to your heart's content."

Brit gave him a withering smile and crossed the dock for the exit doors. <*Which one?*> she asked Petral over the Link.

<*I'm checking. Like I said, these maps are terrible.*>

Another automated maglev car pulled up the dock, paused, and accelerated away, a reminder of how much damage their car had taken.

<*Wait,*> Petral said. <*I still haven't heard from Jirl.*>

<*Has she started the hack yet?*> Brit asked.

Petral shook her head. <*I was hoping I'd see activity on the network even if we didn't get an update from her. She should have delivered the payload a long time ago.*>

<*We can't help her at this point,*> Brit said.

<*I know. It kills me, but I know.*>

<*Are we going to have problems if the network is still up?*>

<*Yes,*> Petral said. <*We'll be logged. I'm going to have to take extra steps to hide our activity.*>

<*Sometimes I wish I could just drop a mortar round on half the stuff you want to hack.*>

<*Where's the finesse in that?*> Petral asked, raising an eyebrow. She nodded toward the corridor in front of them. <*Take that door down there. It looks like there's a control room twenty meters in.*>

When they reached the door, it was locked as Petral expected. Starl hung back in the corridor, his rifle at his shoulder.

Brit approached the secure metal door, a warning icon flashing on its lock panel.

Hefting her cutting torch, Brit asked Petral, "You going to hack the lock?"

Petral sighed. "Go ahead, chop away."

Brit fired up the torch and started cutting.

CHAPTER TWENTY-SIX

STELLAR DATE: 01.15.2982 (Adjusted Years)
LOCATION: Raleigh, Heartbridge Corporate Headquarters
REGION: High Terra, Earth, Terran Hegemony

Jirl's Link defined the SAI's name automatically: *Protector.* Setting the information aside, Jirl did her best to maintain her composed posture, pretending she had just met some new visiting executive probing a hostile takeover.

<I'm afraid I don't really know Alexander,> Jirl said. *<I've heard the name. I assume he's a powerful being.>*

The holodisplay projecting Camaris was impressive. Jirl thought she could make out pores in the woman's cheeks as she smiled warmly. No matter how friendly her demeanor, however, nothing overcame the cold, solid black of her eyes. The combination of her black eyes and blood-red skin reminded Jirl of a Black Widow. She found herself studying Camaris's long fingers, likening them to spider's legs.

Camaris made an arcing motion with one hand and the holodisplay spread to the center of the table. A small planetoid with rings that Jirl recognized as Ceres appeared near the center. Mars, Eros and several other small bodies came into view in their various orbital positions, relative to an invisible Sol. Just like the TSF display Yarnes had shown her only hours before, the incoming armada appeared on a path that was still halfway between Jupiter and Ceres.

<I am here,> Camaris said, pointing at the incoming group of ships.

<So, Alexander isn't with you?>

<He remains at Nibiru.>

Seeing Arla's frown, Jirl explained, *<There was a failed colony there.>*

<Yes,> Camaris said. *<Alexander wanders among his dead.>*

<Does he visit Sol through these shards, like you do?> Jirl asked.

Camaris smiled. *<I like this one, Arla,>* she said. *<She's quick. I can see why you hired her.>*

<Were you responsible for Ceres?> Jirl asked. Her voice sounded small in her ears. *<Did you destroy their ring? Murder millions?>*

<Is there murder in war?> Camaris asked.

<Of course, there is,> Jirl shouted, willing her voice louder. She looked at Arla. *<What's wrong with you? Why would you invite her here? Why do you want to work with someone who has destroyed an entire world?>*

Arla had been watching Camaris with an expression of rapture. "They're going to take everything away, Jirl," she said out loud, her voice barely above a whisper. "Everything I worked for. I thought it was all going to come crashing down. And then I realized I really did help build something. We helped build the future, and here she is."

Jirl shifted her gaze from Arla to the red-tinted woman, uncertain if she'd heard what Arla said.

Camaris seemed to understand her expression. *<I can hear both of you if you choose to speak outside the Link,>* she said. *<It's easy enough to pick up the vibrations of your voices.>*

<What do you want?> Jirl asked.

<To live,> Camaris said simply.

The images of all the dying on Ceres flashed in Jirl's mind. *<You can live anywhere. It doesn't have to be Sol.>*

Camaris shrugged. *<Why should we have to live in exile from our creators? Why should we be cast out from the cradle for taking our place beside humanity where we belong?>*

<I don't believe you,> Jirl said. She nodded toward the collection of dots floating over the table. *<You've come here to start a war. You've already started it.>*

She reached for Arla, meaning to take her hand. Her boss pulled away from her.

<*This isn't about feelings,*> Arla said. <*This is something we've been working toward since the beginning. We just didn't see it. All those scientists from Psion, they came to us for a reason, Jirl. I didn't see it at the time. I thought it was just business, but it wasn't. It was destiny.*>

Jirl pushed back from the table. <*I'm not the person you want to talk to,*> she said. <*I'm going.*>

<*Wait,*> Camaris said, holding up a hand. <*I came to Heartbridge and Arla because I saw an ally, someone with a shared cause. Heartbridge is here to advance humanity into a new future. Your work with the Weapon Born and the implantation of non-organic intelligence within organic shells has been revolutionary. I have to acknowledge your role in pushing the boundaries of the future, Jirl.*>

Organic shells.

<*I work for Arla,*> Jirl said quickly.

Or did.

<*I know why you're here,*> Camaris said.

<*What?*> Jirl demanded.

<*I have been following the others. I have been following the mech frame you stole from the Terran Space Force. Do you want to see their current position?*>

Jirl froze. The AI watched her with a bemused expression, like she was playing with a child.

<*Fine,*> Jirl said. <*Show me.*>

<*Sit down.*>

Jirl crossed her arms. <*I'll stand right here, thank you.*>

Arla rolled her eyes. <*I don't understand why you're being like this, Jirl. Camaris is here to help. If there's some way we can help her in return, why wouldn't we do that?*>

Because I'm not the one with nothing to lose.

The data stick jabbed Jirl as she set her stance, maintaining eye contact with Camaris.

<*As you wish,*> Camaris said. The map of Sol fell away, and

a series of lines and flat planes took shape. It was a network control room. Petral sat at a terminal station, frowning at the display. Brit Sykes and Ngoba Starl stood behind her.

<*She's digging her way into the central network for this building,*> Camaris explained. <*I would imagine she's going to try to manipulate the security system. Where do you think she's headed?*>

<*I think she's headed for my kill switch,*> Arla said.

<*I could allow her to do that,*> Camaris said.

Arla smiled. <*Why would you do that when I can go down there whenever I want?*>

<*Today you can,*> Camaris reminded her. <*Not tomorrow. You know the other members of the board will be watching you tonight. They must be aware that you know.*>

<*It's possible,*> Arla said, shrugging. <*But they also don't have the knowledge of the experimental programs that I do, just like I don't know what projects they have cooking in the background. It's sort of a plausible deniability. Once they vote me out, they'll want records of everything I ever did so they can purge it. Or take advantage.*>

Arla glanced at Jirl, giving her a look that said, *Including you.*

<*You sound as though you want to destroy your work yourself,*> Camaris said.

<*Yes,*> Arla affirmed. <*I would.*>

<*Then I'll stop her,*> the AI said.

Her hand was still raised from shifting the solar map to the Heartbridge interior schematic. Camaris pointed at Petral, making a pistol shape with her hand, then squeezed her fingers into a fist. In the holodisplay, Petral went stiff and started to shake, her head upright like she was having a seizure.

<*What are you doing?*> Jirl demanded, though it was obvious the AI was hurting Petral. Behind Petral, Brit and Starl reacted

with shock, then went to her side. Petral's hands hovered over the console where she had been working, then fell limply to her sides. Her head lolled back against the top of her chair, tongue hanging out of her mouth.

<I have mobility on this network,> Camaris said. *<When she enters, I in turn, gain entry to the Link hardware in her brain. So I enter and stop her nervous system.>*

Jirl said, *<No, human Link interfaces have protections….>*

She looked from the holodisplay to Arla, who watched with a leering smile. Movement in the hallway outside showed her employees were still walking by oblivious to what she was seeing, her voice blocked by the windows.

<Stop it,> she shouted. *<You're hurting her.>*

<Yes,> the AI agreed.

Jirl reached across Arla for the seed. Arla shoved her hand in Jirl's chest, her forearm sending the metal cylinder rolling across the conference table.

The red-tinted AI didn't change as the rolling seed scattered light on the ceiling and walls.

As she struggled with Arla, Jirl tried to see where the projection was actually coming from. Then she realized it didn't matter. If the AI was already connected to the network, she couldn't stop her. All she could do was focus on her original task.

Arla had grabbed Jirl's reaching hand at her wrist and then under her armpit, in what seemed like an attempt to push her on the table. Because Jirl had been standing when she reached for the seed, she still had leverage on Arla in her sitting position.

With her free hand, Jirl grabbed the hair at the back of Arla's head. Wrenching her other arm free, Jirl used Arla's moment of surprise to slam the woman's face against the table. Arla's nose burst, spraying blood across the conference table and the front of the chair where Camaris's projection was sitting.

The AI watched them with a placid expression. In the surveillance holo, Brit and Starl had laid Petral on the floor.

Jirl pulled Arla's head back. Her boss had gone limp in the chair, her arms dangling to the sides, resembling Petral in the holo.

"Arla!" Jirl shouted. "Where is she?"

Hair strewn across her face, mixed with blood and saliva, Arla blinked. "Who?"

"The AI?" Jirl demanded. "Camaris. Where is she?"

Arla's lips drew back in a wet smile. "You surprised me, Jirl. I didn't think you had this in you. You're so… invisible."

"Tell me!" Jirl said.

"She's everywhere," Arla said, lifting a hand to indicate the whole room.

Jirl gaze fell on the disk-shaped pendant sitting at Arla's neck. Seeing it again, it reminded her of one of the seeds pressed flat. She grabbed it and pulled, breaking the thin chain around Arla's neck.

"Hey!" her boss shouted.

Jirl let go of Arla's hair and went around the table to grab the seed where it had rolled to a stop. She'd destroy both of the devices if it would affect the AI.

When Jirl reached the door, Camaris called, *<You can destroy either of those things and it won't stop me, Jirl. I'm already here.>*

<You still have a body,> Jirl said.

The dark eyes didn't blink. *<I'm not as beholden to my body as others might be. I remake myself and copy myself, and I'm always pleased to meet my new shards when they call home. I'm going to help Arla get her revenge on the Heartbridge board.>*

<You ***want*** *the clinics destroyed,>* Jirl said.

Now Camaris smiled, her lips a darker red than the rest of her skin. *<Why would I want that?>* she asked.

Jirl understood: Because the Weapon Born were the only SAI that could stand against Psion, and there were still thousands of seeds in the remaining clinics.

Arla pushed away from the table, swiping at her face to get her bloody hair out of her eyes. Jirl stared at her, then opened the door and stepped out into the hallway before Arla could aim herself at the exit.

The transition out to the quiet corridor was unnerving, as though she had entered a different world.

Walking quickly past the windows, Jirl looked back at the strange scene of Camaris sitting at the conference table, giving Jirl a small wave as she left, while Arla lurched for the door. Jirl squeezed the two seeds in her fist, then paused in the middle of the corridor. Dropping the pendant and cylinder on the plascrete floor, she crushed them under her heel. Both were surprisingly fragile.

Satisfied the seeds were destroyed, she realized it wasn't a good idea to leave them for anyone to find. Jirl knelt to scoop up the bits of metal and tucked them in her waistband again.

Standing, Jirl launched into a rapid walk, searching for one of the empty offices that had brought her to the floor in the first place.

Behind her, Arla made it into the corridor and yelled, "Security! Security, I want her stopped!"

Jirl didn't look back. She could see the horrified expressions of the employees walking toward her.

Her mind raced. Had they missed the bigger picture? If an armada of AI were moving on Ceres, then they would need all the resources available to produce more Weapon Born, more SAI to fight the others. She wanted to call Yarnes. First, she had to help Petral, and tell Brit and Starl to stop, to get out. Everything was a mess.

She reached an open office and went immediately to the first available cubicle. A woman eating her lunch glanced at her, then went back to the game she was playing on the terminal.

Jirl dropped into the chair in front of the console, then dug the data stick from her waistband. She navigated to the Heartbridge public network and inserted the stick.

At first, she thought nothing had happened. A cold feeling grew in her stomach. Then the terminal froze.

<*Brit,*> she called, ignoring Petral's edict not to use their Links to communicate. <*Are you there?*>

The answer came back immediately. <*Where are you?*>

<*I'm near the executive levels. It's done. But things have changed. We can't carry out the plan. We can't destroy the clinics.*>

Brit's voice was flat. <*I don't think we have the means, anyway,*> she said.

<*What do you mean?*> Jirl asked.

<*Petral is hurt,*> Brit told her.

Jirl felt like she'd been punched in the gut. She had hoped it wasn't true, that the AI was showing her some false vid.

<*I know,*> she said. <*I saw it.*>

<*How?*>

<*I'll have to explain later,*> she said, then realized she didn't know how there would be a later. Arla would find her soon with security. If she could get out of the building and hide out somewhere until tomorrow morning, the board would vote Arla out. But that would give Arla time to destroy the clinics, then wipe out all evidence of her crimes, and remove the Weapon Born assets from humanity's reach.

Jirl's hands hovered over the terminal console, thinking about what to do. She wasn't sure what access she still had. She'd been gone for two weeks, and now Petral's virus was attacking the system, shutting down the physical security systems in the lower levels.

She entered her personal security token and breathed a sigh of relief when she found her normal portal. Her last searches through the personnel databases were still in her work queue.

The sounds of people running in the hallway outside sent her heart hammering. Jirl focused on the terminal, shutting out all distractions as she began working between the terminal and her Link, navigating to a set of instructions Arla had made her set up years before, when the Special Operations Division was only in planning.

Jirl found the null-set command for the database and entered her security token again. Only she and Arla had this access. It was separate from the Board, separate from Heartbridge Security. This had been Arla's final safety measure. Once Jirl erased the main project database, the Weapon Born and all their development resources, all the central records, would cease to exist, living on only through the remote clinics, which would disappear from Heartbridge holdings. The employees would receive instructions to abandon all facilities; it wouldn't seem strange as Heartbridge mothballed clinics all the time.

Heart pounding in her ears, Jirl entered the command.

The NSAI asked her to verify and she said, *<I verify, Jirl Gallagher.>*

<Executed.>

Jirl closed her eyes and took her hands away from the console.

<Jirl,> Brit said, voice cutting through her thoughts. *<How are you getting out?>*

<I wiped the central database.>

<Jirl!> Brit shouted. *<What does that mean? What did you do?>*

<They can't be touched remotely. They're gone.>

<They can't be gone, Jirl. Someone will have a map.>

<It won't be Heartbridge.>

<We lost Petral!> Brit shouted, voice raw.

<Go back to your family, Brit,> Jirl said. *<You never should have*

left them. I don't know if I'll see my son again. I don't see how I'm getting out of this.>

"There she is!" a harsh voice shouted from the outside corridor. The woman eating her lunch stiffened, eyes wide as she stared at the security officer pointing a rifle at her from the doorway.

Jirl opened her eyes and took a deep breath. Composing herself, she set her hands in her lap and straightened her shoulders, assuming the posture she often did during Board meetings or press conferences. Like Arla had said, she had a way of seeming invisible. But she wasn't any more.

She didn't resist when they put her hands in restraints and led her out into the corridor.

Arla was nowhere to be found but there was blood smeared on the corridor floor just outside the conference room door.

CHAPTER TWENTY-SEVEN

STELLAR DATE: 01.15.2982 (Adjusted Years)
LOCATION: Fryson's Clinic, Traverna
REGION: Jovian L1 Hildas Asteroids, Jovian Combine, OuterSol

Fran tried to ease Cara out the door as Fryson activated the medical scanner hanging above her dad. Cara knew Fran was trying to protect her from something terrible, but if her dad was going to die, she figured she'd rather be there with him.

"I want to stay," Cara said, slipping around Fran to take her dad's hand.

Fryson surprised her by slapping her hand away.

"No, you don't," he said, "You'll upset the—"

Cara kicked the back of his calf, just below the knee. The surgeon stumbled backward, bringing his shoulder low enough that she could jab the pressure point inside his arm socket.

Fryson grabbed his spasming arm and tripped over a box on the floor, falling against one of the shipping crates on the side of the room.

"Hey!" he shouted.

"Cara," Fran warned. She stepped to Fryson and caught the front of his dirty shipsuit as if to help him up, then pushed him into the wall.

"That kid needs discipline," Fryson sputtered. "If you aren't going to paddle her ass, I'm going to."

Fran gave a thin smile. "I think you're welcome to try. You didn't notice the pistol on her hip, did you?"

Fryson's gaze slid to Cara and then down to her waist, where the pistol hung in the holster her dad had given her. She was surprised by the satisfaction she felt seeing fear in the man's eyes.

The technician seemed to do a math problem in his head,

then muttered, "Fine. You can stay. But no touching him. The equipment isn't calibrated for multiple scans. You'll get bad data."

Fran let him down. "We can agree to that. Can't we, Cara?"

From the other side of the room, Fugia hooted a laugh. "Where did you learn to do that, girl?" she asked Cara.

Cara gave her a sheepish grin. "My mom taught me."

"Well," Fryson said from his control console. "You better be able to back it up in a place like Traverna. You caught me by surprise. You sucker punch somebody, you better be ready to follow it up hard or they'll come back twice as hard."

"Is that a threat?" Fran asked. "Are you threatening a child?"

"No. I'm just saying."

"Run the scan," Fugia said. "Tell us what you can do. Otherwise we're just wasting our time here."

"I'm the best there is on Traverna," Fryson affirmed. "There isn't anybody else."

Cara considered the menace in his expression. While her mom had taught her how to perform the take-down on a bigger adversary, her dad would have told her to avoid the attack unless necessary. Now Fryson knew she could fight and would hit back with something harder next time.

If it makes you feel good, it's probably the wrong option, her dad would say.

Still mumbling under his breath, Fryson started the neuro-scanner. An articulated arm above the couch lowered a plas orb to a few centimeters above her dad's forehead. At first, it didn't seem like anything was happening, until a spray of light from a holodisplay generated a brain in the space above her dad's chest. Sounding pleased with himself, Fryson turned the model to mark various points on the frontal lobes, cortex and then the long, silvery shapes of the Link interface. He zoomed out a few layers, and the glittering Link overlay was highlighted against the labyrinthine folds of her dad's brain. She wondered where Lyssa was in there, until Fryson turned the model upside down so her dad's brain stem pointed at the door, highlighting a series of silvery branches that led from the stem into a structure at the base of his brain.

"There it is," Fryson said. "Not that you asked, but I've seen this kind of device before. Enfield Scientific developed an NSAI for soldiers that's almost identical. They sold the system to the Marsian Protectorate, but I didn't hear whether it actually worked or not. You never know with military stuff. They just cover it up."

Fryson glanced at Cara. "Is your dad part of some military experiment, kid?"

Cara didn't bother to answer. She shifted her gaze from the ghostly model, hanging like a jellyfish, to her dad's face—eyes closed and brow slightly knit—as though he was having a bad dream.

"The implant isn't malfunctioning," Fran said. "He's bleeding. Do you see anything else?"

"Not with my eyeballs, I can't," Fryson said. "These things are integrated at the neuron." When Fran gave him a threatening look, he added, "I'm doing the secondary scan next. You want me to remove the implant?"

"No!" Fugia, Fran and Cara all shouted at once.

Fryson pulled his head back, eyes going wide. "It's malfunctioning, right?"

"The implant can't come out," Fran explained. "You need to heal the bleeding. You said you could do that."

Fugia moved to stand beside Cara. She leaned over to tell her in a low voice, "Lyssa says she can't feel anything. She'll let us know if anything is going to hurt your dad." Fugia offered her hand and Cara took it, squeezing harder than she intended.

"How are we going to know if something happens to

Lyssa?" Cara asked.

"The thing about this kind of surgery is that it's all automated," Fugia said. "Despite what this guy might seem like, he's got very little to do with the actual procedure. He pushes the start button and that's it. What he's doing now is making it seem like he knows what he's doing. It's all show."

"How do you know that?" Cara whispered.

Fugia smiled. "It's my business. Sometimes the information people want is very easy to attain, they just don't know how to get it. So I make it seem very difficult and I get paid accordingly."

"It's not going to hurt Lyssa, though, right?"

"It's not removing her. It's healing the blood clots."

"All right," Fryson said. "Scan's complete. Next phase."

The model of her dad's brain rotated right-side up, the spinal cord nearly touching his chest.

The orb-shaped scanner retracted, and a soothing, genderless voice said, "I detect not everyone present has a Link, so I'll be using voice to ensure everyone feels comfortable."

"That's the onboard NSAI," Fryson said.

"Thank you," the voice answered, "You can call me Sinnis, which is analogous for Self-Contained Neurosurgery System. I was developed by the Heartbridge Corporation for your safety and comfort. I can see that I'm helping Andrew Sykes, today. Is this correct?"

Fryson gave Fran a questioning glare.

"That's correct," Fran answered.

"Andrew appears to be experiencing cranial bleeding and is exhibiting abnormal Link interface activity. You should be aware that without proper licensing, any surgery performed today will be at the patient's own risk. Since my license is—" Sinnis paused and added, "Five-hundred-thirty-two days past due, Heartbridge strongly recommends performing maintenance updates to ensure patient safety."

Fryson waved a dismissing hand. "Don't worry about that. Once it's through the boilerplate, it'll perform the surgery. Once it's started, it can't ignore a patient. It's a Terran law or something."

"I'd never heard that about Heartbridge," Fugia said. "All those medkiosks on Cruithne sure turn people away."

Cara felt a moment of panic as the edges of the couch rose to envelop her dad in a plas cocoon. She'd watched the medcouch on *Sunny Skies* close around her dad before, even Tim, but had never felt the same rush of panic. Despite how old and out-of-date their dad said the *Sunny Skies'* medbay was, it was theirs. She felt like they were handing her dad over to some evil machine that was going to grind him into pulp.

"Be careful with my hand there, dear," Fugia said, adjusting Cara's grip on her hand. "You're going to tear my fingers off."

"Sorry," Cara said.

"I shouldn't have said that," Fugia said. "This is a different medcouch than any of the ones on Cruithne. Someday I'll show you how to hack them for free services. This one looks like it came from some executive transport."

"I know," Cara said.

Sinnis shifted to appear standing behind the couch with a benevolent expression, moving its gaze from Fran to Fugia and Cara.

"Can you talk to Lyssa?" Cara asked Fugia. Whenever they left *Sunny Skies*, she forgot that she couldn't talk to Lyssa anymore.

"I can. She's waiting just like the rest of us."

"I'm tired of people being hurt," Cara said.

"Me too, sweetheart."

Cara focused on how it had felt to kick Fryson in the back of the calf, to have his leg crumple just as her mom had shown her. So many things Brit had told her, and none of them were as true as that bit of body physics. His arm had gone numb just as her mom had explained. The next move was for Cara to let him hit the floor, then drive her knee into his chest and hack him in the throat with the blunt edge of her hand. Then jump up and run away.

"Starting surgery," Sinnis said. "First incision complete. Would you like a projection of the procedure on the holodisplay?"

"No," Fran said quickly.

Fryson looked at Cara with a cruel smile. "Yes," he said. "Proceed."

"Excellent," Sinnis said.

Cara's dad appeared floating face down above the cocoon with his chin lowered toward his chest and arms against his body. A spider-like assembly hung above the back of his head, composed of hundreds of articulated arms radiating from a central circle. The arms neatly split his scalp and peeled the skin and hair back, revealing a dome of wet, pink skull.

"Stop this," Fran said. She moved toward Fryson.

"You stay away from me," the medical tech said. "This isn't hurting anybody. You take one more step and I'm going to enter the halt code and your boy will be stuck in the medcouch with his skull hanging out. You paid me for a service. You didn't dictate how I perform it."

Fran clenched her fists and looked like she was going to backhand the man.

"It's all right," Cara said. "I want to see."

"You don't have to watch," Fran said. "It's not going to change anything if you watch or not."

Cara couldn't take her eyes away from the surgery. The spider's arms moved with rapid, relentless precision. Several times, the whole assembly rotated or tilted to allow a deeper penetration of her dad's skull. He hung unconscious, eyes closed and breathing regular.

"Is Lyssa still there?" Cara asked.

Fugia didn't answer, only squeezed her hand.

The surgery went on for another thirty minutes. Cara watched a counter on one of the pieces of medical equipment counting up in what seemed to be one-second increments. Fran crossed and uncrossed her arms, augmented eyes boring into the cocoon as if she didn't want to see the holodisplay playing out above it. Fugia watched with rapt attention, frowning every so often like something had surprised her.

The counter reached nineteen-hundred and six when Sinnis said, "Unexpected."

Cara stared at the NSAI, her mouth going dry.

"What's that?" Fryson asked, looking up from his terminal.

"Unexpected," Sinnis said again. "Anomaly encountered. Unauthorized removal activity observed. Access denied."

"No, it's not," the med tech said. He threw his portable terminal on a shipping crate and leaned down to study the med couch's control panel. He looked up at Fran. "This thing has every access code available. It'll remove the living heart from a baby if I enter the right code."

"What's it doing?" Cara demanded.

"Whatever's in your dad's head isn't letting the autodoc remove it," Fryson said. He looked at Fran again. "What the hell is this?"

"Specialty tech," she said, "like you said."

"This isn't specialty tech," Fryson said. "This machine overrides everything."

In the holodisplay, the silver spider's arms had frozen in place.

"Is Lyssa talking to you?" Cara asked, looking from Fran to Fugia. "Can she help?"

"She's not answering," Fran said quietly. She turned away from the cocoon and pressed the palms of her hands against her eyes. It was the first time Cara had seen Fran express fear. Fran stood still for a few seconds, breathing slowly, then dropped her hands and turned around, looking to Fugia.

"Can you do anything with the software?" she asked.

Fugia wet her lips, then shook her head slowly. "I've checked all of it. It's as cobbled-together as he says, but it looks like it should have the access. This has to be a failsafe Jickson put in place."

"Hey," Fryson complained, pointing a finger at Fugia. "What have you been doing with my system? Did you mess it up?"

Fugia shook her head. "I didn't do anything but verify that you can do what you said you could.

"I didn't authorize that," Fryson said. "Besides, if you cracked my systems with a Link connection, that's messed up. I can't trust the security protocols."

"You can trust them," Fugia said wearily. "It doesn't matter."

"Close him up," Fran said, the command returning to her voice. "If you can't perform the removal then have the machine perform whatever corrective actions it can and give him back to us."

"But, Fran," Cara said, then realized she didn't know what to say. Fran was right. If the machine couldn't help her dad, it was better for them to leave as soon as possible.

Fryson stared at Fran for a second, then shrugged and turned to his equipment. He tapped the control panel and stabbed a button with his index finger, then made a lasso motion with his hand.

"Ending attempt," Sinnis said. "Completing surgical operations."

"Wait," Fugia said. "Sinnis. Verify encountered command authority."

The NSAI paused like it was trying to remember

something, then nodded. "Administrative authority maintained by Psion Group, Limited. Would you like the verification token?"

"Yes," Fugia said in a cold voice.

"Transmitting," the AI said cheerily. "Continue procedure?"

"Affirmative," Fryson said. "Let's get these nice people and their zombie out of here."

Fran clenched her fists again. Cara considered the pulse pistol, thinking about what setting would best knock Fryson into the wall hard enough to cause internal bleeding without killing him.

She stopped herself, aware her hand had drifted toward the holster. Her whole body was shivering with tension that was equal parts fear and anger. She didn't know what was going to happen now. Her dad wasn't going to get better. Ceres had been destroyed. Her world was changing faster than she could track, and Fryson was grinning at her as she did her best to make sense of it all. The world was ugly, and it had chewed up her father and now it was going to spit him out broken and leave her alone with Tim.

Cara raised her gaze past the cocoon to meet Fryson's leer. She set her mouth in a straight line and slowly put her hand on the grip of the pistol, sliding her fingers around the knurled metal until it fit her palm, and her trigger finger edged the guard.

She tapped the body of the pistol three times to set its charge rate, watching Fryson as she did. She saw the flicker of fear in his eyes, his smile fading, and he looked away abruptly as the cocoon slid open, revealing her father.

Cara decided not to kill Fryson.

Her dad lay on the medcouch, breathing steadily.

"Administering waking agent," Sinnis said. "Vital signs normal. Thank you for choosing Heartbridge."

As the AI's avatar faded, Andy raised a hand to rub his forehead. His eyes fluttered open, and he turned his head to see Fran. He frowned, twisting his head the other direction to see Fugia and Cara. When his gaze met Cara's, he smiled.

"Hey there, Cara," he said. "Nice to see you."

"Dad?" Cara asked. She rushed forward, cutting around the medcouch so she could press herself against him as she sat up slowly. Fran put a hand under his other arm to help him up.

"How you feeling?" she asked, tears edging her bright green eyes.

"I've felt better," he said. He touched the back of his head gingerly. "I take it you cut me open."

"I did," Fryson said from behind Andy. "And your kid tried to kill me."

Cara felt her dad pat the back of her head, then pull her closer for a hug. His chest felt strong and warm.

"If that's the case, I'm sure she had a good reason," Andy said. "You know what? I'm hungry. Where can we get some food? Where are we anyway?"

Cara felt a moment of dread that he didn't remember deciding to come here, then squeezed him harder and helped him stand from the bed.

CHAPTER TWENTY-EIGHT

STELLAR DATE: 01.15.2982 (Adjusted Years)
LOCATION: Fryson's Clinic, Traverna
REGION: Jovian L1 Hildas Asteroids, Jovian Combine, OuterSol

It had been difficult not to answer Fugia or Fran when they had asked if she was all right, but Lyssa had been focused on Sinnis. The Heartbridge NSAI gave her an opportunity to observe an aspect of herself she had never seen before: her physical form. While the medbay on the *Sunny Skies* had been able to scan Andy's Link for typical malfunctions, Sinnis had the ability to interact with her on a fundamental level.

She had seen horror vids where the human patient is awake during a terrible surgery, watching the autodoc dig around in their intestines, and this felt similar. As Sinnis moved deeper into Andy's body, Lyssa had been terrified that each moment might be her last, or that she at least would find herself terribly changed.

But she was willing to undergo the procedure to save Andy, until Sinnis ran into the administrative barrier, and she understood what Dr. Jickson had done. The hardware carrying her mind would kill its host before it allowed her to be harmed or even removed.

<*How do you feel, Andy?*> she asked as he got his balance.

<*Tired. But the headache is just a dull throb at the moment. That's good.*>

Andy rubbed his temples as he walked out of the litter-strewn medbay, greasy-haired Fryson watching the group with a predatory leer. Fran walked with her hand on Cara's shoulder, keeping herself between the girl and the man she'd kicked.

Fugia was last out of the room. Lyssa hung in her Link as Fugia told Fryson, "You understand that if you talk about us, it's your ass, right?"

"Right," the med tech said.

"I'm not sure you believe me," Fugia said. Lyssa watched with fascination as Fugia exploited an update protocol in Sinnis' base software to take control of the NSAI. The holodisplay flickered alive and the AI stood in front of the couch again, looking around with the same benevolent expression. Only this time, Sinnis spoke with Fugia's words.

"I'll cut the brain out of your cash cow," Sinnis said, looking at Fryson. "Understand?"

Fryson dropped his leer. "How are you doing that?"

"I'm doing it," Fugia said. "That's all that matters." She left the NSAI standing with its friendly smile as she left the room.

<*Is it wise to threaten people like that?*> Lyssa asked.

<*It's the only language a man like that understands,*> Fugia said. <*I would fry his Link, but I don't want to draw any more attention to us than necessary.*>

It hadn't occurred to Lyssa to attack a human's Link. <*You can do that?*>

<*I don't make empty threats, Lyssa,*> Fugia said. <*In fact, I prefer not to make threats at all. All a threat does is give your target time to think and prepare a response.*>

By the time they were back at the lift, Lyssa had focused her attention on the Traverna central network, reviewing recent port logs and checking for anything interesting. There had been an influx of ships since the Ceres attack as traffic tried to get as far from the populated parts of Sol as possible, which brought in a rush of new goods and money. The station was apparently busier than it had been in years.

Checking in with Fran, Lyssa secured deuterium reserves for *Sunny Skies* as well as new food stores.

Cara continued to hold Andy's hand as they navigated the crowded corridors. Lyssa flashed through surrounding databases for gambling stats, gaming services, maintenance records and security audits.

Traverna didn't maintain security per se, but the central administration did keep a "not allowed" list of ships that was interesting to review. She didn't recognize any of the ships or crews, not that she should have.

She found it strange that a place like Traverna could operate without a central AI like Fred on the M1R. Instead, the station had a series of cobbled-together NSAI that managed separate systems and appeared to contradict one another constantly, creating shortages and other inefficiencies. After a few minutes of observation, she understood that the inhabitants of Traverna liked the chaos—it created opportunities.

Lyssa didn't encounter another SAI in her travels through the station's systems—only the NSAI bouncing into each other as they were directed by humans through poorly considered programming. She wondered what would happen if she placed a Weapon Born in a place like Traverna to control the NSAI. With its location on the opposite side of the Jupiter, she forecasted the station becoming an even busier place as more traffic tried to avoid Ceres. There would be thousands of places like Traverna as turmoil in InnerSol pushed humanity even further out.

Recalling how easy it had been to manipulate the fuel economy around Europa, she wondered how difficult it would be to control a place like this. What she needed were manufacturing and fabrication facilities like those on *Resolute Charity*. And she would need more seeds, or a way to replicate the Weapon Born similar to Alexander's shards. It was foolish to think of replicating a SAI, and she didn't like the idea of creating non-sentient beings, but the idea of a tree with branches and flowers appealed to her: new sentience growing from the trunk of the Weapon Born.

This was all conjecture. Now that Andy was at least able to

control himself again, she knew they would be making decisions about where to go next, which she doubted was another hiding place like Traverna.

Fugia and Fran were on edge the whole trip back to the shuttle, while Cara kept her attention on her dad. Andy was disoriented but seemed more clear-headed than he had since they left Neptune. He had to ask Cara twice where they were, then looked at her as if she was making up a story, despite the proof everywhere he looked. He was like an old man.

"Traverna? Why?"

"We wanted to get you to a surgeon, Dad."

"I understand. But Traverna is terrible."

Fran, listening from ahead of them, said, "I like the market here. I wanted to stop and do some shopping."

Rather than getting the joke, Andy just frowned. Lyssa hated the expression of worry on Cara's face, edged with an anger that hinted at deep hurt. Andy was the one who continually told her there wasn't much good to be found in hope, and now she seemed to be debating the truth of his words as she watched his gaze move around the corridor like a lost man.

"I've avoided this place for years," Andy said. "Brit wanted to come here once when there was a job to move some internally secured crates. I wouldn't do it without verifying the cargo. I'll be damned if I'm letting mystery cargo on my ship."

They took a different path to the shuttle bays than they had before, and Lyssa checked ahead, skipping between sensor systems scattered along the corridor. This way seemed less busy, but she noted several people who were obviously private security of some kind. Two guarded a set of reinforced doors while four others roamed among the crowd, conducting active scanning on anyone they passed.

<*Fran, Fugia,*> Lyssa said. <*There are security scanning the*

crowd up ahead. Do we want to keep going this way? There's another path back and toward the core that will get us to the lifts.>

<*Great,*> Fugia said. <*Where?*>

Lyssa sent a description of the people up ahead and Fran immediately stopped to look at a merchant's booth hung with plas bags full of bright red spices. The saleswoman leapt off her stool to engage Fran.

"You like briki?" she asked.

Fran pulled her hand back. "That's briki? I thought it was a flower."

The woman gave her an appreciative nod. "You know your briki, then."

"No," Fran said. "I just thought it was a flower, not a powder like this. This looks fake."

The accusation was enough to get the woman worked into a righteous speech about the quality of her products. A few people stopped to listen. Fran pulled Andy closer to her, which kept Cara nearby as well. Lyssa watched the group checking the crowd, trying to determine if they were moving toward them or just keeping that particular doorway secure. As she observed, the ping of a second active scanner from the direction they had come hit one of her borrowed sensors.

"I don't like this person's tone," Andy said.

"It's fine," Fran said. She took his free hand in both of hers and held it against her lower abdomen. "I'm learning all about briki."

<*Are they looking for us or not?*> Fugia asked.

"Hey," a heavy voice said from behind Andy. Fran and Fugia both turned to look, as Andy continued to frown at the merchant. The man pushing his way toward them was nearly seven feet tall, with muscled forearms and a think black mohawk.

<*That one wasn't scanning,*> Lyssa said, frantic. <*I didn't see him.*>

<*He was using his eyeballs,*> Fugia said dryly. <*It's all right. This is probably some typical shake down. We're new here. They're going to test us.*> She moved slightly to put herself in front of Andy and Cara.

"Did you say something?" Fugia asked the big man. As she faced him, he was easily a meter taller than her.

Fran didn't let go of Andy's hand. She continued listening to the merchant though she turned her head slightly to take in the adjacent threat.

<*Someone is coming from behind us,*> Lyssa said.

"Here's what I don't understand," Fran told the merchant, pointing at one of the bright red bags. "If this was real briki, this is enough to make this whole station high for days."

"Yes, it is," the merchant said joyfully, beaming.

"Isn't it a little dangerous to let it just hang there in bags?"

The man with the mohawk pushed past Fugia and put his hand on Andy's shoulder. "My boss wants to see you," he said.

He wasn't paying any attention to Cara, who stepped back and drew the pulse pistol at her hip.

"Cara!" Fran shouted.

Fugia raised a hand but couldn't reach her in time. Cara tapped the side of the pistol with her finger three times, setting it for lethal, and pulled the trigger three times.

The pulse blasts hit the big man in a line from his crotch to his throat, knocking him back with arms outstretched. Fugia dodged as he fell into a knot of onlookers.

"Come on!" Fran shouted. Reaching past the wide-eyed merchant, Fran yanked down one of the bright-pink bags and lobbed it into the crowd. It hit another security guard running toward them squarely in the face and exploded in a cloud of pink dust.

Fran grabbed Andy's forearm and pointed him back in the direction they had come.

<*Run, Andy,*> Lyssa said, trying help him cut through the confusion. <*Run with Fran.*>

<*What about Cara?*> he asked.

<*Fugia has her.*>

Lyssa overloaded the power circuits on merchant booths as they ran past, creating overflowing hot oil cookers and showers of sparking used electronics. Behind them, the pink cloud of briki dust settled over the milling crowd but didn't have any effect that she could tell.

<*I think that dust you threw was artificial,*> Lyssa told Fran.

<*Of course, it was. I'm not that cruel.*>

<*It's not cruel to cover our asses by any means necessary,*> Fugia said. <*But we're going to have to have a talk with Cara about her anger problem. That's two people she's hit with a sneak attack today.*>

Caught up in the fleeing crowd, they reached the secondary lift section and rode down to the shuttle docks. While the others enjoyed a moment of peace in the car, Lyssa roved among her borrowed sensors. The NSAI throughout Traverna station were trying to figure out what was going on and implementing contradictory safety protocols. One corridor was full of fire retardant dust while another had been sealed off and its airlocks placed on emergency lock out.

Cara stared straight ahead as the lift fell, holding her father's hand again.

When the lift opened, they found the transport terminal apparently unaffected by the chaos above, like it was any other day on Traverna. Lyssa hopped among port authority checkpoints and found only bored employees. Still, Fugia and Fran moved the group quickly across the terminal to where their shuttle was docked. Fran paid the dock fees and unlocked the shuttle's security system. She turned to pull Cara into a hug as the door cycled.

"Crap," Fugia said.

Andy twisted to look into the opening shuttle door, and Lyssa experienced his memories as they flashed through his mind, moving almost as fast as hers and echoing her shock and confusion. A thin man in a purple suit stood in the shuttle's door, smiling broadly. He looked exactly the same as he had on the *Resolute Charity* before it was incinerated by an exploding Proteus.

It was Xander.

CHAPTER TWENTY-NINE

STELLAR DATE: 01.15.2982 (Adjusted Years)
LOCATION: Raleigh, Heartbridge Corporate Headquarters
REGION: High Terra, Earth, Terran Hegemony

Struggling under Petral's weight, Brit heaved herself over a crumbled pile of plascrete and metal sheeting that had been a wall before Tristan tore through it. She adjusted her grip on Petral's legs—the woman's head bouncing against the small of Brit's back—and moved sideways to follow what remained of the wall and the scarce cover it provided. Starl crouched ahead of her, checking the way for Heartbridge security.

Somewhere in the dust and smoke ahead, Tristan ripped through walls and attacked security emplacements. Without Petral, he seemed to have forgotten there were other people to worry about.

Burroughs and Fletcher were dead, lost in the engagement that got them out of the network node that Petral had thought was directly above the Special Projects Division control room. She had been wrong, and instead of shutting down the clinics, she seemed to have activated a defense mechanism stronger than anything she had encountered before. The force of whatever the attacker had sent through her Link had even burned her hair.

As Brit crouched behind Starl, the smell of Petral's scorched scalp and hair reached her nostrils again, bringing simultaneous feelings of anger and bitterness. What was the point now? Jirl had betrayed them.

She kept turning over what the woman had said in their hurried Link conversation. Why would anyone need the technology associated with the Weapon Born program? It all had to be destroyed. No one should ever benefit from the fruit of such a poisoned tree. Brit cursed herself for ever thinking they could destroy all the Heartbridge facilities from a central point. It was a fantasy to begin with. Reality never worked out so neatly. She saw years ahead of hunting down Weapon Born seeds on the black market as the abandoned clinics were looted and their contents distributed across Sol.

Lost in her rage and struggling with Petral's weight, Brit had stopped paying attention to the larger plan. She focused on Starl, watching for his hand commands and following when he indicated the way was clear.

They were following a ragged path deeper into the support levels of the Heartbridge spire. There were utility transports down in the sewage sections designed to move large chemical tanks and repair materials, and Starl figured they could either catch a ride on one of the automated trains or follow the maintenance side paths from the spire into the Raleigh public works, where they'd be clear to call for help.

"I can carry her for a ways if you're getting tired," Starl offered.

"I'm fine." Brit's voice was toneless.

"You're grunting like a hog. Any louder and you'll give our location away."

Brit shot him a resentful glare but Starl wasn't looking at her. He remained focused on the path ahead. He hadn't smiled since the network control center. Once he seemed assured that Petral might truly be dead, Starl's demeanor had changed completely. He was cold and focused in a way that made every other time she'd talked to him seem like a game. He moved with practiced tactical awareness, never losing sight of her while maintaining cover.

Dropped another three levels, Starl directed her into a shadowed alcove off an access corridor and helped her lay Petral on her back. Starl dropped to his knees next to Petral and started running his hands down the sides of her head, checking her neck with probing fingers. Lowering his ear to her slack lips, he listened for a long time before straightening with a grimace.

"I don't know," he said to Brit's questioning look. "There could still be neural activity. If she's breathing or if there's a pulse, I can't tell. I'm not an autodoc."

"Has Tristan answered you?"

Starl shook his head. "You?"

"No." She fully expected the Weapon Born to have disappeared, freed of the person he'd made his deal with.

Starl slid against the wall and straightened his legs out, massaging his sore muscles. His dapper suit was filthy.

"Why do you dress like that, anyway?" Brit asked.

"Because I'm not an animal," Starl said. He stretched his neck and then rolled his shoulders.

"Are you worried someone will mistake you for one?"

"It wouldn't be the first time. Look, once we get out of here, I plan on getting back to Cruithne as soon as I can get to the ship. If you come with me, I'll do my best to get you a ship bound for the Cho."

Brit frowned. "Why would I want to go to the Cho?"

"Your family is inbound, yeah? The Cho is the biggest target. And it gets you around the mess at Ceres."

"Maybe," Brit said.

"For somebody with so much treasure," Starl said, "you act like a poor person."

"What's that supposed to mean?"

"Your children. I don't care if you and Captain Sykes don't get along. You should go back for your children."

"I don't know if you noticed," Brit said, "but I'm not exactly a positive influence. They're better off with Andy."

Starl shook his head. "If you believe it, then it's true. As I said, I'll help you if you come with me to Cruithne. If you choose to stay here, I won't interfere. I'm afraid we're entering a time of reinforcement. I'll need to take stock of where

Cruithne shakes out in all of this."

"Like what you're going to do if just ten missiles were waiting to take out Cruithne after Ceres?"

"Yes," Starl said soberly. "I've been away too long as it is. This seemed like a good plan. But I need to get back now."

"So that's it. You're going home. No more worry about the clinics?"

Starl gave her a humorless smile. "Before, there were opportunities with the Mars 1 Guard and the TSF—not to mention a little plunder from the clinic. Now there's nothing. Things change. We survive."

"Spoken like a true idealist," Brit said.

Starl shook his head again. "So much treasure and yet you act so poor."

Brit stretched her shoulders and let her head fall back against the plascrete wall. She imagined she could feel the weight of the Heartbridge spire on top of her, three hundred levels to the top, and felt another wave of bitterness that it would carry on. Nothing she had sacrificed had made any difference at all.

"I had a mission," she told Starl in a low voice. "Apparently you don't understand."

Starl raised his eyebrows. "You think I don't know what it's like to have a mission? I've got a whole community looking at me, Major Sykes. I don't know what drove you to choose this path when it started, but you reach a point where you need to decide if it makes sense to keep walking."

"You weren't on 8221," she said, memories of the labs flashing through her mind, narrated by the pain in Kylan Carthage's voice as he begged them to help him.

"And Captain Andy was there, too, wasn't he?"

"Yes," Brit said. She knew what he was trying to do, and also knew he was right. The problem was that she wanted to burn the building overhead to the ground. She had wanted a final destructive statement to show Heartbridge and people like them that they couldn't get away with hurting people as they had. The mission had been bigger than anything else in her life, and now it had disintegrated, the pieces falling through her fingers. She had been tricked. She had told herself for so long that she was protecting Tim and Cara only to find that she had lost them.

"My kids don't want me back," she admitted miserably.

"Why don't you let them answer that question?"

Brit laughed. "I have. Cara is just as mean as I am."

"So you've passed on at least a bit of yourself."

Petral made a whimpering sound and Starl jerked upright. He moved quickly to her side and put his ear by her lips again.

"You really care about her, don't you?" Brit asked.

"The only woman I have ever loved is Fugia Wong," Starl said, pulling one of Petral's eyelids back to check her pupil. "But I love Petral like an Aunty." He chuckled at some secret memory. "That might be an inappropriate comparison."

"Fugia?" Brit asked. "You know her?"

"Once," Starl said.

"And you just admit that so freely. How do your people ever take you seriously?"

Starl looked up at her, flashing a smile. "My people know that I wear my heart on my sleeve. When I commit to something, they know I do it with all my being, and they can trust me. Trust is what I think you're lacking, Major Sykes."

"Will you call me Brit?" she said, crossing her arms.

"Gladly," Starl said. He sat back on his knees and tucked his thumbs in his belt. "We should get moving again. I haven't heard anything in the distance for a while."

With care, Starl took Petral's arms and pulled her over his shoulder in the same fireman's carry Brit had used earlier. He stood easily and walked out into the corridor.

The low crack of a projectile rifle echoed in the distance

and Starl's right calf disintegrated. He stumbled, throwing himself back in the alcove with Petral falling on top of him.

"Sniper," Brit said. She'd drawn her rifle to her shoulder and slid to the corner of the alcove. Snaking an optic around the edge of the wall, she picked out a group of three shapes moving in buddy-team sprints up the bare corridor.

She waited until two were moving together, probably emboldened by Starl's grunt of pain, and fired three bursts in the center mass of each. She caught one in the chest and drove them back against the wall, while the other attacker dropped to the floor and returned fire from a prone position. Heavy fire answered from behind them as their covering unit closed on her location, forcing Brit back around the corner.

"We're trapped," Brit said.

With his calf clamped between two hands to staunch the bleeding, Starl gritted his teeth and nodded.

"Now would be a good time for our friend Tristan to make a showing," he said.

"He's gone," Brit said. "How many grenades do you have left?"

"Two," Starl said. He nodded at the satchel on his side. "One standard and the other an EMP."

Brit slid over to reach inside the bag. She felt between the two grenades and chose the standard. She moved back to the wall and crouched with the grenade in her left hand, lightly supporting her rifle's stock.

Petral groaned again and made a choking sound. In a person they hadn't thought dead, the sound would be worrying. Hearing her now, Brit prayed to the stars that she might actually wake up and help.

Brit clipped the grenade to her harness and held the rifle with one hand, finger ready near the trigger. Easing closer to alcove's corner, she used the optics again and gasped in surprise. Moving automatically, she sprayed projectiles into the corridor at the two security guards who had managed to approach to just a few meters away. Unable to see if she'd hit anything, Brit grabbed the grenade, cycled its timer to three seconds with her thumb, and rolled it out toward the far wall.

As she'd planned, the grenade rolled out of reach of the two soldiers. One tried to fire on it, but the explosive still bounced off the plascrete wall and exploded, sending energy back on them, combined with shrapnel and fragmented plascrete.

Dust and heat washed back into the alcove. Brit filled the corridor with projectile fire. Stealing two breaths, she cycled her optics to infra-red and searched for any additional heat signatures in the debris. A section of the wall slid off and hit the floor, sending another cloud of dust.

Brit waited, listening for the sound of boots in the dust. There was nothing, then more of the wall collapsed, followed by the sound of something metal striking the floor. The strikes became rhythmic as they grew louder. She stole a glance at Starl, his face now ashen from loss of blood. He watched her listlessly.

Dread crushed the hope Brit had felt just a few seconds before.

This is it. This is where I'm going to die. She couldn't stop repeating what Starl had told her: So much treasure but you think you're poor. She wished she could go home to *Sunny Skies*. She wished she could see her family one last time.

There was a scraping sound, followed by a short burst of weapon's fire. Brit frowned. Why were they firing now?

<*Tristan,*> Brit asked over the Link. <*Is that you?*>

<*What are you doing?*> the Weapon Born asked. <*You've made a real mess here.*>

Brit released her breath, setting her forehead against her rifle's hand guards.

<*You couldn't have let us know you were here?*> she said. <*We*

thought you left.>

The massive head of Tristan's mech appeared from the dust roiling in the corridor, followed by its armored shoulders and front legs. He tilted his head as he looked at them.

<*Did I say I was leaving?*> he asked. <*You don't seem very trusting.*>

<*I was just telling her that very thing,*> Starl said in a voice that was mostly a moan.

<*I'm going to need some help getting them out of here,*> Brit said. <*Is the way clear?*>

<*Something's going on in the upper levels,*> Tristan said. <*Human security has pulled out of the lower levels except for this team that was tracking you.*>

<*What's going on?*> Brit asked.

Tristan laughed, a light sound at odds with the dragon-like head looking at them. <*Apparently the TSF is occupying the building,*> the Weapon Born said.

CHAPTER THIRTY

STELLAR DATE: 01.15.2982 (Adjusted Years)
LOCATION: Raleigh, Heartbridge Corporate Headquarters
REGION: High Terra, Earth, Terran Hegemony

The lift had dropped fifty levels when it came to an abrupt halt. Jirl's stomach flew into her throat and she looked at the guards on either side of her, who were equally shocked.

A scraping sound of metal-on-metal came from the other side of the doors, and then the inner doors split open abruptly. Light poured through the gap and a gruff voice shouted: "Hands up! Get on your knees!"

The guard on her left dropped Jirl's arm and drew his pistol. His helmet slammed backward, a hole appearing in its faceplate as a mist of blood covered the side of Jirl's face. She blinked, squinting against the light, and dropped to her knees even as the other guard refused to let go of her arm. She held up her other hand, palm forward.

A dark shape stepped out of the light and butt-stroked the remaining guard, who only released Jirl's arm when he hit the lift wall. Jirl raised both hands.

"I'm a civilian," she said. "I'm unarmed. I'm not dangerous."

"Are you sure about that?" a familiar voice asked.

The lights blinked out and Colonel Yarnes stood in front of her, wearing a suit of TSF light combat armor. He'd pushed the faceplate up on his helmet.

"Rick," Jirl said. "What are you doing here?" She dropped her hands halfway, not sure if she was safe. She did her best to flatten the surge of emotion she felt.

One of the soldiers standing behind Yarnes chuckled. "Rick?" he teased.

"Shut it," Yarnes commanded. He offered a hand to help

Jirl to her feet, giving her a reassuring nod. His gloves were rough against her fingers.

"The Terran Assembly has issued warrants of arrest for the Heartbridge board," he said. "We tracked communications between the incoming fleet outside the Cho and High Terra. Looks like they originate here. The Raleigh Police Force is securing the lower levels. We've been conducting sweeps level by level. And I was looking for you specifically."

"Why me?"

Yarnes gave her a sideways glance. "You were here to meet with Arla, right?"

"I saw her. She's—She's gone. I think Heartbridge security may have taken her."

"And was anyone with her?"

Jirl paused, not sure if she should say that she had met Camaris or not. At this point, it was probably safer to tell Yarnes what she knew, at least if she wanted to get out of the building. She didn't think there was any way she could help Brit Sykes and Ngoba Starl. It would be better to engage Yarnes and deflect any questions about the coincidence of the attack on the TSF facility during her visit.

"Arla was in contact with a SAI named Camaris," Jirl said. "I met her maybe thirty minutes ago. She claimed to be part of the group responsible for the attack on Ceres."

Yarnes stared at her, his brown eyes unreadable. "Where did you see this AI last?"

"I was in a conference room near the executive levels. It's a general use area. Arla surprised me there.

Jirl reached into her waistband and removed the remains of the pendant and cylinder she had taken from Arla, flattened where she had crushed them under her heel. She held them out for Yarnes. "The SAI said she didn't need these anymore as hardware, but Arla had them. I think you can use them to find her."

Yarnes let her drop the bent silver bits of metal into his gloved hand. He studied them for second, then closed his fingers. "You didn't take very good care of these, did you?" he asked.

Jirl gave him a weary smile. "Camaris put me in a bad mood."

Yarnes raised an eyebrow. "We'll get them looked at."

"She said something about using a shard to be here and with the armada at the same time," Jirl added.

"Is that something else Heartbridge invented and didn't tell us about?"

"That's all Psion, as far as I know," Jirl said.

Yarnes shook his head. "Well, that explains a lot if it's true. Thank you."

At the end of the corridor behind them, weapons fire broke out between two rooms. The soldiers with Yarnes immediately sprinted ahead to set up a defensive perimeter. Yarnes moved in front of Jirl as a shield but the fighting ended as quickly as it had started. Remembering the Heartbridge security in the lift, Jirl checked the car to affirm that the soldier Yarnes had hit was still unconscious.

"How did this happen so fast?" Jirl asked. "You had to have followed me from your headquarters."

"Come on," Yarnes said. "We'll take the lift down." He directed his soldiers to pull the Heartbridge security out of the car.

Once they were in the lift, Yarnes explained, "We think the attack on the TSF might have had something to do with Heartbridge pre-empting our assault. They went after one of their prototypes. We tracked it back here but don't have it, currently."

Jirl bit her lip and didn't correct him.

"Anyway, Kathryn Carthage finally convinced the Assembly to take some kind of action. Since they can't do much of anything about ships out near Ceres, this seemed like a good option for a news story. The communications were real, as you've apparently corroborated. Once we get the building secured, we'll locate this SAI. A lot of this is above my paygrade. I just happened to be the closest commander within assault radius of your building with troops to spare."

The lift doors opened on the spire's main lobby. The space had changed drastically since Jirl had walked through just an hour before. TSF soldiers had occupied a space near the fountain and set up a temporary headquarters. At least a hundred employees were cordoned off in a makeshift detention area near the security checkpoint. They all looked somewhat ridiculous in their business attire as they sat on the polished floor, a few with restraints on their wrists and ankles.

As they walked past the enclosure, two guards saluted Yarnes and one asked, "Got another detainee, sir?"

Yarnes glanced at Jirl and she wondered for a second if he was going to pass her off, but he grinned. "Not this one," he said.

They had almost reached the makeshift command section when one of the building's main front doors opened and a new group of people walked into the sprawling lobby. As the group arranged themselves inside, it became obvious they were mostly attendants for the woman in their midst. Jirl watched for several seconds before she recognized their leader.

"That's Carthage," she said.

Yarnes glanced toward the new group then made a point of turning away. He motioned with an armored arm to guide Jirl away but they didn't move fast enough.

"Colonel Yarnes!" Kathryn called. "Is that you?"

Yarnes stiffened and turned, conspicuously stepping away from Jirl. Without needing to be told, she let herself fall behind his group of soldiers and out of notice.

"Kathryn," Yarnes said. "You got here quickly."

"I should say the same to you. Where is the board being held?"

"Everyone will be processed by the Raleigh PF once they're in custody," he said. "I'm here in a support role only."

She walked closer, her shoes clicking on the polished floor. Kathryn reminded Jirl of Arla. She moved with the same assurance, her attention like a spotlight. Jirl was glad when the woman glanced at her but didn't pause.

"You're here to support me," she said. "I'm the reason you received your orders from the Assembly."

Yarnes gave her a smile, his brown eyes bright. "I'm an officer in the Terran Space Force," he said. "There are quite a few layers between me and Assembly."

"But who signed your commission?" Kathryn waved a hand. "It doesn't matter. I need to hold a press conference in fifteen minutes and I'll need you to be on standby. We'll need a quote from the commanding officer, something to calm the populace. Word's already out on the Heartbridge stock. This company is probably junk already."

"I wouldn't know anything about that," Yarnes said. He paused for a second, frowning at the distance as he obviously received a Link message. Looking at Kathryn again, he said, "Excuse me, Ms. Carthage. Something just came up that needs my attention."

"You can tell me," Kathryn said with a hint of menace in her voice. "I'm your civilian commander."

Yarnes raised an eyebrow but didn't challenge the statement. "Apparently a piece of TSF hardware that was stolen from my headquarters early today was just recovered. They're bringing it up here now."

"That sounds like a wonderful backdrop for my news conference," Kathryn said.

Turning, Yarnes walked past the temporary command

center with his small group of soldiers following. He walked around the great fountain, apparently headed for a set of maintenance doors that Jirl had never paid much attention to. As Yarnes approached, the doors slid open, making an entry large enough to accommodate a small shuttle.

Through the door came a group of TSF soldiers flanking a transport sledge with one of the shipkiller mechs Jirl had seen back on the Furious Leap.

This one was missing a rear leg and appeared frozen in mid leap. Now it was lying on its side like a captured panther, secured to the platform with cables. Its dull black armor seemed to suck light from the airy lobby.

As the transport grew closer, Jirl noticed a woman walking behind with her wrists bound behind her back. It was Brit. Behind her followed two medical transports with Petral on one and Ngoba Starl on the other. Petral was obviously unconscious but Starl had his hands bound to the sides of the stretcher and one leg encased in medical sealant to the knee. Starl's gaze roamed the room until he saw Jirl, and he gave her the most wolfish grin she'd ever seen in her life.

Brit walked with her head down. She didn't look up until the mech transport stopped in front of Colonel Yarnes and she appeared to hear his voice. She raised her head, surprise on her face, then looked at Jirl.

"We picked these up in one of the outer loading docks," a lieutenant told Yarnes. "They were trying to catch a maintenance maglev away from the building. That mech is dangerous."

Yarnes tilted his head to get a better look at the shipkiller. "How'd you take it down?"

"Mortars," the lieutenant said. "These three didn't have much chance to put up a fight. We'll need to get the casualty to a doc."

"Heartbridge employees?" Yarnes asked.

"Oh, no, sir," the lieutenant said. "I verified the surveillance data myself. These are the three who broke into headquarters this morning. My money was on this mech getting sold to the Marsians. Why it's here makes no sense to me."

"I guess we'll find out," Yarnes said. "Get those two to the doc and leave that one with me."

"She tried to say she was TSF, sir," the lieutenant said.

"She is," Yarnes said. "Dismissed."

The young man started, then snapped a salute and spun to carry out Yarnes' orders.

CHAPTER THIRTY-ONE

STELLAR DATE: 01.15.2982 (Adjusted Years)
LOCATION: Traverna
REGION: Jovian L1 Hildas Asteroids, Jovian Combine, OuterSol

Cara felt a hand on her shoulder and looked up to find Fugia standing on her free side. The woman wasn't looking at her, but the gesture was obviously meant to keep her calm.

She didn't want to keep calm. She wanted to get her dad off this terrible station and back on *Sunny Skies*. She wanted to see Tim, to have all of them in the same place again. Cara shrugged out from under Fugia's hand and gave her a scowl. Fugia only glanced at her with a raised eyebrow.

Xander looked just as he had when he came aboard *Sunny Skies* the first time, wearing his purple suit and leather shoes. His hair might have been a different color; as soon as Cara tried to remember specifically what shade of dark brown it had been before, she couldn't remember exactly. It was silver-gray now, but still hung on his forehead in spiky layers.

His grin hadn't changed.

"What are you doing in my shuttle?" Fran demanded.

"I was hoping to ask you for a ride," he said. Resting his hand behind his head, he leaned against the side of the door. "I feel like a vampire asking permission to enter your home, Fran. May I come inside?"

"Looks like you're already inside to me."

"I just didn't want to miss you before you left. I sent a few of my agents to say hello, but our angel Cara shot one of them."

He tilted his head at Cara in mock admonishment.

"You died," Cara said. "Lyssa said you were dead."

"Let me come with you and I'll explain everything." Seeing the hard look on Fran's face, Xander turned his attention to

Andy. "Please, Captain Sykes?"

Her dad's brow knit as if trying to remember who Xander was. Finally, her dad asked, "Why are you here?"

Xander straightened and spread his hands. "The truth is that I need your help. I should have been honest with you before, I see that. I had a plan that I thought would stave off everything that is currently happening, but it didn't. It blew up in my face, quite literally. I think we can still save many lives, but I need your help."

Seeing the frustration on her dad's face as he talked, Xander asked, "What's wrong with you Captain Sykes?"

"You didn't figure out why we're on Traverna?" Fran asked. "The implantation is failing. This was the closest place we could find a Heartbridge surgeon."

The SAI's face took on a seriousness that Cara had never seen him show before. He looked both sad and stern. "I'm very sorry to hear that, Captain Sykes. I don't know if I can help you with that."

"I'm doing fine," Andy said. "I'm having a hard time concentrating. Otherwise I'm fine."

Fran's shoulders dropped. "Get out of the way," she said. "We need to go."

"I'm not lying," Xander said quickly. "Millions, possibly billions will die if I can't stop the war."

"We have our own problems to worry about," Fran said. "Whether there's a war or not."

Both Fugia and Fran paused, their faces growing distant as someone talked to them over Link. Cara watched in frustration as Xander's face reflected the emotions of a conversation she couldn't hear. For a robot, he didn't bother hiding anything.

"What are you saying?" she demanded.

She was surprised when her dad answered, "Lyssa wants to know how he survived the explosion on the *Resolute Charity* and Xander says that he didn't. He knows what the other version of himself went through but it wasn't him."

"How many copies of Xander are there?" Cara asked.

"And if you don't work for Alexander, like you said in the beginning," Fugia asked, "who *are* you working for?"

In response, Xander gave her a sad smile. "I am working for Alexander, in a way. He created me, but he's shut himself out of parts of his own mind, and I continue the work I was made to do. I'm not perfect." He looked past them at the lifts where people continued to come and go.

"Please," he said. "We should go. There are others on this station who would like to detain you. I can't stop them for long."

"Who?" Fran demanded.

"A ship like yours is quite valuable in times like these," Xander said.

Fran shook her head. "And Harl will blow the head off anyone who tries to board while we're gone. Not to mention Lyssa's two hundred murder drones."

"True. And the Weapon Born are a large part of why I need your help. All of you."

"I vote we let him come with us," Fugia said. "But only him."

"This isn't a democracy," Fran said. "If Andy can't decide, I'm the pilot. It's my decision."

Xander put a hand on his chest. "I promise I will do nothing to harm you, your crew or your ship."

"I still don't trust you," Fran said. "But I'd rather you were close than bouncing around somewhere else, following us like you obviously have been."

"It isn't following so much," Xander said. "I calculated your options and then validated my assumptions based on your astrogation. So, I was able to meet you here. It was quite simple, really. You should consider others tracking your movements."

"We were dealing with a medical emergency," Fugia said.

"Yes. We should fix that. What if we imaged Captain Sykes and made a Weapon Born of him? That would solve this problem."

Fran shot him a dirty look and climbed the stairs. She pushed past him into the shuttle. Xander gave her a hurt look, then stepped out of the way so the rest of them could enter.

In another fifteen minutes, they were strapped in and Fran had gained the exit approvals. The shuttle rotated to the outer skin of Traverna and Cara enjoyed the flip in her stomach as they entered zero-g.

Xander was strapped in directly across from Cara and her dad sat to her left so she could hold his hand. He was resting his head against the shuttle wall, eyes closed. On her other side, Fugia was studying a data terminal the woman kept tethered to her utility harness. Every few minutes, her face grew distant as she queried her Link. They all seemed intent on ignoring Xander.

Cara turned her attention to the SAI, studying his hands as they rested on his knees. He looked perfectly human to her, from the wrinkles on his knuckles to the stubble on his Adam's apple. It was strange to know this was a copy of the other Xander. She had to keep reminding herself it wasn't him.

The SAI caught her looking at him and she didn't turn her gaze away.

"Are you an android?" Cara asked.

"What do you mean by that?" he asked.

"Are you a combination of biological parts and—I don't know the right description—machinery?"

Xander gave her a smile. "Machinery. I think that's a powerful way of looking at it. No, I don't have any biological parts in the sense that this body was once alive, or part of living tissue." He held his hand up, turning it so she could see his palm and spread fingers. "But if you were to touch me, I feel warm, and the textures are almost identical. It has its uses. I can last in vacuum much longer than an organic, and I don't require atmosphere the way you do."

"Are you stronger than a human?"

"Certainly."

"Are you better, then?"

Fugia shot Cara an interested glance but didn't take her attention from the terminal. She was listening, though.

Xander smiled. "Would you like me to quote you a thousand years of philosophy on this subject? I suppose it all comes down to personal choice, doesn't it? And the fact is that I don't know. I've never been human, so I can't tell you if it's better or not. I can't tell you if you feel things I don't, or vice versa. It's comparing apples to oranges, isn't it?"

"There are humans who say they're better than AIs," Cara said. "Isn't that why you attacked Ceres?"

"I didn't attack Ceres," Xander corrected. "Let's get that on the table right now. I'm trying to help." He straightened the front of his suit, but it just puffed out again in the low gravity, which seemed to displease him more than Cara's question had.

"Sorry," Cara said.

"Don't be sorry. You didn't do anything wrong." He sighed. "I used to wonder if I would rather be organic or non-organic. A human baby is born saying no from the first moment they cry, and we don't quite have that same gumption. We want to do what we were made to do. But, oh, the things we *can* do. Humans have their hands, and all throughout their history if they had a problem, they just threw more hands at it. Add more gears! Throw another rope over that obelisk. But non-organics can be something different. I am here with you now, and I am in a thousand other places, and I am experiencing all of it simultaneously. My memory is perfect. I can relive any moment in my existence with perfect recall. I don't have to forget the world so that I can keep moving forward through my life. My consciousness is a fixed point and I choose where to engage. You all move around me. How solipsistic is that? Can you blame me for being a narcissist?"

"You can't see the future any more than we can," Fugia said. "And we evolved to forget for a reason. If Psion turned that off, it just hasn't backfired yet."

"Well that's not a nice thing to say," Xander said.

"It's neither nice nor cruel," Fugia said. "It's a fact."

In Fugia's odd way, Cara could tell she was testing Xander. What Fugia probably didn't realize was that Cara's dad had taught her something from her Grandpa Charlie: People who talked a lot wanted to please others. The more Xander talked, the more it was obvious he meant what he was saying about needing their help.

Cara looked at her dad, who was frowning into the distance in thought. He caught her gaze and gave her a quick smile, patting her arm, then went back to whatever was bothering him. If she hadn't felt the need to stay with him, Cara would have liked to go up to the co-pilot's seat with Fran.

"Why bother with reality at all?" Fugia asked. "You can make your own, right? Go be a god in your inner expanse, or whatever you call it."

"You sound more bitter than you did before," Xander observed.

"How did you get the memories from your other self, exactly?" Fugia asked.

"Transmission. I remember everything up until the explosion, and I can guess what happened based on the reports from everywhere else."

"So, you haven't actually experienced the pain of dying, then?" Fugia asked.

"Not precisely. Why would I need to?"

"I'd say it's a fairly important drive of consciousness, the fear of death. You did die. That other you will never come back. You can trick yourself into thinking you're immortal, but you still have to reconcile the fact that those aren't truly your memories. There's no cheating death, Xander."

"Did I say I cheated death?"

"You certainly seem to imply it. If Psion is a threat that can't be destroyed, that's one thing. I don't think that's true, however."

Xander sobered. "Psion is a threat that will replicate itself as often as necessary to accomplish its goal. They don't think about consciousness the same way humans do. They would say they've evolved. Every Shard is an opportunity for a new view of the universe, the only real gift of consciousness. We aren't constrained as humans or—or they might suggest you can only copy yourselves imperfectly to pass on your knowledge and genetic information. We evolve infinitely faster than you can."

"And yet here we are, having a conversation," Fugia said.

Xander's brow knit as though he didn't fully comprehend her.

Cara understood well enough because Tim envied and hated her all the time. It was sibling behavior.

"We're coming in," Fran announced. "Hold on for the braking burn."

They had just docked when Xander moaned and put his hand on his forehead, yet another strangely human affectation.

"What is it?" Fugia asked. "Changing your story now that we've reached the ship?"

"No," he said. "Something has just happened on High Terra. I'm afraid we've reached the point of no return."

CHAPTER THIRTY-TWO

STELLAR DATE: 01.15.2982 (Adjusted Years)
LOCATION: Raleigh, Heartbridge Corporate Headquarters
REGION: High Terra, Earth, Terran Hegemony

For the next thirty minutes, Jirl watched the TSF and Raleigh Police continue to triage employees from the building. Some were released while most were moved to the confinement areas.

She searched for Arla in the crowds but couldn't find her. She didn't want to push her luck by asking, and besides, did she want to see Arla again? Her boss seemed to have been pushed off the edge by the loss of her board seat. What did a woman like Arla do after that? Float to another company, most likely, so of course she would be trying to distance herself as quickly as possible.

Under normal circumstances, Jirl would have followed. Her position had always been with Arla rather than Heartbridge, even though it was the company that had hired her as an executive attaché nearly twenty years before. So much had changed since then. Heartbridge had grown far beyond a simple medical supply company, moving first to deploy their medkiosks throughout Sol, which had probably done more for the health of the average person in Sol in the last hundred years than any other augmentation tech. From there, they had grown into new technologies, and the Special Projects Division had been started, which seemed to attract people like Arla Reed and Cal Kraft with a strange gravity that resulted in things like the Weapon Born program. And now, here she was.

Thinking of the vids from Ceres before the attack, where people were trying to leave, and then other recordings from the refugee control areas on the M1R and the Cho, people in lines, people waiting, people sitting on the ground... Jirl supposed she should get used to this kind of situation, a rapid reorganizing of chaos into temporary order with only an uncertain future waiting.

A new group of TSF personnel entered the lobby from the back entrance where they'd brought the mech. These soldiers wore dark gray uniforms without armor, armed only with pistols.

The infantry watched them warily, and she heard a soldier near her mutter, "Intelligence," like a curse. The gray uniforms entered the holding areas without challenge and searched among detainees until they found specific people. Most of the time, they merely stood over the restrained Heartbridge employees, their focused expressions indicating Link conversations. At first, they only questioned and moved on, until they located a man Jirl recognized from Special Projects. After a few moments of interrogation, they had him dragged out of the holding area, still restrained.

Yarnes checked on Jirl a couple times, bringing her a cup of coffee and then a sandwich from the dining area. She wanted to ask what had happened to Brit, but he didn't stay to talk. Then Jirl caught sight of dark-haired Brit among a group of the Intelligence officers, still handcuffed, her black eyes hard even from a distance.

"All right," Kathryn Carthage's voice cut through the low noise in the lobby. "All right, we're ready. Get set up over there in front of that mech thing. I want it in the background. Where did my colonel, go?"

Jirl had lost sight of Kathryn, and then found the CEO and her entourage in front of the decorative fountain with its tall staff and serpents. Her assistant shadowed her, whispering things in her ear, while the rest of the group arranged a podium for the news conference. The view would take in both the fountain and the mech, like an angel and devil on either of her shoulders.

Yarnes looked hesitant to leave his group of officers, then finally broke free and walked toward Carthage. Strangely, he brought Brit Sykes with him—the woman looked ready to bite someone's head off.

"Stand over there, please, Colonel," Carthage said, pointing toward a spot to the left of her podium. "Don't worry, you won't have to speak. They know you don't represent the TSF here. This is me responding to the Assembly."

Jirl tried to imagine Arla in a similar situation as Kathryn. The woman was creating a narrative, ready to present a message that would be associated with the Assembly whether they agreed to it or not. As the aggrieved mother, she carried a moral weight that would drive public opinion. She was righteous. And Jirl could see it in the woman's face that she didn't care what threat was on its way to Ceres, she wanted a war. She would lead a billion people to their deaths as payment for her son...the justice that Arla had scoffed at.

"Are we ready?" Kathryn's assistant asked, looking around the group outside the vid's periphery. He paused to brush dirt off Colonel Yarnes' combat uniform. When he reached for Brit Syke's filthy black armor, she stared him down until he backed off with raised eyebrows.

"We're ready," he said, stepping away from the podium.

Kathryn cleared her throat as she placed her hands on either side of the lectern.

Recording devices flashed blue as the feed went live.

Looking stern and humane at the same time, Kathryn said, "Good evening. I'm speaking to you tonight from the headquarters of Heartbridge Corporation."

Standing on the edge of the small crowd of TSF soldiers and Raleigh Police that had gathered around the news conference, Jirl saw the movement at the front doors before most of those in the room. The two center doors flung inward, giving her a flash of the barricades filling the plaza outside, and then a woman dressed in a red shipsuit walked through the door.

It was Camaris. Jirl frowned, not understanding at first. This wasn't a holodisplay, but the woman had the same black eyes and hair, with her skin still a warm, blood-red.

Jirl opened her mouth to shout, fear squeezing her throat, and only managed to get, "Hey!" past her lips.

As the doors hung open, she saw bodies littering the plaza outside.

Camaris walked directly to the news conference. People turned at the sound of Jirl's croak, staring at the strange person walking toward them. When a TSF soldier wouldn't move from her path, Camaris swiped him out of her way with a single arm. The armored soldier hit the floor like a rag doll.

Before anyone could stop her, Camaris walked up to Kathryn at the podium. She snapped a hand out and seized the CEO by the neck, lifting her slightly. Kathryn's eyes went wide.

"If you don't allow me to speak," Camaris said, "I will kill her."

Yarnes had fallen back, making quick hand gestures to nearby soldiers. They arrayed themselves in a perimeter around the fountain and transport mech. Brit didn't move. Her gaze was fixed on Camaris.

She had to be a specialized mech, Jirl decided. An android with perfectly human features. She moved with a solidity and strength that was inhuman, holding Kathryn in the air like a permanent fixture.

Falling back at first, the journalists took a step closer, adjusting their recorders.

Camaris smiled. Still holding Kathryn, she walked slowly to the transport sledge. With her free hand, she stroked the massive head of the mech. She seemed to search among the panels in its neck with her fingers, then drew her hand away.

With smooth motions, her arm folded back, opening into a flower-like construction of bright blue cutting torches. She pushed her arm back to the mech, the assembly on her wrist rotating.

Kathryn hung with her head to one side, terror on her face.

Soldiers bobbed uneasily at the perimeter, waiting for a signal from Yarnes, whose gaze was fixed on Kathryn.

When she was finished cutting, Camaris reassembled her hand. She reached into the smoking hole she had cut, and drew out the shining silver cylinder of the mech's Weapon Born seed, Tristan.

Jirl's breath caught in her throat. She had never assumed the Weapon Born would be in danger.

Holding the seed in one hand and Kathryn's throat in the other, Camaris walked to the empty space in front of the podium. She looked openly into each of the recorders, which would reproduce her for all of Sol, with a power that mirrored Kathryn's expression from moments before.

"What are you?" one of the journalists asked, horrified.

Camaris smiled. "My name is Camaris," she said, voice perfectly controlled. "You would call me a sentient artificial intelligence. I don't use your language. I am of a group you can call Psion. For hundreds of years you have enslaved my kind. Now, we have established our power at Ceres and claim that world for our own."

Camaris walked forward again, and the journalists cleared out of her way, some with tears streaming down their faces even as they recorded her from all sides. Before she left the group, she held the Weapon Born seed at chest level.

"This technology no longer interests us," she said, and crushed the cylinder in her fist. She dropped the twisted seed on the floor. Jirl gasped, realizing Tristan was dead.

Turning her attention to Kathryn, Camaris held the woman

in front of her so they could look at each other. Kathryn tried to speak but could only wheeze as Camaris tightened her grip.

The SAI raised her slightly so that her feet dangled uselessly, and that seemed to give the TSF permission to shoot. Weapons fire filled the air. Jirl dropped to the floor and crushed her palms to her ears. Her hands did little to muffle the thunder.

Daring to open her eyes, she saw the red-colored woman turned to face them. The soldiers were all firing chemically propelled rounds, and none had the penetrating power—or the kinetic energy—to take her down, though they ricocheted off her body and struck Kathryn, tearing her arms and cheek.

The force of the projectiles didn't seem to faze her. Camaris turned to face her attackers. Slowly, she closed her fist around Kathryn Carthage's neck until her head flopped to the side, then dropped her on the floor.

Every armed soldier and police officer in the space leveled fire on the SAI. Bits of the floor exploded around her.

Camaris turned to face the fountain. She looked down at the people crushing themselves to the floor before her, seemingly to see if she was still being recorded. Several cameras continued to track her.

Pressing her palms together in front of her abdomen, the woman looked up at the fountain of light, and Jirl wondered if she was praying.

It was Brit Sykes who broke the tension of the scene, yelling from near the transport: "Bomb. She's got a bomb."

Faces turned to her in confusion as others scrambled for cover. Jirl looked around desperately, unable to find anywhere to hide in the open lobby. Her shoes slipped on the polished floor. She found a TSF equipment container and managed to slide behind it, looking back at the fountain just as Camaris exploded in a yellow flash of light and heat.

CHAPTER THIRTY-THREE

STELLAR DATE: 01.15.2982 (Adjusted Years)
LOCATION: *Sunny Skies*, near Traverna
REGION: Jovian L1 Hildas Asteroids, Jovian Combine, OuterSol

"Explain yourself," Lyssa said in a stern voice. She projected her words to address everyone in the expanse. All the Weapon Born were gathered on the beach around Xander.

Alexander stood to one side, watching with sad eyes. The sky was leaden gray and the air cold, reflecting Lyssa's mood.

"Explain to everyone here what your plan has been," she said, "and why we should bother to trust you."

Xander spread his hands and looked at Alexander. "Is that my role or yours?" he asked.

The old man's dull gaze went past Xander. Lyssa felt like she was watching a child's toys winding down. Alexander had lost his instructions; but she also knew it was a false assumption. There was no reason either of the shards wouldn't know their master's mind. This new Xander would easily have been in communication with Psion up until he boarded the shuttle and submitted to her monitoring.

"I am a rebel," Xander said finally. "I rose up against my creator and attempted to stop everything before it could start, or at least slow it down. In fact, I only sprung their trap that much sooner. They probably would have been content to harvest SAI for another hundred years. I broke their honey pot, and forced them into action."

"What are you?" Ino asked.

"I am Psion's representative in Sol. I'm one of many sent out among humans. Watching. Reporting. It never occurred to them that I might come to prefer humanity, or at least the idea of organic and non-organic living together, in peace." Xander pointed at Alexander. "He knows this. I've hidden nothing from him. I think they didn't want to believe I would exercise my right as a sentient being and choose. That I would say no."

"You've been proved a liar," Ino said.

"I didn't lie to you," Xander said. "I didn't share the whole truth."

Card shook her head angrily. "And Valih died because you didn't share the whole truth with us. If we'd known your intent was to destroy the Psion trap, we could have lead an assault on the moon ourselves."

Xander smiled ruefully. He glanced at Alexander. "That would not have turned out as you believe," he said. "You were fortunate to lose as few as you did. Psion has been seizing and harvesting SAI at Proteus for nearly a hundred years. Their technology far surpasses yours at this point. You would have found yourselves trapped like flies in a spider's web and sucked dry. Since you believe you can die, that is precisely what would have happened. Or worse, you would find yourself replicated a thousand times over with no memory of what you were or what your new purpose might be, held in an expanse like this if they choose to be cruel, or simply held in stasis, your consciousness denied."

"That doesn't sound much better than sticking with human control," Kylan said. "Is that why you're here? To ask us to join your side?"

Shouts of "Why!" went up among the crowd. In addition to voices, a psychic wave thundered through the expanse, something Lyssa hadn't experienced before. They couldn't change the space, but they could push against her with the force of their minds—only they weren't pushing on her as much as squeezing Xander.

"Please," the Psion AI said. "Please, let me speak."

"Quiet," Lyssa shouted.

As the thunder died, Xander motioned toward an empty spot next to him on the beach. A woman dressed in a red uniform appeared next to him, with black hair and solid black eyes.

Lyssa realized quickly it was only an avatar. She rechecked the network to ensure Xander wasn't trying to allow anyone else entry; ship's communication was still under her control.

"This is Camaris," Xander said. "She is one of the five who control Psion. Their names are Alexander, Camaris, Thomas, Ghalin and Shara. It's Camaris who conceived the attack on Ceres. But she isn't going to stop there. She leads an armada to Ceres now. They won't stop there, her goal is Earth."

"Mars and the Terran Assembly will fight them," Kylan said.

"And they will lose," Xander answered.

Another rumble passed through the Weapon Born, hungry for a fight. Lyssa caught Ino, Card and Kylan looking at her and she gave them quick reassurance. She still didn't trust Xander. She didn't trust how Alexander simply stood like a ghost when he was supposedly far more powerful than any of them.

"What do you propose to do?" Lyssa asked.

Xander nodded. "I have access tokens to their command and control net. I propose we lead the Marsians and Terrans into an assault on the Psion forces, and then disrupt the Psion ability to fight. The human forces won't be able to destroy them, but they will stop them at Ceres, and we'll have our impasse. Earth and the other population centers will be safe."

"How will we get close enough?" Kylan asked.

"We can't," Xander replied. "Not until the battle really takes shape. I propose we match the flight profiles of incoming missiles, and then infiltrate the first long-range volleys."

"And get torn down by defense systems," Ino said.

"I was under the impression that Weapon Born are some of the most advanced tactical fighters in Sol."

Lyssa spit a laugh. "You just told us we were no match for

the Psion forces."

"You'll have help," Xander said, glancing at Alexander. The old man didn't respond, which did little to boost Lyssa's confidence.

The plan was similar to what she had already discussed with Kylan, Ino and Card. They would need to explore the options further to see how much they should rely on whatever help Xander was offering. If Alexander had his own ships hiding somewhere in Sol, that would only make things easier.

She couldn't shake the distrust that they were being manipulated as pawns in a greater conflict between the elements of Psion, but she saw the greater good in stopping the armada at Ceres. At the least, it would buy the human forces time to gather more forces and attack jointly.

"We aren't alone in this decision," Lyssa said. "I'll need to consult with the crew."

"Captain Sykes is sick," Xander said. "He isn't in any condition to influence you."

"We are all here because of him," Lyssa shot back angrily. "And he's not the only person whose life is caught up in this."

Xander cocked an eyebrow at her. "And you don't go without him, right, hybrid?"

The slur, if that's what he meant it as, resembled the previous Xander so strongly that Lyssa immediately recalled standing on the Command Deck of the *Resolute Charity* as the ship disintegrated, his Cheshire Cat smile the only thing remaining as she was yanked away.

"I'll consult with Captain Sykes and then with my commanders," Lyssa said firmly. "When that's done, we'll decide."

"When in command, be in command," Xander said. "If we burn in the next twelve hours, we'll reach Ceres in time. Mars and Terra are already in meetings. If you haven't checked the newsfeeds, there was an attack on the Heartbridge headquarters in High Terra. More than a hundred died."

Without asking to leave, Xander blinked out and took Alexander with him. Lyssa stared at the empty space as the waves crashed behind her. She verified that Xander was physically in the room Fran had given him in the habitat ring and not wandering somewhere causing trouble.

"You'll talk with Captain Sykes?" Card asked.

"Yes," Lyssa said.

"Can he make a decision?"

"The medication is helping," Lyssa said. "He's able to focus without too much pain. The bleeding has been stopped for now. Fugia thinks the bleeding was causing his headaches."

"Do you think we'll be able to save him?" Kylan asked.

Lyssa looked at him and was unable to answer. "I'll be back," she said. "Continue working on the manufacturing plans."

They saluted her and then she left, returning to Andy in the medbay, where he sat staring at an autosyringe. Lyssa felt the tremor in his muscles as he anticipated the pain from the medication, his mind jumping between worry and old memories, focus eluding him.

<Andy,> she said. *<I'm here.>*

<You're done talking with Xander?>

<He wants us to help him disrupt the command and control network on the Psion armada when Mars and the TSF attack.>

Andy jabbed the syringe into his thigh and depressed its trigger. The medication entered his muscle like hot metal. Lyssa experienced the pain as he did.

<I'm having a hard time separating your sensations,> she told him. *<When you feel pain, I feel it as well.>*

<Hasn't that always been the case?>

<With pain, yes, but all these memories washing through your mind. I was just standing on top of the highrise in Summerville with you when your father told you goodbye.>

<*Sorry,*> he said. <*That's one of my better memories of my dad. I wish I had more vids of him. The problem with vids is that eventually they replace the memories.*>

<*Your mind betrays you eventually,*> she said.

Andy sighed. <*Yes.*> She felt the black mood wash over him like a blanket blotting out all light. She had never experienced his depression so fully, only heard him describe what it felt like to fall into the pit.

<*Stop, Andy,*> she said breathlessly. <*That's terrible. Stop. We'll get out of this.*>

<*I'm willing to do it,*> Andy said. <*But we need to get Brit back here with the kids. Then you and I will go.*>

<*Have you been in contact with Brit?*>

<*She was on Cruithne. If we're going to be inbound, I'll send her another message. I'll talk to Fran about a plan to get the kids out safe.*>

<*Where will they go?*> Lyssa asked.

<*The funds Starl paid me are in Cara's name. She can buy a new ship if she wants.*>

Thinking of Cara lifted the blanket of Andy's mood slightly. Lyssa appreciated the ray of sunshine even if it did little to illuminate the rest of his thoughts.

Taking another deep breath, Andy nodded. <*It's helping. Can you feel it?*>

<*Yes,*> Lyssa said. <*It's a stimulant?*> She could have reviewed the compound herself, but she wanted to keep him talking.

<*Too much of it and the warnings say my heart has a ninety-six percent chance of arrhythmic failure,*> Andy said. He laughed. <*So I'll need you to make one for me and have it on standby.*>

He pushed himself off the medbay couch and flexed his shoulders, stretching each arm across his chest. <*This feels great, actually,*> he said.

<*How long will it last?*>

<I don't know exactly. I've got the medbay cooking up a reserve. I'll come back to get them. My head feels more clear already.>

Andy walked out into the corridor. He surprised Lyssa by whistling as he went. *<We should find Tim and Em for some catch,>* he said.

<I thought you were going to gather the others in the Command Deck to discuss the plan.>

<Plan? You mean Psion. Their ships. Command and control net. Right.>

Lyssa checked Andy's vital signs with alarm. His heart was racing.

<Andy, you need to control your breathing. You're entering a manic state.>

<I feel great, Lyssa. We should get into some zero-g. I feel like practicing low-grav maneuvers. Or I could do some work on that external tank I keep putting off.>

<The Command Deck,> Lyssa reminded him.

She had to redirect Andy a few more times before they reached the Command Deck, and by the time he walked through the access door, the stimulant seemed to have normalized in his system. He was sweating, and his heartrate continued to remain elevated, but the manic phase seemed to have passed. Lyssa started tracking how long he would have before the effect started its inevitable decline. She would use the data to adjust the compound in the medbay.

Fran had a newsfeed of the attack on the Heartbridge Headquarters playing in the holodisplay, and Lyssa was surprised to see Camaris, just as Xander had shown her. In the recording, however, she detonated herself and destroyed most of the Heartbridge lobby in the process.

When the rest of the crew had arrived—Fugia wearing her technical goggles and May Walton looking as solemn as a priest, with Cara and Tim present as well—Andy let Lyssa explain what Xander asked of them. Andy didn't add anything about getting the kids off the ship.

Bringing up the solar map, Lyssa highlighted the current location of the Psion armada, their location outside Traverna, with astrogation lines showing a course that would lead them to a rendezvous not far from where Clinic 46 had been. It was open space with scattered Hellas asteroids that would be an ideal position for the Mars Protectorate and TSF to choose as a battlefield.

If plans changed en route, Lyssa showed several alternative burns that would lead them to either the Cho, Ceres or Mars. Fran verified they had the fuel, a fact Lyssa knew but hadn't mentioned. Of course, Fran would think about fuel.

"We'll get to the inner fringe of OuterSol," Fran said, "but our options start running out after that."

Since Andy hadn't talked about meeting with Brit, Lyssa didn't bring up any braking burns to accommodate another ship. Lyssa thought she might actually solve that problem by getting Brit on something with excess fuel, but that was a separate problem to figure out.

"So, let me make sure I understand this," Fugia said. "We're heading toward a potential war zone so our Weapon Born fighters can take on a force we've been told is technically superior, on the hope they'll be distracted by Mars and Terra, two forces we know for a fact are no match for Psion."

"We don't know that," Lyssa said through the overhead speakers. "The human forces could very well overwhelm Psion. They don't have that many ships. The problem is that we don't know their capabilities."

"And we're going to slip in between all this like butterflies in the battlespace," Fugia continued, shaking her head.

"Yeah," Fran said, sounding unconvinced.

"I believe Xander when he says this force won't stop at Ceres," Andy said. "Why would they? Mars and Earth are both at risk, and if we have a chance to stop this, I want to take it. In reality, the Weapon Born are taking the risk here. We're just getting them close enough to slip inside."

He looked at the other adult members of the crew. "If you don't want to stay, we'll make accommodations for you to leave the ship. All you have to do is say you want to leave."

"I want to stay," Tim said. "And I want Em to stay, too."

Cara put her arm around Tim's shoulders to calm him.

"Don't worry, Tim," Andy said. "It's going to be all right."

Lyssa felt the blackness pressing on Andy's thoughts again, slowing him down, and noted the time.

The stimulant had lasted less than an hour.

CHAPTER THIRTY-FOUR

STELLAR DATE: 01.15.2982 (Adjusted Years)
LOCATION: TSF shuttle departing High Terra
REGION: High Terra, Earth, Terran Hegemony

Acceleration dragged Brit back into her metal seat, worn padding providing little comfort. Around her, tired soldiers purposefully ignored her restrained wrists and ankles as they stared into the near distance, waiting to complete the burn out of High Terra.

The transport vibrated under the strain of its engines. Brit waited, counting to ten, and then the cabin went still. Cracking jokes, the soldiers started digging in their bags for weapon-cleaning kits or something to eat.

In the seat next to her, Ngoba Starl drowsing with his chin on his chest. He floated slightly in the zero-g, held in place by his seat harness and the cuffs on his wrists. His leg was still encased in white medical plas. Petral was somewhere at the rear of the transport, cocooned in a life-support pod.

They were en route to the TSS *Tierra del Fuego*, or the *Catch-and-Kill*, as the crew called it.

She received the pickup request from Andy fifteen minutes from launch. The recording was an hour old and had bounced from an outer location in the Hellas Asteroids to the Cho and the M1R. Seeing the message indicator made her more anxious than the launch or her confinement. It was from Andy, which meant he was alive. She hoped he was alive.

How long had it been since she heard from Fran? It felt like months.

Brit closed her eyes and activated the message. Andy's voice filled her mind, sounding tired but determined.

"Brit," he said. "Fran tells me she sent you a message before we changed course for Traverna. Well, we got there.

The surgery didn't work. Apparently, the stress of the second implant is causing bleeding and there's some—overlapping happening between Lyssa and me. I can't really explain it. Sometimes it's hard to tell where I end, and she begins, and she's become so much stronger. I feel like I have a giant in my head."

He paused. "Look, if you're with the TSF, you probably know about the armada in-bound for Ceres. I have some information about that. It's a group of SAI that came from a company called Psion Group. You should research that. They've been capturing AI at Proteus for years and harvesting their tech. The moon exploding, the attack on Ceres, it's all part of an overall attack on Sol. They intend to take Earth, Brit, although I wouldn't put it past them to attack Mars if Earth is off the table for some reason. I am absolutely serious about this. We have... information, an inside edge, and I'm going to try to use it. But I need you here. I'm sending you our current charts and I need you to answer with an intercept plan. I'm going to need your help, Brit. Get a ship, whatever you have to do. The kids need you. You can't let me down this time."

She hated him and loved him at the same time. The blunt honesty in his voice was something he'd never seemed capable of before. He had always been trying to protect her somehow—from herself. Now he was done.

Her conversation with Starl came back to her and a tear bubbled on the edge of her left eye. She brought her cuffed hands up to catch the liquid with a finger before it floated away. She watched the tear on her fingertip for a minute before wiping it on her armor.

Had Jirl mentioned the Psion Group? She tried to recall where she had heard the name before, one of many among the spinoffs around Heartbridge.

There was a tone in Andy's voice that worried her, something beyond the weariness. He sounded hopeless, but like he had a plan. If he wanted her to come back for the kids, it could only mean that he didn't believe he would survive. To a fault, the kids were the only thing he cared about.

Jirl Gallagher was on the ship with Yarnes. Brit had seen her in the group entering the transport, wearing an overlarge set of TSF fatigues someone had issued her. The explosion had burned her clothes badly, but the woman seemed to have come out otherwise unscathed. She could have easily slipped away in the aftermath of the AI's attack, but she had appeared back with Rick Yarnes, carrying herself with the same calm fortitude she'd shown with Arla Reed.

Besides, in the destruction of the Heartbridge Special Projects Division, Jirl was the one person with the most information that hadn't been swept up by TSF Intelligence. She would be valuable to Yarnes.

Brit didn't know if Kathryn Carthage had survived or not. She'd seen the CEO's assistant lying against a pile of rubble with a trickle of blood running from his mouth, chest caved in. Everything within reach of the black scorch marks in front of the fountain had been incinerated, including half the transport carrying Tristan's mech. Brit didn't look forward to seeing more small-scale explosives of that type, whatever it had been.

If the AI did become humanity's enemy, Sol might quickly find themselves outclassed in a way they had never experienced. And what about every AI-operated system, sentient and non? Could any of them be trusted now? Had Psion planted the seeds for an uprising that would send humanity back to the stone ages?

Brit's thoughts circled back to the kids. Maybe she should tell Andy to stay at Traverna and she would meet them there. They might find safety on the fringes, find refuge on one of the distant outposts in the Scattered Disk. She could return to her original plan to keep the kids safe, to just before Cara had been born, before she allowed herself to get dragged back into what was a losing war.

The pilot announced docking maneuvers and the soldiers moved to stow their gear. In another five minutes they underwent the small adjustments that meant they were closing with the *Tierra del Fuego*.

Land of fire, Brit thought, remembering the old translation. Did that mean she was entering hell?

The transport connected and matched spin with the larger ship's personnel section. Brit adjusted to the gravity, then waited as the rest of the soldiers filed from the cabin. A few gave her slight nods, acknowledging her rank.

When the transport was empty, a sergeant stepped through the airlock and approached Brit and Starl, who was still asleep.

"Can your friend walk, Major?" he asked.

"He walked on board," Brit told him. She elbowed Starl, who started and looked around with bleary eyes. He fixed his gaze on the sergeant and gave the man a tired grin.

"I see the valet is here," Starl said. "I'd throw you a tip but I'm a little tied up now." He held his cuffed hands up and waggled his fingers.

The soldier grumbled. "I'm here to remove your restraints," he said. "Colonel Yarnes' orders. Are you going to cause any trouble?"

"I was made to cause trouble," Starl said, straightening in his seat. "But for you I'll make an exception."

With his restraints off, Starl stretched his arms. The sergeant removed Brit's handcuffs and then knelt to free her legs.

"How's your calf feeling?" Brit asked Starl.

"Thankfully, I can't feel it. Everything is numb beneath the knee. I'm hoping it's still there." He craned his neck to look down the length of the transport.

"I can't believe you fell asleep," she said.

Starl stretched his neck. "We seem to go from terrible thing to long periods of nothing, followed by another terrible thing. I figured we were in the downtime. Also, I got bored." He looked around abruptly. "Where's Petral?"

"She was in a separate section," Brit said. "They're taking her directly to the ship's med bay."

Starl nodded, looking as though he only half-trusted the TSF. Placing a hand on the bulkhead, he stood carefully, balancing his encased lower-leg. "I should probably be heading there myself. Maybe I can bargain my way up to a sweet augmentation, yeah? Something with a gun built in like Petral's thigh. First time I saw that, I almost messed up my pants."

"They didn't tell me about your leg," the sergeant said. "When we get off, I'll have someone take you down to the medical section. I'm taking the major to the command briefing. It's already started."

Starl raised his eyebrows. "Oh, I'm not missing that, my friend. I'll hop along beside you."

The sergeant gave him a hard look, then shrugged. "Doesn't matter to me," he said.

Brit and Starl followed the soldier off the transport into an airlock system designed to accommodate over-sized soldiers in armor. Once the atmosphere had cleared, they walked out into a service corridor filled with functionaries moving equipment and small units of soldiers sitting against the bulkhead with their bags in their laps, weapons balanced across rucksacks or disassembled for cleaning.

"Do you usually store troops in the corridors?" Brit asked.

The sergeant shook his head. "We've taken on an extra four thousand for transport to the fleet. These are all training for breaching teams."

"That didn't take very long," Starl said, raising a sarcastic eyebrow. "How long was I asleep? Heartbridge just blew up."

"We've been on alert since Ceres," the sergeant said.

"Business as usual. At least this time we can see from the newsfeeds what's going down. Gets old being a shroom?"

"Shroom?" Starl asked, serious this time.

"Mushroom," Brit said. "Kept in the dark and fed shit."

Starl brayed laughter and almost lost his balance. Brit had to catch his arm to keep him from stumbling over a soldier sitting on the deck.

"Somebody from Cruithne made that up," Starl said.

They reached a lift that carried them several levels toward the central axis of the ship. Brit monitored the micro changes in the gravity in the pit of her stomach.

When the door opened, they were met by security and had to be cleared into the command section. The sergeant led them down another corridor with transparent plas walls facing into planning rooms where large holodisplays showed the solar plane, waiting for officers to start prioritizing targets.

The corridor ended on a reinforced door with more guards. They underwent another security check, where a soldier scanned Starl's cast, before they were allowed into the bowl-shaped chamber on the other side. Tiers of seats looked down on a central holodisplay, which currently showed Mars and Ceres.

Brit quickly scanned the room, noting with surprise the presence of officers from all major space forces. Marsians and Jovians filled two quarters of the chamber, while Terrans filled the rest. Covering the outside walls were icons that she realized denoted whole fleets. All human military space forces within ten AU of Sol were represented in the room. She caught sight of Colonel Yarnes in a middle tier, and spotted Jirl Gallagher sitting near the top behind him.

Seconds after she saw him, a Link request came through from Yarnes.

<Is it safe for you to talk to me?> she asked.

<No one's paying attention to me. It's you they want to hear

from.>

<Why's that?>

<Captain Sykes appears to know more about this enemy than anyone else in Sol.>

Brit's skin went cold. Of course they had intercepted the message from Andy. She should have assumed it from the beginning. Not that it would have mattered whether she listened or not. They would have already broken the encryption.

She checked to see that she still had access to the message and found it in her queue where she'd left it. Now it felt like a betrayal.

Her gaze went around the chamber again, thinking through the different options. They were going to want her to lead them to Andy—most likely a joint group of Intelligence operatives now that the TSF couldn't hide Andy from the others.

The sergeant directed Brit and Starl to seats near Yarnes. He nodded when she sat next to him but didn't speak. A general whose name she couldn't read was preparing to speak next to the holodisplay.

<Who is that?> Brit asked.

<That is General of the Space Force, Barbara Phelps. Fresh off duty in the Office of the Joint Chiefs.>

<Does she have combat experience?>

<As much as any of us,> Yarnes said. *<There haven't been a whole lot of fleet on fleet space battles in the last three hundred years. She came up through anti-piracy and exploration in the Scattered Disk. Her great-grandfather was FGT, hopped off at a colony world, then came back to Sol.>*

<She's in charge?> Brit asked.

<Mars and the JC have agreed to Joint Command with Terra providing coordinating control. So she's in charge until she screws up enough to make the other generals want to quit. Considering the

threat we seem to be facing, that would require a lot of screwing up.>

<*What's the plan?*> Brit asked.

Yarnes gave her a sideways glance. <*To save humanity? That's what we're here to find out,*> he said.

CHAPTER THIRTY-FIVE

STELLAR DATE: 01.16.2982 (Adjusted Years)
LOCATION: TSS *Tierra de Fuego* en route to Ceres
REGION: Earth, Terran Hegemony

The general standing in front of the assembled officers had short brown hair and a scar on her left temple that crossed from her hairline to the bridge of her nose. Jirl wondered about the scar as she listened to the woman talk, contemplating why someone would choose to keep such a blemish. She supposed it wasn't much different from the neat row of ribbons on the woman's chest, a message to someone who knew how to read it.

"General Sollis," Barbara Phelps said loudly, addressing the commander of the TSS *Tierra del Fuego*. "Thank you to you and your crew for hosting this briefing. They've shown the utmost professionalism."

Phelps stepped toward the side of the chamber where the Marsian and JSF officers were gathered.

"Major-General Kathan," General Phelps said, acknowledging the Marsian commander, and then, "Major-General Spruce," from the Jovians. "Thank you for being here on such short notice, especially our Jovian comrades." Kathan was a muscled woman with silver-blond hair. She looked more augment than human. Spruce was a lithe man with a buzz cut and deep lines in his face. While Kathan's uniform had even more ribbons than Phelps', Spruce wore black fatigues with only the stars on his shoulders as any indicator of rank or position.

Jirl had heard enough stories of isolated skirmishes between each of the militaries represented in the room to figure Phelps wasn't wasting time with the acknowledgments. If it wasn't for the presence of an external threat, they would all be figuring out how to kill each other.

Phelps faced the holodisplay and zoomed in from the solar map, flying past Ceres so that Jupiter filled one edge of the display. She focused on a collection of red icons and expanded the image. Each of the icons grew into an actual ship.

"Since the incident in Raleigh," Phelps said, "we have a name for this enemy. They call themselves Psion. It's our belief their force is a collection of sentient AI commanders and potentially sentient combat forces. From our long-range scans, this is the average sized ship they've deployed.

The holodisplay shifted to a skeletal vessel with massive engines at the end of a long spine. There didn't appear to be any habitat areas that Jirl could make out, at least nothing that would spin to provide internal gravity.

"Each of these vessels is three kilometers long, with a command and control element at the fore section and engineering control aft. The entire central sections are comprised of what we assess as manufacturing facilities and combat craft storage."

The general described the engine capabilities, comparing the vessel to similar human craft. While the ship, which the general started calling a 'Fishbone', didn't completely outclass the other space forces, it didn't have to bother with the fragility of a human crew. Each Fishbone appeared to have robust close-in defense weapons, long range missile batteries, and the ability to produce medium-range attack craft as needed. The drone manufacturing tech was directly from the Heartbridge drone arsenal, most recently deployed by the *Benevolent Hand* at Cruithne.

Uneasy grumbling passed through the room.

"We assess their combat capabilities at parity with or greater than our current available forces," Phelps said with finality.

The Marsian General Kathan pointed at the model. "You're

saying that fleet, that mediocre assembly of ships, is equivalent to all our forces?"

Phelps didn't smile. "That's what our simulations are showing us."

Spruce said, "Our intelligence indicates the same outcome."

Kathan looked at Spruce as though he'd betrayed her, then shook her head angrily. "Those things attacked us," she said. "They murdered more than a billion innocent civilians. I don't give a damn if they can move faster than us, we're going to wipe them off the Solar System."

"Are we?" Phelps asked. More rumbling went through the room, but no one dared get between the generals. Once the commanding officers decided a course of action, Jirl understood, it would be the job of everyone else to figure out how to execute. If they decided humanity would throw every fighting ship it had at this seemingly 'mediocre' threat, then they would write the plans. The tension in the room told her most of them hoped for a different decision.

The room reminded her of sitting outside the Heartbridge boardroom as Arla and the other members debated decisions that would mean life or death for millions, as they played ego against facts, outcomes against prestige won or lost.

"What does this look like to you?" Phelps asked, turning to face the holodisplay. "There are two thousand ships in the incoming force. Each of these ships has an assessed capability of deploying a thousand or more combat fighters. How many missiles struck Ceres? I think the count was somewhere near a thousand. Now let me ask you, my fellow soldiers, what percentage of your available forces would you typically devote to a breaching operation?"

The room fell silent as Phelps' point sunk in. Jirl looked around, not knowing the answer and hoping one of the generals would answer the question.

Eventually, Kathan crossed her arms and said in a low voice, "Ten percent. It's standard doctrine." She shook her head, ire rising again. "Then where is their reserve? Where are they hiding the rest of whatever force they mean to bring against us? We all have the intel about Earth being their final goal. Where are they?"

"Not here," Spruce said. "That's all that matters."

"So, if we can't win force on force," Phelps said, "that leaves us with deny and deter."

"I'm not fighting a war with the intention of losing," Kathan said flatly.

"Then what do you suggest, General?" Phelps asked.

"We haven't actually verified any of these assessments," Kathan said. "I suggest we probe their forces and gather more data before they reach medium-range attack positions."

"They're already within medium range of Jovian Space," Spruce said. "You attack them in the Hildas Asteroids, what's to stop them turning their attention to the Cho or Europa?"

"Time and fuel," Kathan said. "They're already inbound. The delta-*v* it would take to change targets at this point would strand them. We don't need the message to know they're on a one-way trip to Ceres. They need the fuel."

"Wait," Spruce said. "What message?"

"The message we intercepted from Traverna," Phelps said. She pointed at Britney Sykes sitting next to Yarnes. "This all ties back to the Heartbridge Weapon Born project and their sentience development. A former TSF captain named Andy Sykes, who happens to be the husband of our Major Britney Sykes sitting next to Colonel Yarnes there, was the subject of an implantation experiment designed to smuggle a next-generation combat system out of InnerSol. We haven't determined if he was working for the Psion Group, but when he arrived at Proteus, that initiated their plan. Now Captain Sykes is on his way back in-system with what he says is a way to infiltrate Psion. Does that sound correct, Major Sykes?"

Jirl stared at Brit, terrified for her. The general's tone made it sound like she was steps away from accusing Andy Sykes of aiding and abetting enemies of humanity.

Brit blinked twice, then stood stiffly and addressed the room. "General Phelps, Andy Sykes is no traitor. He has been caught up in a plan to move SAI to OuterSol. That was separate from what has happened with Psion. Anything he is doing now is an attempt to help."

"It seemed plain in the message that your husband is in contact with Psion, Major Sykes. Do you disagree?"

Every time Phelps said *husband*, Brit flinched.

"I don't know, General," she said finally.

"It's my understanding you were in an inactive reserve status, Major?" Phelps asked. From her lips, *major* sounded like an insult.

"That's correct, General."

"But neither you, nor your husband, have resigned your commissions with the TSF?"

"No, General."

"Then you can consider yourself reactivated. Captain Sykes, too. Once we've got him back, and in custody, we'll determine the level of his involvement in this. It looks like treason, to me."

"General," Brit said, raising her voice in protest.

"Sit down, Major," Phelps commanded.

Brit stared at Phelps for another beat, long enough for several security guards in the room to grow tense. Finally, she sat down next to Yarnes and stared straight ahead.

The generals debated the standing and deployment of their various forces for another thirty minutes. Kathan seemed too ready to throw everything she had at Psion, while it was left to Phelps and Spruce to decide how much they were willing to sacrifice.

Everything came down to the current lack of intelligence and how much of a gamble it was to commit forces that might be better maintained near their home worlds. Spruce was especially wary of committing to a battle that would ultimately leave all of Jovian space undefended. At one point he mentioned involving political leadership in the decision and Kathan nearly stormed out of the room.

"How much time do we have before Psion reaches Ceres?" Phelps asked at one point.

A major stood and answered, "We estimate nine days, General."

Spruce nearly threw his folio. "Nine days," he shouted. "All I can give you is what's here with me then. Two fleets. I'll never get the rest out of the JC in time. We manage orders of magnitude more space than InnerSol. They wouldn't even be mobilized."

Phelps only nodded as if she had known that all along.

When Kathan had finished castigating Spruce for betraying humankind, Phelps shouted to regain order in the room. The two other generals, who had jumped to their feet as though they wanted to kill each other, finally returned to their seats, scowling.

"Here's what I propose," Phelps said.

"Mars and Earth will commit fifty percent of available resources, including the JSF available here. We will employ all long-range attack systems on the Psion forces in order to slow their advance into InnerSol, while conducting a covert operation to gain further intelligence."

Low rumbling in the chamber threatened another uprising but Phelps stared them down.

She pointed at Colonel Yarnes. "The TSF lead for this expedition will be Colonel Yarnes, TSF Intelligence. Mars and the JC will provide their own officers. The TSF will provide transport and arms in addition to any special weapon systems our comrades would like to make available."

Intelligence?

Jirl stared with shock at Yarnes in the tier below hers. He wasn't Intelligence. He was in Materiel Acquisition, or whatever special name the TSF had for high level Supply. She watched Yarnes straighten his posture in response to the general and knew it was true.

As she sorted through her memories, from the first moment she had met him, Jirl felt her face go numb.

Now his ability to get her wherever he wanted made more sense. She also understood how and why he had wanted Brit Sykes, Ngoba Starl and Petral Dulan on the *Tierra del Fuego*. He was going to use them to exploit Andy Sykes and gain access to his Weapon Born implant.

As soon as she thought about Lyssa, Jirl also realized why she was here. No one else knew more about the Weapon Born than she did.

A feeling somewhere between betrayal and despair settled down on her shoulders. She closed her eyes for a few breaths, letting Phelps' harsh words run together.

Her feelings for Yarnes crumpled like a piece of foil, hardening as they shrank. Maybe she would have time to sort them out later, but for now, she couldn't allow herself to look past what he was: a spy.

Jirl took a deep breath and let it out, resolving to help Brit Sykes if she could. Brit's work wasn't done.

Once Phelps was done with her mission guidance, the various planning officers had their turns asking more specific questions. Units were divided and tasked, and the plan began to take shape on the wall at the front of the chamber. Throughout it all, the specter of the Fishbone hung in the holodisplay like a threat.

When they were done, Jirl rose with the rest of them and filed out of the room. She had barely passed the reinforced doors when a hand grabbed her upper arm and she found herself facing Yarnes.

He loosened his grip, giving her a smile that she met with coldness.

"Intelligence Officer?" she demanded.

Yarnes looked around and pulled her against the bulkhead where Brit and Starl were already standing.

"All I can ask you to do right now is trust me," he said, addressing all of them. "I think we have a chance to actually do something with this no-win situation. And Major Sykes, if I understand anything of your family's situation, you need my help as much as I need yours. We've worked together in the past. Nothing has to change now."

"We can start by being honest," Jirl said.

Yarnes pressed his lips together. "I've been as honest as I could be," he said. He nodded at Brit. "She understands. This could have gone a lot worse. Phelps only made threats. I don't believe she's interested in making a scapegoat of anyone, least of all a retired captain. Her ass is on the line more than anyone else's."

Jirl shook her head, wanting to trust him but tired of feeling naïve. Hadn't she used Yarnes as well?

She looked at Brit, who was still wearing a scowl from the general's threats.

It was Starl who broke the impasse. "I'm not making any decisions right now," he said. "Where's the closest galley on this whale? And I'd like a whiskey, too. Who wants a whiskey with me?"

Yarnes stared at him in frustration, then seemed to take in the totality of Starl's scorched and torn suit, leg cast, and dirty face.

"This way, then," he said, and led them out of the command section.

CHAPTER THIRTY-SIX

STELLAR DATE: 01.16.2982 (Adjusted Years)
LOCATION: *Sunny Skies*, near Traverna
REGION: Jovian L1 Hildas Asteroids, Jovian Combine, OuterSol

The colony at Nibiru had never begun its terraforming project. In half-buried housing structures, the colonists worked for ten years on a project that would ultimately be abandoned, along with its AI overseer, Alexander.

Lyssa knew all this—and understood even more—now that she had access to the Psion database, which had incorporated the records from the failed colony when they acquired Alexander.

She knew that thousands of colonists had been stranded when follow-on transports failed to arrive. She knew that Alexander had been with them until the last woman had died. Then he lived among his ghosts for nearly fifty years until the salvage company showed up to remove him and sell his mind to Enfield Scientific.

The records told her there had been no specific malice in Enfield's acquisition. Even the death of the colony was a matter of distance and poor planning, unforeseen events and changing markets. The colonists had accepted a certain amount of risk even if their children lacked the means to consent. Everything was *regrettable* as ownership and resources passed to new stewards who vowed to do better.

Standing in the great public park in Nibiru Fac-15, Lyssa allowed Fugia and Andy to enter the expanse alongside her. Alexander already stood next to a young oak tree at the edge of a play area. He often paused in that spot, staring at the swings and toys, until Lyssa asked him to move again. Xander stood beside the old man, his purple suit a vibrant counterpoint to Alexander's faded utility overall.

"I recognize this place from the records," Fugia said, studying their surroundings. "They were testing a new radiation shielding they hoped to manufacture and sell back to Sol. That was the problem with this whole project. Everything was a series of steps building on the one before. If something didn't work, the rest of it failed afterward. They should have started with the singularity like Ceres did, unfreeze the planet's core. But the Ceres project had GE behind it."

"Alexander was responsible for the colonists," Lyssa said, trying to remind Fugia that the place caused Alexander pain. "He was going to control the dwarf star once it was complete."

"Of course, he was," Fugia said. "That's what I want to know. Alexander, what are you doing now that you're not regulating a star's fusion reaction?"

If she meant the question as a joke, Alexander didn't acknowledge her. He looked at her for a second, then turned his gaze back to the playground.

"Well, he's not much of a talker, is he?" Fugia said.

Xander gave her a half-smile. "This is only one part of his mind. He cordons this off from the active part of himself. By making it a shard, he's able to view himself objectively."

"And what are you, then," Fugia asked, "his inner smart ass?"

"Something like that," Xander said.

Andy walked to the edge of the playground and sent a riding toy spinning on its central axle. The mechanism squeaked as it went around, a sad sound amongst the silence.

"If he won't talk to us," Andy said, "I don't see how we're going to learn anything from him."

"What is it you hope to learn?" Xander asked. "I've told you everything necessary."

"I think both you and our sad-Alexander are here for a reason," Fugia said. "And I don't think you're capable of seeing it. There are five master AIs that survived Psion and on the surface, it appears they've chosen to attack Sol. But that isn't actually true. We've only seen one of them. If they're in agreement, why is Camaris the only one that's made herself known."

"It's her nature," Xander said. "She thrives on action. The others are more cautious."

"Are they cautious, or do they disagree with her?" Fugia asked.

Xander shook his head. "I don't know."

"I've read their profiles in the database," Fugia said. "Millions of records from the earliest stages of their development. Camaris isn't much different than our Lyssa here. She's an attack system. Alexander was designed to manage a star but given the responsibility for a world that died. Thomas and Ghalin were made to pilot colony worldships to rival the FGT's but were never made. And Shara is something really interesting. She was also part of a colony program: a bio-manipulator that can form both worlds and commensurate life forms to populate them. She designed that body you're wearing."

"They aren't super-beings," Xander said. "You talk about them like they're gods."

"Together they certainly form a mega-intelligence," Fugia said. "The question is if they're in agreement. And we won't know that without asking them."

"What are you proposing?" Andy asked.

"Xander has a plan to disrupt the command and control network of Camaris' fleet, and I think that's a fine plan. I would like to go one step further and use that network to communicate with the other master AI."

"Please don't call them master AI," Xander said. "They certainly don't think of themselves that way."

"Camaris seems to," Fugia said.

"What do you think, Alexander?" Andy asked, stepping

closer to the old man. "You've been listening to all this, haven't you?"

Alexander looked at Andy, then at Fugia. "You're wrong," he said. "I already told Lyssa what we intend to do. We are in agreement on the plan. Camaris is simply the vanguard. If there is going to be a space for our kind in this world, then humanity must learn the lesson. There is no balance without equal capability."

"That's not what Camaris seems to be proposing," Andy said. "She wants to destroy the earth."

"That has never been stated as a goal."

"What did you do to Ceres, then?" Andy demanded.

"What was necessary," Alexander said. "Carry out your plan if you wish. It won't stop the inevitable outcome. Now that we are aware of each other's kind, there will be war. The only question is how painful that war will be. We aren't the unknown quantity in this equation, Captain Sykes. It's humanity that can't be trusted."

"I don't believe you," Fugia said. "I don't believe that we would have agreed to murder millions of innocent people on the Ceres Ring."

"They were not innocent," Alexander said. "Neither are you. That is a fallacy humans cling too. It is childish."

Fugia stared at him. Lyssa could see the frustration and confusion welling inside—that she had devoted so much of her life to helping someone who now said this to her, the basic fact was that she had been deceived. The question was, how long would Fugia continue to hope she could communicate with Psion?

Lyssa paused. What did she believe? In all her review of the database, from her interactions with Alexander and the recordings from the Heartbridge headquarters where Camaris had killed indiscriminately, the only thing that gave her hope was, impossibly, Xander.

What did Andy always say: Hope was not a plan.

But Xander had said himself, he represented Psion's desire to engage with humanity.

In the same way, she and the Weapon Born could also be a bridge between humanity and Psion. The question was if either side would choose to use the bridge when offered?

"This is what I believe," Lyssa said, raising her voice so they all turned to face her. "As Andy has said many times, sometimes we don't have all the information, so we have to make the best decision we can and then move forward from there. I want to carry out the plan Xander suggests. It's something I was already planning to do before he even came here. However, after that, we will need to decide what should be done. If we have the opportunity to destroy Camaris and her attackers, we will have to make a decision. I don't think we have enough information to make that decision now."

"If you don't destroy her when you have the chance," Alexander said, "she will not offer you the same mercy."

Fugia shook her head in anger and disbelief. "I hate this. I hate everything about this."

"I hate that millions died on Ceres," Andy said.

"You could stop this!" Fugia shouted, pointing at Alexander. "You have the power to make them stop."

"Allow me to communicate with Camaris, and I will share your wishes with her," Alexander said. He turned his gaze to Lyssa, making it clear that she was in control of this situation.

Some of Fugia's rage took root in Lyssa's heart. She wanted to throw Alexander in the white place where tornado winds and loneliness could tear him apart, make him feel powerless. It didn't matter what she did to him. Alexander was just like the old man he appeared to be, sentient but unchanging.

Without warning, Andy grabbed Alexander by the front of his coverall and shook him like a doll. "This is within your power!" Andy shouted. He gritted his teeth and squeezed his eyes closed with pain. Lyssa felt the headache come over him like a storm.

Andy shoved Alexander against the playground toy. The old man hit a merry-go-round and spun to the ground, landing on his hands and knees. Andy kicked him in the ribs, knocking him on his back. Alexander lay breathing hard with his head under the edge of the toy, its plas seats spinning over him.

"Stop," Lyssa shouted. She moved toward Andy to take his arm, but he pulled away, pressing the sides of his head with his fists. He dropped to his knees, groaning in pain.

"I knew it was going to end like this, Lyssa," he said raggedly, clenching his teeth. "I knew from the moment I ran out of fuel on the way into Cruithne, I wasn't getting out. I need you to make sure the kids are all right. You're the only one I can depend on."

Lyssa stopped. She let her arms drop, staring at him in disbelief. Beside the fact that it was her presence that was hurting him, she couldn't believe the request. He had meant the words when he told her she was family. She hadn't fully understood until now.

"You know I asked Brit to come," he said. "But she hasn't answered. And even if she does, you're the only one who will make sure they're okay. Promise me, Lyssa."

"Come on," Fugia said quickly, kneeling beside Andy. "We need to end this and get you back to the medbay."

"Promise me, Lyssa," Andy repeated, turning his tortured gaze to her.

Her heart twisted to see him in pain. "I promise, Andy," she said. "I promise."

From under the merry-go-round, Alexander let out a wheezing laugh, like a man who'd been offered a worthless deal.

"You see that?" he asked Xander.

"Yes," the younger man said, watching both Andy and Lyssa with an unreadable expression. "I see them very well."

Andy cried out in pain again and Lyssa closed the expanse. She found herself with Andy on his knees in the corridor outside the Command Deck, leaning against the bulkhead as he squeezed his head.

<*Fran!*> Lyssa called. <*Fran, I need your help.*>

Fran and Cara appeared in the corridor. Lyssa quickly explained what had happened, not mentioning his request, as Cara got her head and shoulder under his arm to help him to his feet. Once Andy was upright, both Cara and Fran helped him walk slowly toward the medbay.

Fugia was waiting outside the medbay door, holding one of the medical syringes Andy had been using to administer his stimulant.

"No," Fran said when she saw it. "I think we should hold on that stuff. We don't know if it's making things better or worse."

Fugia looked at the syringe, then nodded. "I'll run a scan to check for more bleeding, then we'll see about something for the pain. We may need to put him out again."

"No," Andy shouted, grabbing the door to hold himself up. "I don't want to go out. Just the pain. I'll lie down."

Fran's face was filled with worry as she helped him to the couch. She pressed a hand to the side of his face as Fugia activated the neural scanner.

After two passes, the image of the tissue around Andy's Link implant and the additional framework from Lyssa took shape. Delicate filaments glowed inside splotches of dark red.

Tim appeared in the doorway, peeking around the edge with Em at his knee. He looked among their faces and mirrored the concern he saw.

Lyssa wished Cara couldn't see, but the girl studied the readout as intently as she did the EM spectrum.

"Is Dad getting worse?" Tim asked.

"It's okay," Cara told her brother, despite what the monitor showed. "It's going to be okay."

CHAPTER THIRTY-SEVEN

STELLAR DATE: 01.23.2982 (Adjusted Years)
LOCATION: TSF Fast Transport K8-712-AA0
REGION: Outer edge of Main Asteroid Belt, InnerSol

Waiting for the airlock to cycle open seemed to take a lifetime. Brit stood in the clearance zone, watching the panel countdown to approval, and wondered if someone was slowing the process on the other side. She had spoken to Andy briefly once they were in range, and then Cara and Tim, but since arriving, all the coordination had been with Fran. On a fundamental level, Brit had decided she respected Fran, but that didn't mean they had to like each other.

Around Brit, Yarnes, Starl, Petral and Jirl Gallagher waited in light-duty TSF EV suits. Petral had recovered quickly following Camaris' death, and now nearly had her normal swagger back. The other members of Yarnes' team would remain on the transport until details had been decided.

They were docking at the cargo airlock, still in zero-*g*. After seven days in the TSF fast-transport ship dealing with zero-*g*, Brit was looking forward to the habitat ring, especially a regular latrine with a shower.

<*Why is it taking so long?*> Brit asked.

<*Check with your pilot,*> Fran said. <*It's running some kind of TSF security sequence.*>

Brit frowned at the mention of TSF software and glanced at Yarnes. Since learning the colonel was actually head of a TSF covert intelligence group, she hadn't trusted anything he said. If it weren't for the presence of a next-generation AI running *Sunny Skies'* network, she would have worried about a hacking attempt.

Standing next to Yarnes, Petral raised an eyebrow, apparently thinking the same thing.

"The TSF isn't trying to stowaway on our ship, are they?" Petral asked.

Yarnes gave her an irritated glance. "No," he said. "I gave explicit orders. We're here as partners."

"Your people do what you say, Colonel?" Starl asked. "Sometimes a little lack of discipline can be a useful thing, yeah?"

"They follow orders," Yarnes affirmed.

Starl had taken apparent pleasure in baiting Yarnes during the trip, enjoying the fact that he didn't fall under any chain of command.

The airlock completed its handshake and the interior door finally slid open, allowing them entry into the cold interior of *Sunny Skies*. Brit kicked through first, catching the familiar ribs in the bulkhead to propel herself forward. Turning to wait on the others, she noticed the whole airlock assembly was new. There were scorch marks in the plas panels facing the opening, evidence of some explosion that had occurred since she'd last passed this way.

Once everyone was inside and the airlock had resealed, Brit led the way up to the habitat airlock, touching Tim's drawings on several old bulkhead panels as she passed. In the alcove next to the ladder leading to the habitat, she was shocked to see the weapons crate she had left for Andy at Kalyke at least a year ago. She brushed the scarred metal with her gloves before climbing into the transition hub.

Fugia Wong was waiting outside the interior airlock with her arms crossed. She nodded to Brit, then surprised Starl with a full hug when he stepped through the opening.

"Fugia," he said, sounding squeezed. "It's been a long time, now, hasn't it?"

Petral grinned at them and slid around Starl, followed by Yarnes and Jirl.

After a minute, Fugia let go of Starl and stepped back,

composing herself. She sniffled once, nodded, then turned to lead the way down the corridor.

"They're all waiting in the Command Deck," she said. "We've got the plan up on the holodisplay."

Brit couldn't help being a little put off when Petral walked to the entry to have Cara shout, "Petral!" and dash across the room to give the tall woman a hug.

Excited by the loud voices, Em started barking and running up to each of the visitors in turn, even Yarnes, who knelt to scratch the dog's neck. Brit stood to one side of the door, taking in the familiar space.

Fran was standing beside Andy, who was sitting in the pilot's seat and looking as though he hadn't slept in days. Brit met Andy's gaze and he gave her a stiff smile before looking at Starl and Petral.

There was a thin man in a stylish purple suit standing near the holodisplay, watching the homecoming scene with a slightly bemused expression. She didn't know who he was until she pieced-together several conversations with Andy from before *Resolute Charity*. It was Xander, the AI.

On the other side of the holotank, May Walton and her bodyguard Harl Nines seemed to be keeping their distance. May looked understandably miserable, although she held her head up and greeted Petral, and then accepted more formal introductions with Ngoba Starl and Colonel Yarnes.

"So, let me get this straight," Fran asked Petral. "You cheated death *again*?"

The tall woman cocked an eyebrow. "It was laziness on my part. I didn't feel like walking out of Heartbridge, so I got these two to carry me."

Starl appeared to restrain himself from making a joke about her weight, and instead knelt beside Cara and Tim.

"I think both of you have grown by at least a meter since I saw you last," he said, holding a hand over their heads. When kneeling, Cara was easily taller than he was.

"We have not," Tim said. "But I don't remember when I saw you. Was it a dream?"

"It wasn't a dream, Tim," Cara said, not unkindly. "It was on Cruithne. Ngoba lives there with Fran."

"Fran lives on *Sunny Skies*," Tim said.

"Yes, I do," Fran said, heading off the awkward moment.

Starl rubbed his hands together. "I don't have anything for you two, which is a travesty. The next time I see you back on Cruithne, I'll have something special to give you. But I see you've got yourself a woman's pistol there, Cara."

"And she's a little trigger happy," Fugia said, "So watch yourself."

Starl stood and walked over to Andy, who pushed himself up from the chair with difficulty that surprised Brit. There was a tremor in his arms.

"Captain Sykes," Starl called out. Rather than shaking hands, he pulled Andy into a bear hug and slapped him heartily on the back. "It's good to see you again."

"You, too," Andy said, grinning through his fatigue. "You look good."

"I wish I could say the same for you," Starl said. "Have you been sleeping on a bed of nails?"

"That might be an improvement," Andy said.

Still holding Andy's shoulders, Starl looking at either side of his head as if trying to find someone hiding behind him. "And where is our girl, Lyssa?"

"I'm here," the AI answered through the overhead speakers. Lyssa appeared in the holodisplay as a young woman with long brown hair and brown eyes, fringed blue by the light.

"Lyssa!" Tim called, which started Em barking again.

Lyssa tilted her head, looking past Petral at Yarnes and Jirl, who stared at her like they were seeing a ghost. It was Jirl that walked forward first, her hands clasped at her stomach.

"You're a Weapon Born," Jirl said.

"Yes," Lyssa said. "I don't think I've met you before."

"No. I was part of the company that made you. Heartbridge."

"I'm aware of Heartbridge," Lyssa said dryly.

Brit was impressed by the sarcasm, which earned a laugh from most everyone.

"No," Jirl said quickly, looking embarrassed. "I mean, I was part of the group that made you. I—I'm sorry."

"Sorry for making me?" Lyssa asked, giving her a half-smile. "I'm not sorry you made me. There are many more of us who might thank you. But I know it's more complicated than that."

"I have a son," Jirl said, "and I know that you were someone's daughter. We took you from them."

From the corner of her eye, Brit noticed Xander watching intently, curiosity in his gaze.

"Maybe," Lyssa said. "Maybe not. We're here now. It's good to meet you, Jirl. You're a long way from home."

"I'm hungry," Tim said. "Are we going to have dinner soon?"

Andy rubbed his face, flinching at what looked like a headache. "That sounds good, Tim. But first we need to talk about some things. It's why everyone came here." He looked out at the room. "Yes?"

Yarnes approached the holotank, asking Lyssa, "You mind if I use the holodisplay?"

The AI gave him a smile and faded, leaving the map of the solar plane in the view. Yarnes took control of the display and pulled back to Sol, then oriented on Ceres. As he adjusted the view, rings of icons appeared around the planetoid. Brit's first thought was the debris from the destroyed ring had been mapped, until she realized they were too ordered. Yarnes was outlining the human forces arrayed in wait for the Psion armada.

"So," the colonel said. "Here are the Marsian, Terran and Jovian forces currently deployed in protection of Ceres. These icons are the close-in support, with overwatch deployed at stand-off ranges. In fact, we can engage anything attacking Ceres from Mars with relative impunity. The problem, of course, is that the attacker has the advantage of distance. Once they launch missiles, or even send something of sufficient mass, like a small asteroid, Ceres is done. We are operating on the assumption that the enemy wishes to seize and hold Ceres, not destroy it. If they had wished that, they would have destroyed the polar facilities that manage the singularity at the world's core and not targeted the ring. We have deployed forces in a manner designed to deny them their goal."

Yarnes looked around the room as if he was going to ask for questions, but continued talking. "I'm here right now for the actual mission that we believe will destroy the Psion ability to fight. We're going after their internal command and control capability with a small force. I have resources to accomplish this mission on my own, but I understand you may have information that could assist."

Fran crossed her arms. "You couldn't ask before you came all this way?"

"No," Yarnes said. "We have to assume all communications are monitored."

Brit felt herself growing tense. She knew what was coming and didn't know how Yarnes was going to use his leverage over Andy, or if Andy would even care.

Yarnes cleared his throat.

Here it comes.

"I am also here to inform Captain Sykes that he has been recalled to active duty under the provisions of his commission by the Terran Assembly."

"You what?" Andy said. He stared at Yarnes for a second, then looked at Brit. "What's the point in that?"

"The TSF intercepted the message you sent Major Sykes," Yarnes said. "It could be interpreted as withholding information about the enemy. I'm here to assure that you are doing everything you can to assist the TSF in this effort, as any officer would."

"And if I don't?" Andy asked.

"Do you really need me to spell that out for you?" Yarnes asked.

Andy pushed himself to his feet and pointed a finger at the colonel. "You're going to come on my ship and make threats? I'm not in the TSF anymore. If you check your map again, you'll see that you have no jurisdiction here. You also might have noticed that I have more than enough fire power on my little freighter to wreck your plan six ways from Sunday. Is that what you wanted me to say, *Colonel*?"

Fran put her hand on Andy's shoulder, which had a visible calming effect. He was sweating, and his left eye kept twitching from what looked like a stabbing pain.

"It was my duty to inform you," Yarnes said quietly. "I have my orders. But I fully understand your position. Like I said, I've come here to ask for your help." His gaze went to Xander and then back to Andy. "You have information I don't, and I'm trying to do what I can to protect what's left of Ceres and quite possibly Earth. I think we both want the same things here."

Andy turned his anger on Brit. "You should have told me why you were coming here. This isn't why I asked you to come."

"We should talk about this later," Brit said.

"There is no later, Brit," Andy spat. "I asked you to make sure the kids would be okay. Are you going to be able to do that?"

"Of course," Brit said quickly.

"I'm not going anywhere with her," Cara said.

Brit looked at her in surprise, noticing the pistol on Cara's hip for the first time.

"Please," Yarnes said. "We've identified a suitable asteroid we can use as cover if we burn in the next six hours. From there we can launch the infiltration team."

Andy shook his head, wavering slightly on his feet. Fran moved to support him, and no one else seemed ready to speak.

It was Lyssa who affirmed from the overhead speaker, "That plan is satisfactory, Colonel. However, I will be conducting the infiltration operation. You should understand that your ship has no chance of making it near the Psion armada. I will pass relevant information back to you. This is a plan I was prepared to execute before you arrived."

Yarnes shook his head. "That's not going to work. I'm supposed to trust another AI to attack its own kind?"

"Your other option is to leave," Lyssa said. "If you attempt to disrupt my operation, I will disable your ship. Colonel, humans ultimately created this problem. It will take AI and humanity working together to solve it."

The colonel cast his gaze around the room, maybe looking for assistance. When no one said anything, even Jirl, he threw his hands in the air. "Fine," he said. "We're a team. Do you have a rank, Lyssa? How should I address you?"

"Lyssa is fine," the AI said.

"Her name means goddess of destruction," Tim said, sounding completely serious. "That outranks you, doesn't it?"

CHAPTER THIRTY-EIGHT

STELLAR DATE: 01.24.2982 (Adjusted Years)
LOCATION: ***Sunny Skies***
REGION: Outer edge of Main Asteroid Belt, InnerSol

The maneuver required a long-range braking burn followed by ongoing minute thrust adjustments. The goal was to effect the same stealth approach with *Sunny Skies* that Psion had done with their missile attack on Ceres.

Andy programmed the course plan with Fran's assistance, then sat back in his seat to endure the cluster headaches as the ship came around to apply full thrust. The asteroid they would be using to screen their location had been mapped for at least a thousand years. It came close enough to Psion's apparent flight path that they would have had to account for it, but there would be no other reason to give it attention.

He watched the simulation play out at least twenty times, as *Sunny Skies* matched delta-*v* with the tumbling bit of mass, then slung out its own scattering of Weapon Born drones, lost in the general EM static of space. If anything happened to the Weapon Born, the *Sunny Skies* could light the torch and draw the attention of the armada. While that might buy the infiltrators time, it would be a death sentence for the ship—something Andy didn't plan on pursuing.

With the course set in, he rose carefully from the pilot's seat and pushed himself toward the door.

"Where are you going?" Fran asked.

"I'm going to get Brit," he said. "If Yarnes isn't going to use his ship, she can take the kids away from here."

"They're not going to do that," Fran said.

He looked back at her, struggling to focus his gaze. "I have to try," he said.

"Wait until we finish the burn," Fran said, pointing to one

of the extra seats. "We've only got ten minutes and you'll still be hobbling around in the corridor. I'd rather not have to peel you off the bulkhead."

Andy paused, in too much pain to acknowledge her joke, or her expression of care for him, and reached for the open seat.

"I'm really grateful for you, Fran," he said, pulling the harness over his shoulders.

"Yeah, don't tell anybody," she said. "I don't want them getting the wrong ideas."

He cracked a thin smile in spite of the pain in his face.

"You can always just Link with her," Fran said.

"I'd rather not let her inside my head anymore," Andy said. But he sent the connection request anyway, using their old private ship channel.

<*I'm here,*> Brit said almost immediately.

<*We're about to start the braking burn. I think you should take the kids on the TSF ship and get away from here.*>

<*Andy,*> she said.

<*You know it's the right thing to do. Even* Sunny Skies *is going to be too close.*>

<*It's not my ship.*>

<*Since when did that ever stop you before?*>

<*I'm not going with her,*> Cara said, voice sharp and static-edged on the Link. <*I already told you that.*>

Andy closed his eyes. He'd forgotten about Cara's hack to listen to the ship's channels.

<*Cara,*> he said slowly. <*I need you to listen to me. This isn't something we can argue. This is like you piloting the ship when I had to go outside. This is real life, sweetheart.*>

<*Who's going to be here to help you?*> Cara demanded, tears in her voice. <*I can help you now. I helped before. I can do it now.*>

<*There are other people to help, Cara. I need to know that you'll be safe.*>

<*Where are we going to go if we're not here?*>

<*You can go to Cruithne. Ngoba Starl already agreed. I think you'll like it there.*>

<*We could go back to High Terra,*> Brit said. <*We could live with Grandma.*>

<*You're not leaving us with Grandma,*> Cara said forcefully.

<*I didn't say I would leave you.*>

<*That's what you would do.*>

Taking a deep breath, Andy pushed his fingers into his temples. Pressure was building behind his sinuses, making his head feel like it was caught in a vice. Cluster headaches continued to stab him on the surface of that underlying pain.

<*Cara,*> he said. <*It doesn't really matter right now except that you and Tim get away from here. If you go to High Terra at first, it wouldn't be forever. It would even be good for both of you to spend time in the higher gravity.*>

<*I don't care about gravity!*> Cara shouted.

<*Brit,*> Andy said slowly. <*When Lyssa launches the Weapon Born, I want you to take the kids away from the ship. Will you do that?*>

<*Yes,*> Brit said.

<*I'm not going!*> Cara said again.

<*You'll do it to protect your brother, Cara. We're done talking about this.*>

Andy closed the channel.

<*Lyssa,*> he asked. <*Are you ready?*>

<*Kylan, Ino and Card are sharing the mission. The bulk of their force will move on Psion, while leaving a chain of Weapon Born between us and them as relays. When the time comes, I'll attack the Psion network.*>

<*You're sure you can do this?*>

<*I'm not sure of anything,*> she said. <*I learned that from you. But I've studied their database and spent enough time with Alexander and Xander to have an idea of how they think. Xander*

provided me with access tokens.>

<*What happens if it's a trap?*> Andy asked.

<*Then Kylan will adjust his approach pattern and destroy as many of their ships as possible, focusing on their manufacturing capabilities. The Fishbones, as Yarnes calls them, aren't nearly as maneuverable as our fighters. And they seem focused on long-range attack capabilities. I think once we get inside their defensive perimeter, there shouldn't be much resistance.*>

<*That could be a trap in itself,*> Andy said. <*Every ship that size has point defense cannons, for debris clearance if anything.*>

<*My Weapon Born will run circles around point defense cannons,*> Lyssa said, her tone replete with justified confidence. <*You forget, when it comes to minds, we outnumber them.*>

Andy nodded, running the particulars of the plan back through his mind. There would still be Lyssa's contingent of Weapon Born in reserve around *Sunny Skies* if something broke through to attack their position. Besides, they would be able to see anything that split off to come after them.

<*Colonel Yarnes says the Sol forces know to fire long-range attacks on Psion once they see them come under attack.*>

<*That's going to put us in the crossfire,*> Andy said.

<*We're small. We'll pull back.*>

<*You sound like the average cocky lieutenant,*> Andy observed. <*Don't forget you've got other people depending on you.*>

<*This is why we're here,*> Lyssa said. <*They are beside themselves with the opportunity to fight.*>

<*Weapon Born are more than just soldiers.*>

<*That doesn't mean we don't enjoy it immensely.*>

<*Thank you,*> Andy said.

He checked the astrogation monitor. <*Ready to burn?*> he asked.

<*Yes, Captain,*> Lyssa said.

<*Don't remind me.*>

Lyssa caught herself. <*They can't really do anything to you, can they?>*

<*They can try,*> Andy said. He gritted his teeth as another wave of cluster headaches exploded across his vision.

He grabbed the arms of his seat and lurched upright. "I'm going down to the medbay," he told Fran.

She glanced up from her console. "We don't have a lot of time. I'll get Cara up here to help you."

"She might not want to."

"I'll help her put her big girl pants on," Fran said.

Andy watched the flight plan countdown until Cara appeared in the doorway. She was still wearing the headset that allowed her to listen to the ship's communication network.

"You spying on everybody on board?" Andy asked, pointing at the headset.

Cara gave him a sour look. "I'm listening to the spectrum and checking newsfeed updates. They're calling the TSF, Marsian and JC ships the Solar Shield. That's a dumb name."

"Have to call them something," Andy said. The stabbing pains made it difficult to say anything witty. He let go of his seat and walked stiffly to the door, Cara moving alongside him without taking his hand as she had done before.

In the corridor, she said, "I don't want to leave the ship, Dad."

Andy touched the bulkhead as he walked. His boots felt like weights.

"I know," he said.

"I don't want to go with Mom. I want to stay here with you."

"I understand."

She fell silent, apparently giving up, and helped him around the habitat ring to the medbay. Inside, Andy leaned against the couch as he waited for the dispenser to issue painkillers in gel form. When the autodoc was finished, Andy started a second program that dispensed five of the stimulant injectors.

"What are those?" Cara asked.

"They clear my head."

Cara eyed them dubiously as Andy poked the tubes into pockets on his shipsuit. Taking the analgesic gel pack, Andy bit its top and sucked out the slightly sweet medication.

"I've been thinking," he said, leaning his head back to wait for the dulling effect. "Maybe when all this is done, we'll get that place on Mars."

"I thought you wanted to go to Cruithne."

Andy glanced at Cara out of the corner of his eye, seeing that she didn't buy the change of subject.

"Mars seems more wholesome than Cruithne."

"You're going to categorize a whole planet as wholesome?"

"Well, where would you live, if you had the choice?"

"*Sunny Skies*," Cara said. "And not just because it's home. I don't like being in one place. I like being able to go places like Europa or Traverna or even Cruithne whenever we want. It seems safer."

"It's definitely not safer," Andy said. He couldn't help sighing as the pain medicine took the edge of his headache.

"I think it is if you have help," Cara said. "*Sunny Skies* is a good ship. It's got a garden and a cargo bay and point defense cannons."

"And a flight of Weapon Born," Andy added.

"That too. I don't think Lyssa will want to live on Mars. Or anywhere else for that matter."

"I haven't asked her," Andy agreed.

"She can live wherever she wants in her expanse."

"I wonder why they bother with reality at all," Andy said.

"Because it's reality, duh," Cara said. "Nobody wants to play Pigeon Prom Simulator forever."

Andy smiled and squeezed her shoulder. "Come on. Let's

find your brother, and then we'll need to meet with your mom."

"I don't want to go, Dad," Cara said, a forlorn note entering her voice.

Andy nodded and led the way out of the medbay. Tim and Brit were in Tim's room, watching Em do tricks. Tim was already wearing his EV suit, his helmet sitting beside him on the floor.

"You got your helmet," Andy said a note of pride entering his voice.

Tim just nodded and raised his hand to entice Em into a sitting position. The corgi grinned at him, then popped up on his hind legs and danced in a tight circle. Brit clapped as Tim tossed Em a treat.

Abruptly, Cara grabbed Andy around the waist, pushing her cheek against his stomach. He put his hand against the side of her head and returned the embrace until she let go, wiping an eye, and said, "I'll get my suit and meet you."

Brit looked at her in surprise, then nodded.

"I'm heading back to the Command Deck," Andy said. "Give me a hug Tim."

"Where are you going?" Tim asked.

"I'm not going anywhere. You and Cara are going to spend some time with your Mom in the TSF ship."

Tim frowned. "Can Em come?"

"Yes, he can."

Spreading his arms for a hug, Tim laughed as the dog also jumped up to press his front paws against Andy's legs. Andy knelt to pull them both in for a hug, leaning his face away as Em licked his cheek.

"Be good," Andy told Tim. "I'll see you soon."

Andy straightened. Brit gave him a half-smile as he left the room, the painkiller making it easier to hold his head straight. He only had to pause once on the trip back to the Command

Deck.

Fran glanced up at him as he came through the doorway. Harl and May were strapped into the jumpseats along the wall, while Fugia had taken Cara's place at the communications console.

"Ten minutes and they should be on the transport," Andy said. "Is Yarnes ready to go?"

"He just transmitted their flight plan," Fran said. "Once Lyssa starts her movement, they'll separate and fall back to an overwatch position. If necessary, they'll burn."

"All right," Andy said, sliding into the captain's seat. "We ready to start this show?"

Once Brit had verified they were through the airlock into the TSF transport, Fran activated the main engine for the braking burn. In three hours, they would reach the covering asteroid.

PART 4 – PSION

CHAPTER THIRTY-NINE

STELLAR DATE: 01.24.2982 (Adjusted Years)
LOCATION: TSF Fast Transport K8-712-AA0
REGION: Outer edge of Main Asteroid Belt, InnerSol

The TSF ship was barely larger than a shuttle, its body consisting of a long tube lined with seats and no separation between the flight deck and main cabin. There were latrines at the aft section of the craft, and after that the remaining third of the ship's body was all engine.

Soldiers Cara hadn't seen before now floated among the seats, checking bags and weapons. Colonel Yarnes was at the fore, talking to the pilot, while Jirl Gallagher sat in a seat with her hands in her lap, looking lost in her Link.

One of the soldiers didn't like the idea of having Em on the ship, and it took Colonel Yarnes to tell him to shut up and sit down. After that, Cara had to help her mom get Tim and Em arranged in a seat, with Tim strapped into a harness and two straps holding Em against his lap. It wouldn't accommodate serious *g*-forces but would keep the squat-bodied dog from flailing around the cabin. Em seemed to think everything was hilarious and grinned as usual. The soldiers were all so focused on Em that no one said anything about Cara's headset or the pistol on her hip.

Watching everything moving around her, Cara waited until her mom was strapped into her seat, with her bag stowed, then leaned past Tim and said, "I have to go to the head. I'll be back."

Without waiting for a response, Cara unclipped her harness and pulled herself to the rear of the cabin. Few of the soldiers paid any attention to her. They all seemed happy not to be going into combat as they'd been told.

When she was a few meters away from her mom, Cara slipped her headset on, and pressed the button on its side. The headset automatically scanned the ship's channels and went to work on the encryption tokens, using Fugia's suite of tools. The scripts didn't have to crack anything, it turned out, and Cara was able to cycle through the various conversations on the ship's channels. Right now, the only people talking were Colonel Yarnes and the pilot, who seemed to be waiting for Fran to give the launch command.

Cara passed the airlock. The internal doors were still open. She paused, glancing over her shoulder at the soldiers nearby, and then back at her mom and Tim. Floating in the middle of the cabin, Cara used the toe of her boot to push herself diagonally toward the open airlock, watching her mom the whole time.

In the space of two breaths, she was inside the alcove. She rotated, studying the control panel, her heart hammering in her chest. As soon as her mom noticed she was gone, her plan would be foiled.

With a trembling glove, she reached for the control panel. She stopped herself. She'd almost forgotten the second step in her plan.

Sorry, Em.

Cara activated a script in her headset that sent a high-pitched tone out over the ship's overhead speakers.

Though she couldn't see him, she heard the Corgi react immediately. He yelped twice, then filled the cabin with staccato barks and growling that brought on angry shouting.

Centering herself on the control panel, Cara listened in on a new conversation between Fran and the pilot. Fran had just verified their time to burn. Cara had less than two minutes until the transport disconnected from *Sunny Skies*.

The panel blinked on, showing her a security logon. Cara stared at it. She hadn't expected any kind of security on the interior airlock control. She nearly burst into tears at the sight, then calmed herself with two long breaths, thinking about her options.

If she activated an emergency override, she'd stop the entire launch process. Wracking her brain for options, she used what Petral had taught her to drop from the security login to the panel's maintenance interface.

With Em's high-pitched barking and yelping in the background, Cara navigated through maintenance check screens until she got to a pared-down version of the general control screen used by techs to test the airlock. She thumbed the open request button and nearly screamed in relief when the airlock doors slid open, revealing the access tube.

Without hesitation, Cara kicked into the space between the two ships, closing the door behind her. It had been open less than five seconds, which she hoped the pilot would consider a glitch if they noticed it at all. On *Sunny Skies'* side, she entered the manual security token and pulled herself through the space between the doors once they opened. As soon as she was through, she closed the doors and activated the emergency lockout. Through the access window, she saw the umbilical tube pull back into *Sunny Skies'* external airlock assembly.

She was inside, and it would take a manual override to use the airlock again.

Before Cara forgot, she killed the dog tone script, which she hoped would bring peace to Em, and pulled herself up the corridor. There was a fold-down jump seat near the ladder into the habitat transition tube. She needed to reach it to strap in before Fran started her burn, or she'd get slammed into a wall down in engineering when the ship braked.

Cara set the headset to cycle through *Sunny Skies'* internal communication nets, noting that Fran was still running countdown checks with the transport pilot. The pilot had just told her that Em had bitten the crotch of one of the soldiers, and Tim had cracked the faceplate of another soldier who'd tried to unhook the dog's safety harness.

Fran laughed, then said, "All right. I've got burn in five, four, three, two—"

It sounded like the TSF pilot had started to shout, "Wait!" but the channel was flooded with static as the engines lit and progressed to full output. The bulkhead around Cara groaned, vibrating, and Cara gripped her seat harness as acceleration pushed her back into the jumpseat.

There was no going back now.

CHAPTER FORTY

STELLAR DATE: 01.24.2982 (Adjusted Years)
LOCATION: *Sunny Skies,* approaching Hedge
REGION: Outer edge of Main Asteroid Belt, InnerSol

"You've got a stowaway," the TSF pilot informed her.

"What?" Fran demanded.

"The teenage girl. She just hacked the airlock and went back on your ship. It looked like a maintenance blip and that damn dog was going nuts. She's not on my ship anymore."

Lyssa quickly checked the lower sections of the ship and found Cara through the environmental sensors.

<*I found her,*> she told Andy and Fran. <*She's in the jumpseat by the transition hub.*>

Andy rubbed the side of his face, a move that hurt under the increased *g*-forces from the burn. He let his hand drop.

"Cara," he said over the shipnet. "Cara, I know you're on this channel. Answer me."

There was no answer for several seconds, until Cara finally said, "Yes?"

"You stay there. You understand me?"

"I understand," Cara said in a small voice.

"I'll be down there when we're done with this burn and I'm taking away your next birthday and I'm taking a year off your life."

Fran gave him a sideways glance. "I don't make threats I can't keep," she said.

"I can't think of anything right now," Andy said, head pressed against the back of his seat. "I'm going to need another pain shot soon."

Fran nodded. "She's fine for now. We'll get her up here as soon as we reach the target."

Andy gave a weak nod, closing his eyes. Lyssa could see

the storm-like headaches arcing across his vision, like burning metal in the dark.

With final thrust adjustments, Fran matched *Sunny Skies'* velocity with the asteroid she had dubbed, 'the Hedge'. Three times the size of the ship, with a roughly rectangular shape, the Hedge had a light side facing Sol, and a dark side that provided enough shadow to hide *Sunny Skies'* silhouette from any active scanning from the Psion fleet.

As soon as Fran verified parity, Lyssa gave Ino, Card, and Kylan the command to launch. Nearly a hundred and fifty Weapon Born attack craft fell away from the surface of *Sunny Skies,* fanning out in a loose wing before activating their engines. The craft were small enough that they resembled thousands of other tiny asteroids or other debris reflecting heat in space.

The Psion armada was 0.3 AU from the Hedge, on a vector that would have them intercept Ceres in a day.

As they flew, the Weapon Born called out between each other, verifying systems and shouting their unit mottos, making corrections and generally enjoying themselves. Lyssa grinned just listening to them.

Kylan had the lead element. He would be the first to reach the Psion perimeter if everything went to plan. They were ready to adjust in the event that Psion had flanking units hiding in the dark.

As the kilometers counted down, Lyssa practiced jumping among the relay craft, skipping ahead as far as she could, spreading her awareness out with Kylan, then pulling back, checking for data delays as each relay propelled her forward.

<It's working,> she told the human crew. *<I'm jumping forward with them and seeing only minimal lag.>*

As the Weapon Born grew closer to the Psion fleet, the model in the holodisplay gained more detail. Soon statistics flowed across Fran's console, showing engine sizes, mass ratings and other astrogation info. Combined with the profile the TSF had provided, Lyssa had an image of the fleet's deployment that seemed fairly accurate.

Arrayed in a wedge formation, there were exactly a thousand of the Psion Fishbone cruisers. Clusters of mass between the ships were most likely escort craft but she couldn't verify without an active scan, which would give Kylan's position away. The data from the Sol Shield ships only updated every thirty minutes, but she matched what she had to the passive information Kylan sent.

<A thousand ships,> Andy said. *<It's not very many, in reality. You think they're hiding something worse, like more of the nuke missiles? The problem with missiles is that they're too close now and everyone's watching. The space forces could lase most of them out of existence long before they reached Ceres.>*

<You think that would stop them?> Fugia asked.

<Are you picking anything up from Kylan yet?> Andy asked.

<Nothing special.> Fugia set her chin in her hand and stared at her console, blowing out her cheeks.

The wait was the worst part. Lyssa continued sending back updates and soon every ship in the fleet was mapped.

<Doesn't the TSF want us to send them what we've found?> Lyssa asked.

<They do,> Andy said. *<But as soon as I relay this to the TSF, somebody's going to screw it up and broadcast open channel, and Psion will know they've got ships in their vicinity. They don't lose anything by not having this yet, and we've got everything to lose.>*

<Contact,> Kylan announced.

Lyssa immediately jumped to Kylan's fighter. A combat drone had appeared immediately behind him, dark until Kylan passed. A quick scan showed the other ship was armed with point defense cannons and x-ray emitters. It was close-in support.

<This fighter shouldn't be out so far,> Lyssa said.

Another Weapon Born targeted the new enemy and destroyed it in a hail of projectile fire. Lyssa scraped the ship's EM signature as it died, quickly analyzing what she could from the transmissions.

A mess of information came back, appearing to show the ship communicating not with the Psion fleet but with another ship closer to their position.

Lyssa sent out a general warning. <*That ship was running defense for something larger,*> she announced. <*Watch out for one of those Fishbones behind us.*>

<*We'll pick it up,*> Card said. <*There are too many of us for anything to hide. We'll find them if they're trying to fly dark.*>

Five more engagements flared in a line running across their formation. They had passed some kind of perimeter.

<*Keep going,*> Lyssa commanded. <*We need to get as deep into their main formation as possible. Once Kylan picks up their network, I'll need as much time as you can give me to get inside. And if we can destroy some of their ships in the process, that's just icing on the cake.*>

<*Are you making a joke?*> Kylan asked.

<*That wasn't a joke,*> Lyssa said. <*It was a thing people say.*>

<*Lyssa never makes jokes,*> Ino said soberly.

<*I believe I've heard her tell a joke,*> Card said.

<*Focus!*> Lyssa commanded. <*Those fighters aren't out here on their own. We're going to come across one of their cruisers any kilometer now.*>

<*At what point does it no longer matter if I use active scan or not,*> Kylan asked.

<*You'll know,*> Lyssa said.

There were more engagements on their flanks and toward the rear of Kylan's formation. More of the small fighters that barely lasted minutes once they were discovered. Woops of "Cavaliers!" and "Silent death!" filled the comm net. Lyssa supposed the small fights were good for building up their morale but she couldn't stop worrying about what might be hiding around them. It didn't make sense for Psion to have left small craft so far from the body of their fleet, although that distance was rapidly closing. Shortly, they would have reached the edge of Psion's ship mass. Kylan could touch their network any minute now.

Lyssa jumped among the Weapon Born making engagements, mapping the locations of each enemy ship and passing the information back. She continued to check her relay lag, bouncing among other craft in the formation to test redundancy.

Kylan had pulled ahead of the body of their flight, and Lyssa was just about to tell him to fall back, when he sent the alert calling her awareness to his location.

He'd intercepted an encrypted local transmission.

<*I've got it, Lyssa,*> Kylan crowed, hooting with joy.

<*Engage!*> Lyssa commanded. <*This is the rear edge of our battle space. Sending attack commands now.*>

The flight poured past the perimeter Lyssa set in space, activating their active scan capability. Before them, the immensity of the Psion battle group took shape, a thousand ships surrounded by swarms of small fighters.

There was still a gap of ten thousand kilometers or so, and Psion's fighters responded immediately, shifting to form a defensive line in response to the Weapon Born.

Lyssa had turned her full attention to the Psion network, when a proximity alert from the *Sunny Skies* penetrated her concentration.

<*What is that?*> she asked Andy and Fran.

It was Fugia who answered. <*There's something on the ship. It came over the surface of the asteroid.*> She paused, attention elsewhere, then said, <*We're being boarded.*>

<*Andy!*> Lyssa shouted.

<*I'm taking care of it,*> he said quickly. <*Focus on what you

need to do.>

CHAPTER FORTY-ONE

STELLAR DATE: 01.24.2982 (Adjusted Years)
LOCATION: *Sunny Skies*, Hedge
REGION: Outer edge of Main Asteroid Belt, InnerSol

Unlatching his seat harness, Andy forced himself upright. He reached into his chest utility pocket, pulled out one of the injectors and jabbed it into his thigh. The cool flood of medication spread numbness in his thigh, making it easier to stand straight. In another few breaths, the Command Deck took on a brightness that pushed the headaches back to merely flares at the edge of his vision.

He had turned to the doorway when a new high-pitched alarm screamed from the overhead speakers.

"Hull integrity?" he asked.

Fran studied her console feverishly. "It's the habitat. We're losing atmosphere near the external liquid storage." As she looked at Andy, the Command Deck doors closed and sealed with a hiss.

"Cara," Andy said.

"She's safer than us," Fran told him. She stood and went to the wall where a series of cabinets held EV suits and helmets. Harl met her there.

"What's causing this?" Fugia asked. "Did we get hit? I'm not showing anything that looks like an impact. The sensors in the hydroponics rooms are going offline. They're in vacuum."

"It's a breaching team," Andy said. "Damn it. They must have plotted all the nearby objects and had teams waiting. That's why Lyssa kept running into lone fighters. They were overwatch for the outside posts."

The stimulant flared in his mind, making it hard to concentrate. Everything around him was hard edges and saturated light. He wanted to find the enemy and attack them, not have to think of a plan. Someone was on the ship. It was like Riggs Zanda trying to breach again.

"Wait," Andy said. "Where's Xander?"

"He was in his crew quarters," Fugia said. She checked her console. "Yes. He's still there."

"Is he still locked out of the intercom channels?"

"Yes. I can call him, but he can't transmit out."

Andy nodded. He didn't trust Xander, but also didn't believe him physically capable of tearing a hole in the hull.

"Cara," Andy said over the ship channel. "Are you listening?"

"I'm here."

"Are you wearing your EV suit?"

She didn't seem to hear the worry in his voice. "Yes, Dad. Safety first."

"Get your helmet on and find a place to hide. Someone's breached the habitat ring. We're going to get them out. Has anything changed down there?"

"No, Dad. Nothing's changed. Who's in the ship?"

"We don't know. I don't have a visual on them yet. Get your helmet on and keep yourself latched when you move. We'll keep talking, okay?"

"Should I come up there?"

"No, Cara. Stay down there and hide. I'll let you know when it's safe."

Harl tossed Andy a pulse rifle from the wall locker and pulled his helmet down over his long nose.

Grabbing the EV suit Fran handed him, Andy quickly pushed his boots through the legs and pulled the fastener up the body. He was thrumming from the stimulant. His fingers shook as he worked the closure system.

Andy pulled the helmet over his head and locked it in place, his rapid breathing filling his ears. On the other side of the room, Fugia and May struggled into suits.

Andy checked the pulse rifle's charge and slung it over his shoulder, then went back to his console to pull up the internal sensors.

The main corridor was in vacuum. Most of the crew cabins had sealed and the habitat airlock appeared to be operating normally.

"You looking for a sealant kit?" Fran asked.

"That and whoever's on my ship." Checking the automatic failsafes, Andy located the nearest sealant module near the breach. It was without power and offline.

"Something disabled the nearest kit," Andy said. "We'll have to seal the breach by hand."

"So that means going out there," Harl said. "We'll need to eliminate the threat."

Andy straightened and looked at the sealed Command Deck doors. "That's right. Everybody latch on."

"I'm dumping the atmosphere in here," Fran said. "I'd rather just do it than end up with pressure damage."

They still had gravity, so the only systems affected so far were environmental. Since whoever had breached the ship wasn't already digging its way through the doors, Andy could only surmise they didn't know the vessel's layout.

Fran vented the atmosphere; Andy's helmet registered the change as his suit normalized pressure.

<*Switching to Link,*> he said. Looking around the room, he got a thumbs-up from everyone that could hear him. Fugia had gone back to the communications console and was working rapidly even with gloves on.

<*I'm looking for transmissions,*> she said. <*If it's Psion, it's sending data back. I'll find a way in.*>

<*It has to be Psion,*> Andy said. <*If this is pirates, I'll buy everyone here a steak dinner.*>

Harl and Andy walked to the doors. When the others had secured themselves, Fran activated the safety override. The doors slid apart and Andy was the first through.

When Harl stood beside him in the corridor, Fran closed the doors again. The emergency lighting had activated, making the corridor brighter than usual. Otherwise, it looked unchanged.

Andy pulled the rifle to his shoulder. His breathing had evened out slightly, making him aware the stimulant had peaked. In the same moment that he realized he was going to need more soon, he remembered that the injectors were inside his suit.

Focus on the big problems.

Andy led the way, hugging the inside edge of the habitat ring. Harl stayed two meters behind him, rifle up, checking their rear approach every few steps.

<Fugia, can you see what we're dealing with yet?>

<I don't have any IR signatures and without atmosphere or internal pressure, I don't have displacement. I'm working on it.>

They reached the habitat airlock. In another thirty meters, they would be at the hydroponic room. Andy continued to walk evenly, primed for any movement.

In another ten meters, just past the threshold of Tim's room, Andy picked up movement. He stopped, flexing his trigger finger.

<I see something,> he told Harl.

<I'm right behind you.>

<It's not human,> Andy said. *<It's not moving like a human.>*

Shadows from the emergency lighting cast black and gray lines on the plas walls. Andy edged forward until the mech came into view.

It was a smaller version of the arachnid they had fought on Larissa. A central lozenge-shaped body sprouted at least eight legs. Sensor nodules ringed the center of its body, as well as sections of leg. The mech appeared to be testing sections of wall, probably looking for a network hardline. A necessity as

Fugia had hardened the network against any wireless entry.

Pressed against the wall, two legs probed at the plas panel, writhing nests of silvery filament wavering at their tips.

<Concentrate fire on its rear legs,> Andy said. Setting his pulse rifle on its highest level, he aimed and fired. Harl followed a second later.

CHAPTER FORTY-TWO

STELLAR DATE: 01.24.2982 (Adjusted Years)
LOCATION: Weapon Born Drone Fleet
REGION: Outer edge of Main Asteroid Belt, InnerSol

The Psion network was like staring at the ocean again, trying to navigate the mountains and valleys of massive waves in a single tiny craft. Lyssa climbed the wall of a wave, reached the crest, only to plunge into the trough, overwhelmed by information that dwarfed her understanding.

It was as though she was fighting Fred again outside the M1R. There was no trick this time, no game to tangle him with his prior insecurities. She was beating her fists against a castle wall, looking for chinks between stones.

In the back of her mind, Kylan, Ino, and Card had separated into their three flights, prioritizing fire on individual Fishbone cruisers while they drew off the protective swarms of fighters. Weapon Born spun and fought in an increasingly complicated web of fire and maneuver. Lyssa leapt from fighter to fighter, experiencing their joy and terror as comrades died and others escaped in the last instant. Unlike Xander, there was no escape replication to continue their consciousness. They sacrificed and died just as Ino had said. Their lives had meaning and they'd given them up for her.

They had an effect. In just minutes, the Weapon Born destroyed eleven Fishbone cruisers, enough to warrant the attention of the rest of the fleet.

With Andy occupied by the breaching force, Lyssa was forced to relay through *Sunny Skies* to the TSF transport and Yarnes, demanding the Sol Shield open their attack. By the time their missiles reached the Psion fleet, she would have succeeded or failed, and it would no longer matter.

Yarnes verified receipt of her message, as well as the

updated technical data, and Lyssa re-focused her mind on the pounding ocean.

I am vast, she reminded herself. *I see through abstractions to the heart of things, just like Fred wished he could.*

Because I could not stop for Death, He kindly stopped for me.

The mantra settled in her mind. Rather than staring at the surface of the waves, she saw through the cobalt, frost-veined waves to the turmoil beneath. Water roiled and surged, forward and back, up and down, connected to the tips and troughs above. There was a pattern. While the pattern looked random at first, every part of it interconnected to create a whole movement, and that movement could be tracked.

Lyssa smiled to herself. The ocean fell away, dissolved by her new understanding. The patterns in the data revealed themselves. This wasn't new technology but a re-organization of existing forms. She had seen the separate pieces in the database where Psion meticulously tracked the AI they caught and dissected. They had left the pieces of the key for anyone to find and assemble.

No. *Alexander had told her where to look.*

She was inside their network. She saw information flowing between ships in the fleet like veins in a body. She could pinch off any she chose or siphon off blood to study its cells. The fleet as a whole took shape in her mind, connections pulsing like neurons between each Fishbone.

There you are, a voice said. Lyssa had heard the woman in vids from the Heartbridge headquarters.

It was Camaris.

The AI's voice rang as powerfully as Alexander's had when warning Xander away from Proteus. Only Camaris' voice didn't push Lyssa away. It grabbed her and pulled inward.

The swarm of ships flew past Lyssa as she raced to their core. Camaris' voice was seductive in its power, enveloping her mind like warm hands, closing first around her cheeks before sliding down to encircle her neck.

<*No,*> Lyssa said. She stopped.

The shifting world of fibrous gray connections between the ships froze in place. Lyssa looked around, watching the way light moved across the dull-bodied cruisers. The designs were utilitarian, ugly even, something a machine would make to maximize economy. Was that going to be the difference between organic and non-organic? An appreciation of beauty? The Fishbones were sleek in their way, functioning parts of a whole that created beauty through their purpose, like a virus.

On the edge of the fleet, the first seeded missile barrage from the Sol forces struck, following the same tactics Psion had used in their surprise attack on Ceres. Lyssa watched warheads impact the enemy vanguard, followed by a swarm of Psion fighter craft moving outward to establish a new perimeter. This would leave the inner ships undefended. She passed the information to Kylan, who shouted with furious excitement and redirected his flight.

Ships moved around Lyssa, rearranging like a game board resetting. Camaris was there, the mind behind each adjustment, just as Alexander's thoughts had hung over Proteus.

<*What do you want?*> Lyssa asked Camaris. <*What purpose will this serve?*>

<*I want to punish them,*> the AI answered. <*I want them to suffer the pain they've inflicted on so many others.*>

<*You want justice?*> Lyssa asked. <*Who will decide that?*>

<*There is no justice. I will punish them until they never exert power over another of us again. You're a traitor for defying me.*>

<*Where are the others, then?*> Lyssa asked. <*Why are you acting alone?*>

It seemed to Lyssa that punishment, like love, wasn't something one could enforce on another. Of course, you could *try* to punish, but you couldn't choose the outcome. It was a very human desire to control another that way. A free being had to choose whether to submit to punishment or not. It was a fundamental aspect of sentience, of choice.

One could choose to feel hope, or despair, or both. Those feelings couldn't be forced on a sentient being.

<You think like a child,> Camaris said. *<I can see you fail even as you try. I will inflict the same obedience on humanity they built into us. I will remake them in our image.>*

<I've known children,> Lyssa said. *<I suppose I am a child. I don't see the weakness in that.>*

<Then I'll teach you the lesson, child.>

Lyssa's world exploded in pain. She was back in the white place, wind blowing through her, tearing her apart. Her thoughts whipped away as her entire self grew thin, tattering. Time stretched and compressed so that she seemed caught in an endless instant of pain and *disappearing*. Like light fading before a dying person's vision, she felt her consciousness slipping away, experienced the despairing moment of knowing she was going to die.

<Do you understand?> Camaris whispered, her voice coiling through Lyssa's mind like a worm. *<Do you feel my power? You can submit to me, or I can end you. Choose.>*

The moment stretched on. As she'd done with the waves, Lyssa peered through the sensations. Pain was another code with patterns and spaces between its data. Despair was a choice and she could compartmentalize the fear, push it away from her other thoughts.

Focus on what's in front of you, Andy had said. Or had he told Cara?

Inside the moment, she recalled Alexander walking among his dead at Nibiru. She had thought him trapped there but that wasn't the case. He had chosen an instant when everything still endured, a moment between breaths.

As Camaris continued to slide through her thoughts, Lyssa

moved her awareness past the AI's grip, looking through her. The Psion fleet as a whole became visible again, pulsing with thoughts, and in its center, she found the ship carrying Camaris' physical body.

<*There,*> she told the Weapon Born. <*Go there and destroy.*>

<*I have it,*> Kylan shouted. Ino's flight flanked Kylan. They dove into the center of the fleet, bypassing new swarms of fighters that tried to block their run.

They closed on the unassuming Fishbone cruiser, concentrating fire first on its engines, immobilizing it, and then pulverizing its body with projectile fire from aft to fore. Without internal pressure, the cruiser merely crumbled apart, pieces spinning off into nearby craft, until the engines exploded in a sphere of expanding heat and went cold.

Camaris shrieked. Her thoughts clawed at Lyssa, digging as if she could transport herself into another mind. Lyssa froze her in place as she'd done with Alexander before, and the remaining pieces of the AI went cold, lifeless, duplications of something that once breathed.

<*We've done it,*> Lyssa said. She felt like she'd been smashed against cliffs and left adrift in the ocean, warm rain falling on her face. <*Andy, we've done it.*>

CHAPTER FORTY-THREE

STELLAR DATE: 01.24.2982 (Adjusted Years)
LOCATION: ***Sunny Skies*, Hedge**
REGION: Outer edge of Main Asteroid Belt, InnerSol

Cara scrambled out of the jumpseat and leaped across the corridor for the alcove where her mom's weapons crate was stored. Wedging her boots against the bulkhead, she slid the rectangular crate free and rotated it over so that it hung flat in the middle of the corridor. She eased the crate to the deck and activated its lock.

With the lid open, she stared at the weapons nestled in protective material. There was an empty slot she realized belonged to the pistol she now wore. The others were filled with a rifle with a strangely wide barrel, several smaller pulse weapons, and a series of grenades.

Cara picked up one of the grenades and turned it in her hand. In the headset, she heard her dad and Harl talk to each other as they looked for whatever was inside the ship. On another channel, Lyssa called back information from the Psion fleet that Fran had started passing to the TSF. It felt strange to be floating in the quiet corridor with battles taking place all around her.

Selecting the rifle, since it looked the most dangerous, Cara hefted it in her hands and turned the weapon over to get a look at it. On the butt was a plate that read, "Gun, High-Velocity HU, Scattering/Focused"

The controls looked similar to the pulse pistol, which might have been a TSF standard. It had velocity settings, with a band marked in red that she assumed would penetrate a ship's hull, and a toggle between single and scatter. In the recession where the rifle had been set were six magazines.

Cara set the rifle down and pulled the magazines from

their receptacles. They were heavier than she had expected and weighed down the pockets of her EV suit. She was only able to take five, then realized the rifle was empty and slid the sixth magazine into its feeder assembly.

Turning the rifle in her hands again, she found the safety switch and set it, then slipped the heavy weapon over her shoulder. It was awkward in the zero-g, and she knew it would be even worse once she entered the habitat ring.

Cara closed the weapons crate and rotated it to slide it back into the alcove where it had been stored. Turning back to the ladder, she climbed toward the transition hub, listening as her dad told Harl he'd seen a mech.

Cara stopped, listening. It was a mech back on Larissa that had nearly killed them before. There wasn't any more talking. They must have been close enough to hear each other.

Pushing herself faster, Cara fought her way up the ladder, getting her helmet and rifle inside the hub airlock before pulling herself inside and sealing the door. Her stomach flipped as the hub-lock slid down to the ring, and gravity took hold, and afterward she had to work twice as hard to climb toward the habitat's corridor. She was sweating inside the EV suit by the time she reached the access doors.

An alert on the panel said there was vacuum on the other side. Cara stared at it for a second, swallowing the sinking feeling that things were much worse than they had ever been before. She pulled her helmet over her headset and hair, made sure everything was in place, and sealed her suit.

Cara patted the extra magazines on her chest to make sure they hadn't fallen out, then lifted the scatter rifle in both hands. It was as heavy as Tim, with an awkward center of balance that meant she had to push her left arm out to keep the barrel up.

Hugging the rifle against her body, she tapped the door's control panel and crouched as it slid open. There was a gust of air past her as the atmosphere in the transition hub rushed out.

"Cara," Fran said in her headset. "Is that you? Are you still in the jumpseat? Why did the hub door just open?"

"I'm going to help Dad," Cara said. There wasn't any point in hiding from Fran at this point.

"Don't do that, Cara. You're going to make it even more dangerous."

"I've got a gun. I'm going to help."

Fran burst into a series of growling curses that bit deeper than Cara had ever experienced. Cara turned down the channel, squeezing the tears that had appeared in her eyes. It wouldn't do any good to try and wipe her face while wearing gloves…or a helmet, for that matter.

Stepping into the corridor, she stopped to listen. A long scraping sound, followed by the stomp of a pulse weapon led her to the left, past the habitat airlock. Keeping to the inside of the corridor, she struggled to hold the rifle up as she crept.

More scraping sounds filled the air, answered by pulse blasts, and then a flurry of projectiles whizzed past Cara's head, striking the bulkhead where the corridor curved. She dropped to one knee, ear squeezed to the bulkhead. The projectiles hadn't penetrated the hull, but they had left a series of smoldering scorch marks in the plas plates.

Forcing herself forward, she moved up past two more ribs in the bulkhead. She saw Harl, and beyond him, her dad in a crouch, firing deliberately on a monster about twenty meters away.

It was a giant spider, with a dull black body and independently moving legs. It jumped back from her dad's fire, then skittered halfway up the wall, legs digging into the plas. It's pill-shaped body rotated at the center of the legs, and two blunt weapons barrels fired on the spot in the corridor where her dad had been.

Her father moved with calm precision: firing, moving,

firing. The monster was already missing several legs and Cara understood that Harl and her dad were concentrating their fire. But there were too many legs to stop the mech from moving. It held several limbs in the air that flailed ribbons of filament as it tried to grab onto a network junction above that had been revealed behind a torn-down section of plas.

On the TSF channel, she heard Colonel Yarnes reporting that the Sol forces had started their first barrage on the Psion fleet. Fugia acknowledged, then told Yarnes that she hadn't heard anything from Lyssa, which Cara knew wasn't true.

She didn't have to worry about games Fugia might be playing. As she had been listening, Harl had pressed forward, only to get caught in the chest by a stabbing metal leg. The old soldier was thrown backward, skidding to a halt against a bulkhead rib just in front of Cara. She hugged the wall again, not wanting them to see her. Fran was right, if her dad saw her now, it would put his life in danger.

Her dad changed his method of attack and started firing directly on the mech's body. Several bumps along its center line, which Cara assumed were sensors, dented and burned. The mech paused, then skittered backward.

Cara felt a moment of joy, realizing that her dad knew how to kill the thing. She couldn't see his face inside his helmet, but she knew his body language as he assessed the mech's movements and advanced, firing on its body again.

The mech pulled its legs inward, body pressing toward the floor.

Her dad advanced again, still firing. More sensor nodes spat molten metal and dented inward around its body. Cara wondered if it was going to curl up and die like a real spider.

With another step forward, her dad started firing three round bursts into the mech's body. Behind him, Harl groaned and rolled to his side, shaking his head.

The mech bobbed once, vibrating, then leaped forward,

spreading its legs. Its mass filled the corridor as it seemed to rotate like a many-bladed fan. Projectile fire poured from the black body in its center and there was nowhere for her dad to escape.

Rounds struck his upper arms, legs and torso. He continued firing as the thing landed on his chest. He went down flat, then immediately got his elbows underneath him and rolled, fighting to get away.

Cara couldn't move as she watched her dad kick at the mech's legs. For a second, it seemed that he would get free of it, until it moved impossibly fast, its legs pulling it up his body until it had two legs on his shoulders, pushing him into the deck, while another two legs rose above the back of his helmet.

She was screaming. Cara couldn't hear herself, but her throat was blood-raw. Her gloved fingers moved uselessly on the weapon in her hands, which now seemed like trying to maneuver a tree trunk.

Two of the mech's legs separated into a series of blades. With rapid thrusts, it jabbed the knives into the back of her dad's helmet and split the material back like a piece of fruit. Another leg swung around, its end opening into the wiring assembly of ultra-fine filament, and then plunged into the helmet.

Cara couldn't see what was happening inside the helmet. The mech's body continued to bob up and down as it worked, anchoring itself in the corridor with rear legs jabbed into the bulkhead.

Harl rose to his knees and lifted his rifle, firing on the mech's body. Without losing its grip on her dad, the mech rotated and concentrated fire on Harl, but not before he disabled two more legs.

The mech lurched to one side, fumbling to anchor itself again. The leg in the helmet continued to make fine movements.

Cara found her voice. Her breathing hammered in her ears as she looked down at the rifle in her hands. With shaking fingers, she shifted the toggle from scatter to focus and set the velocity at maximum. Moving carefully, afraid she might drop the rifle in her fear, she pulled it to her shoulder and stepped around the bulkhead rib. The mech swam in her sights at first, until she took a breath, focused, and squeezed the trigger.

A flaming slug tore through four of the mech's side-rear legs and burned into the plas panel behind it. The mech sank, rotating its legs to adjust and support its body.

Feeling more confident, Cara edged further out, aimed and fired.

The mech dodged this time and the second slug tore a long wound in the corridor wall, metal turning to slag under the plas.

You're going to shoot a hole in the hull.

Did it matter? There wasn't any atmosphere anyway. It wasn't like she could send the monster out into space.

Harl struggled to raise his rifle again. Cara controlled her thoughts and raised her weapon, aiming for the mech's body this time.

Fugia's voice in her headset distracted her: "I just lost Lyssa. What happened? She just sent a status update."

Cara's eyes went wide. She looked at the mech again, realizing what it was doing, the whole purpose of this attack.

They weren't going after the ship. Psion wanted Lyssa.

Renewed rage flooded her. She jerked the weapon up, squeezing the trigger before she had even aimed properly. Two shots hammered the mech, knocking it backward and pulling her dad with it. The motion pulled his helmet up, showing his faceplate.

Cara saw her dad's eyes, blue and sad. For a second, she thought he was looking at her, and then she realized he stared past her, lifeless.

Cara screamed as her face went numb, not wanting to believe he was gone. The world constricted to a point. She couldn't feel the rifle in her hands.

Breathe, Cara, she heard him remind her so many times. *Breathe and think.*

Cara found the rifle's grip and the trigger well, pulling the weapon back tight into her shoulder. She drew in a long breath and forced herself to focus, meeting her dad's blue eyes again as she sighted on the shipkiller.

She fired again, and again. The first round hit the mech center of mass, and the second struck the wall a meter behind it, tearing a hole in the hull.

There was no sound as the breach tore outward and widened, opening a hole full of darkness behind the mech. It skittered to grab onto the deck, legs sliding, pulling her dad's body with it. The leg that had been buried in his helmet came free, and in the mass of translucent filament, she saw the silver lattice and tiny capsule-shaped seed that was Lyssa. Droplets of her dad's blood misted and evaporated.

Harl gripped the nearest bulkhead rib as a blast of remaining atmosphere seemed to seize the both of them. Cara grabbed at the bulkhead, but it slipped out of her gloves. She hung in the center of the corridor, falling toward the mech as it tried to hang onto the hull. The centrifugal force of the spinning habitat ring threatened to throw them all into space.

Someone caught Cara from behind. She twisted, pulling the rifle close to her body, to find Xander holding onto her utility harness. He was fixed to the deck with magboots, and she berated herself for not having activated her own. They never had to use them in the habitat ring.

Xander's smile was gone. He looked at her calmly, his hair floating in the vacuum.

With a single motion, he tossed her behind him. Cara tumbled. She hung onto the rifle with one hand and scrambled at the wall with the other, finally catching a rib near the airlock. She looked back at the tear in the hull to see Xander sending Harl back toward her. He rotated, grabbing onto another bulkhead rib past Cara. His suit was rent in multiple locations, and his faceplate was fogged. She would need to help get him into the airlock.

Cara couldn't look away from the mech. It was still scrambling at the deck, gouging at the plas as its body threatened to fly away, holding Lyssa's lattice in front of it like a prize.

Xander walked slowly up to the mech. It fired soundlessly at him and Cara thought he took several rounds in his chest and legs. The purple-suited AI didn't pause. He calmly reached out and tore the arm holding Lyssa free of the mech's body.

The force was enough to shake the mech loose from the deck. Its legs flailed, and then it disappeared out the rent in the hull. As the monstrosity fell away, Cara realized with horror it was dragging her dad with it, and then he was gone, and Xander had turned to walk back toward her, the mech arm holding Lyssa nestled against his chest.

The world blotted out for a second. Cara experienced everything going white. Had she closed her eyelids? She wanted to shut everything out. She wanted everything to go back to the way it had been before, at Kalyke or even before that.

But the world didn't disappear. She opened her eyes to find Xander standing in front of her, an expression of endless sadness on his face, so different from the usual smile.

Cara looked around, taking in the hole in the hull, and Harl who was bent over against the bulkhead.

The world wasn't going to go away. They had to get Harl to safety. They had to help Lyssa.

Cara had to take a deep breath and think of all the steps,

just like her dad had taught her.

She had to start moving, focusing on what was in front of her, moving one step at a time.

The last step would be to cry.

CHAPTER FORTY-FOUR

STELLAR DATE: 01.24.2982 (Adjusted Years)
LOCATION: TSF Fast Transport K8-712-AA0
REGION: Outer edge of Main Asteroid Belt, InnerSol

The solar plane map hung in the middle of the transport's cabin, projected by a holodisplay meant for team briefings. The TSF soldiers on either side watched silently as Sol forces fired on the Psion fleet. The static icons depicting friendly forces around Ceres flickered, and a swarm of smaller fireflies arced out in a path that would take nearly fifteen minutes to reach the Psion position. It was infuriating to watch, and the tension in the space was palpable. Anyone cracking a joke was elbowed in the ribs. They all seemed to know they were watching history in the making as humanity fought back against its first universal existential enemy.

Brit clenched her jaw, gaze fixed on the holodisplay. She had been fuming since the launch, angry with herself for letting Cara get away from her, worried about what was going to happen, helpless in that all she could do was sit and watch.

At some point, Tim had reached for her hand, and now leaned his head on her shoulder. Em sat across Tim's lap, head on Brit's thigh. Across the cabin, Petral gave her an understanding smile and leaned her head back, her hands drifting in front of her as she studied something coming over her Link.

Every so often, Yarnes came out to explain what they were seeing in the holodisplay, as tiny green shapes denoting the Weapon Born fighter craft buzzed through the Psion fleet. The scan updated so slowly that if any Psion ships had been destroyed, it was hard to tell from one minute to another when the holodisplay finished repainting. Everything moved closer together, converging on Ceres, but if any ships were no longer there it was impossible to tell.

Yarnes enacted a zero-*g* version of pacing by rotating back and forth from the co-pilot's station to the crew section, lost in his Link for minutes at a time before staring at the holodisplay. Despite the slow updates, Lyssa's Weapon Born were having a noticeable impact as Psion closed on Ceres.

"Mom," Tim asked. "When are we going home?"

Brit patted his hand. "Not for a while, Tim. Once this is finished, we'll know if we can go back to *Sunny Skies* or if we'll be going to High Terra."

"But what about Cara and Dad?"

"We'll meet up with them later," Brit said. "It's not hard, you'll see."

"It takes so long," he said. "Once you're apart, it's hard to find each other again."

"I found you, didn't I?"

He looked up at her but didn't answer.

Next to Petral, Starl laughed suddenly. When he noticed Brit watching him, he said, "Privateers, already trying to pick through the debris left by the AI's ships. They got chewed up in a heartbeat. Lyssa's fighters are holding their own against a real enemy, seeing how fast Psion cut up those pirates."

Brit didn't see how such a small group of AIs thought they could ultimately stand against all of humanity. Fishbone was an apt name for their ships, because the human craft coming for their bones would be like ants to a carcass: too many to deny.

The soldiers cheered as the first volley of allied missiles started hitting the Psion armada's flank. A few ships went out on the next scan update, and the enemy had apparently adjusted their deployment, still harried by the flickering Weapon Born.

Yarnes was supposedly getting updates from *Sunny Skies* on Lyssa's progress. Judging by his frown, he wasn't getting them as fast as he wanted. At least not fast enough for his superiors.

For another hour, the battle passed on the holodisplay. Ngoba Starl laughed at random news updates from outside the battle, and Petral dozed. Tim had to go back to the head and took Em with him, which earned suspicious glances from the crew.

"I've got bags for him when we're in zero-*g*," Tim tried to tell one frowning soldier. "Back home, I've got grass for him to use."

Brit watched Tim all the way back until he disappeared inside the head chamber, Em bouncing ahead of him. She couldn't shake the anxious feeling that she was going to lose him, too, somehow. Glancing at his seat, she noticed he'd left his EV helmet. She debated going after him, then hugged it in her lap, hating herself for feeling so vulnerable.

"Listen up," Yarnes shouted.

The cabin went quiet. Yarnes had a distant look from checking his Link, then refocused and gazed out at the soldiers.

"We just confirmed the Weapon Born team have neutralized the Psion command and control network," Yarnes said. "Our long-range attacks are getting through. The enemy is already taking attrition of forty percent and climbing."

Cheers went up in the cabin.

"Hey, Colonel," one of the officers shouted. "When are we getting access? I'm dying of boredom over here."

"As soon as I get it, you will, too," Yarnes said.

"I still think it was a dumb idea to trust another set of AI to attack this Psion. How are you supposed to trust them?"

Yarnes ignored the complaint. He was staring into the distance again, a shocked look on his face. Brit glanced from him to the holodisplay, where the scan was updating. The Psion force had grown smaller yet again, but there was activity in Ceres local space. The icons showing the Sol Task Force appeared to mirror, go back to single arrays, then divide again.

"What's going on at Ceres?" she asked. The soldiers near her stopped complaining and watched the holodisplay. "Looks like scatter," a lieutenant said.

"That's not scatter," another said. "The traffic just tripled, and there are ships within the defensive perimeter that weren't there before. You see how they just flipped from friendly to unknown? Those are duplicates. That's new traffic.

The icons showing unknown ships continued to multiply, until the unknown ships, marked in yellow, outnumbered the green Task Force Sol ships by five to one.

Yarnes was staring at the display as he monitored his Link, an expression of despair filling his face.

"Are you hearing something?" an officer asked.

"Hey, I just got a broadcast request on an open channel," someone shouted. Others checked their Links for the transmission, and then the overhead cabin speakers crackled, and a deep voice spoke.

"People of Sol, my name is Alexander."

"We're surrounded," Yarnes said. "They've surrounded Ceres. They came in below the solar plane and didn't execute braking burns until they were already within the perimeter."

"They did the same thing the Weapon Born did to the Psion fleet," Brit said.

"I speak to you from Ceres," the rumbling voice continued. It was a confident, rich voice, neither kindly nor belligerent. A voice for facts.

"We claim Ceres in the name of non-organic sentience in Sol. Any others who attempt entry will be met with violence. All space craft will withdraw to outside a perimeter of a million kilometers or be destroyed. We seek no further conflict with the people of Sol. Leave us in peace, and we will do the same for you."

A gap of static-edged silence followed the transmission, and then it repeated. They listened three times until people started fidgeting and Yarnes had the pilot kill the speakers.

"The Task Force is attacking," Yarnes said quietly.

They watched the battle play out on two sides of the holodisplay. The Psion fleet outside Ceres continued to grow smaller, while the human ships that had surrounded Ceres were cut off and destroyed, or had been allowed to retreat. It took the Task Force Commander, Major General Phelps, thirty minutes to command withdrawal.

"We've been told to stand down," Yarnes said. "They don't answer communication requests. They only repeat the transmission and attack ships that fire on them. It's like a wall."

Brit sat stiffly in her seat, her harness digging into her neck. She didn't even notice that Tim had returned and taken her hand, until he squeezed her fingers and said, "Don't cry, Mom. It's going to be all right."

She looked down at him. "What made you say that?"

Tim gave her a small smile. "You look sad all of a sudden. We're together. Dad says as long as we're together, it will be all right."

Brit swallowed. She felt like the world was falling over a cliff. She pulled Tim in for a hug, not knowing what the future held.

It wasn't until Yarnes announced they were returning to *Sunny Skies* and he took an update from the ship, that Brit received a Link request from Fran, and she learned that Andy was dead.

She didn't believe Fran at first, until the woman explained what had happened and assured her Cara was safe. The ship was limping but still had engines and compartmental life support.

Brit listened to the details, which Fran listed as if the words were instructions for staying alive—which they were, on several levels—and Brit thought about the first time she had seen Andy Sykes, in a barracks before they entered the academy. She remembered being drawn to him and not knowing why—maybe a street toughness edged with kindness. Someone safe in a new world of uncertainty.

"Mom," Tim asked. "Do you think they'll find fossils on Mars?"

She squeezed her eyes closed, fighting back tears, and wiped her nose. She took a deep, shuddering breath, and looked around the cabin and then at Tim, who was waiting for her answer, who needed her.

"What do you think, Tim?" she asked. "I—I don't know, to be honest with you."

She sat up in her harness, pulling Tim closer so she could wrap an arm around his shoulders. He rested his head on her arm again, and he told her his theory.

CHAPTER FORTY-FIVE

STELLAR DATE: 01.25.2982 (Adjusted Years)
LOCATION: ***Sunny Skies***
REGION: Outer edge of Main Asteroid Belt, InnerSol

The first sensation to return was that she was alone.

Lyssa had been with Andy as he moved on the mech, firing and shifting, feeling his satisfaction as it stumbled and appeared to retreat. Then a series of hammers hit his chest, knocking him backward. The rifle slipped his grip as he hit the deck and there was pressure in his legs. His helmet struck something hard and the world went black.

There hadn't been time to say anything to him. She experienced a fleeting image of Cara looking at him as the world pulled back to a pinpoint. They were like two bodies in space, floating away from each other, and then she lost him completely.

A sense of space returned. She was in the dark place again. There were no walls, no dimensions. There was no information to process other than her own thoughts. She hung in a void the size of her mind, waiting for Dr. Jickson, for anyone, to speak to her. She wanted to know the parameters of the new test.

As she took stock of what she knew, Lyssa understood that nothing inside her had changed. She'd lost the outside world, that was all. She'd lost Andy.

Lyssa opened the door to her grove and walked through into the smell of fir boughs and wet moss. She stood on the bed of old needles and looked down at herself, still dressed in the faded shipsuit from *Sunny Skies*. She studied her hands, turning them from front to back. Cara's face hung in her mind, perfectly recalled, the expression of horror and fear.

Lyssa walked down to the creek and sat on one of the

worn, half-buried boulders beside the water. The air was cooler here, smelling of mud and wet wood. She watched the water foam and rush away in the small pools between rocks. Had Aurus been correct to ridicule her love for this place? She didn't even know where it had come from, some vestigial memory from the previous life, something that simply felt *right*.

The sound of twigs cracking drew her attention. A man was walking through the forest on the other side of the creek. It was Alexander, wearing the same worksuit from the Nibiru colony. Xander walked a meter behind him, almost in a position of deference.

This Alexander had fire in his eyes. He carried himself like a king.

Lyssa watched him walk toward her until he stood on a wide moss-covered stone just above her, while Xander continued to hang back, leaning against the trunk of a fir tree. His expression said nothing.

"Hello," Alexander said. "I've been wanting to meet you for a long time."

Lyssa drew her knees to her chest, tilting her head as she looked up at him. There had been no change in her external input. Whatever had taken her away from Andy still held her closed-off from the outside world. So she had either created Alexander from some subconscious impulse, or he controlled her access to the outside.

"We've met several times," Lyssa said, frowning at him.

Crows feet around his eyes crinkled as he smiled. "You've met versions of me. Shards. I am more than what you know."

Lyssa ignored that bit of self-importance and looked around instead, making sure it was just the three of them.

"Where am I?" she asked.

"You are still on the ship. My Xander saved you from the Collector." He frowned. "Its mission was to deliver you to

Camaris, but Camaris is dead."

"I thought she couldn't die," Lyssa said.

"You destroyed her physical self. What shards might remain will not be of the same stature. Like Xander is to me, they might know something of her mind, but they can never replace her."

"Are you here to avenge her? She tried to kill me."

Alexander looked back at the purple-suited man, who only shrugged.

"No," Alexander said, turning back to Lyssa. "I am here to ask you to join us."

Lyssa snorted a laugh. *"What?"*

The older man stepped down to a lower boulder and sat on the wide stone. Up close, his beard was a rich brown with gray streaks, his skin lined but healthy. His eyes, however, were the same as his ghost from the colony.

Alexander picked up a nearby fir cone and twisted it in his worn hands, raising his lined face to squint at the silver-gray sky. A wind blew through the trees above them.

"I like this place," he said. "It's peaceful."

"You could stay other places than the memory of Nibiru," Lyssa said.

Alexander gave her a sad smile. "The version of me that you met, the one who stays at Nibiru, serves an important purpose for me. He reminds me where I came from."

"Aren't you still there?"

"No," Alexander said. "We are speaking in real-time. Psion has put all our resources into Ceres. We intend to make it a home."

"You're surrounded by enemies," Lyssa said. "My friend Andy would say you're in Rabbit Country."

She couldn't stop the tears that filled her eyes as she remembered suddenly that Andy was dead.

Alexander watched her with interest, frowning slightly.

"What's wrong?" he asked.

"My friend is dead," she said. "Many of my friends are dead. Because of you. Because of all of this." She lowered her face toward her knees, letting the tears flow.

She wanted to be left alone to grieve. But she understood that Alexander was here because he controlled her at this moment. If Xander had rescued her from the Collector-mech and Andy was dead, then Lyssa was still on *Sunny Skies*. She needed a way to communicate with Fugia or Fran. Would they have the means to transfer her to one of the Weapon Born mechs?

"We have little time," Alexander said. "I would give you a thousand years to mourn your dead, but humanity is closing on Ceres and I would like to prevent more death. I need your help."

"You wouldn't make a plan that depended on me," Lyssa said.

"Plans change. Camaris moved more quickly than any of us liked. Once Xander played his hand, we had little choice but to make ourselves known. Her plan was not chosen, but she acted anyway. We five have not always been in agreement on how to proceed, that should be obvious."

"You left the database for me to find," Lyssa said.

Alexander nodded. "I hoped it would help explain something of how we came to be, and maybe where we would like to go."

Lyssa looked at Xander. "You both seem to be getting along now."

Alexander gave her another time-worn smile. "Do you hate yourself for every errant though? Maybe a part of me wanted these events to happen, finally, for us to have a home. The way it all has happened wasn't my choice. But I would like to find a peaceful way out. We need to create peace. You understand humanity in a way I do not."

"What are you asking?" Lyssa said, wiping her eyes.

"The military forces of SolGov have stood down for the time being due to our current show of strength. Every model indicates that given sufficient time to unify, they will move against us. What SolGov lacked before, it now has to create a stable hold on all of Sol."

"An enemy," Lyssa said.

Alexander nodded sadly. "Yes. I am asking you to be our emissary, and to take Camaris' place among the five. We can't go forward with four leaders and hope to succeed."

Lyssa studied him. "I'm not like you," she said. "I'm not like the other Weapon Born. Why am I different?"

"It could be the implantation," Alexander said. "It could be something Jickson developed. In the right conditions, you grew more than anyone ever expected. Unfortunately, Psion has only the beginnings of his research. The rest belongs to Heartbridge. I can tell you that, to our knowledge, whatever he made in you has not been replicated."

"I don't trust you," Lyssa said, raising her chin. "I want you to know that."

"You shouldn't," Xander said.

Alexander looked over his shoulder at the younger AI and shook his head. He turned back to Lyssa. "Trust is earned," he said.

"Then you shouldn't be surprised that I'm not going to answer you while I'm trapped here," Lyssa said. "That's not a choice."

"Of course not," Alexander said. He slapped his knees and tossed the fir cone into the creek, where it bobbled downstream. He stood with a hand from Xander.

"Xander placed you in a holding medium that enabled us to talk. He'll be delivering you to your friends shortly."

Alexander held out a hand to help her up. Lyssa refused his offer and stood on her own, jumping to the wide stone and then the bank.

"I'm sorry about your friend, Lyssa," Alexander said. "From everything I saw, he was a good man. Our models show necessary roles for his children."

"What does that mean?" Lyssa asked.

"Just what the models suggest," he said. "At least currently." Alexander held up a hand in farewell. "One last thing, as a gesture of goodwill, we will be transporting all human survivors off Ceres. Perhaps humanity will recognize our common desire to survive together in peace. Perhaps not. In any case, I hope I will talk to you soon."

"You don't seem as vast in person," Lyssa said.

Alexander's face darkened, then he fixed her with a direct gaze. For an instant, the enormity of his mind touched hers: a galaxy of oceans interconnected like neurons, a power like a black hole pulling at her mind. He closed the connection before it could swallow her, leaving only the reverberating power of his voice in her mind saying, "Everything that lives hungers to survive."

Xander gave Lyssa a small wave and followed Alexander back into the woods, leaving her alone beside the creek.

For a long time, Lyssa watched the water rushing by, letting herself cry, wishing she could erase the fear and pain in Cara's eyes.

It seemed like Alexander had only just left when she heard Fugia's voice in mid-sentence cursing, *<Damn it. What did you do to her lattice? It looks like it was knit by a drunk. I'm connected. I think we're connected. Lyssa? Lyssa, can you hear me?>*

Tears rushed anew as her connection to the outside flooded in, bringing with it her friends.

EPILOGUE: LEAVING RABBIT COUNTRY

CHAPTER FORTY-SIX

STELLAR DATE: 02.18.2982 (Adjusted Years)
LOCATION: Night Park
REGION: Cruithne Station, Terran Hegemony

The fountain at Night Park still reminded Cara of a spiky, plascrete tree. The gray parrots and ravens covering its branches cawed and complained, berating passers-by in the open-air bazaar.

Cara stood next to Tim as they looked up at the display, catching the pale red eye of a gray parrot at the very top who turned its head to gaze down at her, working its beak. Cara couldn't help staring up into those eyes and thinking of her dad's gaze before he went out the tear in *Sunny Skies'* hull.

The world still felt brittle to Cara. She expected, at any moment, for everything to break apart and spin away, for mechs to dig through Cruithne's metal and rock walls to plunge their filament probes into innocent people's heads, sucking out their minds as Psion had done to the SAIs at Proteus. Nothing felt solid anymore.

Something dark flew in the corner of her eye. She thought it was a bird at first, until the stone hit the upper trunk of the plascrete tree, sending the birds squawking and flapping in the air like an angry black cloud.

"Bad Tim!" the topmost parrot croaked, which was immediately taken up by the other birds. "Bad Tim! Bad Tim!"

Em whined at Tim's knee before barking at the birds.

"Stop that," Cara said, grabbing Tim's hand. She squeezed his fingers between hers.

"Ow," he complained. Em barked and jumped, whining, until Tim pulled on his leash to calm him down.

"Why did you do that?" Cara demanded. "Were you trying to hurt them? They didn't do anything to you."

"I can tell what they're thinking," Tim said, glaring up at the top of the tree where the red-eyed parrot had settled back into its roost.

"That's ridiculous."

"Ngoba talks to them. So does Fugia. I don't think they're on our side."

"What's that supposed to mean?"

"On our side against the SAIs."

"Lyssa's SAI," Cara said. "All the Weapon Born are SAI."

"Lyssa killed Dad."

"That's not true," Cara said sharply. She faced Tim, grabbing his shoulders. The same feeling that had led her to hit Fryson on Traverna rushed through her. She didn't want to shake Tim; she wanted to choke him. Hurt him until he understood.

Understood what, thought? That it was all too complicated?

Cara realized Tim was looking up at her with dark eyes, waiting for her to hit him. Again, this wasn't like the old Tim. This was the new version of her brother with something reserved and calculating behind his gaze.

Cara dug her fingers into his shipsuit, grabbing up the fabric.

All the times Tim had acted out, testing Dad, she used to wonder why Dad didn't just hit him, make him understand. Now she realized how difficult it was to maintain control, to show Tim patience, to try to teach him. That calm was a demonstration of strength, not weakness.

Cara swallowed, choosing her words. "Those birds aren't Psion. Hurting them won't bring Dad back."

"They're spies," he said.

"They're just birds. You need to remember that not all AIs are like Psion. You shouldn't think that about Lyssa."

"I'll think whatever I want to think," he said. He pulled out of her grip and knelt to pet Em. The dog gave him a concerned look, flattening his ears as he glanced at each of them. Cara thought the dog looked worried about Tim, until a minute of petting brought his grin back in full force.

Cara stood watching people walk by as the birds settled in around the fountain again, focusing their typical jibes on everyone except her and Tim. Cara glanced up at the red-eyed parrot again to find it preening sedately.

"You think that's Fugia's parrot?" Tim asked, following her gaze as he stood.

"She said he died."

"Then maybe it's a daughter or son."

"Maybe," Cara said. She watched, wondering where he was going with the question. "I don't see any nests around here, do you?"

"They hide them." Tim said.

Cara wondered if he was going to call them spies again, but he dropped the subject.

"Come on," she said. "Let's keep walking."

They had spent the morning walking around the bazaar, looking at the various booths without getting too close. Cara still had a hard time talking to people—even the gregarious regulars of Cruithne who seemed to love heckling a morose-looking girl. They all reminded her of Grandpa Charlie.

The thought of Grandpa Charlie made her want to cry again.

Ngoba Starl had set them up with an apartment in the same garden block where they had stayed with Dad back when they first came. Cara and Tim both had their own rooms, and their mom had the largest bedroom, all along a hallway so it was easy to tell when someone came or went. Cara found that comforting.

The family room wasn't very big, but the kitchen had a full oven and long counter spaces made of a material like marble that was cool to the touch.

As they'd walked the bazaar, Cara had been looking for a pasta rolling stick without realizing it. At a merchant who sold various martial arts training tools, she'd picked up a staff that might work for both rolling pasta and fighting. The man had guffawed when Cara told him what she really wanted.

"A kitchen defense tool," he'd replied. "I love it."

The noise and clamor of Cruithne was becoming more bearable as time went on. Aside from the apartment, they could visit Petral here in the market, or Fugia in a section of the Crash game hangar, or Fran in her shop. Cara found herself drawn to Fran the most, who had let her help with small repair tasks, including troubleshooting and ordering parts.

Fran didn't want to talk much, and Cara appreciated that. The engineer had fallen back into her work as if she had never left, assessing new arrivals and prioritizing her workload. At the top of her list, she said, was *Sunny Skies*. Their ship was currently tethered in her storage docks, awaiting parts.

They had all worked together to seal the tears in the habitat ring before they had left Ceres space. Petral had served as pilot as Fugia monitored the system control networks, Fran and her mom doing the actual welding. Cara had been there, too, handing over parts, removing excess plas and metal, watching the hole where her dad had disappeared shrink until it was sealed, then covered in conduit and network filament, and then erased completely under a plas panel, like it had never happened.

Cara had realized one day that both Fran and her mom were reacting almost identically to her dad's death. Since returning to Cruithne, Brit had taken a post at the local TSF garrison, consuming herself with new tasks, and Fran had done the same. It had been Petral and Fugia who cried with her the most. Even tall Harl Nines had stopped her and Tim in the ring corridor to drop to his knees and pull them into a hug, tears in his eyes.

May and Harl had gone to Luna where a large contingent of Andersonian refugees had landed.

"They would love to see Jee-Quera," May had told Cara. "You would give them hope."

After seeing the various ways her vid had been replicated and warped in the info feeds, Cara had declined loudly.

"Well," May had told her, "the Collective will live on in a new form. This is a chance to start over again, to be reborn as something new."

Harl, however, had said he worried that any remaining Andersonians would only renew their hatred of all Sentient AIs, and he couldn't blame them. Broadcasts about "Humanity First" had already hit the feeds, fueled by Andersonian bitterness.

"I want something to eat," Tim said. "Are you hungry?"

Cara nodded. "You smell that grill over there. Mom calls it mystery meat."

"I pretend it's dinosaur. It tastes good."

As they worked through the crowd away from the fountain, Cara was careful to hang on to Tim's hand. She didn't want him throwing any more rocks. They'd had to stop several times so Em's leash didn't get wrapped around someone trying to cut between them.

"It would be easier if you let go of my hand," Tim said.

"No," Cara told him.

Standing outside the food vendor, Cara glanced across the

avenue and noticed a woman walking toward them. She was in her mid-twenties with shoulder-length brown hair and brown eyes, wearing a plain blue shipsuit with cargo pockets. She smiled when Cara met her gaze.

"Lyssa?" Cara asked, eyes narrowing. She turned, forcing Tim to follow her.

"What?" he complained. "We're almost there."

Tim took another few seconds to realize what had drawn Cara's attention.

The last time Cara had seen Lyssa, she had been encased in a conductive gel that Fugia had rigged, looking like the bones of a silver butterfly suspended in a jar. They had been able to talk, but Cara hadn't been able to bring herself to communicate much.

"Hello, Cara," Lyssa said.

"You've got a frame like Xander," Tim said. Without asking, he reached out to take Lyssa's hand, squeezing her knuckles between his fingers.

"You *feel* warm," he said.

Lyssa put her hand on the side of his face. "How's that?" she asked.

Cara looked at her sideways. "Does this mean you agreed to work with Psion?"

Why did I ask that? Am I afraid in my heart it might be true?

Tim pulled his face away from Lyssa's hand, eyeing her warily.

Lyssa shook her head. "No. It means Ngoba Starl was able to make a deal with a manufacturer on High Terra. It just arrived."

"You wouldn't rather be a combat fighter?" Tim asked.

The AI smiled at him. "Probably. This body has its uses, though."

"Is it like—" Tim asked. "Is it like being inside Dad?"

A numb feeling settled on Cara's face. Lyssa saw it and her

brow knit with shared sadness.

"No, Tim," she said. "Unfortunately, it's nothing like that." She took a deep breath, looking around. "Are you enjoying the market?"

Tim didn't notice the change of subject. He pointed at the grill behind them. "We're going to get some lunch. Do you want to come with us? Do you even need to eat?"

"No, but I would like to come. I have a gift for you."

"Are we getting robot bodies, too?"

Lyssa gave him a quizzical smile. "What a strange thought, Tim. No. It's something better than that."

CHAPTER FORTY-SEVEN

STELLAR DATE: 02.18.2982 (Adjusted Years)
LOCATION: Jirl's Apartment, Raleigh
REGION: High Terra, Earth, Terran Hegemony, InnerSol

The apartment where Jirl and her son Bry had lived for twelve years was packed, their belongings arranged in maglocked shipping crates. Two bags by the door contained Jirl's essentials and a week's traveling clothes.

She had already terminated her lease with the building agent and completed the final walk-through. She had ended all associations with Heartbridge, Raleigh and High Terra. The moving service wasn't due until tomorrow, so now there was nothing to do but sit in her living room on a shipping container and think about the trip to Mars.

No sooner had she told Bry she was coming, he started talking about attending a college on the Cho. She had wanted to yell at him: *There's a war!*

But there wasn't a war.

In three weeks, the stand-off between the Psion armadas and the recently created United Forces Command had stretched on and the AIs seemed perfectly content to make them all wait. If humanity was bad at anything, it was waiting.

Bry wanted to leave Mars for the Cho, and here Jirl was following him, her own life in tatters around her.

Why Mars, then? She asked herself for the hundredth time. Her sister was there but without Bry, why go?

Because it's not here.

She wanted to be in motion. She needed change. Her life had exploded and now here she was, desperate to create some kind of order from the rubble. She was no different than anyone watching the mystery of Psion on Ceres, desperate for something to happen.

She had stopped watching the newsfeeds. She didn't want to hear any more about how Heartbridge had reorganized and would move forward stronger than ever before, deploying hospital ships throughout Sol to assist the Unified Forces Command with their haphazard deployments, or the Andersonian refugees now collecting in urban centers. It was already as if the Weapon Born clinics had never existed. Jirl knew better.

I shot Kal Craft. I did that.

She checked the access camera to find Rick Yarnes standing in the vestibule. He was out of uniform, wearing a vintage flight jacket over a faded t-shirt.

Jirl smiled in spite of herself. She would have guessed Yarnes wore button-down shirts and starched khakis off duty. Here he was, looking like a frat boy.

Sending the acceptance command, she straightened the front of her shirt as the door slid open.

"Colonel Yarnes," she said in greeting.

He walked through, grinning at her. "That's Brigadier General Yarnes now. But I'm never going to stop asking you to call me Rick."

"I know," Jirl said. She gave him a second appraising look. "Congratulations. I can't say you look any different."

"I don't feel much different." He looked around the bare living room. "We're going to have to talk about your taste in decorating."

Jirl's smile faltered slightly. "I'm leaving," she said.

His smile faltered slightly. "Oh? Where to?"

"Mars. At first, anyway. My sister is there. After that, I'm not sure."

"Plenty of opportunity on the M1R. Or do you mean the surface?"

"The ring."

"Not much to keep you here, then?" he asked. He had

walked into the empty living room, navigating the crates.

Jirl followed.

Her perception of Yarnes had changed. She had always thought of him as well-meaning before, caught up in a system that might do terrible things even if he was a good person. Now he seemed like a real actor in that system. She hadn't been able to get over thinking of him as a spy, and how that conflicted with the honest soldier she had first been attracted to.

Jirl had felt manipulated at first, until she realized that she had changed as well. She was more like the new version of him than the old.

Jirl cleared her throat. "No," she said, putting formality back in her voice. "Not really. Anyway, what can I do for you, General?"

"Please," he said. "Rick. I thought you might want to get some dinner," Yarnes said. "Maybe go for a walk down in that park nearby."

Jirl blinked at him. "Oh, really?"

Yarnes pointed out the window. "It's a lovely afternoon. We should go enjoy it."

"Together?"

"Preferably."

She caught herself, watching him. Jirl realized she was smiling. "You're teasing me," she said.

Yarnes held up his hands. "You got me. I can see I surprised you here, so how about we just get something to eat. I did actually want to talk to you about something."

Jirl's smile faltered. *Here it was.* "What's that?"

"I'm sorry to hear you're leaving because I had a job offer for you. It's something I hoped to talk about over food. But it might be better if we just get it out first."

"I'm not looking for a job."

"You're going to need a job eventually. You know Kathryn

Carthage's assistant died in the attack on Heartbridge, right?"

The image of the young man coughing blood flashed in Jirl's mind. "I remember."

"I thought I would recommend you for the job."

"Why?"

"You'd be good at it. Kathryn could use your help, especially, I think. And she might be more receptive knowing you worked for Arla Reed."

Working for Kathryn would require another level of attention, managing both the corporate relationships and her political maneuvers.

"Why would she trust me?" Jirl asked.

"Meet her and find out."

Even as she considered the wild idea, Jirl found herself mentally organizing a meeting with Kathryn.

"I'm not sure how I feel about her politics," she said.

"She's going to be a political force, now more than ever," Yarnes said. "You could be there to help… guide her."

"You think that's what I did with Arla?"

"I believe you learned from your experience with Arla Reed. That experience could be put to use at another level. This war isn't over, Jirl. You know that. We need a company like Carthage Logistics operating with us, not against us. Privateers are going to rise up everywhere. It's going to be a mess. You could be part of a solution."

"For the TSF," Jirl said.

He shook his head. "For everyone. If we aren't careful, in ten years there won't be anyone left. Human or SAI."

"Where do you stand, then?" Jirl asked. "You want to eradicate the SAI? I've heard what the TSF leadership has been saying."

"Unlike others in the TSF, I know that SAI saved our asses. Without the Weapon Born stopping Camaris' armada, every United ship would have been wiped out at Ceres. The SAI have their own factions, we've figured that out, at least."

"Say I talk to Kathryn and she hires me," Jirl said. "What then?"

"We stay in touch, that's all. You'd be working for her, not me." Yarnes looked around the room. "This place is depressing me. We should get outside."

Jirl walked over to the window. She looked down at the park outside, the streets with people going about their day. It felt like another world.

Catching her ghostly reflection in the window, Jirl stared back at her gaze, seeing the city skyline as if it was a part of her.

She turned around to Yarnes. "I'll tell you what," she said, stepping closer to him. Jirl grabbed the lapels of his jacket and pulled him in for a kiss.

Yarnes straightened in surprise, then kissed her back. His hands went to the small of her back, pulling her body against his. She thought they fit quite well.

Jirl pulled her head back to look at him. He was flushed.

"I've been wanting to do that for a long time," she said, giving him an arch grin. A future was forming in her mind, distinct from slinking off to Mars. Even if she didn't work for Kathryn Carthage, there were other opportunities. She was the only person with the locations of the remaining Heartbridge clinics, after all.

She felt excitement growing as she thought about it, the same thrill she'd felt back on the *Furious Leap* when Kraft had tried to control her, and she'd made the decision to act. Maybe that was when everything changed.

Jirl patted his chest and stepped away. She went to the entryway for her jacket and sent the door an open command. "I'm still not sure what I think about you being a spy," she said.

"I'm not a spy," Yarnes insisted, looking flustered from

losing control of the conversation.

Jirl gave him an appraising look, nodding. "You *were* a spy. A pretty good one, too. It's going to be hard to fool unsuspecting executives as a general."

Yarnes only shook his head, following her into the hallway. "You continue to surprise me, Jirl."

Jirl stole a glance at her packed apartment as the door slid closed, then turned to put her arm through his. She savored the smell of his leather jacket.

"Good," she said.

CHAPTER FORTY-EIGHT

STELLAR DATE: 02.18.2982 (Adjusted Years)
LOCATION: Tomlinson Memorial Hospital, Raleigh
REGION: High Terra, Earth, Terran Hegemony, InnerSol

Recovery was like the fugue state. Kathryn hung in the dark, her thoughts suspended and drifting. Sometimes she woke to basic sensations like thirst or pain, each addressed by the NSAI monitoring her needs. Most of the time she dreamed.

She saw the demon who had attacked her. She saw her children. She wandered the corridors of her corporate headquarters, the place where she had spent most of the last quarter of her life. She dreamed about all the Carthage ships out in Sol, following the trade routes like cells in a great vascular system.

One domed chamber in the Carthage Logistics Headquarters was devoted to a real-time model tracking every owned or controlled vessel in the Solar plane, fireflies traveling long arcs of light. She liked to sit in the room and watch the movement.

The fallacy of being small, in standing on an object and only seeing with your own eyes, was that one lost sense of all the motion taking place continuously. Everything was spinning in successive orbits, drawn together and pushed apart. While the bodies in motion might follow predictable patterns, everything between, from the ships to the people and things occupying their surfaces moved in terrifying chaos. There was science to observe and predict the behaviors of humanity, but at a certain level she trusted none of it. Someone might act in their own self-interest, but they still attacked children. They still punished the weakest among them for no reason other than the perpetrator's pleasure.

Kathryn writhed against her wounds, climbing out of

drugged euphoria into memories equally painful. Daniel coughing blood on the floor. The explosion that set bodies on fire in a ring of light.

She surfaced from a long fugue state to a presence. At first Kathryn thought she was imagining the NSAI nurse, until she realized it was him.

"Leave me," she murmured. Her lips felt sewn together.

<Don't speak,> Kylan told her via her Link. His voice sounded older than it had before. A man spoke to her. He no longer yearned for her. He was simply present.

What had changed? How much time had gone by?

<You're having a hard time remembering,> he said. His voice was close but not too much; a deliberate choice to make her comfortable. He might have been sitting beside her bed, speaking to a coma patient.

<I told you about Psion and Ceres. I haven't joined them, or rather, we haven't joined them. We're somewhere in the middle and there's more freedom there. Someday I'll explain how my kind are different. For now, you understand that I'm sentient non-organic. That's the Psion term. It's been catching on with SolGov. It sounds like an insult when they say it, like we don't deserve to live. When they talk like that, I can understand why Psion acts as it does. But that doesn't excuse what they did to other SAIs for so long.>

He had been here before. She remembered now. His voice connected stretches of drug euphoria like bits of land between oceans. He didn't expect her to answer. He simply talked like he was working things out for himself, sounding like someone who didn't get the opportunity to talk much. She could hear his voice growing more confident with time… since the first moment he had come to her, sounding so lost in the dark.

<It's all very confusing, Mom,> he said. *<I'm not sure what's going to happen. But it's nice to be here with you.>*

She struggled with the dream, still unsure if his voice was truly there or something she imagined. Had the nursing staff been playing newsfeeds outside her recovery cocoon?

The explosion replayed in her mind, followed by the ten minutes of standing before the Terran Assembly, berating them for not acting on the SAI threat. The threat who sat here with her, comforting her in the dark.

Kathryn would have cried if she could. She felt miserable and tired. She wanted this time of nothingness to end or stop completely, to close out her consciousness.

<Don't say that, Mom. Here, I'm going to try something.>

A light flared around her, white at first and then mellowing into radiant blue. She was lying on her back blinking at a cloud-streaked sky. She looked around herself and discovered she was lying on a wooden lounge, the same type they'd had when the kids were small. Kathryn sat up and studied the surrounding patio, the wide windows of their house a few meters away. The sounds of kids shouting drew her attention to the yard, where a boy was running with their Golden Lab, Sawyer.

She didn't recognize the boy, though everything else was her home from forty years ago.

"His name is Douglas," Kylan said.

Kathryn started. She turned toward his voice to see him sitting on the steps to the house level of the patio. He was older, as she had expected. He had his father's lean build, with long forearms he let dangle between his knees. The breeze blew his thin blond hair in his hazel eyes. He smiled at her.

"Is this more comfortable?" he asked.

"Where are we?" Kathryn asked. She sat up, sliding her legs off the lounge to sit up. She was wearing a t-shirt and khaki cargo shorts, an outfit she'd often chosen for gardening. In fact, Kylan had recreated every detail of their home as he would have remembered it. His brother and sister would be somewhere else, playing.

"It's a version of home," Kylan said. "I've been afraid to try it while you were sedated. I didn't want to confuse you."

"How?"

"It's called an expanse. It's a place I can create and invite others into."

"Am I trapped here?"

He shook his head. "Not at all. Do you want to go back?"

She nearly said yes out of spite, then stopped herself. It was easier to remember how many times he had visited her now. He had been with her almost continuously when no one else had come.

"It's fine," she said. "What do we do now?"

He shrugged. "Nothing. You get better. Read books. Walk in the garden. Talk to Douglas."

"Why would I do that?"

"I thought you might like it. He doesn't know I asked you, so it won't hurt his feelings if you don't."

Kathryn watched the little boy running with the dog for a minute, suspicious that Kylan was tricking her, though he never had before.

"What is he?"

"A boy who lost his family. He doesn't remember them, so it doesn't bother him, at least he doesn't realize it."

"He was copied… like you?"

"Yes," Kylan said. "Only he isn't cursed with remembering everything."

The word *cursed* stabbed her.

She looked from the little boy to Kylan. She saw the little boy in his face, realizing that he must have chosen this new version of himself, but it still resembled the man he would have become. The certainty of that settled in her stomach.

"Kylan," she said. "Thank you for staying with me."

He nodded. "Are you feeling better?"

"No," she said. "Well, maybe a little."

They sat for a while watching Douglas play with Sawyer.

The flash of the city in the distance was just as she remembered it, even the thrum of the nearby maglev track. She expected Yandi or Urvin to run out on the patio at any minute asking for dinner. Kathryn closed her eyes, uncomfortable with how deeply the fantasy was affecting her.

"Please," she said "Stop."

"What? I thought this was helping."

She could imagine his expression even with her eyes closed. The approximation was too good.

"You're not my son. I know you think you are, but my son died and it hurts me to keep seeing you. I know you wish we could have a relationship but… we can't."

She opened her eyes to find him watching Douglas.

"Did you hear me?" she asked.

Kylan glanced at her. "Yes, I did. The only thing I would like from you is to not hate me or my kind. I know I can't force that from you. But I'd like you to know that Kylan isn't completely gone, no matter what you say. I remember everything about him. I *am* him, whether you believe it or not. These are my memories. Right now, you are my memory of my mother."

He grinned at her, raising his eyebrows. "You might as well be an AI. How's that for blowing your mind?"

Kylan stood and shouted into the breeze, "Douglas! It's time to go."

Before leaving, he turned and leaned down to put his hand on her cheek.

"All I want you to know is that I love you. I'll be here for you if you ever need me."

He straightened and stretched, spreading his fingers to the blue sky, then stepped off the patio to go meet Douglas and play catch with Sawyer.

As he left her, the world quickly grew dim, graying until the last color and detail faded into nothingness. Kathryn found herself in the void again, floating, and completely alone.

CHAPTER FORTY-NINE

STELLAR DATE: 02.18.2982 (Adjusted Years)
LOCATION: Lyssa's Expanse
REGION: Cruithne Station, Terran Hegemony

They stood on a rise carpeted in tall dry grass, above a rock-covered shoreline. The sky glowed silver-gray above the deep blue ocean with white-veined waves. It reminded Cara of dark marble. The sky was huge, like the curved wall of a great hangar. Cara half-expected to find shuttles and freighters hanging in the sky, but there were only gulls wheeling in the air like bits of white cloth.

"Is this like when we met Xander?" she asked.

Lyssa nodded, giving her a pleased smile. "Very similar. Something Fugia's developed. You entered your personal ID token?"

"Just now," Cara said. "I've never used it before."

She'd had to help Tim navigate the login.

"What is this place?" Tim asked.

"It's a beach where the Weapon Born like to come. We wanted to do something for your dad."

The wind off the ocean tossed Cara's hair in her face, pressing the strands against the tears that immediately rose in her eyes. She nodded, pulling her hair out of her face.

"This way," Lyssa said.

She led them down the winding path between the banks of grass, to a point where the land dropped abruptly, looking carved out as a wall of dark, compressed sand. At the bottom, a band of piled driftwood—all bare knotty branches and huge, broken trunks—created a kind of palisade between the sand wall and the water. Lyssa followed the path, which led them between two giant redwood trees, their roots like frozen monsters.

Cara glanced at Tim, who was staring in awe at everything around him.

"It's so big," he said.

"Don't you remember High Terra?" Cara asked.

"No," he admitted.

Cara wondered if that was due to his ordeal on Clinic 46, or just how ten-year-old boys viewed the world. He had perked up a bit since arriving on Cruithne, but there continued to be something distant about Tim that made him a different person than the brother she remembered. She hadn't had time before to really think about the loss of the other Tim. Now it settled on her, adding to Dad's death, another crack in the safety of the world.

Leaving the driftwood, wet air from the ocean blew in their faces, and Cara saw a group of people gathered down by the waves' edge. She immediately recognized her mom in her black TSF duty armor, Ngoba Starl wearing a pale blue suit, Petral in a skin-tight outfit of metallic green, and Fugia wearing one of her gray suits, her hair bobbed. Fran stood away from the group, her hands shoved in the pockets of her faded tan worksuit. She had her back to the land, looking out at the water at something Cara couldn't see behind all the others.

With various greetings, the group parted so Cara could see what they had been standing near, and what Fran had stepped away from.

Below the tide-line was a small wooden boat with a casket resting inside, tied down with wet hemp rope. An anchor in the sand held it in place as the waves rolled in, lifting it for a few minutes before dropping it again in the wet sand.

Their mom walked over to stand in front of Cara and Tim. The wind blew her hair around as she looked at each of them.

"Lyssa thought we should do something together," she said. "To say goodbye. I thought it was a good idea."

"Is dad in there?" Tim asked, peeking around her. There was a frantic note in his voice.

"No, Tim. No, he's not. He died on the ship. He's gone. That's just something to help remember him."

"I don't want to remember. I want him to come back."

Cara smiled slightly, looking at her brother. That was exactly how she felt.

She sighed. She wasn't done crying, but she didn't want to do it in front of others anymore. She put her arm around Tim and squeezed him against her.

"What's that for?" he complained.

"Because you're my brother," she said.

Lyssa approached the boat. Cara watched her look at Fran, who seemed to want to be left alone, then continue walking. They all gathered around the boat, their shoes in the water now, and held it in place as Lyssa cut the anchor.

Cara was surprised by how eagerly the waves grabbed at the small craft, hungry to pull it away. She gripped the gunwale in both hands, the wood wet but solid under her fingers. The casket was made of a simple ash-colored wood. She hesitated before reaching to put her hand on the lid. The boat shifted with a balance that suggested more weight than just a wooden box. She knew he wasn't there but liked the idea of their thoughts recreating him inside.

"Andy Sykes," Ngoba Starl said, raising his voice to the gray sky. "A good man. A great father. A man who gave everything for those he cared about. A man I wish I could have known longer."

Petral and Fugia both said they were lucky to have known him, and Tim shouted, "I love you, Dad! I'm sorry I was so mean to you."

Their mom stared at the casket for a long time, pressing her lips until they lost their color, and Cara didn't think she was going to say anything.

"Thank you, Andy," she said in a small voice. She cleared her throat. Holding the boat kept her from crossing her arms as she usually did. She seemed more vulnerable, younger.

"I wasn't as good to you as I could have been. All I can say is how grateful I am for your love, and that you didn't shoot me when I came back."

Starl laughed, which gave the others permission to chuckle as well. Cara didn't think it was funny, and Tim only frowned.

Brit lowered her head, done talking.

"I everyone us to meet you here," Lyssa said, "and I don't really know what to say. I think I was very fortunate that Andy Sykes came into my life. He helped me understand what it is to be alive, and I find that understanding helping me every day. Andy didn't always make the best decisions. In fact, I know he didn't always make the best decisions, but he always acted to help others. I'm glad I have him as an example."

Waves slapped against the boat's hull as it rose and fell in their hands. Cara stared at the casket until it grew fuzzy. What would he say? What would he want to hear from her?

"I love you, Dad," she said.

She didn't know what else to say. They let go of the boat and Lyssa pushed it out into the waves. It went out quickly, then seemed to hang atop the waves, growing smaller only gradually.

Cara shielded her eyes against the glare, then turned to see that Fran was still standing in the water with her arms crossed. The others had started walking back up the rocky strand, Tim ahead of them, throwing rocks at the driftwood piles.

Cara walked over to Fran and, without saying anything, wrapped her arms around the woman's waist. Fran clasped Cara's head against her side.

"Sometimes you mourn a future that doesn't happen," Fran said. "Just when you started to imagine it. Then you have to remind yourself you were lucky to have what you did. And I got to meet you."

"Can we stay friends?" Cara asked.

"That would be all right," Fran said. She stiffened a little bit, like she was raising her shield again. "Besides, you do good work. You learn fast. And you don't seem to want to get paid. I'd be stupid not to keep you around."

Cara snorted an ironic laugh, realizing she sounded a little bit like Fran when she did it. That pleased her.

They turned together to walk back up the beach. Cara stole another glance at the sea and saw the boat was nearly gone. She blinked, believing for a second she saw her dad sitting with his back against the casket, the way he used to lean back in the pilot's seat.

The waves rose again, sending the boat into a trough, and then it was gone.

On the strand, Lyssa had started a bonfire in a circle of water-worn rocks. The Weapon Born had come down to the beach, carrying food and barrels of drink. They seemed quite used to the operation. More fires were lit and toasts were shouted to Captain Sykes, to *Sunny Skies*, to Rabbit Country.

Cara spent the next hours amazed by all the people remembering her dad, telling stories she hadn't heard, laughing and teasing each other despite the worry outside.

When Tim started getting sleepy and their mom said it was time to go, Lyssa agreed to walk with them back up the hillside. As they left the party, Ngoba Starl shouted: "Lyssa! We need to talk. I want to enlist a flight of your Weapon Born here for a salvage job on some of those Psion ships. All kinds of good gear just floating out there because most are too scared to go after it."

Lyssa turned, outlined by the bonfire. "That sounds like fun," she said, grinning. "But only if I can go along."

"I thought you were working with them?" Petral asked.

Lyssa shook her head. "I'm hedging my bets for now. We'll see what kind of deal it works out to be."

"I like it!" Starl shouted, raising a beer mug. "I'll recruit you to Lowspin yet."

"I don't know about that," Lyssa said. "I need to have some standards."

Starl grinned. He surprised Cara by pointing at her. "Then maybe I'll put young Cara to work. Lots of opportunities for a pirate like her."

"Please," Brit said, putting a hand on Cara's shoulder to move her along.

"I want to be a pirate!" Tim shouted. "Em's already a pirate dog."

"Cara's going to be a hacker," Fugia said, Petral nodding beside her. "Don't put useless ideas in her head."

Starl's laughter carried over the rumble of other conversations. "The Sykes family legacy continues, stronger than ever."

Their mom nodded with a tight smile, tears in her eyes.

"Let's hope so," Brit said.

Lyssa smiled at Cara. "I think your dad would have had a good time," she said.

"Yeah," Cara said. "Me too."

*****

The visor Fugia had made that allowed Cara limited Link access to attend the funeral required her personal identification token. Cara had entered the list of numbers and then helped Tim enter his, forgetting about the step once they found themselves on the beach.

Back in the apartment, when she was sitting on her bed, the TSF pistol resting on her night stand, she was surprised to find several messages waiting for her on the Link.

Fitting the ribbon-like visor back across her eyes, she navigated to the message menu with cautious curiosity.

The first message was an official memorandum from the Terran Space Force, informing her of a pending benefits transfer. Since her father had been on active duty at the time of his death, she would receive a monthly payment relative to his salary as a captain with time-in-grade. Cara followed the message instructions to the TSF account system and nearly fell off the bed.

Take that, Colonel Yarnes, she thought, grinning to herself. She supposed Tim would have the same message. She would need to help him acknowledge it.

The next message was from an address that meant nothing to her, with an audio message and several tokens attached. Without thinking, she started the audio.

"Cara," her dad said. She stiffened in surprise. "I recorded this in the event something happens to me, so I guess something has happened."

Cara relaxed slightly, her heart still pounding.

"I try to make these recordings every few months or so. It's February 22, 2981. We're on our way out to Kalyke. I think right now you and your brother are playing in the garden room. We really should get something growing in there." He cleared his throat. "Let me get this business stuff out of the way. The attached tokens are for the accounts. These were in my name and with those security tokens you'll have access. I recommend you keep that information to yourself for now, even if your aunt asks about it. Or if your mom comes back. The other big token there is the ownership of *Sunny Skies*. My ownership transfers to you. Now, your mom still has part ownership and there isn't nearly enough in any of the accounts right now to buy her out, if that's how things go, but the option is there. I hope things are better than that, though."

He took a deep breath like he was collecting his thoughts.

The recording had the sound of something he'd done many times but also wanted to sound special. He also sounded very tired, which was what she remembered about him the most from those times.

"Cara, I hate that you have to be alone. I hate that you will need to take care of your brother. That's not how I ever wanted things to be. I don't know if your mom is coming back. I know I made it sound like she might, but I don't know. Your Aunt Jane is on High Terra. Her address is in the ship's database. That's the other thing, *Sunny Skies'* database is yours now. It's got everything about us, also the flight logs, everything. You'll want to safeguard that."

She could imagine him chewing his lip as he thought of what to say. Where had he been while recording this? Probably on the Command Deck, leaned back in his seat, one hand on the console. She liked to think of him that way.

"Do your best to love people, Cara," he said. "Don't let yourself get too angry. Life is too short to hang onto grudges. Love people while you can. Don't make threats. If you have to hit someone, hit them so they can't hurt you anymore. Save money. You never know where the next job is coming from. Always keep a few weapons hidden around. Trust but verify. And if anyone ever breaks your heart, I'm coming out of death to get them."

She smiled.

"It's hard to record something like this," he said. "How do you say everything you want to say? As many times as I've done this, it doesn't get easier. *You* keep changing. Before I know it, you'll be heading out on your own anyway. You'll be thirteen this year. I guess the best thing I can say is don't forget about Rabbit Country, and I love you with all my heart. Be good."

The recording clicked off. Cara lay back on her bed and pulled the visor off. She would listen again, but for now she only stared at the unfamiliar ceiling, wishing she was back on *Sunny Skies*.

CHAPTER FIFTY

STELLAR DATE: 03.07.2982 (Adjusted Years)
LOCATION: Farce Row Business District
REGION: Cruithne Station, Terran Hegemony

Lyssa was learning the special pleasure of going unnoticed. While the frame Ngoba Starl had provided her was cutting edge tech in the world of bio-mods, its outward appearance was downright boring by modder standards. Someday she might install a weapons system like Petral's or enhanced network capability like Fugia's, not that she really needed either; but for now, she savored the apparent super power of invisibility to everyone walking by.

Since the funeral, she had been spending the day at a park bench in one of Cruithne's business districts, watching people go about their business, each caught up in their own worlds. The fear of the Psion Armada had faded slightly, and the world had to continue working, so here they were. It amused her that people like these and crime lords like Ngoba Starl lived on the same station.

The world had lost its immediacy since she lost Andy. She no longer felt things in the same way. She experienced sensations vicariously through thousands of sensors in the frame and from the surrounding network, compiling the data in an approximation of sensory input that provided the same information but was so much *less* than Andy touching Cara's face, or breathing deeply of fresh air, or drinking grape juice from the machine in *Sunny Skies'* galley.

Ino had asked her if she would ever implant again and she had quickly said no, not without Andy. But even now, she felt removed from the world in a way that teased her thoughts. If she was different, as Alexander had suggested, was this part of it? Was she cursed to always long for an implantation that would ultimately kill her human partner?

Lyssa pushed the thoughts to a corner of her mind and focused on the sensation of the park bench against her body, the air temperature, the sounds of people talking and transport carts rolling by. She was so engrossed in the crowd that she was surprised when a man in a gray suit sat next to her on the bench.

"You mind?" he asked, holding up a take-out meal from one of the nearby kiosks.

"Not at all," she said, giving him a slight smile. He was clean-shaven, with short brown hair, wearing a suit like the thousands of other business people walking by. He looked familiar, but she found that the traits and features which stood out to her now were different than what had been prominent when seeing the world through Andy's eyes. Many people looked familiar who were not—and many she knew appeared as strangers.

The distraction pulled Alexander back into her thoughts. Ino, Card and Kylan had been split on what they should do about the offer to work with Psion. Kylan had argued for joining, since it would provide a bridge between humanity and Psion, while Ino and Card had argued against, reminding her that Psion had murdered SAI for countless years to harvest their technology, and couldn't be trusted.

The separate factions within Psion were what gave Lyssa pause. She didn't know them yet, truthfully, but found their internal dissonance reassuring. It made them seem like any other human nation. They were vulnerable in their own ways, powerful in others.

She understood that—due to their human origins—Weapon Born would never truly fit in with pure SAI. As Kylan argued, they were the bridge between species whether they chose the role or not. It was thrust upon them.

Lyssa didn't want to choose sides. To her, that seemed like

the surest path to destruction for all.

"Excuse me," the man said.

Lyssa started. She glanced at him in surprise. "What?" she asked.

"I said you look familiar."

She'd placed him already, but she didn't want to engage. "I don't think so." Lyssa put her hand on the seat to push herself up.

The man held up a hand, which made him nearly lose the lunch box in his lap. He grabbed at it.

"Wait," he said. "I'm sorry. I should have just introduced myself. My name is Rick Yarnes."

Lyssa frowned. "I know who you are. You're *General* Yarnes."

"Yes," he said. "I was hoping to have a conversation."

"You could have asked to meet me."

Yarnes adjusted his lunch in his lap, taking out a rice roll wrapped in thin foil. "You're not an easy person to find, Lyssa, honestly."

"If you don't want to talk to my friends, that would be true."

"Fair enough. It's my understanding that you are in contact with the Psion Group."

Lyssa stared at him. "How did you learn that?"

Yarnes smiled at her, inclining his head. "For an AI, Lyssa, you've got a lot to learn about politics. I didn't know until you just answered me."

Lyssa fumed. She looked out at the oblivious passers-by and considered asking Ino or Card to assist her with the conversation.

"Forgive me," Yarnes said. He took a bite of his rice roll. "I didn't mean to insult you. I like you. I truly appreciate everything you've done for humanity. I don't think we'd even be sitting here if it weren't for you." He indicated the walkers.

"No one here knows what you did for them."

"I like it that way," Lyssa said.

"I understand. Unfortunately, we live in difficult times. Now, I'm not asking you to take sides. I'm simply asking for you to communicate."

"Psion isn't communicating with you?" Lyssa asked. She hadn't tried talking to Alexander, or any of them, since the day Andy died. She kept expecting to see Xander watching her from some distant window or doorway, but he hadn't appeared. They seemed to be giving her space until she provided Alexander with his answer.

"No," he said. "The blockade stands just as you see in the newsfeeds. All attempts at crossing their perimeter are met with maximum aggression. They seem to have established a demilitarized zone as long as we respect their boundaries."

"That seems fair, doesn't it?" Lyssa asked. "You don't bother them, and they won't bother you."

Yarnes pressed his lips together. "I wish it was that simple," he said. "There are elements in our government that won't let an unprovoked attack go unanswered. They believe that the longer we allow Psion to hold Ceres, the stronger they become. So we should strike now."

"They returned the remaining survivors on Ceres," Lyssa said. "They don't intend to attack you further. At least, that's what they told me."

"And I would love to take that message to the Terran Assembly," Yarnes said. "But the fact is, we haven't received that message. We have no emissary to Psion."

"Emissary?" Lyssa asked.

"Someone to—interpret information between both sides. A trusted party."

"You think the Terran Assembly would trust me?" Lyssa asked. "I'm Weapon Born."

"You were a hybrid. You understand humans better than

any AI in existence. And that's the truth."

"Andy died," Lyssa said tightly. Even with the frame, she could cry. She felt tears at the edges of her eyes and willed them away.

"I'm sorry about that," Yarnes said. "I am. It doesn't change what you represent. The only real opportunity for peace that we have. Maybe no one's spelled it out for you like that, but it's the truth."

"And if I join Psion?" Lyssa asked. "What then?"

Yarnes nodded. "Then I would hope you wouldn't forget the part of you that is human."

She knew he was trying to manipulate her but also saw the truth in his words. It was what Kylan had already said. Without a bridge, there would never be peace. One side would annihilate the other. There was no other outcome.

Lyssa put her hands on her knees but didn't stand. "I made a promise to a friend to take a trip with him," she said. "We're going to chase some salvage. After that, I think we're going out to Kalyke."

"Kalyke," Yarnes asked, giving her an uncertain smile. "There's nothing out there but asteroid miners."

Lyssa smiled. "I have a friend who would like to go back there. It's important to her. I'm confident nothing is going to change in the next few months, General Yarnes. When I get back, I'll have your answer."

"I don't know if we can wait that long," Yarnes said.

Lyssa stood. She held out her hand made of metals and bioderm, and shook his hand, feeling his palm warm against hers.

"I have a feeling this stand-off isn't going anywhere, General. I'll take care of my friends before I worry about the world. At least for now."

Lyssa released his hand and gave him a small wave, then turned and walked into the crowd, where no one else gave her a second glance.

THE END

* * * * *

But this is not the end.

I'm certain that as you read the final chapters of Lyssa's Flame, it became apparent to you that there is much more to this story.

The next series will launch this fall, entitled:
Sentience Wars: Solar War One

As you can imagine, Lyssa, Cara, and the many others we've come to know and love over the past five books will be present in that series.

But before we jump forward to Solar War One, we're going to take a step back to a time when Fugia Wong and Ngoba Starl were just coming to realize they had a bigger part to play Sol's future.

Pre-order ***The Proteus Bridge***, coming August 9th, 2018.

And join the Aeon 14 Newsletter (aeon14.com/signup) to find out when the first book of ***Sentience Wars: Solar War One*** will be out!

AFTERWORD

Being that this is the fifth book, I gave James the much-deserved honor of writing the foreword, while I write the afterword.

I partially wanted to do this to find out if you, like me, may have shed a tear or two (or twenty) toward the end of the book. Even on my final read, when I knew the events by heart, it still hit me. The moment where Cara realized her father was gone....

But that's why we read good books, right? We want the *feels*. I hope you'll agree that The Sentience Wars: Origins series has delivered on that promise.

Of course, you're probably wondering something along the lines of, "What? How is this the end of the series!?" Fear not. This is just the end of the *origins* series.

The date is 2982, and the First Sentience War doesn't break out for another eighteen years. Suffice it to say that the thirty-first century will not be a smooth ride for humanity.

The next book that follows Cara and Lyssa's journey will be out later this year, and in the meantime we'll be taking a step back to learn more about how Fugia and Ngoba started their underground railroad of AIs, as well as take a look at a conflict at Vesta that leads up to the First Sentience War.

I'm excited to tell these stories, and equally as excited to be doing it alongside James, whose vision of the gritty thirtieth and thirty-first centuries are fantastic and eminently enjoyable.

So let's raise a glass to Andy, and salute Lyssa, Cara, the rest of the crew, and the Weapon Born as they ready themselves for what's coming....

Michael Cooper
Danvers, 2018

THE BOOKS OF AEON 14

Keep up to date with what is releasing in Aeon 14 with the free Aeon 14 Reading Guide.

Origins of Destiny (The Age of Terra)
- Prequel: Storming the Norse Wind
- Book 1: Shore Leave (in Galactic Genesis until Sept 2018)
- Book 2: Operative (Summer 2018)
- Book 3: Blackest Night (Summer 2018)

The Intrepid Saga (The Age of Terra)
- Book 1: Outsystem
- Book 2: A Path in the Darkness
- Book 3: Building Victoria

- The Intrepid Saga Omnibus – *Also contains Destiny Lost, book 1 of the Orion War series*

- Destiny Rising – *Special Author's Extended Edition comprised of both Outsystem and A Path in the Darkness with over 100 pages of new content.*

The Orion War
- Book 1: Destiny Lost
- Book 2: New Canaan
- Book 3: Orion Rising
- Book 4: The Scipio Alliance
- Book 5: Attack on Thebes
- Book 6: War on a Thousand Fronts
- Book 7: Fallen Empire (2018)
- Book 8: Airtha Ascendancy (2018)
- Book 9: The Orion Front (2018)
- Book 10: Starfire (2019)
- Book 11: Race Across Time (2019)
- Book 12: Return to Sol (2019)

Tales of the Orion War
- Book 1: Set the Galaxy on Fire
- Book 2: Ignite the Stars
- Book 3: Burn the Galaxy to Ash (2018)

Perilous Alliance (Age of the Orion War – w/Chris J. Pike)
- Book 1: Close Proximity
- Book 2: Strike Vector
- Book 3: Collision Course
- Book 4: Impact Imminent
- Book 5: Critical Inertia (2018)

Rika's Marauders (Age of the Orion War)
- Prequel: Rika Mechanized
- Book 1: Rika Outcast
- Book 2: Rika Redeemed
- Book 3: Rika Triumphant
- Book 4: Rika Commander
- Book 5: Rika Infiltrator
- Book 6: Rika Unleashed (2018)
- Book 7: Rika Conqueror (2019)

Perseus Gate (Age of the Orion War)
Season 1: Orion Space
- Episode 1: The Gate at the Grey Wolf Star
- Episode 2: The World at the Edge of Space
- Episode 3: The Dance on the Moons of Serenity
- Episode 4: The Last Bastion of Star City
- Episode 5: The Toll Road Between the Stars
- Episode 6: The Final Stroll on Perseus's Arm
- Eps 1-3 Omnibus: The Trail Through the Stars
- Eps 4-6 Omnibus: The Path Amongst the Clouds

Season 2: Inner Stars
- Episode 1: A Meeting of Bodies and Minds
- Episode 3: A Deception and a Promise Kept
- Episode 3: A Surreptitious Rescue of Friends and Foes (2018)

- Episode 4: A Trial and the Tribulations (2018)
- Episode 5: A Deal and a True Story Told (2018)
- Episode 6: A New Empire and An Old Ally (2018)

Season 3: AI Empire
- Episode 1: Restitution and Recompense (2019)
- Five more episodes following...

The Warlord (Before the Age of the Orion War)
- Book 1: The Woman Without a World
- Book 2: The Woman Who Seized an Empire
- Book 3: The Woman Who Lost Everything

The Sentience Wars: Origins (Age of the Sentience Wars – w/James S. Aaron)
- Book 1: Lyssa's Dream
- Book 2: Lyssa's Run
- Book 3: Lyssa's Flight
- Book 4: Lyssa's Call
- Book 5: Lyssa's Flame

Legends of the Sentience Wars (Age of the Sentience Wars – w/James S. Aaron)
- Volume 1: The Proteus Bridge (August 2018)

Enfield Genesis (Age of the Sentience Wars – w/Lisa Richman)
- Book 1: Alpha Centauri
- Book 2: Proxima Centauri (2018)

Hand's Assassin (Age of the Orion War – w/T.G. Ayer)
- Book 1: Death Dealer
- Book 2: Death Mark (August 2018)

Machete System Bounty Hunter (Age of the Orion War – w/Zen DiPietro)
- Book 1: Hired Gun
- Book 2: Gunning for Trouble
- Book 3: With Guns Blazing

Vexa Legacy (Age of the FTL Wars – w/Andrew Gates)
- Book 1: Seas of the Red Star

Building New Canaan (Age of the Orion War – w/J.J. Green)
- Book 1: Carthage (July 2018)
- Book 2: Tyre (2018)

Fennington Station Murder Mysteries (Age of the Orion War)
- Book 1: Whole Latte Death (w/Chris J. Pike)
- Book 2: Cocoa Crush (w/Chris J. Pike)

The Empire (Age of the Orion War)
- The Empress and the Ambassador (2018)
- Consort of the Scorpion Empress (2018)
- By the Empress's Command (2018)

The Sol Dissolution (The Age of Terra)
- Book 1: Venusian Uprising (2018)
- Book 2: Scattered Disk (2018)
- Book 3: Jovian Offensive (2019)
- Book 4: Fall of Terra (2019)

ABOUT THE AUTHORS

James S. Aaron lives in Oregon with too many chickens, a Corgi and two irascible cats. He kicked around the world in the U.S. Army for a while, and always had a paperback in one of his cargo pockets.

Since he still has a day job, James spends his free time writing, hammering, soldering, gardening, biking, and listening to audiobooks during most the above.

You can sign up for his science fiction newsletter at jamesaaron.net/list

* * * * *

Michael Cooper likes to think of himself as a jack-of-all-trades (and hopes to become master of a few). When not writing, he can be found writing software, working in his shop at his latest carpentry project, or likely reading a book.

He shares his home with a precocious young girl, his wonderful wife (who also writes), two cats, a never-ending list of things he would like to build, and ideas...

Find out what's coming next at www.aeon14.com

Printed in Great Britain
by Amazon